SIGHT

SIGHT

"Let their eyes close. For that which is temporal can be seen, but that which is unseen is eternal."

Justin Smith

Published by Tablo

Published in 2023 by Tablo Publishing.

Publisher and wholesale enquiries: orders@tablo.io

20 21 22 23 LSC 10 9 8 7 6 5 4 3 2 1

ACT I

The Pledge

Part 1: The Pain Comes First

6,205 days left.

According to my spies, the group was in their usual commorancy, a makeshift hideout that leveraged the catacombs of old beneath the royal family's home. The place was damp, dimly lit, and haunting. The catacombs were largely forgotten now, not having been used since wartime to smuggle the royal family out—the only sure way to ensure the Cara Royale line lived on.

Before all this, I was given a choice: Either bring the entire nation under the most invasive surveillance system it had ever seen, or risk sending out more spies than we ever have. We chose the latter, going with individuals from the old world that our people had never seen. In either case, one thing was certain: there was no turning back now.

"It's easier for you to suggest, when you're the diplomat credited with keeping the peace, Gaius," Damian signed. He was typically in opposition to Gaius's methods. He hadn't been pushed yet to challenge his leadership. But he was nearing that point.

"My concern is simply this: how can we continue to ensure our anonymity?" Tudor asked. He adjusted his glasses—his only sign of weakness—before continuing to sign. "The nation is changing, technology is catching up. We cannot move like we used to."

Tudor was right, for they were being watched from the very beginning. Our spies were unlike any other; they held a supernatural ability to read minds, alter their appearance, and uncannily adapt to ever-changing situations. The only risk, and it was a substantial one, was potentially exposing them to the public. Our people still were not ready.

"And speaking of being unable to move like we used to, we are also getting too old for this," Damian added.

Gaius unfolded his arms but further furrowed his brows. Conflicting body language.

"I am asking you all for one last mission. I am asking you because I need you—all of you."

According to Isa, my lead spy, Gaius looked again to Damian as he signed. When he pointed his finger outward, he swung it out to each member before him: the twin brothers, Tudor and Tora; Damian Cala; Timothy Aquinas; and Gregor Bastian.

"We had a 'final mission' once before, Gaius," Damian protested. "And that time we lost a brother. We took Maya's father from her. *We* did that."

Gaius stood abruptly. Damian, with swagger, stood to meet him. They met nearly eye to eye, though Damian was two and a half inches taller.

"I *know* what I did, Damian. Do not push me. What did *you* do?"

Tudor stood too and placed himself between the men. He put a hand on each of their chests. "What we must agree upon is that we all sinned that day," Tudor added. "However we reconcile it, we must admit it was sin for all, not sin for one."

Tudor was right. From one perspective, one could say it was one of the last nudges needed to encourage continued peace during a time when it seemed like the conflict would result in the loss of nearly a billion people. The lesser of two evils. However, others could say it was an unsanctioned murder at the least and a hate crime at the most.

I am of divine royal blood. To that end, the Old Guard will be held accountable when this is all over, but I am an engineer first. It was this conversation that showed me that this work can no longer continue with a craftswoman—it now required a diplomat and a soldier. I asked Isa to find a way to record what they observed. The observations exceeded my expectations.

Isa, along with the rest of her ancient race, will be the key to saving Vedere when the time comes. I have to trust them, there is no one else. From this point on, Isa and I have decided to keep these matters close; Isa has chosen two of her trusted colleagues, Gabrielle and Avis, to inform on those who choose to work against us.

"What I did, Gaius, was follow orders. *Your* orders. And what I am doing now, after all those years, is still adjusting to the crimes I committed." Damian backed away on his own, returning to a stool.

Timothy joined the conversation. He was the most devout religiously, and also the most dedicated to Gaius and his cause. "We are not starting this journey now, my friends. We are ending it. Let us see it through to the end."

Damian bounced his shoulders quickly in a flippant response. His only source of restraint came from the reminder that now was surely not the time to stage a coup.

"Our target is the last daughter of the Davis family," Gaius reported. "This comes directly from the Viceroy. Her name is Talia Davis. We are tasked with eliminating her and her family—then we are done."

Damian calmly stood and walked to the center wooden table used for planning. He flipped the table into the adjacent wall. Papers lightly fluttered onto the stone floor. "So we kill more children. That's our task," Damian replied.

The rest of the group lowered their head or looked away. Tudor stared off into space.

"I will never ask you to hunt down a child again. Ever," Gaius signed.

Damian stormed out of the cave. Thomas placed a comforting shoulder on Gaius as the others slowly filed out.

"I am with you to the end, brother," Timothy signed. "Please just tell me this is the last time."

I waved my hand over the screen to shut off playback. I was all but certain now that the end would truly come within my lifetime. And that would change things.

***

Tora McDaniel, 513 days left

The group that Tora had been spying on was delicately passing around a collection of handwritten notes on a dozen sheets of old paper.

"Those notes are written in a language long dead—with symbols and logograms that would baffle most scholars," Tora signed. He had his twin, Tudor, with him and a younger clergyman. The young man's face twisted into a tight snarl. He had been radicalized.

The group of seven had met during an odd time. Though complete darkness in Vedere was impossible, it was still considered the end of what Vederians called the Productive Period. The streets were empty as less than optimal light tinted the landscape. Odder still, the group met in a fairly dim room hidden in the basement of a hotel.

The group knew the dangers of their meeting, prepared for it, but still failed to predict the immediacy of a possible attack, Tora thought. Their activities were illegal, as was their meeting. Tora would see to it that they faced justice, but not everyone was as passionate as he was, especially his brother.

"Tora, this looks like a family studying together, not planning an attack," Tudor suggested. "There is no immediate danger to this district."

Tora McDaniel could not be more different than his brother. Tudor was an artist and poet with a thin frame and contentious disposition. He would argue with you knowing his argument was flawed, and yet would debate it until you either tired or gave up. Tora, on the other hand, was a devout Vaeli, a reverent man whose beliefs bordered on fanaticism. He excelled in one of the few places men could in Vederian society—the church. He'd dedicated his entire life to the faith and it showed in all of the typical ways: he was superficial, judgmental, and impatient.

Tora and Tudor were taken from their orphanage when they were four. No one knew much about them except for the unique skillset they possessed. Tora and Tudor were trained killers—two of the best.

"This is the job," Tora replied with a shoulder shrug. "Kid, make sure you're ready to run." Tora backed his drone off from its vantage point and assessed the hotel one last time before detonating the bomb. It flashed a white sphere around the entire hotel, then imploded the entire building. He contacted the Ophori to inform them of a Cophi terrorist attack. That lie was part of the explicit directions he and Tudor were given before the hit.

"I hope all of these people suffer. How dare they turn their back on the nation?" the young clergyman signed with sharp fingers. Tudor briefly stared at Tora before getting up to leave, shaking his head.

***

Valerie, 340 days left

"This is where you cannot blink—otherwise, you'll miss it. The wool is now being pulled from your eyes. Did you feel it, Brother?" Valerie leaned in and lowered her shoulders, trying to show what she was explaining was gravely important. He didn't take it that way.

Valerie's brother scrunched his lips and pointed with his chin toward Mother. The color of Victor's skin brightened into a pale light brown—he was upset.

"All things exist in the light of *now*, sister," Victor retorted. He was normally pious, patient, often focused. But now his arms were folded tight like a straitjacket. His hand had a tight grip on his bicep, wrinkling his sleeve.

Victor was the youngest and the smallest of the Cara children. He often mistook Valerie's confidence for condescension, but he usually knew when to back down. This time, he stood a bit straighter as he pushed back his hair and straightened his black turtleneck.

He was going to spar with Valerie. "The concept of hiding something is not even a part of our culture. There is nothing our people have to fear," he explained.

In the mirror across the room, Valerie could see her skin turn a dark brownish-red. She wanted to snap his neck. Instead, she turned to Mother and touched her forehead, linking their minds.

"I fear, Mother, that you too are blinking. The nation is trying to tell us something—and you are blinking. Do you know what I fear? I fear what our people will think."

Victor looked at Valerie out the corner of his eye. He didn't like Valerie's theatrics, as he put it. Valerie looked at Mother; she let her eyes alternate from the floor to her emaciated face and back again, hoping to see a response. All she did was stare at Valerie with wide, soulless eyes. Her body shook as she sweat profusely. Valerie's mother pried her gaze away from her only to jolt her bony frame at the next observation.

It was strange behavior indeed, but it was expected. Valerie's royal family was no exception to a common albeit misunderstood illness. It also came at the worst possible time: a time of political turmoil as their nation poised itself to split once again.

This was no longer Valerie's mother. She couldn't even call her by her name, Vera. After a nearly two-century reign as Ægæliphi, she had become horrific. She ruled with an unfathomable dominion, presiding with a political and religious authority that she now seemed to have no interest in exercising. The real power was with the Viceroy—but even now, they remained a mystery to Valerie.

Vera retreated into a fetal position. The fetal position was new. Vera was coming undone. Her sickness had begun to take its toll—absolutely terrible timing.

Valerie observed her weightless frame, curled and twisted onto itself. She didn't realize how tightly she held her bedsheets. There were a few damp dots there too, where tears had fallen. *"The absolute power of the known world, unable to leave her bed, reduced to tears. What had we become? Someone has to change this course,"* Valerie thought to herself.

"This is weakness. It is weakness and the people sense it. They rebelled against your mother, and they will soon rebel against you. Who can see you like this, Mother? How long can we protect your honor?" Valerie asked. She yanked the sheets off her mother's bed and threw them in the vicinity of Victor. Mother furrowed her brows and shut her eyes. She smacked her ears with her hands and clawed at her legs until navy blood dripped from her fingertips. Victor rushed over to calm her.

Valerie threw her hands up and walked away. She wandered over to Mother's enormous annular bedroom window. From our palace, she could peer out through the near-panoramic window into almost any direction. Ræ wasn't just their home. It was a beacon that represented splendor, wonder, and the advancement of the nation of Vedere.

Valerie backed away a few steps, in awe of the pure white marble and granite castle of discs and cylinders stacked in an ancient design. The structure was built on an island with an impenetrable wall encircling it in a way that made it difficult to tell which came first—the marble or the earth around it.

Valerie looked at what they owned: around the island was the district of Arælia, the capital city of the nation of Vedere. It was sovereign territory and belonged completely to their family, the Cara Royale. Surrounding Arælia was the city of New Redemption, which was the political seat of the continent. Valerie looked at the twelve bridges that linked Ræ, Arælia, and New Redemption. This had been their land for thousands of years.

"We are Vedere, Mother. 'This is what history tells us. This is the truth. This is how the Earth began...'" Valerie hoped quoting a portion of the national

anthem would appeal to whatever principle her mother had left. *"'We are Vedere. And we are the race of the world.'"*

Victor was crying. Blood was dripping out of Mother's ears—another common symptom and unfortunate sign that her sickness was much more advanced. She would die soon.

"It is our job to maintain order, Mother. This is a duty we cannot forget."

Mother, Vera, gently placed her hand on Victor's as she turned toward Valerie. She stared at her with those piercing icy blue eyes that they all shared. Due to age, all of her hair was gone—save for her razor-sharp eyebrows. They were a deeply contrasting white that clashed against her deep brown skin. Valerie saw herself in her.

"Who are you? Victor, who is this woman?"

And Vera saw a stranger in Valerie.

Vera was over two hundred years old, a testament to advancements in Vederian biology and gene therapy, as well as the nearly perfect living conditions that their family enjoyed. She was well past the average age of one hundred and sixty-five and, though an old woman, her skin still held firmly to her prominent cheekbones and her established nose.

Valerie observed those same cheekbones in herself. She remembered the vibrant, pure white, waist-length hair her mother used to have. This was how she preferred to remember her these days.

According to Valerie, she was strong and determined then. Her greatest achievement had been ushering in an era that later generations would come to call the Great Renaissance. Post-war Vedere needed someone to cling to and the young queen helped her nation find its culture again. *"Where had that woman gone?"* Valerie thought.

Valerie recalled the single thick braid Mother would tie her white hair into before going out into the courtyard. It took no effort from her to enchant her constituency. She would enter a room and all things stopped. A bustling market would freeze in place. A panoramic lightshow near the city center would reschedule if she were strolling by— Valerie was in awe of her grace. But her mother had changed.

Valerie also remembered the frequent trips to the flower garden, the stories just before bed. She remembered the weight of Mother's almost-translucent crown, which she would try on while she applied makeup to accentuate the elaborate facial tattoos she'd received upon becoming Ægæliphi, ruler of the halos.

Before the conflict, the nation of Vedere was split into states or parishes called halos. Each halo was governed by a royal family—one of seven original families. The matriarch of each family was given the title of ræ, a Vederian sign that meant eldest mother. When a ræ died, the title was passed on to the next eldest woman in the family. It was a millennia-old system that worked relatively well up until recent history.

To see a dwarf where a giant once stood was almost too much for Valerie to bear. She signed to her mother as she turned around to slump against the window's frame. *"I'm sorry, Mother."*

Valerie was taught that the Cara Royale was established when a great ancestor, Vaia, brought the waring rings together in culture and religion. Vaia's zenith as ruler represented the power that ran through the veins of their family—the power to coalesce.

Valerie wanted to return Vedere to Vaia's splendor, but that was not to be her destiny. Valerie was second in line, after Vega. Her destiny outlined a life as regent—less power, even lesser influence. It made Valerie's chest swell with pressure like a balloon. It was there, in her mother's bedroom, that she first decided she'd have to act.

Valerie looked out past the vast circular chasms that carved the nation into rings, ever circumnavigating outward. She stretched her vision even farther to inspect the circular barriers that Vaia's granddaughter, Vivian, constructed around their family home. She soaked in all she could see. She wanted to be clear on what she was going to be fighting to protect.

Valerie was convinced that it was time for renaissance. In fact, she felt they were overdue. "I was taught that family comes before everything," Valerie signed, as the rings on her fingers danced in the light. She noticed her gait slowed as she neared her mother's bed. "So I wonder, Mother, who among your family will you respond?"

Valerie's upbringing was not pleasant. Vega was given the special tutors. New clothes were sewn for her for any public appearance. Valerie believed she was the burnt loaf of bread. Dark, hardened, and forgotten.

Valerie wasn't facing the direction she entered from, so she jolted when the center partition of the floor rose to reveal an icy-colored cylinder carrying an occupant veiled by frosted glass. It was Vega. She lightly touched foreheads with each of the family members, establishing the mental connection.

Vega remained formal, as she always did, requesting permission to enter her mother and brother's preexisting torphi through the Second Language, signing. *"I humbly request to proceed into torphi with my mother and sister."* Vega exhibited perfect posture, establishing her six-foot-two frame.

Valerie let her eyes roll. To her, it was as if Vega went out of her way to remind everyone of her etiquette.

"Mother, how are you feeling?" Vega sat onto the bed next to her. Victor playfully jumped on the other side of the bed. Valerie grabbed his wrist in response, but Victor snatched it away from her grip.

Vega turned, but only slightly, to ask a question. *"When will I ever catch you two embracing? What have we but family? Any ideas?"* Valerie frowned as she felt her sister was always this condescending. *"Val, you really must employ couth. Do not berate our mother or our brother at this time."*

Valerie let her face twist with anger. Most of the time her face displayed like a flat pane of glass. But she knew they could feel her emotion in the torphi.

"At this time, Vega? Can you describe to me a more apropos instance at this juncture?" Valerie couldn't stand her sister's vocabulary.

Vega raised an eyebrow in surprise as Victor stood up to cross his arms. Nothing could be hidden in torphi. There was no lying or deceit. Once you were linked, you were vulnerable.

Valerie stood over Vega, who was sitting. *"You see, I find the timing more than apropos. We are nearing a second civil war, Vega. The Cophi are threatening to reclaim the city and the distribution of our nation's wealth continues to strain the Royale. When will the timing be more appropriate? When the nation is burning with our people in distress? When we have to throw your children in a bunker? In the darkness?"*

Vega stood up, reestablishing hierarchy, before turning to face the window. Victor decided to chime in, appealing to the family. *"Our mother is in distress. As Ægæliphi, our mother is the nation. Won't we attend to her?"* Victor sat back down on the bed. Valerie understood his point, but she didn't like it. It wasn't enough for her.

Vega returned from her view. *"Our nation is growing, Valerie. Distress is to be expected, is it not?"* Vega bit her lip softly just before pulling her white hair up into a bun.

Valerie narrowed her eyes as they stared each other down. After a few seconds, she gave her a smirk. *"I don't expect distress, Vega. I expect clearer vision. We are the people of sight. That is our gift from the goddess Vedere, and what I see is a problem."*

Instead of attempting to regain superiority in the argument, Valerie resigned. *"I see a problem that it is our duty to fix. This is what we are defined by as a family. I put this duty above all."* This was the statement that had come to define Valerie. The family had not realized it yet, but the beginning of the end had come. Valerie had a plan.

Victor decided to respond. *"Are you saying that you will place the duty of our people over your own blood?"*

"Duty is our blood, Victor," Valerie replied.

"We are placed as we are to make the decisions necessary to ensure the best quality of life for our people," Vega added. *"We make these decisions because we are trusted that we know best."*

And now, here they were at the crux of the issue. Valerie was not trusted.

"Do you trust what I think is best?" Valerie asked.

"Valerie, you worry me. I expect so much more from you."

"I wish you hadn't said that," Valerie replied. But she got the answer she was expecting. *"I wish there was another way."*

What Valerie didn't expect, of all things, was how painful her plan would truly be. She was certain she had taken everything into account—everything except the pain. In that moment she learned that sometimes, when you have to do the hard thing, who you are controls what you will do—even if you're unsure you want to do it. Tonight was the beginning. *Tonight would be progress*, Valerie told herself. Tonight would begin not just her future, but the future of her people. Her face would be the last her mother would ever see. Matricide had always been in her heart, but today it had seeped into her mind. Valerie would kill her mother, the queen of Vedere, but the pain would come first.

***

The Journal of Georgette Davis, 57,300 days left

Day 1

I reminded the team today that we have the blessing of the Ægæliphi. The result of our endeavors can reshape the knowledge of our entire nation. We do not know exactly what we will see, but we have prepared and taken all necessary precautions to ensure the brightest minds our world has ever known remain protected during this endeavor. I tell them we have a blessing, but the truth is that whether we're blessed or not, if we do not succeed, we will not have a world to return to. This has to work. We have to find proof.

We are all broken by what is above us, and yet our team, today, is fresh and anxious. I think we are all a bit afraid—afraid of failure, of us wasting precious time and resources, of us returning to the war-torn world above us with nothing. Many of us have devoted our entire lives to this expedition; many of us cannot afford to be left empty-handed.

"I believe that we will make it, my darling. I say this because I truly believe it in my heart, but also because I believe in you," Rory, my beautiful husband, signs to me as I write. "The breathers work perfectly!" he continues.

I can tell he is smiling from behind the mask as his eyebrows raise and the corners of his eyes cinch. I trust in him as he trusts in me. We've spent so many years together—planning this great task, tallying countless hours of research and experimentation—and it has become very much a part of our lives as anything else we do. I cannot remember a time we did not speak of our goal. That we did not work, sleep, and work again in this very office I am currently sitting in. We have put decades in an impossible task and yet, I am still worried. I believe, but I am worried.

My husband believes in me as I believe in him. He has loved me through my obsessions. He has held my hand through marathon nights as I buried myself under books he knows he will never read. He has brought me a cool cloth when I worked in the lab in the middle of the day. He has grabbed my cheeks—one in each hand—and pressed his forehead onto mine as we share a smile. He jokes that I love the Underside more than I love him, but how that's just fine to him because he just wants to be wherever I am.

He is as beautiful as he is an educated. His work as an engineer cannot be considered anything short of genius. His designs are brilliant and, without him, our expedition would have been impossible. We will be able to breathe down there because of Rory. Our environmental suits will be portable, durable, and easy to repair. Our scientists will be unencumbered as they conduct their research. Seventeen years of work, seventeen years of marriage. But that is not the only partnership I have made. I also have kinship. My sister, Chelcie, prepared the itinerary. She has developed a stellar plan.

Step one is to complete a final systems check and inventory all last-minute additions to the caravan. We will then take the hovercars to the southernmost point of the Habitat Zone—aptly called the Reach—with our team of over seventy-five of the nation's best scientists, theologians, political delegates, and philosophers. We will have to rappel the entire team and our gear past the Mouth of Vaia, where the gravity will shift to nearly a quarter more than it is here on the Topside. (This is one of the components that I worry most about; we've trained for the increase in gravity, but I'm concerned that the prolonged exposure—even with training—may not be enough to prevent irreversible consequences to our physiology.)

Step two begins when we pass the Mouth of Vaia. At that location, we will establish our first base camp before we trek 7,500 meters to where we will set up our more permanent compound. We hope to process any biological samples and archeological discoveries there. If we bring anything back home—anything that definitively proves the origins of our civilization—we can save our world. I can truly only hope.

Next, beginning with the security team, we'll conduct reconnaissance, review aerial surveillance data from our drones, establish a testing perimeter, and confirm the barriers of our artificial habitat in order to create a safety radius. Naturally, we will use our synths to construct our habitats and begin testing.

Following construction, we will allow the natural sciences division time to retrieve samples and conduct the necessary series of tests of the surrounding flora and fauna. This will help us better understand the Underside's ecosystem and determine if there is any safe vegetation for any number of purposes.

At that point, we will then conduct a summit with our philosophers, theologians, and political delegates to decide how to plan the rest of our expedition. Once that is decided, I will personally lead our Alpha team farther into the Underside to find specific signs or clues attributing to our origin. We will have our alpha of Security, Ava Bastian, a brilliant military strategist and former Ophori leader; Richard McDaniel, alpha of Theology, who will be leaving behind his pregnant wife for this expedition; Saven, our alpha of Philosophy, Viceroy-appointed; and, finally, Nubia, the most brilliant ecologist I have ever met and close personal friend. We will compile all evidence and finally return Topside with our findings.

It felt good to write that all out. I am now more excited that I was before. I try not to think about how dire the situation is here in our nation. I can only hope that this work will mean something. I have to believe that it will.

***

Part 2: Birth Comes Second

The Journal of Georgette Davis, 57,299 days left

Day 2

It is so strange now—being here. I was certain I was mentally prepared to be here, but now that I am physically here, I have been challenged. And of all the things I should be worried about, it is not the mission that worries me. I'm worried about my marriage. Our marriage has never existed without the expedition and now that we are at its gates, I'm unsure of how I feel. It scares me.

We had only one goal with this expedition: to determine where we came from. We have put together the best team that the United Nations of Vedere can offer. The brightest minds, the best critical thinkers, the most composed, balanced, and level-headed team that we could possibly assemble. Yet it is not our work that scares me. What does that mean?

Logistics: We have set up camp and everything seems to be in order. I know I keep saying this, but I truly believe this mission will be a success. We may discover wonders our minds have yet to comprehend. Who knows what the Underside holds? One thing I am proud to say is that we all understand that we have a responsibility as students, biologists, theologians, philosophers, and teachers. Our team believes we are best together. We have a duty to seek out that which we do not understand. And we agree. That is why I sense success.

So far, everything is going as expected. In the nearly two decades of planning, we have prepared every contingency we can possibly conceive. We have team members so dedicated you could argue they are more prepared for life down here than up above. Some of the scientists on our team grew up planning this mission. We have members on our team that come from two and three generations of the same family.

Around ten years ago, we began sending probes to the Underside to get a rough mapping of the terrain and its geology. We discovered that the Underside is composed of almost identical terrain to ours, except for one major difference—it is shrouded in almost complete darkness. The temperatures range from 0 to -4 degrees Celsius, with some liquid water in pockets speckled across the landscape. We know it is impossible for many of the plants to photosynthesize, so we are unsure of how the plants get nutrients. We have been unable to find any animals or insects.

Five years later, we began launching beacons to the Underside to illuminate the areas we would be studying. The strategic placement of these beacons became our study radius. The area that our drones scouted as ideal showed images of stone structures that our anthropologist believed were built by our earliest ancestors. We chose that area as our epicenter and worked a radius outward. We hope to find anything that points to where we began and how we developed. From our probes, we decided on a location near a basin with a mountain range to its east. This would allow us to investigate the ancient structures and surrounding area. Each beacon stood three hundred meters, creating a visible area about the size of the capital city of Arælia. It is a fantastic plan.

With a study area, we employed Dr. Chelcie's synth technology for all Underside construction, as we believed the air to be unsuitable for Vederians. Each synth could be programmed much like a drone and could be powered for six months on a single solar charge. They were designed to be bipedal, torphi-responsive, and nearly indestructible. Standing three meters tall, they were also about thirty times stronger than the average Vederian. For our mission, we had the resources to design and build seven synths and, after beacon construction, we had them return to be reprogrammed for our expedition. We assigned two synths to the security team, two to the geological team, two to the ecological team, and one to myself personally.

We know the synths will be intimidating to work with, but we've briefed the team and stressed their importance. This is the most important work of our lives. We have a responsibility to employ every tool and innovation we can to ensure a successful mission. I am certain we will be fine.

For further contingency, we have assigned a few doctors and psychologists to assess any needs our teams may have. We anticipate stressors. We will be isolated from the world for at least three months. It will be hard on the body and the mind—but I believe in our preparation. The pain always comes first. It hurts to begin, and it hurts to continue, but we've been through the pain of preparation. It is now time for commencement.

***

Athena Saroyan, 4,013 days left, a decade before the death of the Ægæliphi

Halo Raphaela is the second halo of the nation of Vedere. The continent completely encircles the first, Michaela, and is two-thirds the size of it. Halo Raphaela has one of the fastest rotations in the nation, making travel to and from difficult for travelers. Those native to the halo are also acclimated to the slightly stronger gravitational pull the halo boasts. It is characterized by its large mountain ranges—some of the highest in all of the nation—and various research centers. Most of the continent is speckled with laboratories, museums, and national fields.

My husband wanted to live here because he needed, in his words, "to be closest to the capital, without actually being in the capital." I suppose I never quite understood what he meant. If fact, I think it took me entirely too long to realize that I almost never understood what Gaius meant. He always eluded me. All the way to the end.

A year and one month ago, I remember, vividly, sitting, legs folded on the floor next to one of our bookshelves in our library. Gaius was having a conversation with our son, Balien. He didn't speak to him as if he were *our* son, however. He, as always, only spoke to Balien as if he were *his* son.

I remembered how that bothered me.

"What does your history tell you, boy?" Gaius asked, shifting his weight from one arm of the chair to the next. Before him, our five-year-old son sat, wide-eyed and smiling, with his legs folded.

"It tells me the truth, Father," Balien replied, almost reciting.

"And what is truth, Son?" Gaius asked, his eyes now locking with Balien. Before his son answered, Gaius replied, *"I will tell you."*

Balien adjusted his sofa pillow before his father began in torphi: *"In the beginning, there was the quinqu. Before the quinqu, there was nothing. All that exists owes its life to them. As gods in their own right, the five came together, creating beings never before seen, and when it came time to make woman, the world was forever changed. This being, woman, would be wise, unmoving, and astounding. Vedere..."*

Gaius paused to straighten his back, blinking a few times and shaking his head as he prepared to continue. He was confused again. He had seen this exact moment before. It was what Vederians called shading. Often, in torphi, the passing of time as perceived is not linear. Memories are grounded in emotion and emotions are not bound by time. They are also extremely unreliable. During typical torphic conversations, time can loop and spin, especially if the present strongly resembles the past. This was not the first time Gaius recited the religious history of Vedere to his son. But it would be the last.

"Repeat after me, Son," Gaius asked. His son unfolded his legs, mimicking his father's posture. *"Vedere."* Gaius's hands opened in front of him, forming a "V" shape with palms up. The fingers were pointed slightly toward his son.

"Vedere," Balien replied. Balien mimicked the sign, pointing back at his father.

"Hören, Gan Dong, Odore, and Nusdvagisdi," Balien mimicked again as Gaius continued—Hören, parallel hands held up, with the left thumb forming a perpendicular crossbar; Gan Dong, a sideways pointing right hand that moved further right as it turned away from the body; Odore, cupped hands in the shape of a bowl but turned so that there was no bottom; and Nusdvagisdi, a fist with the thumb tucked under the pointer and middle finger, placed directly on the chest.

"Each god wanted their likeness in us, but Vedere disapproved," Balien recited.

"Very good, Balien," Gaius replied, grabbing his son's hips as he placed his son directly in front of him.

"See me, this is the most important part, son. As the scriptures state, Vedere, the wisest of the gods, offered to step aside, which motivated the gods to compromise. Through this act, Vedere emerged as the most suitable template." Balien nodded vigorously, and if Gaius had kept count well, which he had, this would be the seventh time he'd had this conversation with his son.

"Vedere's likeness would be used for the new being," Gaius explained, as if he had never uttered this truth before. He continued, using both torphi and tanna.

"This new being, called Vederian, would be the gods's greatest creation. For Vedere sees all. Nothing can hide from her. Vederians would experience the world through Vedere ... through sight." Gaius's body rocked and swayed with each motion. Tanna is about facial expressions as much as it is about the motion of the hands. Eyebrows would raise and lower as the entire face matched each sign's meaning.

Balien was transfixed. He refused to lose eye contact; he was excited, but also didn't want to be disrespectful. Breaking eye contact during telempathic dialogue would completely disrupt communication. For tophi to operate properly, full focus and eye contact is required. Once torphic dialogue is established, eyes cannot break gaze, though there are a few exceptions. Balien is one of those exceptions. Unlike every other Vederian, Balien has to blink to keep his eyes moisturized. But by this age, he has mastered the feat of not blinking well enough to even fool his own father. Balien was better at assimilating than I was, and he was still a child.

Balien was special. There was no denying that. He was already so acutely tuned in. It was astounding. At such a young age, he had already mastered concepts that would challenge most adults. No one can enter torphi by accident or by force unless a mental invitation is extended. Both minds must be prepared. Either Balien didn't require such a mental practice, or he had the ability to circumvent it.

Vederians share memories, emotions, past experiences, and impressions though torphi. It's something that makes for very little secrets, and very few lies. And though torphi is an inherent ability to all Vederians, it's important to understand that torphi is *still* an ability, much like any other skill that has to be perfected. Some are better than others. Visions more intense, emotions more personal. It can be overwhelming for some depending on their ability and even then, some things simply cannot be shared and those who suffer from certain mental illnesses struggle to communicate as well.

Nevertheless, torphi is still a language. A mental language. And it was built on a complex mixture of emotions and memories. For Vederians, instead of speaking and using words to convey ideas and concepts, torphi directly imbued the recipient with the desired concept. And when supplemented with physical hand signs, very complex ideas can be shared almost instantly. Torphi is fluid thought—thought that can be turned on and off like a faucet.

For us, our reference point for vision-based language is linked to the other senses. The opposite is true for Vederians. All they know is sight. This presents unique challenges when we engage with them. For example,

Gaius is proficient in both tanna and banna, which was a rarity, as most men did not receive the necessary schooling in Vederian culture. Learning the skill of tanna was a necessity in most sectors, as many Vederians preferred it over torphi for privacy and convenience. Though it's common to see Vederians casually communicating using tanna, there are purists who regard torphi as the most educated and respectable form of communication.

When we chose to have Balien, Gaius intended for his son to thrive in Vederian society. I intended something similar, but for entirely different reasons. Becoming fluent in all forms of communication would be a skill Balien would have to have. We both at least agreed on that. But ultimately, Gaius could never know what his son *truly* was. I didn't have to hurt him in that way. But I made a choice. I'm certain he knew our child was different, but I believe out of love he ignored those differences. This was one of the rare few instances he got to be with his son, so instead of questioning what his son was, he focused more on who his son was becoming. That was the part he was missing.

Gaius continued, but his demeanor shifted. This was turning into a completely different conversation. I didn't want to have to step in. I remained in my office as the two went on with their conversation.

"Balien, we were made to see, and I believe this with each beat of my heart. We are the observers. We are keen and we are perceptive. It is these traits that have allowed our people to outlast every other civilization before us. We are truth-seekers, Balien. And to that end, I want you to know something, Son. I am not who you think I am."

My body froze. I had become a statue of marble so still I was certain I had been noticed by the two in the room across from me. I listened acutely to hear my husband's heartbeat speed up. This was going to be truth, whatever it was.

This time, Gaius intentionally shared past emotions—knowing his son could look through his vestment. He was initiating a sæ, a rare Vederian ability in which a trance-like state is initiated. It's a realm that only exists in a collective consciousness and, according to my understanding, only

Vederian women could enter it. This was an ability Gaius had to have *learned.* Learned from someone extremely important.

I closed my eyes and focused. I would have to hijack the sæ. I connected using my son's heartbeat as a conduit. We were now all traveling together, but Gaius would not know.

Gaius had taken us to the past. This had to be at least twenty years ago, as remnants of the Civil War were more evident.

"Son, the history of Vedere is brimmed with suffering," he began. Though Vederians cannot *physically* feel pain, their emotions are close enough. Gaius stood with tears that traveled down his cheeks. Time was being manipulated as well. This was very advanced torphi. Gaius's age began to fluctuate and his clothes changed color and style. This is what I feared. The ability that Vederians had, the sæ, was in fact incredibly powerful. In reality, time is linear, but in a sæ time is no longer confined. Time's true form is liquid. It is as vast as the ocean and as responsive—like rippling waves when anything comes in contact with it. And, like water, if you were not careful, you would drown.

Gaius was aging, as was Balien. First, he was an eight-year-old boy, yet also a man of thirty, almost simultaneously. He was a remarkably smart man, nearly seven feet tall with a head of hair kinked tight, eyes green, and large hands. This was something Gaius was not supposed to see.

Gaius squinted his eyes as he attempted to make out the setting of the mental palace he was creating—a bright, modern house with stone tables and wooden floors. I recognized the architecture. It was partly Vederian, but partly something else as well.

Gaius could not know yet that he was nothing like his son. I still had to raise Balien. Teach him how to assimilate, as my father did. Teach him how to deal with men like his father.

Gaius represented the old guard. He was the model for Vederian men everywhere. He was a believer. A religious soldier, priest of the goddess, and now, a father. He trail blazed the path for men in leadership roles in his day. Before him, the Ophori was an elite class of warriors and clergy that accepted only women. The priestesses served as liaisons to the goddess. The female governors relegated men to the more physically demanding roles. The highest role in the world, the Ægæliphi, embodying nothing short of truth and justice, was a female-only position by royal blood. And though the nation of Vedere was not made for man, Gaius was content. He held fast to this truth. He fought for the world his son now had and though he prayed to the goddess for a daughter, he still loved his son and he loved his nation. He would die for it. And still, Balien was nothing like his father. He never would be.

I searched for a window of opportunity to interrupt the sæ. I couldn't allow Gaius to see Balien as a full adult. He wasn't ready for that truth, not yet.

"But it is a history that you must see. You are about to see something extremely painful." Gaius was fixed, looking ahead into the mental construction he was building. The modern house began to break down, another structure was being built now. He had not yet noticed that Balien's age was fluctuating as his was.

Gaius was building the throne room. He was young, handsome, and in peak physical shape. He kneeled among some twenty or so other men all dressed as Ophori. Gaius was not *just* a priest in the Order of the Ophori. He *was* Ophori. When I married Gaius, I knew I was establishing a house of secrets. But I never imagined I was married to a liar on par with myself.

"This is a memory I am showing you, Son, because I want you to learn a very important lesson: pain always comes first. Son, we are in the throne room of the Ægæliphi. I am being given a mission that was truly a sinful act. And though I never realized it then, my brothers and I are allowing our hearts to be turned away from the goddess forever."

The chamber was so bright, it was as if the Ægæliphi were made of pure light. She communicated only in tanna. Her ebony black hands, which deeply contrasted with her unblemished white toga, moved smoothly and calmly. She was asking the men to murder an entire village. And they didn't flinch.

"Balien, I was a part of an extremely secretive group. By trade, a battalion of priests, but we had also become something else entirely. We called ourselves The Old Guard." Gaius's face grew old, his hair growing down to his waist and then back up to his ears as he became younger again before continuing.

"In that time, there was an offshoot group of called the Heretics of the Civil War. Their descendants became the people we now call the Cophi. We believed that they were motivated by the Va Dynasty. We were told that by covertly neutralizing a resistance leader, Kamali, and most of her family, we would be effectively restoring order to the halos. We truly believed that, Son. I want you to know that."

I could not believe what I was seeing—could hardly process it. As tears streamed down my face, the scene changed again. We were sinking deeper into the liquid. Deeper into time. Gaius was one of the assassins who killed my grandmother. It was now painfully clear how convoluted things had become. I had to come up with something. Something very quickly.

It was now the night of Prince Victor's birthday, Gaius and Balien were in the middle of a heated argument. Gaius and his son stood eye to eye. This was dangerous. Dipping this deep into a sæ could drown you.

"The Residuals are nothing but superstition, Balien!" Gaius maintained. He was dressed in formal wear, as was Balien. They were at the capital. "The study of such is witchcraft and blasphemy and you know this. We were made in the likeness of the goddess Vedere, the goddess of sight. We were made to see. What do you think this means?"

Gaius flinched as he watched himself in the stairwell with his son; this was the old guard speaking. The context of this conversation was now clearer. Gaius was revealing a secret to *save* his son.

"Years ago, it was the resurgence of these fanatics that nearly cracked the nation into shards."

Gaius looked back at his son just as his future self did the same. They were beginning to meld. They were running out of time. We all were.

"Balien, we cannot stay here much longer, but I want you to see for yourself. You are the very embodiment of an idea, a good idea. But if you do not stop, if you are not wise with your thirst for knowledge and truth, you will begin to entertain the likes of charlatans." Gaius was disgusted and it showed. "You cannot become this, my son. I have broken an oath I vowed never to break. I have divulged the *keep* to you. And I have done it to save you. No one knows of what I will share with you next."

Gaius placed his hands behind him in a gesture that did not match the conversation. Future Gaius had placed his hands behind his back to follow after the Present Gaius. Soon they would become the same man. I had to do something, but I couldn't move or shout.

"It was the idea, Balien, the small, infectious idea that absolute truth could not exist that spawned religious fervor into anarchy. An idea that started as merely a simple hypothesis."

Gaius was preparing to make one last appeal. To Gaius, Balien was his greatest achievement. But he was still in the dark. It had been a miracle that the secret of our son's heritage had been held within the walls of our home for this long. But even more miraculous was the fact that his father still wasn't aware of exactly *what* Balien was.

"You are so inquisitive," Older Gaius continued. "There are not many secrets that can be hidden from a mind like yours. This was something I now have known and something that you have always known." This was it. Gaius could no longer communicate in the present tense. His mind was starting to buckle under the strain of the sæ. Drowning.

"Father," Adult Balien replied, "I am what I am. You have to accept that." In an instant, everything was pure white. We were finally exiting Gaius's sæ. I stumbled out of my office chair and fell flat on my back. I heard Gaius's body thud on the floor as he collapsed. We were back in the present. Our son was a child again. And he too was laid flat on his back.

The majority of Balien's knowledge about who he truly was came from me. Everything he knew about being Vederian still came largely from books, but it was now clear that this was the beginning of Balien inching toward a mindset that Gaius viewed as horrific. This was a breaking point. Gaius had only ever seen that mindset lead to death. To Gaius—and I now understood this—this was about a father saving his son's life from something he did not fully understand: curiosity. Balien was not just a boy growing up in a matriarchal society, he was an alien living in a completely different culture. Gaius was knocking at the door of this fact. And I suppose now was as good as time as any.

"Balien, do you understand?" Gaius signed, wiping the blood from his nose. He was relentless. He wanted to know just how inquisitive his son was. The flashback, the flash forward, all of it to make a simple point: do not ask too many questions. It was practically a threat.

"Gaius, is everything alright?" I asked, interrupting. This was becoming too much and Gaius was not letting up.

"Balien, do you understand?" Gaius asked.

Balien paused for a moment.

"You could never understand what you've just done," I sign. I am at my breaking point.

Gaius immediately stood up and gave me a customary nod. "Athena, I—I'm sorry."

I ignored him, opened the door, and ushered him out. I then turned around to Balien and winked. "I hope you're OK, little man."

Balien nodded. "I am tough. And I remembered what you told me. The truth is that this is what history tells us. This is how the Earth began. We are Vedere. And we are the race of the world—"

"But what?"

"But there's more than meets the eye," Balien replied.

We both smiled.

Athena Saroyan, two days later

This garden was one of the most beautiful places I had ever known. The shada flowers, the ones that would change color each time you look at it, the hopi trees that formed a canopy over the ground it protected. The stories I read here. The stories I was told here.

It was in this garden that my father, Genet, explained to me who I truly was. He sat me down here, underneath the hopi tree, and explained to me who our family *really* was, where we truly came from. He explained why we lived here. Why we should always stay here. And even when I was old enough to understand why he was right, I still resented never seeing the world like he had and his mother before him. But it was still beautiful. It was still one of those places that just felt right. It felt like home. And though I spent nearly my entire life here, I still found peace here.

This was also one of the most beautiful places Balien had ever seen. Each petal, each leaf, glimmered and danced in the sunlight. Rays shined beams onto vibrantly lit flowers and brilliant trees. Farther down, past our land, the forest was covered with Osra, giant trees with bioluminescent trunks, roots, and stems. The soft glow of their roots led early Vederian settlers as they established walking trails and roads.

"We used to travel in twos and threes," my father would say. He spoke in our language, the one of the tongue. "It lit our path, and we were never lost."

My father and his people were so brave. What they aimed to do. Who they had to turn against. I don't know if I could have done what his ancestors did. But I do know that it is now time for my son to know who he is and why he is different. It is my turn to light his path, so that he may never lose his way. So I will be brave too.

"Sit down, Balien, I want to tell you a story." I patted a spot next to me. "I want to tell you about another boy and his mother."

When my father first told me of our origin, I didn't believe him. When he taught me to speak I still thought it was a game. When I began to *hear* the sounds as they slowly creeped into my conscious mind, I was still slow to believe. It was all too much too fast. But it is always too much too fast.

Balien sat and folded his legs. He winked at me and squeaked out a smirk. "Is this an object lesson? Or a real, true story?" Oh, my boy is smart. Maybe too smart. He is the type to try and understand the things you are telling him before you even begin. And even if he's wrong, he'll adjust. He'll do that quickly as well.

"This story is completely true, I will not lie to you," I sign. I know he'll take to spoken word very quickly. I have no doubt of that. But I'm worried about his curious mind. Once he is aware of our family's deepest secret, he will be a target. He will be in danger from now until the final breath he draws in. I feel the swell of fear rush up into my throat. I wonder if this is the fear my father felt. It was so scary.

"Years ago there was a woman who lived in the hills. She was different. She looked different than all her friends, she acted differently, she believed differently. You see, she was convinced the world she was in was missing something. She had this nagging feeling that so much was being left out. What she was seeing was not truly the world—not really, not to her. Over time, she began to see the world in a new way, but it was not long before she realized she was the *only* one who could do it. Many, many people called her crazy. They said she was a liar and only intended to create a more divisive world. But she didn't give up. She gathered the courage to tell others about the new world that she saw. She wanted everyone to be able to experience the world as she could. But there were others who disagreed. It caused a terrible war. A civil war, in which she nearly lost everything. And in the end—and I'm sorry but you must know—she was killed by one of her closest friends—"

"Mom, I know this story," Balien interjected. "You're talking about Kamali."

"Yes, yes, the leader of the Kofi. You're very smart. Tell me what you know." He likes the encouragement. He's six, so he's extremely competitive. He has also become even more powerful.

"The books say that Kamali was a traitor, but you told me not to use that word. She was assassinated by an unknown person. She believed in the Residual and tried to tell everyone about it. Everyone thought she was crazy." Balien crossed his eyes and used his pointer fingers to spin around his ears.

"Very good, Balien. You seem to know quite a bit. But there's more to this story than you know. There's more than meets the eye." I point to my green eye and smile and wink with my brown eye. "I know you never met my father, Genet. He died before you were born. The same was true for me: I never met my grandmother."

Balien perked up. This was the first time I had spoken about Balien's grandfather and great-grandmother. I could tell he was interested.

"What was your grandmother's name?" he asked.

"Kamali," I signed, grinning. The hand sign was a shape in which the thumb is placed between the pointer and middle fingers. You take that shape and lightly push it upwards.

"What do you mean Kamali?" Balien asked, confused. "You mean I'm related to Kamali?"

"Yes, Son," I reply. "And your great-grandmother was not a traitor, nor was she crazy. She was just not like any of the people around her."

I took a pause for effect.

"Your great-grandmother could experience things that no one else could. She knew things that others could never know."

Balien was still much too young to understand who we were, but I had to plant the seed now.

"Alright, that's enough for today. How about we get you swinging from this hopi tree?"

Balien jumped up with a smile.

***

Talia Davis, 216 days left

The journal entrusted to Rory was extremely worn. It had creases lengthwise along the spine as if its cover had been folded over itself hundreds of times. It was full-grain leather of the highest quality. You could tell that it initially began as a rustic light coffee brown—until you inspected its corners, which through a healthy amount of wear had faded into the deepest of browns, as if it were made up of thousands of layers of similar hue all pressed into one.

It was a color that identically matched the brown of Talia's hands. She knew she was right, not in her mind, but her heart: both had come from the same origin, as it were a living book of skin that held the words of her grandfather, ordered meticulously and cautiously with countless pages of diagrams, arrows, circles, and highlights.

Talia pored over it, as she had done thousands of times. As she thumbed through the pages, her mind flashed back to the day years ago it was first placed into her hands. Talia's father, David, had been the original keeper of the journal; he was a librarian and writer himself. He loved books and chronicling. He placed immense value in books and their power. He taught his daughter to love books in the same way, just as his father had taught him.

"This journal, Talia, it lives as we live. It speaks and causes thoughts to spring alive," he would always say. "The thoughts you develop as a result are its offspring. As such, they too must be cared for, raised, and nourished."

David had always intended to withhold the secrets the journal held until Talia was ready, but that time came sooner than he intended.

On a particularly bright, clear day, David was stabbed sixteen times the moment he crossed the threshold of his home. The air was so crisp on that day it was almost sharp, as if glass were in the lungs. Breaths had to be stolen between the sobs of Vedere's newest widow and her child.

When he fell, a flurry of papers flickered up the air before landing over his sprawled, lifeless body, his navy messenger bag half open, resting on his quarter-turned hips.

David's wife, crawling toward her husband's folded feet, found the presence of mind to reach into David's bag to remove a full-grain leather journal with creases along the spine. She knew his walks and journaling were partners in habit and that his father's work always stayed with him.

Talia was in school that day. When she reached her house she was less shocked to see Ophori at her door and more astounded at her mother's calm demeanor while speaking with the warrior-police force.

With her eyes, she told Talia to freeze in the way only mothers can do. Talia cemented and dug roots into the terrazzo sidewalk. An iciness jolted through her body, as if a stalactite had fallen into her curly crown. She knew now that obedience would mean the difference between life and death.

She took a moment between her shallow breaths to observe and analyze her situation: was there time for tears?

First, it was clear her father was dead. Second, the presence of the royal guard in such a short time frame most likely meant he had been killed. Third, her mother's lack of tears and stoic demeanor meant she was thinking; she'd seen that face before a decisive chess move. Fourth, none of the Ophori were questioning her mother, with the majority of the battalion inside the house, stepping over her father with each reentry. They were looking for something. Fifth, her mother's request kept Talia just out of eyesight, meaning a threat was still present or there was something that she needed Talia to do.

Talia lowered into a crouch as soon as she realized that—her mother had thrown the journal into the nearly landscaped shrubs that shrouded her from the Ophori. She only had a few seconds, which she took. Her only final regret was that she didn't allow her gaze to linger just a bit more on her mother. She knew she would never see her parents again. Talia was twelve. And all she had left was a journal that she'd never read.

***

Talia Davis, 184 days left, two days before the death of the Ægaeliphi

When Talia was taken to live with her aunt, her aunt took her to see someone every week. Every week for seven years. And with all of that, it didn't help her. Talia's behavior borderlined on agoraphobia. She had become even more bookish and reclusive. She was curt, almost always, and her voracious reading caused her to be deeply critical of nearly everything. But she still had a few relationships.

Talia left the school library and took an automated hovercar home. She was met at the door by her aunt.

"I want you to freshen up, baby. I know you just got home, but I'm headed to a fundraiser," Talia's aunt signed. Her aunt was a former law professor who lobbied often and was a huge supporter and best friend of their district's proveyor. "I think you should leave the house and come with me."

Talia tucked the corners of her lips back so that her deep dimples flashed. She rolled her eyes while motioning for her aunt to step to the side.

"Talia! Don't be like that, please. I actually think this is something you'll enjoy. You'll be among some of the smartest minds in Vedere: historians, biologists, ecologists, even etymologists like your grandfather."

Talia thought about it for a moment. Her aunt made a valid point. There could be some serious benefits to making some scientific friends, but she had to be careful. Her parents were killed, for reasons she still didn't fully understand. But the prospect of meeting someone who could help her with the journal was something she couldn't pass up. She looked up and smiled.

"Alright, I'll be ready in twenty minutes."

***

Valerie, 2,554 days left. Six and a half years before the death of the Ægæliphi

There is an enclave that is formed from an arch made of marble. It's a threshold that separates the lower quarters from the keep. It's a central location with a view of the seven cardinal directions Vederians use. In school, Vederians learn of north, south, east, and west. They are also taught of tan, ban, and sæ, or forward, toward, and above, respectively. The final three refer to a range of directions that apply to different planes of existence. Since their recent discovery, the understanding of how tanna and sæs work had drastically improved. But even before the advancement of technology, this archway served as a gateway.

Vedere's earliest leaders, both Vo and Va, all used this spire. From this archway, a person could see the entire nation. All four cardinal directions. And if they happened to be a sær, they could also see the nation from the other three cardinal directions as well.

This spire was where Valerie spent a lot of her time. When she was a child, she would peek just above the ridge of the keep. She felt as if she were the mother and the view was her child. The sky was the child's mind: clear, crisp, and innocent. The land was the child's body: alive and bustling, curious and inquisitive. She would imagine the people as they lived. She asked herself what they painted and what led them to dance. And when she needed to simply think, the stillness allowed for the unencumbered flow of honest thought. This is where Valerie learned that she could sæ.

Vera knew of all her children's favorite spots around the castle. Vega would sleep on the Ophori training ground looking straight up at the sky. She'd lay on the cool concrete motionless. She'd have to be called in for dinner. The youngest, Victor, could almost always be found in the library with a book between his small fingers. He was small enough to curl between the bookshelves and would treat the cutout as if it were the bottom of a bunkbed. Valerie's spot was the keep, where she would endlessly stare out into the world.

This time, Vera asked her guards to wait at the edge of the courtyard, just northwest of the keep where Valerie was standing. Vera stood alone in the courtyard for some time. She took a few deep breaths and lifted her head up toward the sky. The twenty-one-year-old ducked under the ridge spire to remain out of sight. Her mother was only looking up at the amberlight, enjoying the pink and purple clouds as they blended across the sky. Vera slowly rolled her head down to a neutral position. She met eyes with Vega, standing at the opposite end of the courtyard.

"I'm no longer surprised that you know where I am, but rather, that you know *when* I am here," Vega began. She embraced her mother and kissed her cheek. Valerie peeked above the edge of the spire. She had a perfect shelf to rest her chin.

"I always knew that if I could not find you, you would be here, off to yourself," Vera replied. "I also know when you are bothered. Tell me what is troubling you, my dearest."

Vega let in a sharp inhale and furrowed her eyebrows in a way that made them appear as a single, horizontal line.

"It is just so cliché, Mother. It is me, thinking about age and my own thoughts. The older I get, the more I feel the weight of the throne."

"And you have become so strong."

Vera leaned against a sculpture of her grandmother. All of the Ægaeliphis of Vo were placed around the courtyard, facing inward. Some were posed as warriors, others poised in philanthropic positions handing out books or fruits. Vera's grandmother was seated reading, one hand in a book, the other on her chin.

"Your family is the throne, child. You were born royal, you will live royal, and you will die royal."

"I know, Mother, and when my time comes the Viceroy will give me absolute power. I will be responsible fo—"

"You are a woman, Vega. You already have absolute power," Vera interrupted. "And you are not given power, you *are* power. The Viceroy cannot give it and they surely cannot take it away."

Vera was correct in that the Viceroy had no political power. They were simply matriarchs who were highly revered and respected in Vederian society. They had been established since ancient times and had remained present through both dynasties. The ceremony, the traditions, it was all a show. Ultimately, power only transferred from woman to woman, from mother to daughter. This was how it had always been—until very recently.

Vega was still skeptical and despondent. With a huff, she let out a deep sigh and lowered her forehead onto her mother's shoulder.

"I think it is time I tell you," her mother began. Vega's head peeked back up over the makeshift fort she had created with her mother's draped clothing. "It is time I tell you of how I came to be Ægæliphi. Do you remember my other grandmother?"

Vega nodded.

"She was a great woman. An honest woman. You must never forget that."

Vega nodded again.

"Now, do you remember our family tapestry?" Vera asked. "The one that had the loose thread that you liked to pull when you were a child?"

"Yes, Mother." Vega smiled. "You punished me for an entire month for pulling that thread."

Vera looked out over her kingdom. "Yes. An entire month. And do you remember why?"

Vega pulled her hair back and thought for a moment. "You told me that pulling a single thread could ruin the entire tapestry."

Vera nodded back in response. "Yes, my child. Exactly that. And so, as you are now older, there is something that you must know. Our family has pulled a thread. There is a single lie in our land, my child. Just one. But it is a lie that could unravel the entire world."

Valerie felt a pull in the pit of her stomach. She had never heard of an actual lie. She knew what it was in concept, but she had been taught that actual lies no longer existed in society.

"See me, child. I know this frightens you, but you have to know this truth and no one else. Not even your sister Valerie. My grandmother hid something from the world. And now you must do the same."

"What is it, Mother?" Vega replied.

"Your grandmother kept a secret from the nation. She protected it from the existence of someone who could shake the very foundation of our world. A baby. A baby that was nothing like us."

Valerie's eyes widened.

***

Record NGV #291, Avis Reporting, 513 days left

Gaius forced a mechanical smile as he took several steps back to exit to the party. To say that Gaius was not sociable would be an understatement. He was gruff, curt, and narcissistic. But he was also effective, pointed, and direct. He knew how much he could take before his introverted tendencies began to set in and he knew how to read a room. He left the main atrium and climbed the stairs of the spire to overlook the capital. With a light tap to the temple, he disengaged his kokoto from the main mindstream so he could exit the conversations in the atrium.

In modern society, when a Vederian wanted to be a part of the larger conversation, all they had to do was connect their kokoto to the Oro. Within it, they could select from various interwoven streams of mental conversations and connect.

Gaius climbed the stairs of the spire to take a look at the view. The amberlight, or the lesser light, as it's also known, felt calm and still. Amberlight's transition is marked first with silence of the birds, though a Vederian would not notice, and a cool breeze, though this too would go unnoticed. Gaius brought in a shallow inhale and let out a long exhale. He signed a short prayer and adjusted his formal clothing. He was ready to rejoin the party.

As the final arriving family members were seated, Valerie stood up from the royal table and raised two fingers into the air. She instantly had everyone's attention. She smiled and beamed with a sparkle in her eye. Her body moved as if it floated underwater; her arms and hands flowed peacefully as she turned her eyes to her brother.

"My brother, Victor, is the most beautiful baby I have ever seen." The crowd lightly bounced their shoulders and waved their hands, the Vederian form of laughter. Victor was turning nineteen.

"He will go on to be a great member of our family, I'm sure—well, maybe." A few in the crowd jumped again. "But let us not forget that before we can be great, before we can grow and develop, pain comes first. Birth comes second. So on that thought, happy birthday, Victor, may you become all that you were intended to be." It was a curious traditional saying. Vederians didn't feel physical pain. However, they did experience extreme mental distress. It was pretty close.

The chandelier's sparkles mirrored the crowd's jewelry. Both flashed as the crowd's shoulders bounced again in agreement. Valerie took two sips from her glass before handing it to a bartender, as she went to greet Gaius and the other priestesses.

By raising her hand, Valerie showed her palm to greet Gaius as they came together. He too raised his hand, palm exposed. It was a greeting that meant peace.

As a devout Vaeli and priest of the Church of the Vedere, Gaius rarely ever felt comfortable in the palace when it didn't include his typical affairs. The Vael, as the church had come to be called, was extremely powerful. In the past, Gaius's job had been to enlighten the minds of the people as consort to the goddess, Vedere, but in recent years his job had morphed into a kind of rehabilitation of the minds of the new generation.

Over the decades, belief in the Residual had seen a resurgence. Now, they called themselves the Cophi and though they were believed to have been completely wiped out, many were believed to still be in hiding in the more remote areas of the nation. The Cophi was seen by the Church and the Viceroy as the nation's biggest threat.

"We were made to live as Vedere would, in order, in respect, in honor." Gaius was responding to a councilwoman from Ajax. "Our nation was lost, ma'am. The halo rulers of old pushed our world into disgrace. The accursed Cophi and their beliefs nearly broke our nation."

"It was our recommitment to order, to technological advancement, and to our adherence to Vael that has catapulted us past the wildest dreams of our ancestors," Tora McDaniel added. Tora passed a familiar nod to Gaius. They had not seen each other in quite some time.

"Our history outlined our ancestors' mistakes and their imbalanced rule is what made them inferior. There was no order, no respect, and no honor," Gaius added. "It took Civil War and nigh tearing of our nation in two to restore greatness." Gaius paused to allow those words to land.

This was Gaius in rare form—it's amazing how well I knew him. Rarely did Gaius speak of his younger days. Standing six-foot, four-inches, even at middle age, he was still in immaculate shape. His long white hair was parted into two braids reaching nearly to his waist. His dark skin was weathered like expensive leather, but smoothed over as if it has been damaged. His gray eyes had a glimmer of peace, but looked out as if they have seen plenty suffering.

Gaius was a priest now, but he was once a warrior and one of the best, second only to Maya Durham, widely regarded as the greatest Ophori to ever live. Gaius Saroyan had committed thirty years to the Church's cause as he fought in conflicts after the Sisters War, but he told no one—not his wife, and surely not his son.

Before Balien was born, the world was very different. The city of New Redemption did not experience the peace its citizens enjoyed now. Entire families had died to restore that order. Peace was reestablished, but the shroud of chaos was returning. Gaius knew that everything was about to change.

"I am following along quite well, gentlemen," Valerie replied. "We are due for a return to order. Everyone is so afraid of conflict, but I welcome it. We have citizens who experience a peace that came at a price they do not understand. I think it is time they understand how much peace costs."

Whether the constituents agreed with Valerie or not, no one would openly disagree with anything she said.

"Our princess does indeed know the price of peace," Tora added, hoping to change the subject slightly. "How did the saying go? Out of ch—"

"But out of that chaos, solidarity emerged," Gaius interrupted. "Valerie was that solidarity."

Valerie had become a household name after the Sisters War. In a conflict that spanned eight decades, multiple generations were dragged into a bitter battle between two family lines, Vo and Va. Valerie was not expected to see any battle, but she trained and fought nonetheless. In the waning days of the war, it was Valerie who led the final efforts to stamp out Va soldiers.

Valerie was a personal friend of Gaius and was one of the few who knew he was trained as an Ophori. Together they fought on covert operations as a perfect pair. Valerie and the Old Guard were unstoppable. Their ruthlessness and precision helped close the chapter on the Sisters War.

Vega was to become Ægæliphi, but it was Valerie who, at twenty-five, held the heart of the nation. She was determined and strong, and Gaius also came to love her immensely. There was a story that came from one of the Sisters War's covert operations: Valerie infiltrated the home of a known Cophi spy with the help of seven Ophori warriors, using a new technology called the *hala,* a harnesslike device that protected the body with super-heated rings of light. During this raid of the spy's home, Valerie discovered that the rings of light could be used as projectiles. By the time reconnaissance arrived, everyone—including the Ophori—had been reduced to ash, save for Valerie. She intended to be victor, even if that meant being covered in the ashes of her own women.

"Agreed, Valerie the fierce warrior," a proveyor from Puresh added. She stuck her tongue out while she signed. "The fiercest of them all."

An awkwardness crept into the great hall. At the high table, many of the world's important leaders were present, proveyors, members of the council, Viceroy, clergy, and the royal family. But Valerie was not universally loved. She had skeptics in the more independent halos further away from Cara Royale rule. Many from the interior believed it was the outer rings that were responsible for keeping the line of Va alive and supported.

"How is Puresh, Proveyor?" Valerie asked.

"We are blessed by the nation," the proveyor replied. "How is the Cara Royale?"

It was a direct, threatening question. Though explicit details were kept from the public, it was clear something was wrong with Ægæliphi Vera. It was coming up on a decade since her last public appearance.

"Our family is tighter than ever," Valerie replied.

"Please give my blessings to your mother," the Pureshi proveyor replied. "I have a long journey home—if you'll excuse me."

Valerie narrowed her gaze. "You are excused."

There was no crime higher in New Redemption than divulging the Keep, which was defined as any knowledge of the personal affairs of the Ægæliphi and/or her family.

If there was one thing that was clear at the table it was that in this case, the Keep was simple; Valerie was keeping a secret. Her mother might be lost, Valerie was not.

***

Dr. Fallon Sylvan, 2,555 days left

When Vega first approached Dr. Fallon Sylvan, his heart shook in his chest. Her unmistakable entourage formed a small parade as the caravan snaked down the embankment to the sea. The sleek, polished silver ships descended from above and hovered just above the beach. From the Tyree coast, Dr. Sylvan's lab peeked just over the horizon. The sand was iridescent, with colors that danced back and forth between pinks, greens, and blues. The water was so clear it was almost unnerving swim in it. You knew there were millions of eyes looking back at you. The doctor's research called for a close proximity to nature. There was a special place in his heart for those millions of aquatic eyes that looked back up at him.

The embankment was so smooth, you'd have to get down on your knees and press your nose to the sand to see the granules. The craggy embankment had razor-sharp rocks of browns and grays that cowered in the shadow of the Galavad, which could be seen a continent away.

The Koi mountain range that floated above was believed to be the remnants of a continent above Halo Michaela, one that clearly had been shattered. All Vederian continents floated in the sky, and, in some places, there were still levels. The Galavad was built within a range that was high enough to deter intruders for a reason. It was the royal garrison and armory for the entire nation of Vedere—the country of continents that called the sky home.

Dr. Sylvan clenched his teeth and his fists as his tiny island became threatened by seven veiled palanquins—the veils were standard practice to conceal the person who was the true Cara Royale. They formed a semicircle in the sea just fifty meters from his island. He knew that whenever anyone of the royal family traveled, they brought with them a spectacle equal to none other: enough warriors to challenge a city and floating ships armed and at the ready with every energy weapon, spear, and pair of eyes pointed directly at you.

Fallon folded his arms behind him after wiping his sweating brow. As the first dense satin veil unfurled, he saw her: Heir Vega. As she extended one foot outward to step into the water, a servant rushed around to present a saucer-sized stone disk for her to stand on. As she took her next step, another servant sprang into action, catching her other foot without her making an adjustment to her stride. It appeared as if she walked on water. The servants were content to be soaked.

With a splash, two giant figures entered the water as the whole company began their walk to Dr. Sylvan's island, Sciya. Where the depth of the water would top the head of the average Vederian, it only reached just under the chest of the two giant figures, now close enough for Dr. Sylvan to make out—Ophori. The faithful servants had now placed the stone disks on their heads as they held their breath and trudged beneath the water.

Much about the Cara Royale was still a mystery to the public—including what they looked like. This was the first time Fallon had seen Vega. Prominent cheekbones and deep brown skin glowed. She was clothed in a dark lavender silk, crystal eyes pierced through her veil.

Directly from stone disk to sand, she continued her gait as her servants coughed up water. The Ophori looked past the doctor as they surveyed the lab. Though slightly hunched over, Vega still towered over the doctor. She then did something Dr. Sylvan was not prepared for—they lightly touched foreheads. *"Dr. Fallon Sylvan, genius of the Science Church of Vael, I thank you for your time."* Fallon felt his legs weaken.

Fallon's eyes were hazy with fatigue; he was completely unprepared to accept any visitors, let alone a princess. Embarrassed, he regressed into formality, responding as he had been taught to respond.

"Heir Vega, I am your servant. What do you wish for me?" The two Ophori bent down at the knee to support the weight of their queen as she sat on their thighs. Anywhere a princess sat became her throne. She stretched out

her legs, her sandals pushing fresh grooves into the sand. Anyplace her foot landed became her jurisdiction.

"Dr. Sylvan, you are the brightest mind in the nation. You champion Vederian biology. You are talented." Heir Vega paused to turn her head. Her body shook for a moment before she continued. *"We have much to discuss. The utmost discretion will be required, for the task I set before you will not be easy, but it is simple."*

Fallon froze. The heir had approached him unannounced. To his relief, she wanted to work *with* him, not kill him. In all his years of study, he had only hoped his research would be published. She looked him in the eye—as a friend.

Vega continued, *"To complete this task, you must first take your first step."*

"You are absolutely correct, Queen. The journey starts with just one step," Fallon replied with an absent mind. He quickly realized his mistake. *"Forgive me, but, what exactly is the first step?"*

Vega's cheeks warmed into a bright red. *"Indeed, Fallon, but I meant it quite literally—you haven't moved since I arrived."* The rings of her fingers danced in the light. They sparkled just as the waters glistened, reflecting the sun's light.

"Be calm, Fallon. Just call me Vega—I insist. I've come to you because I need your help and I have put my trust in you. Will you place your trust in me?"

Fallon's eyes wandered, only for a second. He looked up to his left, noticing an Ophori loosen up a bit before tightening her grip on her staff. *"Of course, Vega. I trust you,"* he replied.

Fallon noticed the weight of Vega's hands on his shoulders. It reminded him of the burden he'd just agreed to, and just the same, as she lifted her hands from his shoulders, he felt relief.

"This must be Sciya, your island laboratory. I'll require a tour." Vega motioned to the main glass door of Fallon's lab. It wasn't just the lab commissioned to him by order of the Viceroy; it was also his home. Fallon chose the location of an island for the peace the setting brought. The air was light and salty and though the sun provided its perpetual light to all of Arælia, near the water it sparkled. Fallon had spent a decade at sea studying the ecosystems of Arælia: the fauna, the animals, all of it. Fallon motioned

toward the main entrance, straightening his back and placing his hands behind him.

"Are you married, Fallon?" Vega asked, stopping in the foyer of the atrium. One Ophori stood at the door. Another shadowed the heir's every move. Fallon turned to Vega as he felt his body sink into the floor.

"I was," Fallon replied. *"Her name was Ava. She was killed in a fire, here, at Sciya."*

"What terrible news, Fallon. I am deeply sorry."

As they crossed the threshold of the atrium, Vega and Fallon entered the largest structure of the lab.

"The door is motion-sensing, mind your step." Fallon forced a smile before motioning to the main forum. *"This is an area I like to call the Grand—I designed it myself. It serves as the central hub of the entire lab. Around it are similar domes like the Grand, though smaller, positioned as a spiral. Each dome is made of a totally transparent surface to aid my research. As you can see, in the center we have the main console with surveillance and my proprietary AI system that manages the entire lab for me. I designed her from the ground up. She is apt to respond to any voice commands and has the ability to appear in holographic form for ease and accessibility."*

Vega placed her hands behind her back as well. *"Holographic technology is still bleeding edge in most sectors, Fallon. Well done. I also understand you have developed near-field teleportation."*

"Oh, I forgot! Absolutely, yes. Near-field is how I travel to the other domes across the island. This is required for many of the domes because some are positioned midair, such as the aviary and the fitness center. The marine study lab dome is situated about two hundred meters away, on the surface of the ocean floor. As of right now, that is the maximum distance at which I can transmit living matter."

"Excellent, excellent. And I understand that at the Science Church of Vael you completed your thesis on Vederian genetics," Vega pressed.

"Yes, Vega, that is true, though my thesis was amended by the Viceroy for infringement, as I'm sure you're aware." Fallon stepped over to the console to produce a 3D map of the entire island.

"Yes, and I understand that as punishment, you were commissioned away from the capital to study here at Sciya."

Fallon nodded. *"Yes, Vega."*

"Such a brilliant mind. We could have used you in the capital. At the time I was not fully aware of all of the affairs over at the Science Church, I studied privately at the Arœliac Institute. I was told you were incredibly close to fully mapping the Vederian genome. You believed it was the key to preventing a number of diseases."

"In my collegiate career, I was ambitious. I believed that with the proper knowledge, there was no disease that I could not eradicate. It was audacious. I pushed for the impossible. I was lucky to have the Viceroy throw out my thesis. I'm surprised they didn't do worse." Fallon lightly touched a few domes on the map. They changed from a light blue to a green.

"Fallon, let me be direct. You are the brightest mind in Vederian genetics. I consider it your specialty and it is, in fact, linked to the nature of my visit. What I have come to ask of you may very well be impossible as well. I came to you because I still believe in that same ambition. I need your audaciousness. I need you because I haven't much else of a choice." Vega paused for a moment. *"Fallon, I am sick. I am sick and I don't have much time."* The heir rolled back her veil and removed her wig. Her bald head was speckled with white spots and her posture loosened to reveal a much more emaciated frame.

Fallon's eyes widened. "By the Goddess! Heir, I will do everything in my power to cur—"

It was only now that Fallon realized that Vega had been using all her strength to stand. She nearly collapsed to her knees before Fallon and an Ophori could catch her.

"No, Fallon. I do not wish to be cured. You can't cure me. And even if you could, you'd waste too much time. It is too late for me. What I ask for is a task only you can complete."

"Anything, Vega."

Vega let out a series of coughs and her navy blood spattered on the back of her hand.

"I need you to clone me," Vega replied.

Fallon searched her eyes for any deceit, though he knew the Cara Royale never lied. They were both now sitting on the floor.

"Vega, I—I—I'm not sure I can do what you ask of me. The technology, it—it simply is not there. I would need at least twenty years, Vega." Fallon sat back on

his knees. He looked up at the sky and then back down to the marble floor of the Grand.

"Fallon, you will have seven years, maximum," Vega replied as one of the Ophori stood, cradling her as if she were a newborn. Vega rolled up her sleeves to reveal her arms, covered in sores from the elbow up. *"Within seven years, I will be dead and when I die, my younger sister, Valerie, will ascend. Fallon, listen to me, I cannot trust Valerie with the kingdom. No one can. She is not for the people. She is not like me."*

Fallon furrowed his brow as he began to stand. *"But Vega, what do you actually plan to do?"*

"I need a replacement. I need it to look as if I never died. I need my clone to be me and I need no one to know about it. I know the technology is there."

It was true. The basis of Fallon's research in genetics was that with the proper facility, funding, and oversight, it could be marginally possible, but the entire genome would have to be mapped. What Vega asked for was possible in theory, but the needed resources would be unlike anything ever provided.

"I—I would need ... billions," Fallon began.

"Done."

"I would have to essentially build another lab. And it couldn't be this close to the coast."

"Done."

"I would need unprecedented access to Vederian records, medical histories, charts—"

"Done. Anything else?"

"I would need you to believe in me, Vega. I can hardly believe in myself." Fallon had no other vulnerabilities to hide. It was all out there now.

"Fallon, you are the smartest man alive. I would not have come to you were that not the case. Now, let's get started."

***

Fallon, 2,120 days left

Work on the Vega II project began nearly a week after Vega visited Fallon. He entered his lab early, when the halos were still out of sync. Each continent, or halo, orbited the one preceding it. Time was marked by their rotation and the shadows caused by their movement.

He walked over to his desk and placed his tablet down. He began a prayer in which he cupped both of his hands in front of him, palms up as he kneeled. His numen was hung on the wall, placed above all the other objects in his office. He fixed his eyes on it as he prayed. Vederians cannot blink, so his eyes remained focused on the sacred object.

It was not uncommon to see believers praying with tears streaming down their face, eyes, and face red from the strain. It was believed that the longer one could go without losing focus, the more connected to the goddess they were.

This morning, Fallon prayed for guidance. He feared he would not be able to complete the task Vega requested of him. Though typically not very religious, Fallon figured it couldn't hurt to enlist all the help he could get.

The first thing Fallon had to do was sequence Vega's DNA. When she arrived, late afternoon, he took her to his newly redesigned lab—the entrance of which was now permanently guarded by Ophori royal guard just inside the glass. He began by swabbing underneath her fingernails, inside her mouth, her nose, and ears. He took hair samples and skin cells and compiled them in a file under the name, *Vega II*. Vega also provided him with the highest clearance possible—unmitigated access the main information system of Vedere, the Oro.

The Oro was the collective knowledge of the entire civilization of Vedere—a digital network of thousands of years of data stored in tiny hubs called kokotos that could be accessed mentally. When the Elder Vederians discovered that these stones—found naturally in the earth and sea—could house vast amounts of information, they mined and cultivated the precious minerals.

Once it was understood how complex computing could be driven by these minerals, kokoto technology exploded. Embedded in the earth, they were used for mapping, tracking threats, monitoring weather conditions and agricultural growth patterns, and even locating more precious minerals. Later, they were used for surveillance, security, and data processing, and eventually fashioned to store power, transfer it, and even serve as a conduit for weapons.

Over time, the stones took different shapes, with development extending beyond spheres to cylinders, cubes, cones, and hexagonal prisms. The primitive understanding was that the larger the kokoto, the more potential energy. Further study and theory addressed the potential utility and power in constructing new shapes of kokoto. As the carving technology became more sophisticated, cones became the standard for projection and holographic technology, hexagonal prisms were used for system computing and accessing the Oro, and cylinders and spheres powered vehicles and weapons.

In 72 Æ Vex, a little-known scientist, Dr. Julian Parish, theorized that kokotos contained traces of molecular compositions that resembled organic elements. Dr. Parish believed that it was this unique property of the mineral that allowed for the variety of functions and abilities. Dr. Parish also postulated that it was that same "soul matter" that could also be found in Vederians themselves. He suggested later in life that a tesseract-shaped kokoto had the potential ability to interface with the Vederian biology, specifically the mind. In 109 Æ Vex, the first kokoto tesseract was constructed and presented to the current Ægæliphi, marking a day that would forever change Vederian culture and life.

The unique properties of the tesseract provided a Vederian wearer with the ability to not only link their mind with the Oro, but with other Vederians as well. Communication via the tesseract came to be known as the ni'oro, a virtual communication in which locations, thoughts, and emotions could be augmented and shared to convey concepts and beliefs.

Soon, all religious services were held in the Oro, with recreation and sports following suit. Within fifteen years, access to the Oro started to be monitored. By thirty, it was overrun by the consumer industry, constantly monitored by the local and parish governments. New kokoto shapes were designed and given to the newly established Ophori, a police-like force designed to help enforce and protect Vederian citizens both in the real word and the Oro.

Since the beginning, there were always those who rejected kokoto technology. Fundamentalist Vederians believed that communication should be conducted in the "old way," with hand signs, *tanna*, and *farq*, which used a portable light that could be flashed at varying durations to communicate. Many were hesitant to adopt technology as a part of their everyday life. A few never did—this allowed for a select few to exist off the Oro entirely.

Nevertheless, several hundred years later, kokoto technology was commonplace. It was implanted at the base of the skull of newborns or even genetically engineered as soon as the zygote was formed. Data was constantly added to the now fully established digital system, the Oro, which could be accessed through the bioengineered kokoto.

Initially, knowledge was free and available to all. But this eroded over time. Information was now sectioned into coteries the Viceroy established. The first tier was called Base and was considered common knowledge. It contained access to everything from basic Vederian history to math and philosophy. The second tier was called Advance and gave members access to a broader knowledge of common knowledge, as well as details about the government's extended functions.

The final tier was Æ, reserved strictly for the royal family. This clearance provided access to the entire network of the Oro, including all secret groups, assignments, and details about Vederian existence. For a number of years, this system worked spectacularly well.

In 80 Æ Vy, a delegation from the parish of New Redemption formally requested additional access to the Oro. Their request was denied. In 89 Æ Vy, New Redemption again formally requested additional access, this time along with the delegates from Halo Gabriela. They were again denied. Following a three-halo revolt, which almost turned into a civil war, the Information Pact of 90 Æ Vy was introduced.

It ensured that access to previously restricted files would be made public and that future documents could be released per formal inquiry, with the Ægæliphi providing the final decision. The people trusted the Æ and were satisfied with the pact.

With information now more accessible, adjustments were made to the Vederian educational system. Students were given placement tests to determine their place in the Oro. The size, color, and grooves of the secondary kokoto denoted the information tier and clearance level. It would ultimately determine their coterie in society as well.

The Medical Coterie was associated with a blue kokoto and became standard equipment for doctors. It housed all the collective data available on Vederian biology and similar disciplines. Red kokotos were given to the Ophori and other peacekeepers within the Safeguard Coterie, while green kokotos were given to clergy and philosophers—members of the Religious Coterie. Later additions were made: orange kokotos for the Labor Coterie, silver kokoto for advocates and barristers, and the black kokotos, which were only given to the Cara Royale and were custom made for each member of the family.

Over the decades, as kokoto became essential to Vederian life and work, style integrated into how the technology was used. Most Vederians wore their kokoto around their necks as a necklace—this was most common among the Cara Royale—or around the wrist. The Labor and Safeguard Coterie wore their kokoto around their bicep and barristers and doctors typically wore their kokoto around their head, with the kokoto itself at the center of the forehead.

Computers were designed to support kokoto technology, coming equipped with a cutout for the kokoto to rest. Kokoto could power devices, transfer data, and verify payments. Kokoto tech also became prevalent in defense designs as well. Weapons were powered by kokoto and could focus various intensities of light at a target, either stunning or killing them.

By the modern era, Vedere had become completely dependent on kokoto technology and was the standard for nearly every task in society. It became the main determinant for success in society, as kokotos were often passed down or transferred between close families and friends. Crimes involving kokotos also became very common, as citizens who wanted to exploit the information that kokotos held made careers of theft and forgery. With the right set of tools and patience, some kokotos could be reverse-engineered or surgically altered to reveal the information they had: currency, personal information, anything.

This is what Fallon needed to do to access to the Oro while remaining anonymous. He already had help—Vega provided him with her personal kokoto—one of the most powerful objects in the entire nation, but Fallon had to ensure it continued to look as if it was being used as designed. This required the work of an excellent forger and kokotosmith. Fallon would travel to meet an old friend, Yanne, who lived on Halo Asa.

Lush and full of bioluminous flora, Halo Asa was the fifth circular landmass and rotated between Halo Penelope and Halo Davina. Those born on Halo Asa called their halo *Brica*, the Brilliance, or the Brilliant Ring, for the way the halo perennially glowed. The people who lived on the Brilliance were traditionally traders and merchants that had an affinity for mining and gardening the raw minerals and plants that produced light. Brilliants, as they came to be known, were typically experts in bioluminescence, mineralogy, and botany.

Less known, though, was the criminal reputation Brilliants had as hackers and kokotosmiths.

Fallon always knew where he could find Yanne. She'd already told him which home she would die in—the same home her mother died in and her mother before her. It was a quaint, traditional Asan home: pyramid-shaped, crafted from solid marble, nestled between a half-moon moat to the right and a sizable garden to the left. It was just as he remembered it; there was an intentional neatness to the space, each gardening tool placed in a perfectly parallel row on the shelving near the garden.

Fallon flashed the door light and waited. It was the middle of the day. Yanne could have been out at the market. Just as Fallon considered checking the market, the door opened.

Yanne's hair was a lion's mane. It was white and gray and formed endless curls and coils that buried her face. She hid her typical wide smile behind her hand, a habit she developed when her head was smaller yet her teeth and smile the same size as they were now. She allowed her chin to point toward her chest. She brought her arms together to fold them, displaying a glowing ring on each finger.

She had dyed her eyebrows a deep black that sharply contrasted her olive skin. They matched the black tattooing on her arms and face. She held onto the awkwardness for as long as Fallon could stand until she cracked a smile.

"Don't worry, Fallon. To see you, it is good," Yanne signed in the way that most Asan Vederians did. Her hands were a bit closer to the body and the shapes a bit more closed. Their dialect also placed emphasis on what was being observed first.

"To see me, I know you didn't expect. I have a task. You must know I've come because the work I am to do is extremely important—"

"And private," Yanne responded. She took a few steps back from the door's threshold and allowed Fallon to come in.

Yanne's home was extremely neat for the work that she did. Despite that, there was a plethora of drawings, schematics, sketches, paintings, and sculptures in every corner. Her plants covered almost every table in her home.

"You have to see it. There's no real way to explain it," Fallon signed as he placed the black, marble-sized kokoto on her kitchen table. "I'm realizing I'm just jumping straight into this, but it's a matter of time, you understand?"

Yanne nodded, but remained where she stood. She took a few moments before walking over to her cupboard and pulling out two glasses. She filled them with water and carried them over to her kitchen table.

"Cara Royale kokoto. Of course I understand," she began. "But I have to know—where did you get a Cara Royale kokoto?" Yanne tapped the side of her glass with all of her fingers before taking another sip. "What I have built here, Fallon, do you see it? What I've done with my mother's home, do you see what I've done? I've maintained it. I polish the marble every day. I maintain the garden. I keep her plants alive. I've done this in honor of her. What have you done?"

Each of Yanne's questions poured the weight of a gallon of liquid cement onto Fallon's lap. In between each of her questions was an implication that was very clear: Fallon was threatening everything she had built by coming to her home with such a precious item. The act alone called into question whether or not he even cared about her.

"I've mourned as you have mourned," Fallon replied, giving up his poor attempt at an Asan accent. "I have remained obedient to my Ægæliphi, and to my commission. I am here because what I require is a task no one in the seven halos can do but you. I need your skills just one last time."

Fallon finished his signing and clasped his hands. His eyebrows were upturned. He sat there motionless, save for the single tear that trickled down his dark cheeks.

Yanne stared Fallon down, her face growing redder as time passed.

"I needed you, Fallon!" Yanne stood and threw her cornucopia across the room.

Fallon quickly looked away as if one more gaze would burn out his eyes. He sniffed up a fit of tears. His breath sped up. His shoulders rose and fell sharply, cadenced, labored.

"I loved your mother as I loved my own. You know that. It hurts me more that you know that and do not recognize it. I had a duty, Yanne. What was I to do?"

"Save my mother," Yanne replied calmly. "To this day, you are still the brightest mind in Vederian biology, possibly ever. I know how fixated you can become. My mother died of cancer, Fallon. No one has died of cancer in over a hundred years. All I wanted you to do was say yes. You could say yes to everyone but us. You let mother die. If there was anyone who could have saved her, it could have been you."

Fallon had no rebuttal. Yanne's mother had a type of cancer doctors had never seen before. They had lost the battle before it began. But while Fallon was busy helping Vega, he knew he could have done *something.* He prepared to gather his things and reached for the small, black kokoto. But Yanne wasn't done.

"And now you are here. You are here and you need my help. You come in here and place an object on my mother's table that could literally get us both killed. What am I to do, Fallon?"

Fallon remained in his seat. He had been defeated. He knew that he had to at least try, but without Yanne nothing more could be done.

"Thank you for your time and I am sorry for all that I have done to you." Fallon finished his glass of water and pushed in his chair.

"Remember this conversation when the task is done," Yanne signed carefully. "I am not you. I will always be true to myself. What of you?"

***

Fallon, 2,024 days left

Fallon was pacing his genetics lab, a place where he now spent the majority of his time. "Now, let's try it again," he told Ava. "This time, we'll set the power output to a dynamic range. We'll adjust it as we see fit. I'll be relying on your computing."

Ava's hologram nodded. "We'll do it on my mark. I will do my best to pay attention to the storm."

With a nod, they both flipped the switch to open the power grid. Fallon's lab had its own hydroelectric power source, but they had come to learn that their work required additional power. Fallon had rigged a few solar panels to pull the necessary power, but that was not enough either. The plan was to harness one of Vedere's strongest electrical storms.

"Fallon, we can only give it one more spin before we lose the entire kokoto." Ava switched to the nearest screen to Fallon. "If we do this, it will set us even further back. We'll have to craft a whole new kokoto. At the required size, it would take at least a week." Ava was right. They had custom-designed the largest kokoto on record. It was shaped as a prism, the size of an average bedroom. The idea was to use the prism's power to jumpstart the most difficult task—the cloning.

"Fallon, Yanne has arrived."

"I didn't think she'd come after helping us with the prism." Fallon walked over to the nearest stool and plopped down.

Yanne walked in and pulled up her hair. She was sporting the same lab coat she wore when they were in school. "Fallon, get over to the teleportation hub. Time is of the essence."

Fallon rushed over to the teleportation hub. In nearly two years' time, Fallon's research and genetics lab had turned into an entire wing. Three separate hubs now formed a network of labs dedicated to the Vega II project. The power conduits were centralized in one hub with a four metric-ton kokoto carved directly out of the Mount Vaia. The second chamber housed and converted the energy to the third chamber, called the Clay, which housed the organic material for the cloning process. The desired result would be a fully aged clone. One that Vega would work with personally to ensure a smooth transfer of knowledge and understanding.

Fallon teleported to the Clay to review the genetic material. "Ava, on screen. Can this body take one more shot?"

"Let me crunch the numbers," Ava replied. This was the second fully grown body that Fallon had attempted to develop—progress at this point was no longer optional. The plan was to imprint the body with Vega's backup kokoto, though no one knew for sure the amount of data needed for a full transfer. Ava's math checked out. "We can give it one more jolt, Fallon."

The only limiting factor in kokoto technology was design. That is what made the technology so revolutionary. A skilled kokotosmith like Yanne could fashion thousands of three-dimensional shapes to perform hundreds of thousands of varying tasks and processes.

Various shapes could even be fashioned to fit into others to combine functions. It was Ava who originally hypothesized that encircling a tesseract kokoto in a hollow sphere could allow for a unique spin of the tesseract itself. She theorized that the power generated by a known mind-linking kokoto could allow for a harnessing of that power that could be funneled into the Vederian brain. The problem, however, was not in the design, but in the execution.

"Fallon! Wait!" Yanne feverishly tapped Fallon's shoulder. "I know what the problem is and I know how to fix it! We will be down to the millisecond."

This was their third attempt.

With hardly a warning, Fallon's island was bombarded by the ravenous electrical storm. The windows surrounding the laboratory came alive with purple light as the sky flashed and burned through the dusk of Vedere's amberlight. Though typical Vederian amberlight only partially tinted the landscape, the storm had darkened the island enough to send a jolt of fear down Fallon's spine. In the commotion, his lab's power had cut out—just before Yanne's epiphany.

"Yanne, tell me what I need to do. We may never get an opportunity like this."

Yanne pushed up her sleeves. "OK, Fallon, but you must manually establish a connection. I can adjust the routing, but you have to go outside the lab and place a kokoto above the Clay's facility." Fallon immediately rushed for one of his deep sea suits. He postulated that the rubber should be enough to protect him. He also put on one of his own designs, a clear visor he could flip down over his face like a blacksmith. This way he could see what Ava saw.

"See me, Yanne. No matter what happens to me, continue the experiment to the end. I know I don't have to make you promise."

"This is your life's work, Fallon. I believe you. But I need you to come back."

Fallon teleported directly into the water, the furthest the conduit could take him, and from there he swam around to the outer ring of the Clay and began his climb.

"Fallon, you should know that the odds of the kokoto vaporizing you in this lightning storm are—"

Fallon immediately interjected. "Ava, I don't want to know. Just calculate when I need to hold my breath."

A peculiar light flashed in Fallon's peripheral, near the mainland. At first, Fallon assumed it was a lightning bolt connecting with a tree. This light, however, was so unnatural and bright that it could have only been caused by one thing: a hovercar. *Who could possibly be traveling at a time like this?*

Yanne interrupted Fallon's train of thought. "Fallon, you are nearly to the top. You will likely only have one chance at this, so make it count. Remember, it's magnetic, so you only need to get it close. It's the timing that will be difficult."

Fallon removed the kokoto dangling from the clip on his harness. Almost instantly, it took hold of the Clay's roof, establishing a connection that sent 97 mA of electricity thorough Fallon's body.

Fallon saw nothing but pure white light as his body slammed back into the sea. His body went limp as it sank to the bottom.

"Fallon!"

"Fallon!"

"Fallon, please!"

Ava had been using the strobe light on one of Fallon's drones to help him regain consciousness. She began displaying instructions on his visor. Yanne rushed down to the teleportation hub.

"Fallon, you only have forty-five seconds of air left. You have to swim up now."

Fallon's mind felt like it had been put in a blender. Weakly, he worked his feet back under him and pushed himself toward the surface. It was during his ascent that he saw it: a young man floating in a fetal position just below the surface of the water. Fallon swam up to the young man and pushed his chin toward the surface.

Exhausted, he let the waves carry both of them back to the beach. "Ava, please scan his vitals. I'm going to go check for more survivors." Legs still trembling, Fallon worked to stand up on his feet.

By the Goddess, what happened here? Fallon thought.

Fallon tripped and dented his knees into the beach sand. He quickly removed his gloves and shuffled back to his feet as he followed an eerie purple light just over the ridge.

There was only one thing that could produce that color purple. It was exactly what Fallon was worried about: a hovercar crash. Fallon gathered a few quick steps and turned them into a jog. The crash site left a twisted metal trail that skidded into the sand, but the vehicle was gone. The kokoto had used the electrical storm to channel the majority of the power, but the excess had ricocheted off, leaving a black beam of singed earth.

"By the Goddess, Ava, what have we done?"

***

Record NGV #292, Gabrielle Reporting, 2,017 days left

Gaius could usually be found standing just to the right of the Ægæliphi. As Avis explained to me, he was an æsir, a kind of guard and diplomat. Day to day, he would assist in the majority of diplomatic processes between the halos, draft edicts for review, and serve as private security for the royal family. He had come a long way from mercenary.

Initially, regents, or ræs as they were called, were given jurisdiction over their entire halos and allowed to lead as they saw fit. The Trinity, or the first three halos—Michaela, Raphaela, and Gabriela—developed a summit that grew into a coalition with all ræs coming together once a year to council and perform political tasks: everything from discussing trade policies to infrastructure and development. During the time of the Trinity, the Ægæliphi held absolute power. This became a point of contention for the less patriotic halos. And with each halo having a differing opinion on the Vo and Va dynasties, allegiances were difficult to predict.

Eventually, the outer halos planned rebellion, citing concerns with how precious minerals such as platinum and kokoto were being mined in their territories. At an unknown date (though believed to be at least a century ago) the kokoto-rich halo of Davina formed an alliance with the silk-rich halo of Asa. Meetings were held at the capital of Halo Asa, Medisi. The Medisi family was a proud family of explorers—as most outer-halo families were—and they prided themselves in the land they explored. They had their own royal guard, the Ashanti, and they were known to be able to hold their own against Ophori.

The Haven family of the Halo Davina were incredibly industrious, building bleeding-edge technology. They held the largest known deposit of kokoto and harrow stone, and Halo Davina was the home to some of the smartest architects and engineers in the nation.

The alliance discovered that with the technology of Halo Davina, and the fighting might of Halo Asa, a legitimate run for the throne could be made. It also helped that the Haven and Medisi families were loyal to House Amavi, a now nomadic family with dynastic claims to the Ægæliphi that went as far back as written history could go.

Emissaries were sent to Halo Penelope and Halo Maria and by the end of the year, the Outer Four—Asa, Penelope, Davina, and nearly completed Maria—were poised to challenge the Trinity. After an emissary of the Outer Four was denied entry into Halo Gabriela, the war was on. For seven years they fought bitterly, with heavy losses at Halo Gabriela and Halo Penelope.

With another year of war looming overhead, a breaking point was nearing. Halo Penelope was losing structural integrity. Many of the nation's smartest geologists feared that the entire halo itself was susceptible to failure if the war continued on. This is how initial negotiations began.

A new governmental structure was established, weighting the votes of the halo upon various factors and, as compromise, the previous royal lines were asked to step down as ræ and become part of a new structure as "proveyors."

It took decades for many of the outer halos to adjust to their new structures of power and many were still sore from how the war ended. Gaius was there each step of the way, balancing the peace. It was this work that made Gaius one of the most well-known men in the nation.

Gaius scanned the constituency. It looked to be a typical day for the Ægæliphi. She signed edicts, tried cases, and though it was clear she was becoming older and less capable of prolonged public appearances, everything seemed to be normal—that is, until a note was slipped into his hand by an aide.

There has been an accident.

Gaius excused himself from the royal court and hurried to an enclave behind the throne. Before him was a young aide, tasked with the terrible news.

"Gaius, I am so sorry. There was an accident. Athena—"

Gaius quickly interrupted. "Athena? What happened?"

"We've searched the area, Gaius. I'm sorry. No one survived."

As if relying on muscle memory, Gaius leaned his hip into a right hook, leveling the aide. Several others rushed in to restrain him. The veins of his neck bulged and pulsated as they wrestled him to the ground.

It is said that Vederians do not feel pain. That is only partly true. Gaius's heart had dissolved into blood. It could be seen all over his face as he sobbed, kicked, and fought against a wave of grief he was too weak to overcome.

Once calmed, Gaius left to investigate the crash site himself.

I put down Gabrielle's report. This will change Gaius forever, I thought.

***

Seraphina, 1,947 days left

When I first approached the Light in the sæ, he was asleep in the home of the doctor. He was just beginning to remember his name. He wouldn't know me. And I knew he would be confused and disoriented. But this would be the only way. His abilities were sharpening as each day passed. He would be found soon if I did not guide him now. I would have to tell him who he really is and why his time is now. Time is so much shorter than we would have hoped.

I'd never attempted a sæ from this great a distance, but I had to try. He had to know the truth. I chose the form of a pure white eagle. I knew that he would believe it to all be a dream, but he would still receive the information he so desperately needed.

I flew down into a setting that his own mind constructed. It was a beautiful beach with an endless coast stretching as far as the eye could see. The sand was black as coal; the water clear and still—no tides. Balien stood out in the waist-deep water, wading. I flew to him and spoke, "Come to the land, Balien. There you will find truth."

He turned to me slowly. His dark brown skin deeply contrasted with the light blue sky. His pure white hair was short and shaved, cropped close to his ears. This was my first time seeing the Light. His eyes were as sharp as crystal and as light as the sky above.

"Who are you?" he asked, placing his hands behind his back respectfully. I couldn't yet reveal to him who I was, not until he knew.

"Why do you wade in the water?" I replied. Balien cocked his head to the side as he squinted his eyes. He quickly straightened his neck.

"I'm looking for someone," he answered calmly.

"What do you seek?" I began to piece together the construct his mind had created—Balien was still able to perceive sound, as always. He had simply lost knowledge of what it was. The still water was our world of sight, but there was nothing to hear, just water. Any movement created a wave he could see. He was trying to make sense of what he was experiencing.

"I seek the truth," he replied. "I—I've been to this beach before. But it was very different. It was not this calm."

"The truth is made up of light. Come to land with me, we still need you." I transformed from a white eagle to a white koi fish. As I swam, the waves left a path for Balien to follow. He was intrigued by the sound and came with me to land. I then transformed into a wolf.

"Balien, I am only your guide. I was with you in the beginning, but I am not your beginning. There is a plan for you; you are the Light. You will be the example for all people, the bridge between worlds. Some will follow you and some will not, but do not become discouraged. You will save those who choose life. Are you ready for the knowledge you seek?"

Balien nodded.

"Then turn and face the truth!"

In the distance, far out in the ocean, a wave began to grow. What began as a small swell built into an enormous wall of water. It rose so high it blended with the sky—both the sky and the sea were one. Balien began to tremble. It was too much for him.

"Do not fear it! Do not run from it! It is yours! It is your truth!" I howled. As the wall neared it grew in size until it was as tall as mountains. Balien fell to his knees. He turned back to me.

"I can't! It will consume me! I will die!" he shouted.

It was too much for him. We would have to try again.

***

Part 3: Discovery is Third

The Journal of Georgette Davis, 57,298 days left

Day 3

07:00

We are making our way to the Eye of Vaia. Now that we are able to get more accurate scans, we're beginning to see how little we know about the location. Initially, we believed that beyond the Reach the earth would hollow out into a deep valley—more like a cavern. But now that we've arrived at the Reach, it has become clear that the geography may be our first true challenge. We are essentially descending into a pit and digging deeper than anyone else has in history. There will be many firsts during this expedition, but we cannot take any of them for granted.

From a historical perspective, the Eye of Vaia has always been the furthest Vederians have traveled. It has an incredible history. For thousands of years, the Eye of Vaia was believed to be a portal to the underworld. Tradition stated that the soul left the body as the body returned to dust. The souls pass through the Reach to the Eye of Vaia, where Her righteous sight judges where the souls will ultimately arrive. Ancient religions took a pilgrimage here, others have tried to establish a settlement. None of those settlements have been successful, and as the Church of the Vael rose to power as the de facto religion of Vedere, the Eye of Vaia was desecrated. Regardless of the team's beliefs, we witnessed the final tree nearly a hundred miles ago. The land around the Eye of Vaia is essentially a desert—but there is no sand. It's is all deep, soft, lush ground. It looks extremely fertile, yet nothing grows from it. Nothing has ever grown from it. Our alpha of Ecology has ordered samples of the earth. We do not have time to investigate at the moment, but we will file the samples for a later date.

We knew that one of the biggest hurdles of the expedition would be at the beginning. This was largely due to our inability to accurately predict how gravity would work toward the edge of our halo. We were unable to plan our descent as well as we would have liked. Geographically, our understanding of our continent was that it functioned much like a plate or disk. Our initial plan was at the edge of that plate, we would use a "chip" in that plate to walk around the edge to the underside.

However, now that we are here at the site, it is clear that the Eye of Vaia is simply a pit. To get to the bottom of our "plate," we would have to drop down one end of the hole and at a certain point climb back up to the top of the other side—the new topside. The hypothesis now was that somewhere through that hole the gravity would invert. We will test with smaller equipment before proceeding.

15:00

It has only been a few hours, but the effects of the gravity are beginning to take their toll on us. We are so heavy down here, closer to the Eye. We accounted for a quarter of our weight to be added, but I fear we will still have issues with fitness. Tonight, we will be discussing a plan for those of us who will be unable to bear the weight of their equipment. We do not really have the provisions to travel back and forth from the Eye of Vaia to our compound. We will have to figure something else out. We will also send out our first security team for recon. Once everything is cleared, we will proceed to expand our perimeter until we have a sufficient radius to conduct all our tests on the other side. So far, everything is going close to plan. I have asked our security team leader, Major Bastian, to employ the use of the synths for as much legwork as possible. Our workload and efficiency is nearly cut in half by this gravity, much further out from our assumed margins.

***

Record NGV #293, Isa Reporting, 6,204 days left.

There were more gathered today than there had ever been. And the people knew it. The energy was palpable. The excitement was built. The final stages of the plan were beginning.

The new child had already been born. And this time, the timing was right. Generations of work and hundreds of spies later, I now found myself at the front row of our tragic play.

"There are no gods, my friends—I want you to know this. In our world, we are taught that we are the race of the world. From childhood, we are taught that this is the way things are—that we cannot impact our world. Taught that it is the gods who have set up our society and left us to ourselves. And so again I say, there are no gods. Do not believe in them. Do not believe in how we came to be. Do this first and then look within." Justice Afauna was Vederian. But he led a group of people who believed in the Others.

"The question becomes: How do we make it? How do we move on? The answer is simple; We do this by looking to each other. We do this by living for ourselves. We have been lied to, my friends. You stand here before me because you know this much to be true. You've seen the waves in corners.

You've seen the shapes leaving the mouths of your friends and family. You know this is the Residual."

The crowd before Justice Afauna nodded in agreement. They were here because they were skeptics. They disagreed with the religious beliefs of their ancestors. They believed that something changed when Georgette and her people left for the Underside. As Justice locked eyes with the hundreds before him, he let in a deep breath before he continued.

"Do not believe in me. I am not asking you to believe in me. Do not believe in the gods. I am not asking you to believe in them. I am asking you to believe in us." Justice reached forward as his friends carried him to the center of the crowd. He waved off his cane and an assisting hand that was outstretched.

"See me: if I die, our ideals will not. I am not your leader." Justice smiled. "I am your confidant. I am here simply to encourage you all in the work. I know we are all desperate for a catalyst. And so that is why we have risked bringing so many of us together at one time. I want you to know that catalyst has come."

Justice raised one fist in the air as the crowd erupted. With tears taking turns down his cheeks, he searched the crowd for his daughter. Epeë was not there.

"I have been told that the unimaginable has been born." Justice shrugged his shoulders to adjust his posture. "A child we once thought to be lost to time. Incapable of existing in a world like ours."

Justice began to weaken. He motioned for his cane so that he could work his way back to his chair. The entire group had gathered in an abandoned textile mill at amberlight far from the capitol. They had taken every precaution, but they could never be too sure.

Gregor Bastian, Justice's oldest friend and military leader of the Cophi, scanned the audience. He was seated behind Justice, legs folded, just off-center on the makeshift stage created for the unplanned meeting. His face was clear in expressing his disagreement with Justice. Gregor didn't think the people needed to know about the child. He didn't want them to get a sense of how much hope they had placed in the child. The truth was that the child was the crux of their larger plan. But Justice argued that unveiling the truth was what the Cophi was all about in the first place. Justice believed it was for the people to decide. This was how Justice had always been.

"This child has the ability to unite all our people. To return us to a truth we were always meant to know," Justice explained. "And as believers in the Residual, we are not just about knowing a truth and keeping it hidden. It is our responsibility to ensure that others are given the truth—for it is for them to choose to accept or reject."

Justice was a believer who valued the power of choice. It was his goal to ensure that all Vederians could experience true equality through the dissemination of information. Justice measured his life by how many he was able to help reclaim truth from the darkness of deceit. And he did well over the decades—but so much would change.

Gregor felt a double tap on his shoulder. It was one of the guards. "Two closer to the entrance, five on the roof. If we scatter—"

The Ophori had found them. It was already too late.

Gregor quickly pushed the guard out of the way as an arrow whisked by his cheek. He dove on top of Justice to protect him from the roof that had exploded above. The Ophori began systematically subduing most of the group. Gregor's eyes tracked the assailants—there were too many.

"They want me, Gregor. Now please do not argue; they can have me but they cannot have you. Find my daughter. I will be fine."

Gregor hesitated for a moment, but he knew Justice was right. He stepped into an all-out sprint. In the chaos of rounding up as many prisoners as they could, Gregor slipped by with little resistance. He made a break for the tree line, never looking back.

***

Seraphina, 1,722 days left

When I approached the Light in the sæ, it was my fortieth attempt. His mind was still within a different state of consciousness. He still wouldn't know me. He would be confused and disoriented. But this was the only way.

I was becoming proficient at performing a sæ from this great a distance, even in my old age. He had to know the truth. I chose the form of a pure white dove. He would believe it to all be a dream, but he would still receive the information he so desperately needed. He had to wake from his coma.

I flew down into a beautiful field with endless green grass stretching as far as the eye could see. There were no trees—not yet. Balien sat in the field, legs folded.

I flew to him and spoke, "Let us find a tree, Balien. There you will find truth." He turned to me slowly. He was older now. His pure white hair was longer, his hands and feet larger. Such a long time asleep. His eyes were as sharp as crystal and pierced me just the same.

"Who are you?" he asked, as he stood up to greet me. I couldn't yet reveal to him who I was, not until he knew.

"Why do you sit in an empty field" I replied.

Balien cocked his head to the side as he squinted his eyes. "I'm looking for someone," he answered calmly. "Are you who I am seeking?"

"I am not." Balien was still able to perceive sound, as always. He was beginning to understand what it was once again. The open field was our world of sight, but there was nothing to hear, no birds chirping, no trees with leaves that rustled in the wind. Only the light flickering of blades of grass created a wave that he could see. He still was trying to make sense of what he was experiencing.

"I seek the truth," he continued. "I—I've been to this field before, but it was very different. It was not this serene."

"The truth is made up of light. Come find a tree with me, we still need you." I transformed from a white dove to a white fox. As I ran, the bent grass left a path for Balien to follow. He was intrigued by the sound and came with me to a tree in the distance. I transformed into a bear.

I repeated what I always did: "Balien, I am only your guide. I was with you in the beginning, but I am not your beginning. An entire civilization put their faith in you. There are not many of us left. You are the last of us, the example for all people, the bridge between worlds. Some will follow you and some will not, but do not become discouraged. You will save those who choose life. Accept the knowledge you seek, turn and face the truth!"

In the distance, far out in the field, a stampede of buffalo appeared over the ridge. What began as just two or three grew into thousands. Balien began to tremble. It was too much for him.

"Do not fear it! Do not run from it! It is yours! It is your truth!" I growled. As the wall neared, Balien fell to his knees. He turned back to me.

"I can't! It will consume me! I will die!"

It is too much for him. We would have to try again.

***

Fallon, 1,245 days left

"Thank you so much for agreeing to meet with me. I truly had no one else to turn to." Fallon motioned for the heir to sit. He was still not accustomed to having royalty in his home. "Something like this has the potential to shatter our world. I believe that it will change everything."

The heir's eyes widened. She reached down and put her hand on top of Fallon's. "Fallon, we are more than colleagues. We are friends. I'm here for you. Are you in trouble?"

Fallon hesitated before continuing. Had he made a mistake in reaching out to her?

"Vega, I am housing a young man. A very special young man. A young man who opens up an unseen world as large and as vast as our own. I believe this young man is the answer to everything—not just the cloning process, but the Cophi, the Residual, even your mother's illness—"

Vega cut her eyes to her two guards. They immediately left my office to wait outside. Vega softly touched the side of Fallon head and brought his forehead to hers. *"We now must speak in absolute secrecy."* Their minds linked, closing the loop between them.

"What does this mean for my child? Does he help bring my child to me?"

Fallon thought for a moment. He knew that she could feel his emotions as well as he could feel his own. Fallon wanted to communicate as clearly as possible.

"Yes, Heir, but I must ask again that you do not refer to her as your child. I know what she means to you, and how important she will be to our world. But we must make this distinction now. And yes, I truly believe that he can. When I found

him, he was unconscious. I took him to my neurology lab and hooked him up to every piece of medical equipment I had on hand. My computer scanned his brain. It ... it made no sense. I have seen nothing like it during my career. Nothing close. I even hesitate to say that he is Vederian."

Vega leaned back in her chair. Her left knee began to tap up and down. She was ... nervous. *"Have you communicated to the 'special' child?"*

"No, but when he regains consciousness, I intend to do just that. Vega, I believe he is going to be the answer. I do not quite have a word for it, but the young man's brain can sense the world in a way I have never seen. He can detect things our eyes cannot. He has a way of sensing vibrations that travel through the air. Waves that for years our scientists could only theoretically assume existed."

Vega cocked her head to the side and squinted her icy eyes. Her lips pursed and she folded her arms. *"I'm sorry, Fallon. I'm not sure I understand."*

"You see, for years our brightest scientists developed mathematical theories for the way we experience the world. There were always gaps. As if we were missing the rest of the story. We know the first act, but the math says there is an entire play being performed."

Vega nodded.

"The math suggested that there was something else that was a part of our reality. Something we couldn't see, but that affected the things that we could see."

Vega continued to nod her head. She was getting it.

"We were able to define only the absence of something, we were never able to prove the validity of it."

"I see, and you believe this young man can sense the unseen force that affects our reality?"

"Yes, Vega, I've already crunched the numbers. What his brain can do matches the early calculations. Whatever else is out there. He has a way of seeing it, or perhaps he doesn't even see it at all. Maybe it's something that cannot be seen."

"But how can such a thing be possible? How could a Vederia—"

Fallon had to cut her off. *"But you see, that's just it, Vega, I don't think he is Vederian. Vega, I've taken blood samples. He is surely part Vederian, but he is part something else as well."*

Vega's knee stopped bouncing. *"I ... I've been told something like this before ..."*

"What? From whom?" Fallon knew there had to be more to the story. There was no way a secret this big could survive in Vedere.

"From my mother herself, the Ægœliphi. She told me there was a child that was brought to the capital that was nothing like us. But this was years ago. She thought it was merely a story that her mother told her to help her sleep. Do you think they could be related?"

"They would have to be, Vega. It's the only explanation. The young man could very well be a descendant. Or perhaps something else entirely?"

Vega thought for a moment. *"Fallon, what if he is not the only one? We ... we could have an invasion on our hands."*

Vega was right. Fallon was so caught up in what the young man could mean. He hadn't given much thought to whether or not he was alone.

"And see me, Fallon, it is not me that you should be worried about. It's my sister. If she gets word that any of this is true ..."

It would end Vedere's peaceful era.

"But tell me, regarding my ch— I mean, the Vega II project. Are you still able to do it?"

"Yes, Queen. I can do this ... but that is where you come in. What do we do with the young man?" This was the challenge. If the young man's existence got out, it could threaten every religion, every branch of science, every philosophy in the entire nation. The people would not be ready.

"Let's start with what we know," Vega replied. *"I do not have much time left. I worry that I will not be healed and the Vega II project is still months away, which means the window is closing. If I die before my clone can replace me, my sister will be in power. I cannot, will not, allow Valerie to ascend to the throne! If I have to fight I—"*

Vega's first coughs splattered navy-colored blood onto her dress. It was another one of her coughing fits. *"Remember, if there is one person who cannot learn of this young man's existence, it is my sister, Valerie. She is relentless, Fallon. She does not know how to stop. Once she is fixed to a point, there are very few who can stop her. We must do everything we can to keep this young man safe. I have made people disappear, and I can do it again. You may not like my methods, but—"*

Fallon had to ask. He was nervous, but he had to know. *"Why Vega? You've never told me why—not really. Why is Valerie not a suitable replacement?"*

A fire lit in Vega's eyes. *"How dare you ask such a thing! It is a personal matter!"*

Fallon was instantly hit with a wave of anger and fear. Vega had never erupted like this before. She had never directed this much emotion toward Fallon.

"Valerie will not see the throne. Do you understand?"

He didn't.

Vega shook between coughs. Her emotions hit Fallon so hard it caused his head to rumble.

"Fully, my Heir. I have but one more question: how do we hide a young man in plain sight?" he had to redirect the conversation quickly.

"The same way we have hidden mine. We will keep him with you. Now, you have work to do."

***

Valerie, 339 days left

Valerie paused with a sheet of paper between each of the fingers on her left hand. In her right hand, she held a stack of documents thick enough to strain her grip. She was sitting on the floor, legs folded, with her body hunched underneath the sole source of light provided in the deep catacombs beneath her palace. She was brave. No Vederian would ever be this close to darkness.

Water dripped and rolled down the rocky surfaces that surrounded her, though she would not hear those drops land on the dirt behind her. Soon, it would be morning, though it would make little difference from amberlight to day. Valerie's growing underground library was one of the few places shrouded in perpetual darkness—something you could not easily find in Arælia. Arælia was the center of the known world, both physically and culturally. The People of Sight never had to touch darkness naturally. To be in the darkness, one had to seek it out. It had to be constructed. If you wanted to hide something, place it in the darkness. This is what Valerie's Royal Library was.

The documents in Valerie's hands bore words written in a script not used by Vederians for hundreds of years. Valerie's eyes followed each symbol delicately as she took her own notes. Valerie was challenging her own fears to read these secret words. It was not only a fear of darkness that slowly poured into her mind, but the fear that the cascade she had started would spiral out of control. As news of her mother's death traveled to the ends of the known world, soon the conversation would turn to Vega, the beloved. This would make Valerie regent as her sister was before her. If her plan was to succeed, her research would have to prove correct. As Valerie continued her reading, her sixth set of documents revealed just once sentence:

t h e y a r e c a l l e d q u i n q u

Without warning, the underground light went out, encasing her in complete darkness. Valerie's breathing rose to a quicker, shallower cadence. Her body trembled, her eyes shifted uncontrollably. It was her childhood all over again. She was underneath a throne room in the ancient bunker. She was picked up and carried through so many corridors and walkways that she became dizzy. Three women each kept a constant hand on her chest and shoulders. Someone, older, was running alongside her, gently stroking Valerie's hair and signing to her, "We can always find peace, remember? Mama said that we can always find peace, no matter where we are."

The darkness was extracting memories Valerie had forgotten. Why was she running? Who was stroking her hair?

If they were able to hear it, they would have known that one of the giant pillars that circled the throne room had fallen, shaking the walkway enough to cause the small entourage to stumble. Vederian philosophy taught that the effects of impact could be sensed visually, in a way that was called "the respect." The larger the object, the more respect it had. They did not hear the giant pillar bend and creak as it fell, but they did see the causeway tremble under the weight.

It was an ambush that had caused the House of Cara to retreat underneath the catacombs. The Farqi had finally breached the city and their intent to capture the throne was within reach. Valerie remembered men running along with her and the others. She remembered being confused and terrified.

Suddenly, all around her, the walls of the ancient catacombs began to glow with a hot-white color. This was enough to bring her out of her flashback and return her to her secret library. The white symbols adjusted to a greenish hue to reveal complex logograms. As Valerie began to scan the text, words she was initially unable to fully read began to decode in front of her.

The purpose of the House of Cara

As a founding member of the Order of Quinqu, the House Cara, under the commission of the Five, will uphold the ideals of the Order throughout the subsequent generations of the line of Vo. Any deviation from this divine plan will be met with unflinching consequences. Remember.

The Prophecy

And then there will come a Darkness; such an absence of light that madness and despair will swallow the Earth. There will be a Light. A Light that will lead the Heart. A Light that the Shadows will reject, a Light that will endure. And then the End will come; the World forever changed.

The tone in both texts shook Valerie. Her face scrunched as she tried to remember her great-grandmother's name. Something wasn't right. She needed a genealogy to be sure. Valerie accessed her kokoto and signed, requesting a holographic representation of the House of Cara.

[Requested]

[House: Cara, Databasing …]

[The Line of Vo]

[Vo, mother of Vashti, daughter of Unknown]

[Vashti, mother of Valentina, daughter of Vo]

[Valentina, mother of Vana, daughter of Vashti]

[Vana, mother of Valma, daughter of Valentina]

[Valma, mother of Vaia, daughter of Vana]

[Vaia, mother of Vala, daughter of Valma]

[Vala, mother of Vivian, daughter of Vaia]

[Vivian, mother of Vei, daughter of Vala]

[Vei, mother of Victoria, daughter of Vivian]

[Victoria, mother of Vera, daughter of Vei]

[Vera, mother of Veronica, Vega, Victor]

Valerie stood up, eyes fixed on the hologram. Her hands shook as she signed another request.

"Kokoto, are there any errors in this report?"

"No."

"Inquiry: Line of Va"

"No data found."

"Inquiry: Sisters of Vo"

"No data found."

"Inquiry: Veronica"

"Access Denied"

Valerie dropped her papers. *How could my clearance be denied?* Valerie hurried to her study and placed her kokoto in the main computer's groove. She signed commands at the computer's camera to begin inputting a query.

"I need all data on Veronica Cara."

"No Data Found"

Valerie slammed her desk with both fists.

What am I missing? What can I not remember?

Valerie knew what she had to do. Grabbing her comforter, she stormed back down to her catacomb library. Valerie found a comfortable place to sit, then threw the comforter over the light. Back to complete darkness. Then she waited.

She remembered the same scene: running, trying to understand what was going on, who she was with, where she was going.

Then, she remembered.

"We cannot do it, we are out of time," Valerie remembered a man explaining. "We have to call it all off."

Valerie remembered a second man arguing with the first. There were in the Cara Royale's palace, the main atrium.

"We cannot do this with a child. How can she possibly remember? The plan was the mother," the first man explained.

Suddenly, they had to start running again. The first man picked Valerie up, the second ran the opposite direction. Valerie and the first man ran around the corner to hide. He put Valerie down.

"Æræya, see me. I hope you are old enough to understand. I'm sorry, it wasn't supposed to be this way. You are Æræya Amavi. No matter what happens. You are the last living descendant of the line of Va," the man explained.

Valerie remembered who they were running from: four Ophori warriors and a young warrior queen—Vera.

"Do not kill my daughter, please do not," the man begged.

"This was my home," Vera explained. "You ambushed my home."

Vera shot the man in the forehead and the chest. The laser left a small singed dot just above his eyebrows. Vera looked at Valerie and crouched down.

"What's your name?" she asked.

"Æræya ... Æræya Amavi."

"No, my daughter. He was trying to take you away from us. Your name is Valerie Cara. You are a part of our family. I will never leave you in the dark. Never."

Valerie's computer screen flashed. Someone was at her door requesting entry. The faint light flickered enough times to bring Valerie back to the present. She took her hidden stairs back up to her room. At the door was a member of the Viceroy, though it was impossible to determine which as they were all identical.

"Is there something troubling you my child?" the old woman asked. She raised an eyebrow.

"I—no, I am fine," Valerie replied.

"Child, you have been in your room for three days. Tell me, what is troubling you?"

Valerie took a book from her desk and flung it across the room. "I will not be denied."

"Denied what, my dear?" the Viceroy asked.

"Did you know ... did you know that there is some sort of *message* in the catacombs?"

"I did not," the old woman replied. "What was on the database?"

"A genealogy—I think. A mention of a Veronica. A mention of a line of Vo, a line of Va. But it was all mixed up, it's not the family history that I was taught."

"Come with me, child. It's finally time you read something."

The walk to where the Viceroy lived was not far from the Ræ. It had an official name, Oroisha, but it was known by most people as the Hysk. It was the oldest structure in the known world—the original seat of House Cara. The nation's best rulers were believed to have been born there, the Ophori trained there, but what exactly went on in that building was impossible to know for sure.

The old woman led Valerie through a secret passage within the Ræ that was completely underground. The path was lit by a light source that Valerie had only been told of in stories. The light was constant, warm and inviting. The stories that Valerie had been told suggested that the lights could have been lit initially by the earliest Vederian settlers and has remained lit ever since.

Valerie wanted desperately to be a part of the old ways. She was more enamored with how things *had* been done than how things were being done *now*. She believed her family's line was divine and directed by the goddess. To come to such a sacred place, the Hysk, with a member of the Viceroy—it nearly overwhelmed her.

"Just a bit farther, young one. I have to tell you, this visit must remain between us," the old woman said. Her way of signing had its own dialect. It was a bit understated, but it was there: the way her finger would bend at the end. How she slowly tracked her hand when finger-spelling. An unexpected eyebrow raise. Her rings were strategically placed, they looked to be *a part* of her hands, not merely ornaments, but extensions of her hands.

Keeping this visit secret worried Valerie. Vederians could not lie when asked a direct question with eye contact. It would take some cunning.

The Hysk was larger than Valerie remembered. It was equal in size to her home, but carried a more modular design. Its exterior was made almost entirely of the bioluminescent harrow stone from the Hylian mountains.

The first cube was a doorway to the others, which housed a number of transparent cubes that were used to transport occupants to the other stone cubes, both horizontally and vertically. There was also extensive infrastructure below the surface as well. As they entered, Valerie's eyes widened with wonder. The old woman and Valerie entered a transparent cube that quickly whisked them horizontally first, then down.

"We are in the possession of a collection of papers," the old woman signed simply. "We have kept these papers hidden until the proper time and place presented itself. You have proven that time is now."

The cube stopped somewhere deep below the Hysk. The larger stone cube it was within was much larger than the others. In fact, the halls seemed to go on endlessly, intersecting at a point that was dimly lit in rows.

"You have never been this far, child," the old woman continued. "If you continue on, there is no turning back."

Valerie nodded. The hallway was filled with hundreds of young boys quickly walking to and from rooms filled with books, artifacts, and peculiar objects. The old woman took a small boy by the hand and the three of them made their way to an innocuous enclave with a small stack of books and papers in its belly.

"This is your helper, child," the old woman signed. The boy walked over to Valerie and folded his hands behind him. He never looked away from Valerie. "This is what you seek. I suggest you take these papers and this boy to a seating area back up a few levels. Make sure you are in the proper frame of mind for what you will read."

The old woman walked away, leaving Valerie with a short stack of papers and a six-year-old boy. Valerie would spend the next four months at the Hysk. What she would discover would change her life forever.

***

Record NGV #295, Gabrielle Reporting, 220 days left

Some of the most pivotal moments in a person's life involve the decisions they make when they are presented truth. But it—truth—is a precarious thing, isn't it? There is *the* truth and there is *your* truth. And somewhere between there is the truth you accept. The latter is what matters most. When one is presented something it is now about what they chose to do. Do they look away? Do they stare it down?

"Helper, get me the dynasty accords—everything from the previous century to present," Valerie signed. The boy scurried away as fast as he could. Valerie was unrecognizable. She hadn't left her room since the old woman left her there. She had bathed two or three times in that period. She ate one meal a day and slept only a few hours each night. She had become gaunt, eyes lit aflame, lips dry and cracked, toenails and fingernails overgrown. She had become obsessed. The papers the old woman provided detailed a list of family members of which Valerie had never been told. They were a part of a group of other families with very specific purposes. One particular family—her family—had a very specific purpose for Vedere. A purpose she had spent months studying.

The Vederian elders communed with the other original families, called the *quinqu*, and it was the elders' job to maintain a specific world order through their family's line. It was the role of her family, the Amavi, that Valerie became enamored with—and it all made so much sense. All the fault she found in her mother could rest in a higher purpose that she felt her mother ignored. And now, with the evidence she had, she could place blame—but not until she fully understood her family's purpose. Fully understood what her mother *should* have done. Fully understood what she now *had* to do.

The boy tipped in with a stack of books almost too heavy for him to carry.

"Boy, look," Valerie signed. "Amavi is to carry out specifically the bidding of quinqu. Worship of quinqu comes before all duties of the nation."

The boy was rooted into the ground, still struggling with the stack of books. He had no response. "Boy, did you know that our people are not alone? Did you know we had purpose?"

Two flashes at the door indicated a visitor. The boy scurried over to the door and took a step stool to reach the peephole. It was the old woman, along with three other women, each holding a black box. The older woman was holding black clothing, neatly folded. The boy opened the door and the women filed in.

"You've had enough time. You now know enough truth. We are ready for you," the oldest woman said. "We are here to begin your transformation. It will give you discomfort."

Valerie stood, then stumbled. For the last few months, she hadn't stood for very long.

"I am ready, I am a servant of the quinqu. Tell me what I must do."

The oldest woman removed Valerie's clothing while the other three women opened their boxes and produced black ink and needles. She was to be tattooed.

"You must now open your eyes for the final time. The first was to see. The final will be to sæ. It is time your mind woke up. Put on these clothes, receive your tattoos, and follow me."

Valerie nodded and followed.

***

Machiavelli, 212 days left

When Valerie returned, I knew she would be different—but not like this. She had become a completely different person. Thin as a rail. Skin covered in black tattoos in shapes I couldn't understand. Her face seemed permanently twisted into a shape I did not know she could make. She had become reclusive, sensitive, and argumentative. Her helper, the six-year-old, now signed for her whenever she needed to communicate with anyone. She wouldn't even sign to me.

She had disappeared for four months, but her family hadn't taken the time to look for her. I guess they assumed that she had to temporarily escape. She had done something like this before, but never for this long. When they last got together, I had understood things to be partly resolved, but instead Valerie left while her mother's health continued to decline. Vega carried out all duties for her mother. Victor was in and out of the Ræ as well. It felt like things were slowly unraveling. I would have no idea how bad things had gotten. Not until I had a conversation with her.

"My mother is Ægæliphi. This will change soon," Valerie explained through the child. There were no formalities. No explanations and nothing to clarify the four months she went missing. She motioned for her servant, an older man known as Barius, to stand in front of her. When she asked me to meet in the Royal Library—which was essentially a collection of the total knowledge of the people of Vedere—she made no clarifications. Simply a written message explaining when and where. The library's vast halls and bookcases brought with it the splendor of hundreds of years of knowledge, opinions, and journals.

This used to be one of Valerie's favorite places. As a child she couldn't wait for her daily time here in addition to her studies. She was able to absorb so much. Able to be so imaginative. It did not mean she was not troubled, or that she did not have her faults. But she was an object lesson in how complicated people truly can be. How they can believe one thing, say they will do a thing, but show the complete opposite. How they can grow unconscious of how their actions portray their beliefs, of how those actions would be subsequently viewed.

Through it all, I was still certain I knew her, not just as a child, but as an adult. I had hoped this invitation, to one of her favorite places, was a return to form. That she would be back to herself.

Valerie grabbed the boy by the head and pushed him away as she stood—something she rarely did now. She was almost always in a seated position when I would see her in passing, behind a book or set of diagrams. She seemed to care about nothing else; about anything other than the research she was conducting. But today she had put her books down and stood before her oldest and most trusted instructor. And she had requested me, her personal advisor, to attend. Her first real visitors in four months.

"Barius, you've been my servant since I was about three, correct?"

Barius nodded.

Valerie walked around him in an elliptical orbit. Even her gait had changed. She held her posture differently. *What had the Viceroy done to her?*

"You've known my mother for just as long, and I've only known you to love our family like it was your own."

Barius nodded again.

"And so it is for this reason that I ask you one question: Why have you lied to me?"

Barius shook his head as his hands searched for the arm of a chair to sit. His eye contact with Valerie never wavered. "Heir, I swear to you, I have never—"

With no hesitation, Valerie slapped the old man across the face, bringing him to his knees. I flinched with the boy as Barius fell.

He took a moment to steady himself and wipe the blood from his bottom lip. "My child, I have only loved and cared for you. Why do you doubt my truthfulness?"

Valerie responded by kicking Barius in the face, producing more blood. She wiped her bare foot on Barius's beard to clean the outside of her foot. "You are Cophi. Do not think I do not know what you have been up to."

Barius straightened his back, standing with a slight waver before replying. To my surprise, she was right.

"I know you will kill me soon," Barius signed, wiping the blood from his mouth and nose. "So know this, just because you now know who I am, and perhaps, now that the Viceroy has told you who your *real* family is, doesn't mean I didn't love you as my own. Whatever you plan to do next, know that you will not be powerful enough to stop us all."

The bravery displayed in Barius's disposition was amazing. How he managed to be a spy for nearly a century was also a feat in and of itself.

"Oh, but Barius, I will not kill you. You must be a witness. You all must. I've been *exposed* to something. You could even say that I've been infected with something. Do you know what that is?"

Barius stood motionless.

"It's the *truth*. I have been exposed to such a truth that I cannot help but be transformed. It is my goal now that the rest of my people be transformed. And you're going to help me."

Valerie took a moment to return to her seated position. "You've known me to always spend as much time as possible in this very library. I've read all of these books. I've read them all *twice*. I've read and I have learned. And not a single one of these books shed light on what I have learned. You could say I've developed a new perspective on how to rule."

Barius was attempting to continue to stand upright, with a kind of dignity.

"What the people want to know and what they *should* know can be two vastly different things. My mother never gave the people what they truly wanted. People do not want to be free. They don't even want the complete truth. They only want to know what they *should* know. They want to be ruled." Valerie's eyes widened as she stood again and walked toward Barius. He had now taken a knee. He could no longer stand, so she kneeled down to meet him.

"Did you know my mother was never to see the throne?"

Barius nodded. "I helped install her in the war. Your family, the Amavi, they were completely overrun. Vera killed them all, all except you. She loved you."

"She kept me prisoner!" Valerie dug her heel into Barius's hand, the one holding him up. "I have been lied to, Barius. We all have been lied to. There are too many secrets in this castle. Too many secrets in our history. I intend to seek them out."

Valerie closed her hand into a fist and swiftly jabbed Barius in the neck. He choked as he dropped to both his knees.

"Our ancient purpose as a family line was to ensure peace through control. It's bigger than you and it's bigger than me. It's bigger than the entire nation itself. It's about *why* we are what we are. My mother never understood her purpose. I do."

Valerie now turned to me as she tiptoed to a nearby chair, crossing her legs after she sat.

"Machiavelli, fetch me a cloth, I just had my toenails painted."

Since she was a child I have cared for her in ways no one else could understand. Her newfound ruthlessness excited me. Her steadfastness was incredible. Valerie had found a conviction. And I had found mine.

"What makes you think your family is the only one with purpose?" Barius asked. "The work has already been set into motion. You do not know everything Valerie, you do not—"

Valerie gripped Barius's head with both of her hands. She looked up to the sky as her eyes rolled back into her head. Barius went limp as his eyes did the same. Valerie was a sær. A very powerful sær.

In just a few seconds, she had read Barius's mind. The stress she put him under to extract the information also killed him.

"Such a stupid little man." She loosened her grip and let Barius's limp body slump to the ground. "He gave me everything."

Valerie walked back to her chair.

"Machiavelli, see me," she continued, looking past me. "I meant what I said. No more secrets."

Valerie was a consumer of knowledge, she adored books as a child. Now as a sær, there was no limit to how much information she could attain. How had I missed this ability of hers?

"Thanks to Barius, I am now aware of an artifact the Cophi call the Book of Books. I want that book. Someone is hiding something and nothing will be hidden from me."

I nodded, though I was not completely certain what she meant. It seemed clear now that Valerie had been exposed to information that only the Viceroy had. There were always questions swirling around about how the children were raised, and what their mother did to them. But no one suffered more than Valerie. Now I knew why.

Valerie was not her sister Vega. She was not the one the entire court adored. The one considered too perfect for this world. She was the "other." And now she knew why. It was time for Valerie to begin her plan.

***

Quannah, 210 days left

Quannah was certain the letter was penned by Dr. Fallon Sylvan. It made the most sense. It said to come alone to a marketplace in the city of Puresh. He was assured the area would be busy enough for no one to suspect a nefarious meeting between two men. But it was still a risk. Vedere's matriarchal society was structured, but not quite oppressive. Still, caution would be vital.

Traditionally speaking, it was a man's prerogative to remain neatly within societal norms. There was a history of too many allegations and rumors of what *could* happen if someone lived outside of Vederian society and its structure. As far back as Rory Davis, it was clear that maintaining status quo ensured anonymity and safety, but it also guaranteed a life most internally dreaded. For all of Vedere's advancements, it was still not a utopia. And though the majority of citizens lived a prosperous and enjoyable life, there was an undercurrent of fear in many throughout society. The status quo was clear: if you step outside of what was expected of you, you will disappear. This is precisely how Justice Afauna disappeared. Gone without a trace.

Quannah became aware of Fallon during his schooling days at the Citadel. Brilliant mind, sharp wit. He fit in very well in the female-dominated circles of the educational elite and could hold the types of conversations that most men could not. He found a value in paying attention to these conversations, and it served him so well that he found himself invited to aristocratic settings where he could further prove his place among women—that is, until he completely disappeared.

Quannah was only aware of bits and pieces of information, but he gathered that Fallon was commissioned away from the capital to a lab by the sea, but beyond that he had no idea. It was disappointing news, as he was indeed a part of Quannah's plan—though he didn't know it yet.

The disappearance of Justice was incredibly alarming. Quannah and Justice had worked together closely for nearly seven years. They were just about to begin mobilizing—and then everything stopped. Justice fell off the face of the halo. Quannah completely lost contact. He was still not completely sure if even he had been compromised.

There was only one thing Quannah knew for sure: they were running out of time. They were closing in on just over two hundred days left. Whether or not Quannah liked the public meeting with Dr. Fallon Sylvan, he didn't really have a choice.

The one thing Quannah did know about Dr. Fallon was that he had an outstanding family history. The only concerning thing was his choice to live outside of the work his family was known for. But if he was even a fraction of who his mother was, there was a solid chance.

As for Quannah, as an Omega, he thrived within a space of anonymity. By job description, he was asked to be omnipresent but invisible. He dashed through the corridors of the palace swiftly. He knew what was needed before it was requested. He responded when called. This attentiveness had provided him the most powerful currency in Vedere: information. For years, Quannah believed the information he had acquired served little purpose in the grand plan. The truth was he had become disillusioned.

Vederian society didn't call them Omegas. To them, Quannah and others like him were eunuchs. But in either case, his father would have told you that they were within their destiny. Quannah's father, a principled and thoughtful man, would often elucidate on the privilege Omegas had. He would continue on, rambling about the task their family served, their place in this society, how they were so important.

Most Omegas never get the opportunity to know when their day has come—their day of destiny. The day when nothing else will ever be the same. But of course, it was what they trained for—the one thing that brought Quannah personal shame.The one thing Quannah could never understand about his father was his passion for such a subservient role in society. He seemed moved by a purpose so deep and rooting that it seemed it went far beyond any passion Quannah ever thought he'd had. Quannah didn't understand as a child, but it was the very thing he clung to as he got older. To obtain the level of passion and devotion to something, *anything*, like his father had. Quannah hated his role in society, but nevertheless it was his and time was running out. His father's work, and his father's father's work would not rest with him.

Today, though, Quannah had the opportunity to save a life. He saw Dr. Fallon before Dr. Fallon saw Quannah. The crowds were thick enough that one could easily get lost. They were all dressed the same and no faces could be seen as per the custom for Vederian men. Without hesitation, Dr. Fallon walked up to Quannah and they quickly touched foreheads. Quannah could feel his emotions now. Dr. Fallon was afraid.

"The code word is redemption." Dr. Fallon walked straight past Quannah. *"We cannot stop moving."* He craned his neck, scanning the market for

Ophori. *"We are meeting because I believe that what you know can help save a very special child."*

"Understood. I'll continue to follow you until we have to split."

"Talia Davis is the last known relative of the explorer Georgette Davis. I have been approached by her and a young sær. Talia has information that could change the course of both of our lives." He pretended to shop for potatoes. Quannah did the same, but walked a bit farther.

"Her life has always been in danger," Quannah replied. *"But her father has been murdered and her mother jailed. What can we do to save the girl's life? Any idea who is after her?"*

"We must find her and hide her. I have contacts among the Cophi, they know how to keep things hidden."

Dr. Fallon had no idea how much Quannah knew. One part of him was still unsure if he could trust him. The other part of Quannah was almost certain he had no choice. Either way, he could not possibly explain everything here, right now, in this market. The second matter was the Cophi. Justice was missing. They were without their leader. First, Justice disappeared, then Tora was killed. It was clear someone was on the offensive, someone in direct opposition to us.

"My involvement ends when the child is found. So long as you can ensure that she will be safe," I maintained. *"I am extending an enormous risk by even being seen outside the Citadel. I want to be sure you understand that—"*

"You have my word, Quannah, put it to the test. Now, what exactly are we discussing? Why do you believe her life is in danger?"

"I know her life is in danger, because someone has been connecting dots they shouldn't be able to connect. Someone very powerful is closing in on something extremely important. It is now only a matter of time."

"So we're on a timetable?"

"The ferry leaves at ten, we better hurry." Quannah tried to remain calm. A member of the Ophori was patrolling, stopping only briefly to stare directly at them. Dr. Fallon never noticed her. Quannah employed a technique his father taught him: during *torphi*, when you want to misdirect a conversation, you have to think about something that replaces the thought you want to conceal. Torphi is a powerful physiological process, but it

has its limits. The brain does not process everything—just the most recent thoughts and emotions. Sharing and reading emotions is like observing ripples in a river after a stone is been thrown into it. You may not know when a rock was thrown, but you are able to observe the ripples it creates when it contacted the water. Eventually, each ripple that follows becomes weaker as the effect of the rock fades away.

Vederian *telempathy* is very similar in how it behaves. It allows one to move freely from one mind to the next, but only through eye contact. You cannot follow the conversation until you observe the first ripple. Anything before that (the rock) has to be assumed based on the ripple. And if a third observer—in this case, the Ophori soldier—wanted to understand a conversation between Dr. Fallon and Quannah, she would have to quickly make eye contact with both of them long enough to get information. If she chose Quannah, she would read both his initial response (regarding the ferry), and only a faint idea of what Quannah wanted to conceal ("I know her life is in danger"). If she entered Dr. Fallon's mind, only the most recent thoughts and memories would be present. The best the Ophori would be able to conjugate would be "the ferry leaves at ten, we better hurry," with the very honest thought from the doctor being, "So we're on a timetable?"

It was a complex tactic that took some wit and skill to pull off.

Fortunately, the soldier was not at all amused. *"I have no interest in the conversations of men,"* she replied, and continued on.

They were safe—this time. They continued their conversation.

"I believe that she has information that is of interest to House Cara, and perhaps others," Quannah maintained. *"It could very well be related to the same information you were able to obtain as well."*

"Who specifically within House Cara?" Dr. Fallon pressed. He was fishing for something.

"At this time I cannot say, I must be careful," Quannah answered—all of which was completely true. *"I believe Talia's life is in danger because of what she knows. And when she is finally aware of the importance of what she is carrying in her little book, I believe that she will attempt something incredibly dangerous. Something I too have been planning with the Kofi for some time: traveling to the Underside."*

The Underside was a largely unexplored part of the continent. Very little was known about it until Talia's great-grandmother led a daring expedition there.

"Quannah, I know that the Davis Expedition had survivors," the doctor boasted. And it was true—for him to even to have that minor detail was worth my attention. But that would not be enough. *"And I also know that they found ancient ruins, ruins that do not match any anthropological data we have to date."* It now seemed this Dr. Fallon knew much more information than Quannah initially anticipated. But he was not done.

"According to Talia, Georgette left clues for her descendants. She has set tasks for others to complete in the present day. They had to have known how monumental this discovery was. They—"

"They knew how hard someone would work to conceal it as well," Quannah interjected. *"The discovery shatters everything we know. Those in power cherish the delicate balance they have established."*

Dr, Fallon smirked. *"Of course! It must be that other family. The one that started the Sisters War."*

"No, my friend. Much bigger than the royal family. There is a conspiracy that spans millennia. The rabbit hole runs very deep. I'll put it simply: you should be very concerned."

"Quannah, I am already terrified. I don't think you know what's going on outside the sacred walls of the royal family's home. You don't know about the people who have gone missing, the secrets, the lies. More and more of us are beginning to see our world for what it truly is, Quannah, there will be an awakening." Dr. Fallon stopped walking to look back at Quannah, then continued on through the market.

"There has already been an awakening, doctor." Quannah paused for effect. *"It's all so very periodical now, my friend. Every few hundred years the collective eyes of the people begin to open, and each time those eyes aren't simply shut, they are cut out of the skull. You have no idea who you are dealing with and you could not believe the reach they have. Doctor, you are a mosquito; whining and worrying about getting wet, oblivious to the fact that you are flying over an ocean. I'm afraid I cannot help you."* Quannah had hoped this would dissuade him. It did not.

The doctor pulled Quannah into an alleyway. *"They took my eldest sister. And when my second sister went out to find her, they took her too. Now my mother has no one, no one to take up her work, a depressed academic of a son, and an entire dying culture under her wing. And you know what hurts the most? We don't know who took them. We cannot ask the Ophori. We cannot go out ourselves. We are powerless. They are stealing us in amberlight and we don't even know who is responsible!"*

Quannah respectfully nodded his head.

"Quannah, I am already at the end of my rope. It's not just my family, but my friends. We are under attack. Anyone who questions, anyone who thinks outside the will of the Vael and the law of the Cara simply disappears. And I am certain the expedition has something to do with it. I am certain that Talia's book is the key. And I believe they point young Talia to those ruins."

"If we start down this path, Doctor, look, you won't be able to unsee this anymore. Are you ready for that?" Quannah asked.

Dr. Fallon looked Quannah in the eye and nodded. *"I will tell you everything I know."* The pair touched foreheads.

"Let's get to work."

***

Gaius, 210 days left.

Standing at the door was a silver-haired woman in standard Ophori-casual attire. The blue-and-silver garb she wore was formed from a single piece of fabric, wrapped around the extremities first before meeting at the center of her body with a knot. The knees and elbows were protected with black leather cups as the fabric covered the rest of the soldier's body up to her helmet—which covered her face entirely. She took up space, still very intimidating. Her black visor hid all emotion, which could be jarring for a Vederian. She stood motionless, as all Ophori do, but in her own way she looked to be on the defensive, and an Ophori is never on the defensive. Always attacking, their motto.

Her hair was braided into seven individual braids that snaked from beneath her helmet to gratuitously cover her upper body and shoulders. Underneath the coils of blue fabric were revealed intricate white-inked tattoos that covered her arms and legs. They were in stark contrast to her deep black skin. With perfect posture, the warrior stood six foot six—three inches over Gaius—with an athletic physique that accentuated her beautiful symmetry. As she reached toward her helmet, the air became still. There was a moment that felt like time stopped as both individuals sized each other up. After what felt like an eternity to both, the soldier's extended arms revealed her tattoos enough to confirm her identity: it was Maya Durham, First Leader of the Ophori, the highest military leader in the nation of Vedere and one of the most powerful women outside of the Royal family. Upon removing her helmet, she gathered and placed her seven rowed braids to the front her, presenting the mane of a lion before she began to communicate.

"My old friend, may I have the honor of entering torphi with you?" she signed.

Gaius straightened his posture. "Yes, Maya, of course. To what do I owe the pleasure?"

"As you know with us, Gaius, life isn't easy." Maya was referring to the life of a warrior. The life of Ophori and all their secrets.

It had been at least two decades since the final meeting of the Old Guard, when Maya was only three. After the disbanding of the Old Guard, most of the old members wanted nothing to do with the old way of life. Most all of the council members who were appointed during wartime had their memories wiped, a technology that was illegal, as it was misunderstood by even the most brilliant Vederian neurologists. All of the aides, the artists, the writers, the entire inner court of the Ægæliphi—all would never know of the horrors in which they participated.

And, ironically, due to the trauma of war, the Old Guard, the initiators and foot soldiers of the war's most atrocious acts, could not be mentally cleansed—not completely. Many were simply trusted at their word, as some stated they wanted to live knowing what they had done. Others, though, were crushed under the weight of their own guilt. Officially, the Old Guard consisted of twenty-one men. By war's end, only seven were thought to still be alive. Maya's father, Robert Daniel Durham, was a part of that number, as was Gaius. Timothy Aquinas, a former farmer; Phillip Andrew, a former artist; Tudor McDaniel, a former historian; his brother,

Tora McDaniel; and Damian Cala, a former filmmaker, were all who were believed to have remained.

In the early days of the Old Guard, Robert Daniel lost his wife to suicide. Unable to adjust during that time, Robert Daniel would occasionally bring his young daughter to the Old Guard's meetings. Though this was strictly forbidden, Robert Daniel had the respect of his brothers and was known for being a good man, a valiant warrior, and a good father.

But the Old Guard was truly something else entirely.

As Maya and Gaius briefly touched foreheads, the questions began to develop. Why was Maya at the home of Gaius Saroyan? She had also come in casual Ophori dress, but that did not exactly mean she was unprepared for a confrontation. Ophori members were highly skilled in hand-to-hand combat that was built on the strong foundation of only on the most genetically gifted and talented. Ophori were trained to constantly assess an ever-changing landscape of situations. Using sight as their guide, many of their attacks were based on misdirection, disorientation, and blinding.

Official Ophori documents stated that Ophori sparred regularly, with serious confrontations that often ended in the maiming of both parties. The level of training that was necessary for the men to be on par with the female fighting force was highly selective, grueling, and unforgiving. Many of those who were trained as Old Guard never survived.

Still standing in the threshold of the door, Gaius sensed a hint of informality as Maya continued. *"Gaius, I have come to you with the hope that you could give me direction."*

Gaius offered his front room for Maya to sit.

"I see you as my father," Maya explained. *"I have been made aware of something that is very concerning. I am coming to you in confidence. No one can know about this."* Gaius searched for deceit in Maya's eyes, but found none.

"What have you found, Maya?" Gaius asked as he sat down next to her.

"I have ... books. Well, it's a kind of book of books, more like notebooks really. These books belonged to an ancestor of mine, Damien Durham. It seems he was some kind of scientist. I only read a few excerpts, but it seems he was a part of that failed expedition I learned about in school. But none of this information seems to make sense."

"What do you mean?" Gaius asked.

"Well, the details are all wrong. He's talking about plants I've never seen before, and they're books from others discussing ancient ruins and objects. I ... I don't know what to make of it."

"So what concerns you about them? Should we get another academic to—"

"No! No one can see this, not yet. I don't think this is something anyone should see. They're ... they're probably inaccurate, but Gaius, there's some wild information here, and I just want to know what it means, and what happened to Damien. But no one—and I mean no one—can know about this. Only you and I know."

"You have my word, child," Gaius replied. He stood up to go to the kitchen to retrieve a glass of water. He waited until his body blocked the drawer that he slowly opened. *"Would you like some water?"*

***

Balien, describing his most immediate memory prior to the event at 2,024 days left. Transcribed at 157 days left.

When my mother collapsed, the four walls surrounding her turned transparent. I was in the living room reading when she fell. There was a pool of liquid and a limp body encased in a clear box that no longer looked like our kitchen.

It's Vederian technology and it's often taken for granted. In modern Vederian homes, nearly all solid surfaces can turn transparent when necessary; in this case, an emergency was detected in the kitchen, making the room's occupant visible.

Rushing to her, I signed, "Mother, is it time?" I activated her touch-sensitive garment to reveal a squirming human form, stretching and uncoiling herself as she prepared for an escape. It was my mother who taught me that Vederian babies could still hear in the womb. It is upon birth that they are welcomed to a world of silence. As a child, I believed that once I reached my twenties, I'd have a much better understanding.

"Mother," I signed, two inches from her face, "your child is coming and you must stand up. We have a plan, we can make it."

I assessed the situation; we still had some time. If we could get to Puresh, we could safely deliver the baby and keep her hidden. We knew we would require outside help for the premature birth and we couldn't depend on the baby's father, Gaius. I pictured the images of what needed to happen in my mind. I slid around behind my mother—almost slipping—as I squatted to pick her up. Lifting my mother wasn't the hard part. The hard part was picking up a woman in labor. She cried out—something she couldn't do once we left the house. But I expected this as well, knowing there was really no way to calm a mother afraid to lose another baby.

Vedere had been a matriarchal society since its beginning. Womanhood and the power of creation were central concepts not only to various Vederian religions, but ideological and political beliefs as well. Vedere had become a miracle of a place. Advancements in science, agriculture, and sociology had catapulted Vederian society past the expectations of many of its scholars. But not even Vedere's brightest minds could solve the mystery of Vederian biology and its complications.

"I don't think I'm going to make it," Mother explained, trying to get her feet under her.

"If we work together, we can do this, Mother. We knew this would be difficult." I had only met Gaius Saroyan twice before today. He didn't seem to be a mean or cruel man, but he was despondent around me. He would begin each conversation with a heavy sigh, and though he knew he was not my father, he tried his best to treat me as his son.

My mother never spoke about my real father. I knew nothing about who he was, what happened to him, or where he could be—if he was still alive. I only know his name: Balien. And for surnames, I have Gaius's. Balien Saroyan, a junior of a stranger, with the surname of another stranger. My new sibling would be Gaius's child. We hadn't yet thought what kind of dynamic that could become. Today was about first bringing a non-Vederian into the world without anyone knowing.

I locked eyes with my mother as we counted to sync her jump.

One ... two ... three ... up!

I hoisted her into the air and made a break for our vehicle, only to discover it was raining as hard as Vedere could rain. Looking back, I don't think it ever rained as hard in Vedere as it did that amberlight. Mother got into the hovercar first. I started the vehicle up, switching the terrain from "SKY" to "LAND."

One thing I always remember about that day is that flying to the hospital would have saved my mother about four and a half minutes. I was certain we could not risk flying in the storm, but now, every now and then, I wonder if we could have made it. In the end we went with magnetic travel and, regardless of the result, I will always regret it. It cost me too much.

Mother looked out the window, as if she would see Gaius speeding around the corner.

"I'm sorry, Mother, but we have to consider going to the hospital." I knew it wasn't wise to speak audibly, but I wasn't really thinking. It got her attention.

"I will not allow it," she replied. "The moment that child is born, it will be taken. We will all be taken. It will be the end of our entire family."

She was right. But I still wish I had taken that risk.

This is where my memory begins to slip. I remember lightly tapping my mother's forearm twice to get a circulatory scan to begin on her biosuit. I remember seeing her torso and arms light up, revealing all relevant information. I remember how beautiful it looked, every vein and lymph node color-coded and elegantly rendered. The baby looked good, but time was running out.

I looked ahead a few hundred meters for any obstacles. We had passed the genetic research center out past the beach and only had three left turns, a right, one bridge. From there, it would be a straight shot. The road looked clear. Hardly anyone traveled on the ground anymore. Visibility would have been tough for a Vederian anyway, as the rainwater disrupted the many spectra of light Vederians could see, but we were good. I was certain that we were good.

We hit a hard bump, which introduced the bridge. It was at that point that I only remember being exposed to pure, white light. My vision slowly returned as my view of the icy water below the bridge began to get closer and closer. I tried to process how many seconds I had before the vehicle would crash into the water, but I realized too late there would not be enough time for both of us. As we crashed into the water, the last thing I saw was glass crashing into my mother's eyes. Everything went black.

I believed this to be my tomb. Ice cold water, complete darkness. My heart was ripped apart. I had lost everything. And it happened quicker than I could process it.

But that river was not my tomb. It was my cocoon. I was in pain, but I was changing. I was lost, but I was searching. And when I emerged from the water I was never the same again.

Part 4: Simplicity is Fourth

The Journal of Georgette Davis, 57,297 days left

Day 4

Beyond the challenge of arriving, it has been a relatively simple task. The camp has been established and the work has already begun. It is important to note that the more complex parts of this expedition are yet to come.

I have asked Dr. Durham to consider keeping his own journal. He is a very skilled writer and extremely observant. I trust him, and if anything were to happen to us, I know an account of what occurred will be safe with him. We must be sure to employ contingency.

I have also had a long conversation with my alpha of Philosophy, Saven. He believes that one of the tenets of understanding life is to view it in its most simplest terms. Simplicity can be found everywhere—at least according to Saven. He was chosen to be a part of this expedition because of this manner of thinking. And if anyone can make sense of what we hope to discover, it is him. I put my full faith in him as well.

Tomorrow we hope to activate our security team. This will be our first true amberlight in true darkness. We pray our artificial lighting does not fail.

Until tomorrow.

***

Record NGV #296, Gabrielle Reporting, 201 days left

Nothing had changed—except for how much the kid had grown. The lab had developed further. Vega was sicker. The Ægæliphi had made what many believed to be her final public appearance three years ago. And no one had seen Valerie. And as for Fallon's work, he had come close, but he was still mostly unsuccessful. He now had two twenty-somethings in comas.

When Fallon found the young man, it seemed apparent that someone had been to the crash site before him, but Fallon didn't stop to investigate between the deep poundings inside his chest. Had it not been for Ava and the lab, the young man probably would have been dead.

Fallon leaned in closer with his hands behind his back. He called up a 3D model of the young man.

How incredibly alone you must feel; to feel things no living person ever will. You are plagued with fears I will never understand. And for what your life has now become, I am so very sorry. He wasn't even sure what he was looking at—the bloodwork and various scans indicated the young man should be brain dead. Even if he were to regain consciousness, there was no telling how much assistance he'd need to survive.

His shoulder rose as he leaned on the desk for support. *Seven years of work,* he thought as he reviewed the charts. Fallon had committed seven years to understanding the process of cloning, a phenomenon many, including himself, thought to be impossible at this level of complexity. In an instant, everything was realized.

It was the young man who helped him understand what was missing. Where the process was continuing to go wrong was due to the mind, not the body. Fallon was burdened with the task of assisting the clone's mind in accepting reality. Each time he would attempt to wake her up, she would reject everything: who she was, what she was, what the world was. And Fallon still couldn't fix it.

But there was more to it than that. Here was a young man with a genetic code that was completely alien. A wholly unique physiology, totally different biology, with the possibility of experiencing the world in a way Fallon couldn't fully comprehend.

"Ava, run their vitals again, please. I need another update." Fallon turned from his desk and walked over to the young man.

The young man squirmed a bit before calmly opening his eyes. He looked around, squinting as his eyes adjusted to the light. Fallon, stunned, quickly grabbed his desk chair, dragging it along the cement floor.

The young man's blood pressure shot up. Fallon and Ava worked to sedate the young man again, Fallon prying the young man's hands off his ears in order to administer medication.

Fallon and Ava agreed to wake the young man again, but this time they would take a different approach.

***

Record NGV #297, Gabrielle Reporting, 199 days left

Two days later, they were ready once again. Their turnaround was so quick, I almost missed the beginning of their conversation.

"OK, Ava, I'm ready. Everything look good to you?" Ava nodded on screen.

"Let's wake him up. I'll try torphi first, assuming that's how he communicates."

Fallon walked over to the bed and prepared for another potential outburst. *Are we in agreement?* Fallon touched his forehead to Balien's. *He doesn't seem to be able to torphi,* Fallon thought to himself as he began to sign.

"Can you understand signed language?" Fallon motioned. This time, the young man's ears were stuffed with cotton swabs.

"Yes," the young man replied. "I've never been very good at torphi, sorry." The young man had calmly opened his eyes and looked to be at peace.

"Well that's OK. I know it's difficult for a number of the population." Fallon picked up a kokoto and placed it in the form-fitting grove in the wall near the bed.

Balien coughed as he twisted his fingers into shapes. "Where is my mother?" Balien signed as he rolled in the bed, attempting to stand up.

"When I found you, you were alone. And that is the truth. Can I ask who you are? What is your name?"

"My name is Balien Saroyan, son of Athena. We were on the way to the hospital—she was going to give birth to my sister. Just keep it straight, doctor. What happened?"

The truth would have been that the accident was caused by Fallon's experiment.

"It—it must have been the storm, Balien. If your mother was with you, I'm sorry. Your mother is gone."

Balien slumped further into the bed. "What is this place, Doctor? What do you do here?"

"I'm a biologist. I study Vederian biology. I focus on genetics."

"The only thing I can remember, Doctor, is my name. My mother and my name. Perhaps at the hospitals—"

Fallon nodded his head. "Balien, I'm sorry. I don't think you understand. By now, there would have been—"

Balien interrupted. "How long has it been?"

"Balien, it has been nearly five years."

Balien didn't move much, but a tear trickled down his cheek. "So I have nothing?"

Fallon placed his hand on Balien's shoulder. "I will do everything in my power. Ava and I will do everything we can to restore your memory."

Balien nodded. "I'm going to rest a bit now if that's OK."

Fallon nodded..

★★★

Part 5: Truth is Fifth

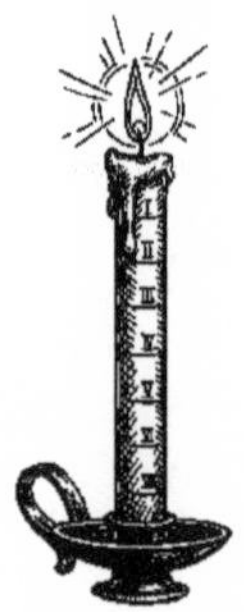

The Journal of Georgette Davis, 57,296 days left

Day 5

Let us get up to speed, shall we? Today was all about the security team and their various tasks. We're past the Reach now. There is an enclave that looks to be the perfect location for our first camp. The synths have already begun construction. I would like to think that with the best and brightest among us, we have nothing but good fortune on our side. We want to answer the most audacious question. Our hearts are so, so ambitious. Who do we think we are?

Priority one was reconnaissance. The Security alpha, Ava, split her team into seven groups, each with a synth. Their job was to build us a perimeter radius for our natural sciences team. We were able to get drone data, a testing perimeter, and 3D mapping of our artificial habitat.

Our immunologist tells us we can only be unsheathed from our suits when we are in our portable facilities. We were asked to be insanely detail-oriented. Head on a swivel, as our security alpha would say. But I cannot shake the nagging urge to remove my visor. I know the air could contain unknown pathogens. I am aware of the hidden, insidious dangers that encapsulate our little camp. But I am not quite yet a part of the expedition either, not yet. It feels like I am watching it happen on a screen. It feels like I am not leading this mission—like it is happening with or without me. I do not like that feeling.

Our physicist told me we have the most advanced scanning technology our world can offer, but it doesn't stop there. We have even brought along experimental equipment, something my husband Rory really pushed for. We have a device that is being called a pressure level meter, or PLM for short. It is a device that responds to changes in air pressure. Our physicist and Rory both believed the unique properties of the Underside could exhibit changes in air pressure that could be lethal. We believe this new device can detect these changes safely and preemptively.

What will we discover? I am still completely enthralled with wonder. It consumes me now. It was a seed in my mind that has now shot up into a giant oak. Maybe we will find nothing, I know it is possible. My life's work could be nothing more than a small news clipping, but I remain determined. How can I call myself a scientist if we leave now? We may find the answer to everything!

***

Fallon, 197 days left

It was one of those days that bled everything into one long moment. The kind where it was unclear what day it actually was or what time.

Fallon sat at his workbench with his palm on his forehead. He was slumped forward and exhausted.

Not even Ava could get the math to work. Fallon had hit a point where he needed help, but who could he ask? Who could be discreet enough for such a project? The illumination of his holographic displays reflected off his forehead and cheeks. Half his face turned blue and the other green. It would flicker and change slightly as he swiped through his screens.

A light flashing in the bottom left corner of the screen called for attention: "New message from Unknown."

Curious, he opened the message. It seemed to make no sense: "EnCt25215a57993ab374e6edcf651969d4bc55ab62cee5215a57993ab374e6e dcf651NSWqQZlfmwGp41a7tl/ JErzjXgkbWlLrmoahlt6AzCs64Rs+PsmDZL7RR6crr3zBlPf2PcqNr5xq9g ==IwEmS."

"Ava, can we get this cleaned up a bit?"

"Working on it now, Fallon. The encryption is 51-bit. Would normally take most standard computers centuries. Just a moment. OK, I understand."

"+PsmDZL7RR6crr3zBlPf2PcqNr5xq9g==IwEmS." It was still jumbled.

"How are we getting this?" Fallon asked.

"It's a door, Fallon, it just needs a key. Let me work the numbers. I'm throwing this up on your viewfinder. I am certain it is an encrypted phrase."

Fallon's dark skin turned a pale blue as the holographic display lit his face. The image depicted waves in varying angles—size and shape.

"Ava, what is this? It looks like a language. Is the key of Vederian origin?"

"It is, Fallon. The math is extremely advanced, I'm not sure any other kokoto could compute this. I'm straining just to get this far."

Fallon started to feel that internal burning you feel when you're in trouble with your parents. He thought for a moment before replying.

"Fallon, that's not all. I'm still processing, but it appears this message was sent directly to you. It's not radiating a message, it's a vector. It—I mean, they have used your mother's name."

"How could it know my mother?" Fallon grasped for a piece of paper and pencil as more and more words flowed across the screen.

Son of the proveyor, seek out the expedition. Find the gift.

Fallon scribbled the words in a rushed hurry. "Is that it? It's repeating, right? That has to be all of it."

Fallon ripped off a second sheet of paper to begin crunching numbers himself.

"Fallon, there's no way you can compute this; it's beyond biology ... it's ... well, I don't know what it is."

Fallon jumped up and began with quick steps that turned into a light jog as papers flew behind him. He grabbed the threshold as he swung around the door. He was headed to his second library. He had to understand the references.

"Ava, jump to the second library and begin cross-referencing the word 'expedition' and 'gift,' please."

"Of course, Fallon. What are you thinking? How can I help you?"

"Well, Ava, not only are you some of the most beautiful code ever written, but you're the most advanced AI in the history of the world. You will be all I need."

"Thank you, Fallon," she replied. "I've already obtained data for your first query. I think we've already hit the nail on the head."

"Where did you learn that colloquialism?" Fallon smiled. "You truly are beyond what I could have hoped. So what do we have?"

"Expedition—Davis Expedition/Century Expedition. This seems to be your best option, Fallon. It's an expedition that took place during the height of the Civil War between the Church of the Vael and the Believers."

"Yes, I remember this. We learned this in school. But it was a tragedy, right? Only two people survived. They found nothing and the queen had completely funded it, instead of funding the Church. Entire books were written on it."

"Well, according to official record, there were four people who returned: The husband of the leader of the expedition, a Rory Davis; an unnamed Sherpa; a security officer; and a Church of Vael clergyman. Their account is that their group was separated and only the four returned to the rendezvous point."

"How did you find this information?" Fallon asked.

"I'm using an entry point via Vega's kokoto. I suppose this was Ægæliphi-level clearance."

"So what are we looking at here? A dead end?"

"Looks like it, Fallon. I'm sorry."

Fallon tapped his temple with his pencil. "OK, well we do have the mentioning of a gift. What do we know about the word?"

Ava began another query. "Gift, standard definition, gift, also known as Epeë, common name for the Hyleians of Halo Gabriela—"

"Hold on, Ava. Seek. Seek the gift. It's a person! I have to check it out." Fallon rushed back to his workroom.

"But Fallon, do you know anyone by that name?"

"No, I don't. Can you check the database?"

"Fallon, it is an extremely common name—wait. I've found something."

***

Epeë, 197 days left

It seemed my family had a tendency to play with fire. We loved how it flickered, the beautiful color, the shapes it could create. And yet it was so dangerous—the perfect killer, as many called it. Put your hand in it, and at first, nothing would happen, until you noticed your bones exposed from your skin burning off.

I'm not sure why fire exists. I remember joking with my father that it wasn't meant for our world. That it seems to be for others, not us. It has been almost seven years since I have seen my father. My mother nearly lost her life trying to find out what happened to him. She went too close to the flames too. And now here I was, doing just the same. I always felt my father was preparing me for something greater, but I never understood what that was.

When I found my father, it was too late. They had kidnapped him and sentenced him already. The edict read: "And for crimes against Vedere, and the six halos that circumnavigate the Capital District of New Redemption, the Order of the Ophori, by the decree of Ægæliphi, the Protector and the Provider, hereby sentences the male, Justice Afauna, to death."

I couldn't find our lawyer in time, but in any case the outcome was clear. If my father's crime was deemed to be treason, he would be forced to confess and be shot. If the crime was murder, he would be killed immediately. I should have been much more prepared for this. My father had always been a renegade and he knew this day would come. He lived up to his name, *Justice*, and he was always prepared to die for equality. But what about Mother and me?

It was practically an all-out sprint as my mother and I raced to the center of town after reading the edict. On our halo, the region to the north of the capital houses all the municipal buildings. This was done to simplify travel for magistrates, dignitaries, scientists, and the like. Given that there hadn't been a public execution in nearly twenty years, many from neighboring halos would be in attendance. As I ran, I tried to formulate a plan. I just wasn't sure how I would get there in time.

Suddenly, a large hand gripped my shoulder. I swung my head around, expecting the worst.

"Epeë! I saw the sentencing! What's the plan?" The tension in my shoulders lessened. It was Tara Abraham, my closest friend. She joined us, without hesitation.

Telempathic communication is difficult when you can't focus your mind. I signed to her, "The plan is to save my father, can you get a hover ring?"

Tara looked at me and smiled. "I'll be right where you need me."

At the next alley, Tara darted to the right, boosting herself off a garbage portal and grabbing a water pipe. She swung onto the adjacent roof. I was reminded that Tara had the potential to be one of the greatest Ophori our halo had ever seen—if she didn't get caught thwarting the direct orders of her own regimen.

Tara is everything the Ophori had ever wanted and, as her best friend, I *wanted* her to get enlisted. She stands six feet eight inches tall and is built to fill out her frame, yet she has the agility of flowing water. Her beautiful hair is usually braided back in a single strand, dancing off her back as she walks. She is strong, beautiful, and menacing, but it was her quick wit that allowed her to quickly move up the ranks. While I struggled to pass my physical tests, Tara was designing them. Had it not been for her, I wouldn't have made it as far in the Order—that is, before my discharge.

I looked over to my Mother. As a capital member, she worked in the inner circle with the proveyors. She was dedicated to uniting our halos and fostering Vedere's next cultural renaissance. She had no idea her daughter was now a failed former member of the Ophori and that her husband was the leader of the resistance. She was just scared. Scared just like I was now, and was all those years ago.

Seven years ago, my father stumbled into our home, covered in blood. He was half-slumped, his mouth moving in a strange fashion as another man helped carry him in. My father was squinting and grimacing, but I couldn't understand why. There were no bright lights in the area, so there would be no reason for discomfort. The stranger pointed to me and moved his mouth as he removed my father's bloody clothing. My father looked at me and collapsed to his knees as the stranger rushed past me to grab some rags and bandages.

The stranger tended to my father's wounds while I remained fixed on the ordeal. The stranger seemed kind and patient as my father thrashed around. After what seemed like an eternity, the stranger, a young man with an eye color that seemed to be ever-changing, stood up, wiped his brow, and approached me.

"Your father will heal," he signed. "Tend to him like a gardener tends to his plants. All will be made clear soon." And with that, the stranger turned and left. The next morning my mother returned from the capital. He told her he had been in a hover ring accident.

Now, as we neared the northernmost part of the halo, the crowd thickened. My mother turned to me and signed, "This must be some sort of mistake. Your father is a lowman. What could he possibly have done to warrant an execution?"

I hate how she speaks of my father. Oh, how Father wanted a social revolution. Since as far back as anyone could remember, women have led our world. I understood the hierarchy, but what I couldn't understand was the mistreatment. Most men were laborers—only valued for their mule-like strength. They were like cattle. My father didn't want that for our society. He believed we could be better.

As I pushed past the crowd, I saw Father. He stood on the court steps, as if he were about to be auctioned. He stood calmly. I didn't want to see my father like this—not when no one knew who he truly was. Not when his wife had no idea who Justice Afauna truly was, not yet.

The morning after that incident, I was barely awake when he opened my door and sat on my bed. He smiled as we touched foreheads.

"Epeë, I know this will be difficult to understand. But you have to trust me—the world you know—from the emotions that you feel to the air that you breathe—it is all a lie. The Vedere you believe in, the Ophori that protect us, the history of our culture ... it is not what it seems. For now, I just want you to understand that there will be a day that I will be in danger and in that moment, remember this: there is more than meets the eye." He stood up and covered my window with the curtains.

"I am a part of something, Epeë. I lead a group of people who the world believes shouldn't exist. Epeë, just ... see me, I need you to join the Order. I need you to be trained and learn about how life in the capital is like. I need you to stay close to the Ophori and pay close attention to the royal family. Can you do that?"

I slowly nodded, though I was not quite sure what he meant.

Father got up and paced from one end of my room to the other before continuing. "I need you to be my eyes in a place I can never enter. I need you to be a spy."

"I won't let you down, Dad!" I replied. I had no idea what I was agreeing to. I just wanted to make my father proud.

"Soon I will explain. But your destiny is greater than the Ophori. It's even bigger than me. When you are older, you will be an incredibly powerful person. So we need to get you ready, OK?"

By the time my mother and I neared the front of the crowd, Maya was addressing the crowd. "We stand for order, peace, and prosperity. Will we let this man take that from us?" the Ophori leader asked as the crowd erupted into a frenzy. Maya turned, looking square at me. "We stand for a principle that is impenetrable. We answer this calling with swift and unequivocal justice."

I looked at Father, bound by the neck, hands, and feet. We locked eyes and he smiled—then he winked.

Everything moved slowly after that. The crowd had raised banners. There were protests and waving hands. I watched as my father was shot up into the air. I dared not lose his gaze. I didn't even notice Tara carrying me away. A fire erupted and the center of town was now chaos. My mind was mush. I understood nothing.

"Tara, Epeë. Listen to me. Your life is now in danger. The Ophori will soon be upon you," a young man with long white hair warned us. I had seen this man before.

Tara put me down and we locked eyes. *What is going on?* I thought to myself.

"There is no time, Tara. Epeë, we must continue running," the man warned. *"I will explain everything shortly. Now, at the end of this corner, turn right."*

"And then what? We're supposed to follow the directions of a complete stranger? This is all really convenient," Tara, the skeptic, responded.

The man spun around. "Upon Justice's death, these were his instructions. You and Epeë are now of the highest priority. Stop at the alley before us."

"This better not be a trap or—"

"Hello, Epeë, Tara. My name is Quannah. And we are now out of time. Sciya is an island where a man I trust has a lab. He researches Veteran biology and his mother was a friend of your father's, Epeë. I—I don't know how else to explain this, but I had no idea it would really be you. I suppose I got lucky. I was given clear instructions to come find you. You and your friend Tara. See me, I'm so sorry it has come at such a time as this, but what I can tell you is that your father was on to something much larger than the teachings of the Cophi."

"What could possibly be more important that the Cophi?" Tara replied.

"Proof, Tara. Proof. Now, we have to get to the lab."

***

Vega, heir to the Throne of Vedere, 157 days left

The most insidious lies are the lies of omission. When you plan decades to prevent something so much greater than yourself, you become obsessive. You have no choice. You become lost in the details. You get so close to aiming for perfection that you begin to leave things out. They're always small. They always seem unimportant. But they multiply. They fester. They build until you know you will be consumed and you have no choice but to succumb to your own mistakes.

My cough began when I was seventeen. And I ignored it because there was nothing that would prevent me from becoming Ægæliphi. I was immortal. I would skip through the great hall, where every Ægæliphi's name, image, and works were displayed. I saw my mother's name. And I saw my own. I would cough, and I would ignore it. But not for long.

But soon, I couldn't ignore my mother either. She had become something worse than my nagging little sister. Much like my nagging little cough. I was infected, not just by disease but by her as well. Her little ideas. Her logic. Her determination. She was so fixated. She was so reverent. So willing to erase, destroy, and remove anything that marred the "ideal"—whatever that was. And as many parts of my daily life began to fade beneath my feet, Valerie continued to rise. As I sank—no, as I drowned—my sister soared. She had wings and yet she was never happy. She could soar past the sun itself. And it still was not enough. You could ask her how she was and se would say, "Not satisfied, not yet," just like my mother.

When Valerie and I were little, we would play out in the gardens. One day—and I'll never forget this—we found an anthill with an enormous colony. I remember letting them crawl onto my hands as I watched them study their environment. But before I could get my notebook, Valerie had returned with a bucket of water to drown them all. I wanted to cry.

Valerie's only response was that she didn't want the garden ruined by anthills.

I became terrified of her. We all did. Her ruthlessness was not what our throne needed. Compassion was what our people needed.

I know now that I will never be queen—not the way I intended. I won't have enough time to be great as Ægæliphi. I would be lying if I said that I didn't resent the fact that Valerie will overshadow me. Why did it have to be me? With all of the diseases we have cured, why couldn't it have been anything else?

I hold the second-highest position of power in the known world. Ten thousand servants would crowd our mother's observatory. Her every word was documented, written, and recorded. Every decree was respected as law. My mother never even had to stand on her own two feet. If she wanted to be carried to and from every room, through every corridor, past every servant, it would have been done. She was queen. She was Ægæliphi.

And like her, I too am carried from room to room, but not because I am magnificent. I am carried because I am sick. I am weak. The weakest heir our nation has ever seen. I can only stand on my feet for minutes at a time. My own servants had to swear an oath of lifetime secrecy under penalty of death just to care for me. The people believe me to be regal. They believe me to be opulent. They consider that I am too good for the ground they walk on. They know me to be strong and principled. They know me to be graceful and kind. They look to me to be the answer to any problems they may have. They see me as too good for my own world. And I cannot stand it. For never setting foot on the ground, I am filthy. I will die from disease, and I don't yet know what the official story will be.

I know that is not all that they think. They treat my mother as if she were already dead, as if no Ægæliphi would ever set foot on our lands again. And what they don't know is that they're probably going to be right. If my plan does not succeed, ruin will visit every Vedere street, every home, and every room. They do not know my sister Valerie. My people cannot be left with her. My sister can never rule, but I fear I am out of time.

The plan that I approached Dr. Sylvan with was fairly simple in concept: When the time was right, a clone of myself would replace me once I succumbed to my illness. My implanted kokoto would be removed and given to her, Vega II, and with it all my memories, hopes, dreams, and ideas. It would be as if she were raised as a normal child. She would grow at an accelerated rate to become me and prevent the mantle of Ægæliphi from being passed to my sister. That was the plan. We worked for seven years and we failed many times. Until now.

Dr. Fallon Sylvan warned me that a procedure of this complexity was extremely risky. "This process will come at a great cost, My Queen," he told me. "It will cost us our morality. It will cause us pain." He was right. It literally shortened my life. The stress made my illness worse. The time I thought I had was shortened. And the complexity that I underestimated hit me full-on.

The first clone died shortly after what would be considered third quadmester. Natural Vederian births require mothers to remain in brighter and warmer climates until the child is born. At Sciya, the doctor's living laboratory, we matched the conditions perfectly, down to every detail. Yet still we lost clone after clone. I was not prepared for how painful that would be. I was paying the price. I was losing my morality.

Under the suggestion of Ava, we engineered two sets of twins. The result emptied me more than I ever thought possible. I became less than hollow. And even today, even with our success, I am empty. I believed that once Vega II looked me in the eye, I would be free of this emptiness, but I now know that I never will.

This goal, for the people, came at a price that was maybe too great. Ava would tell you that we had a 0.05% success rate. She was also brilliantly designed, so she also apologized for being insensitive. We had our one. Our last chance, Vega II, but it came at the price of omission.

***

ACT II

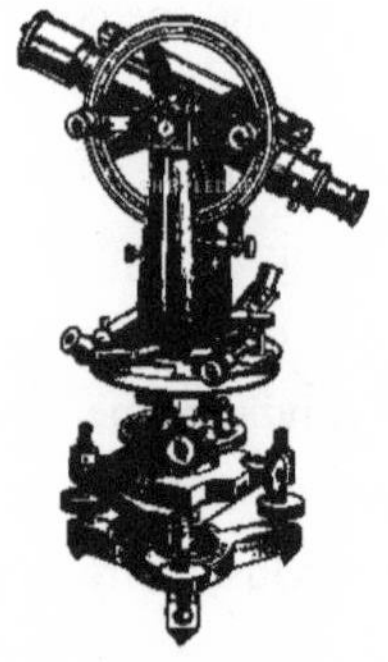

The Turn

Part 6: The Husband

The Journal of Georgette Davis, 57,295 days left

Day 6

06:00

I do not think that I can quite explain what has just transpired. The PLM suddenly started flashing with a pattern that none of us could decipher. The lead physicist, Rory, and I began to document the data and began analyzing. It is still early, but we believe we have discovered what can only be described as a vector.

We still haven't made much sense of it, but we believe it is a directional pulse of air pressure changes that have a source. I am calling for a meeting with all science alphas to vote on the next course of action. I cannot help but plead my case for following the vector. If it has a course, we could be looking at an epicenter! I am talking about a source with possible technology! We could be preparing for a first contact.

But the day is not without complexity. We have had to quell two separate episodes of what I can only describe as madness. We have had sixty-seven separate and recorded seizures, fifty-four counts of equilibrium and balance-related issues, and almost universal aversion to all food. I am nearing calling off this entire operation. I'm so—

12:00

Though we have deduced it is most likely the PLM that is causing the symptoms, we have chosen to follow the vector. We believe that the physiological issues will be temporary and the sooner we find the source of the signal, the better. The ruins we have discovered along the way have been photographed and marked for further study. Along the vector we have built minicamps, each with a proper Beta leader and security team member. All of the Alphas will stay with me. The Gamma leaders will work to build a radius.

The farther we travel, the more it becomes clear that at some point, there was a civilization down here. I am scrapping the rest of the itinerary until we find the source of this air pressure.

14:37

First confirmations of a civilizations—without a doubt. Much of what we have found seems to be a part of a system of probes. My running theory is that our ancestors used some manner of ancient technology that was lost to us to explore this area, or, someone else sent these probes here to help map out *our* landmass. We've only done a cursory check of the technology, but it looks to at least be on par with technology already within our reach if not beyond, though we would know if anything had been sent down here at least within the last couple hundred years.

15:48

We have decided to slow down a bit and really take in all that we have come across. There is so much data to go through, yet we feel the strong need to press forward following the vector. We are going to split up. The PLM's readings seem to exponentially increase as we near the epicenter, so we are sending out a small security team to run a quick check before we continue on. Rory will accompany them, they will return promptly at 20:00.

21:00

The security team has still not returned. We are making provisions for a second team to investigate what happened to the first, but we're going to give it at least a few more hours before acting. We've sent out several messages without any replies. Rory knows what to do in situations like this.

23:36

I will just write it out plainly, so as to not misconstrue what has transpired: Rory has returned with an unidentified child. Near the source of the vector, first contact was established. Communications broke down and there was a conflict. From what we were able to gather, they have weapons technology unlike anything we have ever seen before. Our security detail did not stand a chance.

Rory is explaining what they were like. I will include sketches in this journal as to what they are described as appearing. Despite Ava's questioning, Rory maintains there is a possibility for peace—the baby is proof of that. Rory is convinced the infant was given to him as a show of peace. As for me, I do not know what I believe, but I do know we have lost an entire security detail.

We knew it could be possible that our species splintered off at the beginning. In fact, that was the running hypothesis in many anthropological circles. We had hoped to find migration patterns to the topside of our halos, but this was all under the assumption that we would be discovering people of the same species. What Rory is describing is something entirely different. We have to consider now that we are truly not alone. Our neighbors have been beneath our feet the entire time. Who else is out there?

***

Athena Saroyan, 2,438 days left.

We had to train. He had to hone our skills. No one else could teach him, not like I could. And if something happened to me, he would *have* to know. I can't imagine how alone he would feel if he did not know the truth. If he did not truly understand who he was—if he truly didn't understand who I was.

All a mother wants for her child is to excel. To be all they strive to be. I have trained my son from as far back as he could remember. All he knows is what I have been trying to prepare him for and I've only done the best that I know how. Maybe I shouldn't have started so young. I don't think it's fair to even say he had a childhood. It's all been preparation. All our children's lives have been is preparation, just as my generation's and the ones before ours. It's all our people have become, and I hate it. I hate that we have to raise our children this way. But I don't think there is another way.

Maybe I shouldn't have left Gaius in the dark. Maybe I should have never traveled into the city in the first place. My mother never agreed, but she still supported me. But I have a young man, now. So much is happening to him that he doesn't understand: It's not just puberty, it's his awakening. His brain will be put under strain and, at that point, I can only support him.

"Balien, five minutes," I signed. It's just after amberlight. We have to start our training early.

"OK, OK," he replied. He rolled around in his bed a few more times.

I walked out to our courtyard. The city of New Redemption boasts a climate hotter than most others, but Vederians never feel the temperature. We lived within our domes. A dome for our courtyards, a dome for our backyards. It was the perfect place for training: easy for concealment. If anyone asked what we were doing, we could easily dismiss it as daily prayers.

Balien finally joined me in the courtyard, still yawning and sleepy-eyed. He tripped over the final stair, as always, but caught himself. Now he was fully awake.

"What do you hear, Balien?" I asked. "Let's begin with listening."

Balien plopped down onto the grass and closed his eyes. This was his excuse to fall back to sleep.

"Balien! Remember that Vederians do not sleep with their eyes closed. You need to be prepared."

"Yes, Mother," he replied. "I'm sorry. I hear your voice, Mother."

"Excellent, and what language am I speaking?"

"You are speaking the Second Language, Horeni."

"Excellent, my son. This is Horeni, one of the spoken languages. Could you explain it further again for me?"

Balien rolled his eyes. Yes, we did this every training session, but I needed it deep in his mind. I needed it so deep he could never forget it.

"Sure, Mother." His tone was sarcastic and I frowned as a response. "The Horeni have a number of languages, just as the Vederians have a number of languages."

"Great, and how do we classify them?"

"We classify them as spoken language, with grammar and lexicon, signed language, with grammar and lexicon."

"Good, Balien." As a child he loved the word lexicon. He loved how it sounded. "Remember that signed language has its own visual-manual modality. This is how they convey meaning," I continued. "Language is expressed using a manual sign-stream in combination with nonmanual elements."

Balien nodded.

"What else do you know? I asked.

"Vederians predominantly use tanna, the signed language."

"Correct. What else?"

"They also use banna, their written language."

"And what is the Horeni written language called?"

"Harpsi, raised logograms on paper. They also communicated with instruments, Hopsi."

"Very, very good, Balien, remember it is now our burden to remember. We are the keepers of this knowledge. When everyone else forgets how the world used to be, we will not. Now, let's talk about the mind. How do Vederians speak with their mind?"

"Well, we call it speaking, but it's not words like our spoken language," Balien suggested.

"True," I replied. "But our brains understand it all the same. The words are interchangeable in this context."

"Right," he said. "Vederians speak with their mind through torphi. They establish a physical connection to link their minds, they can then communicate freely."

"That's right, Balien, and today we're going to learn more about torphi. There is a universal language that all people know. It is a conscious stream called the sæ. All people, be it us, the Horeni, the Vederians, we all can connect in the sæ. Consider torphi a dialect of a sæ. Do you remember what dialect means?"

Balien nodded.

"Good, now, take a look at this chart."

Balien got up from his seated position and we walked over to the hologram.

"As you can see, we have mental languages, signed languages, written languages, and special languages. These special languages have their own category, as they are unique to a specific people or context. They don't neatly fit in the other categories. These include, but are not limited, to the Vederian lingua as well as the Horeni language of hokri." Balien studied the graph.

"Both Vederians and Horeni can enter a sæ; there, the minds link at a state so closely knit that the two races can understand each other. They are connected by the mother language. Out of it came torphi and hokri. Do you understand?"

Balien nodded.

"Balien, never forget our work. We have to be the ones who remember. And when you are older, it will be your job to reveal this truth to the Vederians. You represent the work of generations. You are here to bridge the gap when the time is right. This is why I train you so hard, to understand what you hear, to understand what you see. You are the ambassador of these two peoples. The first of your kind."

Balien walked over to me and hugged me.

"I know how much this means to you, Mother. I know how much this meant to your mother and your father before her. I know how much this meant to Kamali. No matter what, I won't forget my purpose. I can never forget."

***

Epeë, 197 days left

Quannah asked us to follow him into nearly waist-length water before asking us if we could swim. "It's fine if you cannot. We actually do not have to go any farther."

Then why were we in the water?

In an odd fashion, the water in front of the island began to lower and we were able to walk up to the building. It seemed the building itself was not the only thing the doctor had designed. I was still trying to understand it all. We hadn't even entered the lab, but from the outside it already looked more advanced than any building I had ever seen before. I was surprised the building was even here. I was certain I had been to this area of the halo before, but I never noticed a building here. Not in the middle of the sea.

We were greeted by a slender man with elaborate facial tattoos. He had long hair and a calm, handsome face—this was the doctor. He described the building as if it were more than his lab, but it seemed too large to be a home—it seemed more like a museum. As we sloshed toward the door, Tara's eyes shifted from the roof of the building back down to the door. She was nervous. I knew Tara couldn't swim. But she would never admit that to me.

The oddest thing about the island was how barren it looked. There were no animals, very few plants—it seemed artificial. The trees were too perfect. The sand was black as ash and carried weight.

"This is Sciya, my home," the doctor explained as he wrung out his tunic. It was a light material that rested lightly on his shoulders and covered the entire length of his body.

"This is government-sanctioned, isn't it?" Tara asked. "This location is not on any map I've seen."

I nodded in agreement. I knew something was amiss. Everything felt a bit *too* contrived.

"Yes, Tara. It is sanctioned," the doctor replied.

"I hold a commission from the heir herself," the doctor continued. "Come, let's go inside."

The doctor's lab was designed unlike any other building I'd ever seen. There were walls and corridors, short ceilings, strange equipment, but there was also very little light—which was odd for a Vederian lab. It was a labyrinth.

"I know this building looks strange to you," the doctor posited observantly. "It was designed this way for me to conduct my research. And yes, it is a laboratory, but it is also my home. It is home to Ava as well."

The doctor stopped in front of us and slightly bowed with his arm outstretched as pixels of light collected on the floor between us. These dancing lights developed to form the figure of a woman. She was youthful, weightless, and completely ethereal. She was made up of so many colors I started to only see white. She smiled. She flowed with a grace only comparable to that of the Ægæliphi herself. She turned to me and raised her palm.

"Hello, Tara and Epeë. My name is Ava. I am an artificial intelligence created by Dr. Fallon Sylvan in the seventy-fourth year of the Ægæliphi Vera, Common date 3176. Do not be afraid. I am before you as only holographic light. My physical circuitry is stored below this complex. My purpose is to process the physical data that Dr. Sylvan cannot detect or process on his own, as well as provide hypotheses, perform and create necessary mathematical formulae, and to predict probable outcomes for our given experiments."

Tara violently shook her head a couple of times. "What is this? This isn't torphi—"

"It is not, Tara. Ava perceives our communication as raw data. Our brain waves are very complex, but the way we use our brains for communication between each other is something that she can understand very well." Fallon smiled. "She simply replies with the same waves we use and directs them to our brains."

Tara turned her head slightly away while squinting an eye. She wasn't satisfied with that explanation. Fallon motioned for us to enter deeper into the maze. It seemed clear that Quannah had been here before. He was not at all surprised by the lab or by Ava.

"Ava does all of the heavy lifting," Fallon continued. "Her processor can quantify data far beyond what we have the capability of doing on our own."

Fallon's demeanor had an earnestness to it. He appeared honest and kind, but was jittery, like he hadn't slept. We walked over to a desk covered in a dozen piles of neatly stacked papers and files. The room was almost a pure white. Everything seemed to be made of the same material and held the atmosphere of a hospital room. Fallon thumbed through a few sheets of paper, then sat on the floor, back propped up against the desk. He froze for a moment. He curled his knees up to his chest and let the papers spill out and down between his legs. He gripped the temples of his head so tightly you could see his knuckles turn white. He silently cried. He took a moment to gather himself and looked up at us.

"You don't need me to tell you how great of a man Justice was and his end hurts me in a way too familiar. He was to religion what I am to science. And without his help, without the intersection of our beliefs, we would never know what we now know."

"So what do you know, Dr. Sylvan? My father never mentioned you," I asked.

"Your father never mentioned me because he could never speak of me. Only a few people know that I am actually still alive," Fallon replied.

"So why all the secrecy?" Tara jabbed.

"I live here in secret, Tara, because of what I do. My thesis was in theoretical physics. My first two doctoral degrees were in genetics and neurology. My third doctoral degree is in—"

"How are you so educated?" I had to interrupt. "I mean, with you, you being—"

"A man?" Fallon smiled as he sniffed up his tears and wiped his nose. "You can thank my mother for that. She's ... important. She was able to pull some strings."

"But explain *here,*" I pressed. "Why are you here? Why are *we* here?"

"I can help with that answer." Ava was now on the wall. It looked as if she could freely project onto any white surfaces. This was technology far past anything I had seen on any other halo.

"We are here because Fallon was exiled. He presented a thesis that almost got him killed. It was branded as heresy by the Church of Vael. He was asked to leave the capital to conduct his research away from the nation. If he were to ever set foot on a halo again, a warrant would be issued for his arrest which—of course—he has recently done."

"So that is why Quannah came and got us?" Tara asked.

"And yes, this is why Quannah came to get you. He came to get you two because he was directed to by a person or group of persons we have come to call the V."

Fallon cocked his head. "Since when?"

Ava laughed. "In the time you three returned. Speaking of which, we have new instructions. The other two will be ready soon."

"The other two?" I asked. "The V?"

Fallon got up from his seated position on the floor and handed Tara and me each a set of schematics.

"I'm sorry, you have to bear with us. Everything has been happening all at once."

The schematics included images and notes of a guy about the same age as Tara and I. The notes suggested his brain functioned differently than expected. His genetic makeup was also unlike anything the doctor had ever seen—per the notes.

"About five years ago, I was conducting an experiment that caused a hovercar to crash over the bridge you passed on our way here. I found a young man in the wreckage and brought him to my lab."

Fallon pulled up a second display on the wall adjacent to us and frowned as it struggled to focus. It showed a detailed computer-generated rendering of a young man with a readout of his vital signs and other similar data.

"The plan was to take him to a hospital as soon as we got him stable, but after we imaged his brain we ... .I—I couldn't."

It was Tara's turn to frown. "So you're keeping this guy prisoner?"

"No, not at all," Fallon replied. "As soon as he gets his memory back, we will get him to his people."

"So he's awake?" I asked.

"Yes. He is awake, though right now he may actually be sleeping," Fallon replied. "He is still quite confused. But I think he may be somehow related to all this."

"So what about the other one?" I continued. "You said there were two."

"Ah, well, yes." Fallon paused as if he was unsure he could continue.

"They are already here, Fallon. And she has already been born. What's done is done," Ava interjected. "We don't know why we are all together. Maybe they can help."

Fallon nodded. "I am also away from the capital because of the commission I was given. Vega, the heir to the throne of Vedere, approached me and asked me to complete a task for her. Something to be done in complete secrecy."

"And what could that possibly be?" Tara asked, folding her arms after signing.

"To clone her," Fallon replied plainly.

"Clone? For what purpose?" I asked.

"To replace her. The heir is dying. There is no treatment. We've already tried."

"I need to pray. Where can I go?" Tara demanded.

"Ava can show you the place to go," Fallon replied. Tara followed the hologram out of the room. Tara was a devout believer. News of such an enormous loss to the throne came not only as a shock to her but a challenge. She saw it as a chance to prove how faithful she was. If she could pray and heal the heir, she would be holier than her sins suggested. If she could petition the goddess and be heard, she would know she was on the right path. It was grief, but it was also her sense of competitiveness.

"The plan was to use kokoto technology to allow the clone to assume Vega's position once the clone's age accelerated to the proper point. As of right now, the clone is in an induced coma and is fourteen. By next week she will be seventeen."

I took a moment to look off into space. I wasn't sure where to look as everything was white, but I needed somewhere to stare.

"I ... I don't think I have to be the one to lecture you on the morality of all this? The rights of the clone?" I suggested.

"I accepted that I would be asking the goddess to leave my presence by completing this task. And if I'm honest, I was never truly a believer. I was asked by one of the most powerful women in the world for help. I could not say no."

I shook my head. "You could have said no. You can always say no. She would have found another."

"Epeë, what's done is done. I know my fate." There was a vapidness in his eyes that accompanied his response and that told me not to push any further.

"So how do Tara and I factor into this? How did you know where to find us?"

"Not long after our breakthrough with the Vega II project, we began receiving communications from an unknown source using a method we had never come across. It was extremely advanced, encrypted end-to-end, and they seemed to know who we were. We refer to them as simply V, I believe. We do not know if it is one person or a group of people, but they leave V as a signature."

"Do you know their motives?" I signed. "How do they know about us?"

"I'm not sure. I didn't even know the two girls that they asked us to pick up were you two. I have been following this along piece by piece. I'm going off of faith."

I didn't like that word. I didn't like how it was signed, and I hated how people used it. I especially didn't appreciate a doctor using it in that way. I'm certain Fallon noticed my furrowed brow. I wasn't trying to conceal it. Not even a little bit. He continued nevertheless.

"Earlier today, we received one of the largest transmissions we had ever received from the V. We're still trying to decode all of it, but it seems to be largely biological data about our people, about Vederians."

"There is more than meets the eye, Doctor. We're at the stage of truth ... and truth is fifth," I added, finishing the sentence. It was a reference to a sacred Vaeli text. Pain comes first, birth comes second, discovery is third, simplicity is fourth, and truth is fifth. It was clear the doctor was very well educated.

We were interrupted by a nearly naked young man, wearing a medical gown that had slumped off one shoulder. On his chest and back were white ink tattoos, similar to Ophori but designed more like the royal family's tattoos. He was lean, tall, his white hair short to a buzz all over his head. Large hands, larger back. He was handsome.

"I wanted to thank you for saving my life. It is a debt I intend to repay," he signed as he made eye contact with me. "I'm sorry. I didn't realize you had company." The man signed with an interesting accent I had never seen.

"I'm sorry, Fallon. I did not realize he had awoken," Ava added.

Fallon gave an authoritative nod. "It's alright, Ava. I'm glad to see he's making a full recovery."

"Well, not fully, Doctor. All I can remember is my name," the man replied. "How old am I now?"

"Well, that will still take time, though it is odd no family has seemed to claim you. There's been nothing reported, nothing on the news. Perhaps we could return to the wreckage site, it could help. And we believe that you are at least twenty-five," Fallon added.

Tara returned from her prayers. "Great, another one," she signed, rolling her eyes.

"I must return to my post," Quannah signed. "I will be in communication with you all in the coming months. There is something else I must do."

"OK, Quannah. Thank you. Well, now that everyone is here, I'm sure all of this will make sense in time," Fallon signed.

The handsome man nodded. For some reason, I felt more comforted knowing he was with us. The doctor took us to a lounging area. "OK, let's get everyone on the same page."

***

Seraphina, 185 days left

When I approached the Light in the sæ, I had lost count how many times I had tried to save him. He had finally woken up, but it seemed that his new reality, without his memories, only confused him further. He did not recognize me. I wondered if he ever would. Still, I knew that this was the only way. His abilities were now fully available to him, but he still did not realize the power he had within him. I will tell him everything. I am too old to do this again. This must be the last time. Time is up.

There was one thing that I was sure of without doubt; Balien's memories had been taken from him, not biologically, but artificially. I did not know how this occurred, but he had to know the truth. This time, I chose my true form. Balien had been overwhelmed enough times; surely an old woman could not be much worse. I knew that he would believe it to all be a dream, so I decided to come to him at a time when he was certain he was awake.

The lab of Fallon Sylvan was incredible. I couldn't fully perceive it as if I were there, everything appeared as dancing stars to me. But it was beautiful in that way. The doctor still did not know his part in all this, but I would leave that work to his mother. Balien was my responsibility. His family traveled so far to complete this work. It was time he understood what they had done.

I startled him when I appeared and spoke; he was reading in his room while the doctor was busy monitoring the clone.

"Put down the book, Balien. I must speak with you."

He turned to me slowly. He was an adult now. His pure white hair was shaved, a short beard was growing. Such a long time asleep. His eyes were as sharp as crystal and pierced me as they always have.

"Who are you?" he asked, as he stood up to greet me. "I'm not dreaming this time, am I?"

"No, Balien, you are not. I have come to you in a sæ," I replied.

Balien cocked his head to the side as he squinted his eyes. He then quickly straightened his neck.

"I do not have much time and neither do you."

"You've been trying to get me to remember," he answered calmly. "Are you ... my mother?"

"I am not," I explained. "Your mother died in the crash that nearly took your life as well. You are now all that is left. You and just one other. I don't have time to explain everything, Balien, I've tried. All I can tell you now is—"

"I seek the truth," he replied. "I—I've had this conversation before, but it was very different. It was not this sad."

"You will need the doctor." I felt my legs begin to tremble.

"For what?"

"To find me. There are still a few on this side who will aid you, and a few on the side below."

"How do I find you? How do I remember?"

"Valvadus. You will know when you are led to Valvadus," I replied before disappearing. It was all I could do to remain that long. I await the young prince's arrival.

***

Machiavelli, 213 days left

There was only one thing that was more valuable than life itself for the nation of Vedere—not beauty, not sustenance, not peace, but truth. Truth was the only currency that mattered. Those who understood this were either already in power, or had killed those too slow to understand. Everything else was crystal clear. Money was simple. The motivation of greed was easy to predict and manipulate. Protecting life, family, beliefs, more complicated, yes, but could still be predicted.

These ideals could be neatly pointed back to the core beliefs nearly all of us held. Valerie came to know this in her quick transformation. She had perfected the skill of observation and manipulation. With her sister and mother gravely ill, her brother in and out of the capital, Valerie was nearly set loose. It was terrifying.

I provided Valerie with all the information she asked of me, and in the process, I discovered a cover-up so large that at first I didn't believe it possible. The implications were enormous. Everything about the history of our people, how we began, it had all been a lie. The question now—the one Valerie was focused on—was who knew and when. We were now neck-deep in the biggest conspiracy in the history of our nation. It was now time to pick sides. It was now *my* time to pick a side.

Valerie was not just unhinged, she was confused. She was losing grasp on who she really was and what was the truth. It took me a few weeks to understand how, but it became clear one amberlight when I stole a peek of her above the spire, a place she frequented as a child. She would spend hours transfixed, staring off into the sepia-tinted landscape. That is when I understood. Valerie was a sær. There were only one or two other women with such a skill, but their identities were not known.

Valerie was trying to end all of this quickly. With power of sight that a sæ provided her, Valerie could obtain all the answers herself; but she was being blocked by someone. Someone more powerful than her. Instead, Valerie was aimlessly grasping the thoughts of billions from moments of the past, present, and future. Each time she entered that realm, she returned a little more undone.

From what I could gather, the plan initially was to simply remove what Valerie deemed as incompetence from her nation and her people. That would be the simple way to explain it, but it was *much* more complicated than that. It wasn't just about rebuilding Vedere. For Valerie, it was about rebuilding her family. The Viceroy had their full influence on her. They intended to return to the days of much more powerful monarchy. Valerie's plan was to exploit one of the oldest Vederian customs, a tradition known as the Tedbik'wali. Tedbik'wali, or the "obscuring" of holiness, was a practice that had established its roots since the beginning of written history, perhaps before.

Since it was believed that the royal family directly descended from the goddess Vedere herself, it was believed that no one outside the family line should be allowed to look upon them. This meant that anyone coming into direct contact with the royal family was expected to cover themselves with a veil. Even the closest servants and aides had never physically seen a member of the royal family. Sight was not only a gift from the goddess—it was considered sacred. A gift that should be met with a gratitude that governed actions. The tradition of Tedbik'wali was such an action, and it was exactly the loophole Valerie intended to exploit.

Valerie not only had the ability to prove her mother's illegitimacy as Ægæliphi, but she also had proof confirming *her* legitimacy as the true royal heir. As Valerie explained it, after the civil war, while a fragile peace was being developed, the true plan of attack began. Over a period of years, the Va Dynasty began to covertly replace royal family members with their own leaders. Just as Valerie was being born, the final replacements were being made in the halos outside the capital. The final plan was to replace a young and more brash Ægæliphi Vera, but the coup broke down as the Ophori fought back at Ræ. Ultimately, Valerie's father, along with the rest of his family, was killed. Valerie was spared and raised as Vera's own. Valerie had felt like an outsider her entire life, and now she finally knew why. She was the last living member of her family line. The *original* family, Amavi.

Valerie moved differently because she finally knew who she was. Vera would have to be held responsible. And it wouldn't stop there. It couldn't. Valerie would have to resolve Vega. She would have to address Victor. And what then? Who would she become as a result?

I met Valerie in her study, a room annexed to her bedroom, which now served as her war room. It had only been a few weeks, but it felt like months. So many had come and gone from this room. So many meetings, requests, secret conversations, and hidden agendas. And at the center of it all, Valerie rarely slept. She rarely ate. She remained relentlessly devoted to her plan. As I entered, she began signing immediately.

"When my mother draws her final breath, that is when Vedere will be restored." Valerie leaned back in her woven chair to cross her left leg back over the right.

"You know it is too early," I replied, as my Tourette's caused my eyebrow to twitch.

"I know that we can be too late. And I will never be tardy. Not when my country needs me." Valerie's icy eyes shifted to a small folder with a few ripped-out pages inside.

I picked up the folder and thumbed through it. It was a scientist's journal. One from the failed Davis Expedition. "How many know that these journals exists?" I asked. "Outside of us?"

"I suspect very few, possibly a few of the other immediate families, maybe less," Valerie replied.

"And how many of the families live?" I continued, as Valerie tilted her head back before grabbing a syringe on the table just within arm's reach.

"There are a few nieces and grandchildren, maybe a daughter." She inserted the needle into her neck and waited a moment before continuing. "I've been told there may be more but we are currently unsure. I want you to enlist whomever you require and bring them all to me."

Valerie had begun taking a cocktail of drugs the Viceroy had convinced her would increase her ability to sæ. There was no evidence yet that it was working.

"As you wish, Valerie. Might I also bring something to your attention?" I took the syringe from Valerie and placed it on a silver tray.

"Go on."

"I provided you with my family's journal because I believed in your plan. But obtaining the other journals will prove a challenge. A descendant of the Davis family lives, one who we previously did not have any information on. A girl named Talia Davis."

"You know what to do," Valerie replied, leaning back into her hair. "There is a conspiracy here. There is more going on here. I do not want any surprises when I take power."

"Yes, of course."

I nodded and placed the clear empty bottle onto the tray with the syringe and left. I cautiously closed Valerie's door behind me, but slowed as I noticed her quickly get up and hurry over to her bookcase. She knelt down and pushed in one of the floor tiles. The floor just to her right unfurled downward, creating stairs that led underneath the bookcases. She took only one look back before quickly descending. I plastered my body to the snaking hallway—making every effort to remain invisible—as she quickly disappeared.

Out the corner of my eye I caught Vega as she briskly walked to her quarters. She didn't notice me.

I looked back at the crack in the opened door and stole thoughts of following Valerie. If her strings were being pulled by the Viceroy, I wanted to know exactly whom I was aligning myself with. I knew this was not information I would receive any other way. I quickly slipped through the open door and skipped over to the depressed staircase, just as that section of the floor moved back to its original position. I became extremely unsettled. Not because I was now trapped in the catacombs—with Valerie surely discovering that I followed her—but because though I continued to descend the stairs, I had the impression I was walking upwards. When I got to the bottom, or the top, there was a tiny sliver of a hallway.

What was an earthen corridor became a white terrazzo hallway that was exceptionally lit. At the end was Valerie, who had not continued farther. She was removing all of the jewelry from her fingers and neck and stuffing them into a concave area in the hallway's wall. At the end of the hallway was a causeway built to cross an aquifer beneath the castle, and beyond that, more catacombs. I allowed my fingertips to slide along the rocky surface of the catacomb's wall and appreciated the smooth transition from rock to terrazzo as I approached the causeway.

Valerie disappeared at the end of where the catacombs began. At the end, a great opening came into view. As light entered the grand underground hall, I was forced to kneel to remain out of view. I was hit by waves of terrible discomfort. First around my temples, then behind my eyes. I began to understand some form of communication, but it was not torphi. It was ... something else.

"*You are not worthy and yet we allow you to live,*" it said. "*You are not beautiful, you are not symmetric. You are not graceful, you are not poised. And yet you still live. That is the grace of the Viceroy,*" The force, both strong and demanding, rushed into my mind like an uncontrollable stream. The rush of emotion caused me to cry as I pressed my palms into the ground, gripping the dirt.

Farther into the great hall, Valerie was also kneeling. She seemed to be experiencing the same discomfort. Slowly, the faces of three people came into the light. It was the Viceroy, no question about it. Three persons of undetermined gender, middle-aged, and clothed in white satin, leather, and silk. They held no emotion on their faces. Their movements were subtle and understated. They were incredibly eerie in every possible way.

"We have chosen to use you. We have chosen to give you mercy, to be drafted in our great plan for the people of Vedere." The three moved in unison, as if they were one.

Valerie frantically scribbled into the dirt floor of the hall.

"What ... would you ... have me do?"

All three raised their left hands. Valerie raised her chin to match their movements, rising to her feet.

"We provided you with the truth. But we require balance. There is an untruth that must be dealt with immediately. The Davis Expedition. All information regarding it, all knowledge of it, must be purged. Burn what you must burn. Kill whom you must kill."

The Viceroy continued to raise their left hands until Valerie was standing on the top of her toes, her chin straight up in the air.

"I am willing," Valerie replied, struggling.

The Viceroy continued in unison:

"There is a man who threatens the very foundation of Vedere. This child risks the safety and ideals of every living being. They must be found and presented before us. Do this and finally return to the work your family was tasked to do over a millennia ago. The work Vera interrupted a generation ago."

"I will do everything in my power to present this child to you," Valerie replied.

"This child aims to go against the will of the goddess. The child is a nonbeliever. A person not of our race, but another. They call upon a false god. They believe they answer to someone else. That is something we cannot allow to exist ... now go."

The race was on. I turned and ran. I knew I would only have small window to escape before I would be noticed. As I ran over the causeway to the entrance, I realized it had already closed. Opening it would cause a suspicion. I frantically searched for anything to help me, but it was too late. Her shadow said she was right behind me.

"It matters not that you saw. What matters is my plan. Let's get to work," she said, wiping the tears from her eyes.

185 days left

Over the next few days, I noted more conviction in Valerie. She took her bidding directly from the Viceroy—without my presence—and directed me thereafter. She had enlisted her own advisors of sorts, as I was deemed no longer sufficient. She had her brother, Victor, milling about the halo in search of some notebook. She'd asked a grief-stricken stiff of a man to seek out the Davis journal, the man called Gaius Saroyan. She'd asked me to research some type of schematic for a type of propulsion system. None of it made sense. I was only given my scene, not the whole play.

I was forced to piece together her plan bit by bit. The Viceroy aimed to stage a coup, and Valerie seemed on a personal plan for vengeance against her adoptive family. But the movements we were making seem to have much, much more at stake that merely replacing imposters. It seemed obvious that the Viceroy intended to extend *their* rule—maybe even to replace Valerie herself. And yet, this was still not the most disturbing part.

Valerie had been preparing herself for some form of ritual. It had taken a considerable toll on her body. Valerie now ate only once a week. She was a rail of a woman and maintained the weight loss was for her "transformation." She told me I would know more in the coming days. Whatever she asked of me, I would do. But I was afraid for her.

She has had several meetings with the Ophori leader, Maya, all ending in stale conversations and shifted eyes. It was my assumption Valerie was building an army as well, with or without Maya. But one thing was clear: Valerie was going insane, and I feared she was becoming too powerful for anyone to do anything about it.

***

Record NGV #298, Avis Reporting, 185 days left

Tara returned from the capital. Her lower half was soaked from wading in the water from the coast. The Tara and Epeë pair had spent five days at the doctor's lab. Epeë didn't need anyone's help understanding they were now fugitives. Whether it was the Ophori, or someone else, it was clear they would not be safe back on the mainland.

"So what I'm getting so far is that the Church of Vael is looking for you," Tara explained. "They aren't out in the open with it, they're just going door to door. Keeping it local."

Epeë perked up. "I still don't think I understand why, but as I've said before, I have no problem speaking to them—"

Fallon looked up from his computer screen. "And I would still advise against it. We both know who your father truly was. He was the key to understanding just how organized the Cophi truly was. And now that answer lies with you."

It was true. Much of what the Cophi was about was passed to Epeë. If anyone could lead the Cophi, it would be Epeë as well. Ava appeared on the nearest wall's display.

"It's also important to note that the large message from the V is ninety percent decoded. We should have more context by the end of the day."

Balien was looking through periodicals, silent films, and history books. He was looking at anything he could latch onto. There was so much that he knew, and yet so much he could not remember.

"Let's go back over everything we know," Epeë suggested. She was tired of waiting. She was tired of hiding. "My original plan was to save my father. We arrived too late. My gut tells me that we should seek out senior members of the Cophi, but I don't know how to find them."

Fallon stood up and walked around his desk, leaning up against the front of it. He took a second to think with his arms folded, then lifted his face as he began to sign.

"So we have a point there. Another point would be that we now know the Church is trying to find you. So we have two points. We still need an end point and a beginning point to connect these dots."

"There's also the V," Balien added. "For some reason, Doctor, they want you, Tara, and Epeë working together. It would probably be wise to see what's up with that as well." Everyone nodded in agreement.

"So that's three points, now," Fallon signed. He used his finger to draw a diagram of the situation on one of the multipurpose walls. Three dots labeled between two question marks.

"Finding the Cophi could be tricky, especially now that the Ophori are seeking Epeë. We can imagine that the Church is actively investigating the Cophi. We don't know how much they know, could be a little, could be a lot."

"I think we should think about this in terms of motives," Tara added. "Look, there are big ideas, here. Regardless of what your belief system is, we have some huge ideals at play. The Church teaches that the Residual is not real. The Cophi believe that it is. Now, we know the Church has been hunting down the Cophi for decades. They were also somehow able to pin Epeë's father."

"Which by the way, how did they do that?" Balien asked. His lack of memories left him in the dark.

Epeë offered the answer. "His charge had to have been treason," Epeë suggested. "There was an attack on a group of believers about a year ago. My father was taken during that attack. Look, my father has disappeared before. It was our assumption that he would appear again soon when the time was right, or that Gregor would bust him out. We had no idea that this time he was captured for good." Epeë lowered her head. "I failed him."

Tara put her hand on Epeë's shoulder.

"My father never asked anything of me," Epeë explained. "He just wanted me to live. To thrive and explore. But four years ago, he had one request. He asked me to join the Ophori."

Fallon rubbed his chin. "To infiltrate?"

"Possibly," Epeë replied. "I got kicked out. I never found out much of anything."

"So we have Epeë's father pinned for treason, a man who led a secret organization that directly opposed the royal family's religion, a swift death sentence, and now they're seeking the daughter. I would first say that it's obvious the Residual is real," Balien said. The room went still. Balien had a solid point. "I mean, clearly the Cophi is onto something that they don't want the general population to know. They want to erase anyone tied to that truth."

"Underpromise and overdeliver," Ava said, interrupting. "I have decoded the message from the V. Or should I say from Veronica. It's a video message. You all should sit down."

Fallon furrowed his brow. "Who is Veronica?"

Ava pulled up the video on each of the walls in the room. "I think you all should sit, seriously. I've read the entire account. It looks like there's way more than meets the eye."

"Hello. I know this will be a lot to process, but time is everything now, so please forgive the rushed nature of this message. First, forget everything that you know, it will make all of this much easier to understand."

Fallon was shocked. The woman looked to be a twin of Vega, albeit a few years older. She had all her characteristics: the same nose, the signature Cara family eyes, the same deep brown skin, the same smile. But this woman was different. It was clear she had spent time away from Vederians. She didn't speak with her hands as well as you'd expect a royal member to sign.

"For the past four generations, a delegate of my family, Cara Royale, has traveled to the Underside to oversee a project known as Long Night. I am Veronica, eldest daughter of Ægæliphi Vera, eldest sister of Vera and Victor. I left for the Underside twenty years ago to oversee the final preparations of Project Long Night, but I have been keeping my eyes on my family this entire time. I can tell you that we have a lot of work to do. Long Night was a result of a landmark discovery Georgette Davis and her team made during the Davis Expedition one hundred years prior. I wish I had time to explain her discovery, but according to our contacts Topside, we are running out of time." Veronica didn't look to be very old, but it was clear she had spent many years worrying. Her worn face held sadness.

"I am contacting you now because we had been working in secret with Justice. It was his job to prepare his people for the coming disaster. That responsibility now falls on you all. Our spies have brought us news that Justice has been assassinated. With our numbers dwindling, with so much work left to be done, we now must take on more risk by asking for help," Veronica explained.

"We have chosen Dr. Fallon Sylvan to lead the new generation, the Young Guild, to assist us in the short rapid works we must complete before the end. We have established friends and allies across the halos to assist you in such a terrible work. But first, context. Nearly a century ago, at the height of the Sisters War, the Ægæliphi was presented a choice. She was losing a war that had already devolved into nonsense. Ideals and beliefs had become blurred, and arguments and been lost to time. Instead of diverting funding to the creation of more weaponry, she chose to fund the Davis Expedition in hopes that the discoveries there would unify our people."

Fallon sat up straight in his chair.

"Through the coalescence of the greatest minds of our generation, Georgette Davis led an expedition to the Underside that not only discovered the origin of the Vederian race, but the fate of the Vederian people as well. Georgette had discovered the truth. Something many embraced while others rejected. For many, it was too much. But there is power in truth, my friends. We are not alone. We are not the only people in existence. We are one of many peoples, and they have come to warn us of our extinction."

Tara looked around at the others, while Epeë and Fallon scribbled notes.

"There will come a day when our halos will be covered in a darkness that will last longer than any of our lifetimes combined. We're talking about centuries of darkness. A phenomenon known as a total eclipse. Again, I know this is a lot to take in, but before the questions start to bubble up, understand that we are already too late. There is nothing we can do to stop it. We do not have the time necessary to use technology to provide enough light for all of our people, and we will lose billions in the hysteria and chaos. It will be the end of our civilization." There was a short pause as Veronica held back a tear.

"So the plan is quite simple, we will work to save as many as we can. We will work to prevent the extinction of our entire race. To do this, we have to work together, bringing our minds together just as Georgette did during her expedition. During the expedition, a number of exchanges were made. There is information that was taken back Topside that we need to complete Project Long Night. We have also worked to track down the majority of the descendants of this expedition—as we believe these are the only people left we can trust with this secret, and the only ones with detailed accounts and records of the history of our people.

"And finally, here is where you all come in: Epeë, you are the only living child of Justice Afauna. Only Justice knew of the Long Night on the Topside. He led the task of preserving our culture. We need you to convince the leaders of the Cophi of the impending danger and seek out the final descendant of Georgette Davis, a girl named Talia. We believe Talia is in possession of the journal of Georgette Davis's husband, Rory Davis. If you find her and the journal, it will be all you need to convince the Cophi. The two of you can then work to obtain the information your father compiled.

"Fallon, we need you to seek out the final descendant of the founder of the Cophi, a woman named Kamali. This will be the most difficult task, as we have little information on her, but our suggestion would be to seek out the oldest of your people for information about her—they should have some clues to her whereabouts. This part of the work is paramount. I cannot tell you why we need this person, not yet, but know that it is of the utmost importance.

"Finally, if you must speak to anyone in my family, you must seek a meeting with my mother alone. If you are unable, then you must then seek my younger sister, Vera, who should be in power. And if all else fails, seek Victor, my youngest brother. Trust them and no one else. In time, I know I will have to return to them to end what I have started, but the work is paramount. Friends, I have taken a great risk to share all of this with you. I do not know if you will keep this secret, but it is my sincere hope that you do. The people cannot know of our end without hope of a new beginning. It has been my life's work to complete this and now it now falls to you. I wish you the best of fate."

The room settled into a stillness as if the occupants were frozen in time. Fallon leaned up against his desk stared forward. Epeë licked her lips and pushed her hair back neatly into its low ponytail. Balien was crouched against a wall, his hands wrapped around his folded knees. Tara was still in the doorway, her arms holding the head of the doorframe.

Ava broke the stillness after a few minutes. "Well, I think the first thing that we should decide is if we believe this message."

More stillness.

"I believe," Balien signed. It was a motion where the hand turned to touch the chest, bouncing as the fingers came together at the sternum. "I do not have all my memories. To me, you are all still strangers, but you are all that I have. I have spent these days trying to read you all. To understand if you all are trustworthy. I have found my answer; I believe in you all and I believe in Veronica's account."

Epeë stood up straight. Her hands began at her shoulders, forming signs using her shin and closed fist. "If anything, I can at least attempt to understand what I seek, what happened to my father."

"And where you go, I go," Tara added. "I can't let anything happen to you, either."

Everyone looked to Fallon, who was still pondering it all. "I believe in Veronica's account. But I don't believe that I am your leader. I think that is for you all to decide." The group now looked at each other. "If we are to do this, if you are to become this Young Guild, then it should be led by a leader of your choosing. We are all here for a reason."

Balien smiled as he stood up. He walked over to Epeë and Tara and put his hands on their shoulders.

"I ... choose to honor my father. I told myself if there was anything that I could do to honor my father, I would do it. Tara and I have been led here. So if we're going to do this, then we do this, let's get to work," Epeë said. "We will do just as Veronica suggested. Tara and I will try to seek out this Talia Davis. Balien and Fallon, you try and find this Kamali."

Ava interrupted, "And our project? What about the Vega II project? The group needs to know if we are to trust each other."

Fallon nodded. "You're right. As a show of trust, I present you *my* life's work. Ava, show them the feed."

On the wall, a display showed a sleeping girl of about seventeen. She was in a pure white room with medical instruments and a giant apparatus over her head. It was a clear dome that was placed over her entire head with a cutout at the bottom for her neck. She was clothed in a pure white gown that came to just below her knee.

"This is Vega II. A clone of the heir, Vega I of the Cara Royale."

Balien, Epeë, and Tara all stood stunned. Epeë reached up a hand to lightly clasp her throat. Tara flashed a slowly developing nervous smile. Balien just stood there.

"I ... I have so many questions," Epeë began.

"I did not believe this technology to be possible," Tara added. "What about her memories, her feelings, her emotions? You can't clone that."

"You cannot," Fallon retorted. "But with the help of kokoto technology, we have been slowly implanting her mind with memories as she has aged. So far she has adjusted to the information load, so long as we induce a coma."

"Then you could do the same for me, right?" Balien asked. His hands flashed with excitement.

"I'm sorry, Balien, but no. When I found you, you did not have a kokoto. Oddly, you also didn't have a scar at the base of your skull. You never had a kokoto implanted."

"Who all knows about this?" Tara asked.

"Other than the three of you? Vega and myself. No one else."

"That's interesting," Balien added.

"What?" Epeë asked.

"It's just, I'm seeing a pattern here. Vega doesn't want Valerie to see the throne. Veronica doesn't want us reaching out to her either. She explicitly stated that if we could not speak to Vega, that we should skip to Victor. What's up with that?"

"Does anyone even know Valerie? I've only seen her in public once. She seems nice enough," Tara posited.

"My father met her, once," Epeë added. "He said she was a lioness in a cage."

"If it were my guess, Valerie must exhibit traits unbecoming of the family. Something has—or is happening—between that family that we know nothing about. And it's enough to convince them that Valerie is unfit to be Ægæliphi," Fallon signed.

"And that must infuriate her," Epeë suggested. "If I knew my sister were dying and didn't tell me, or worse, actively worked to refuse helping me ascend, I would be livid."

"So it's clear we have a situation brewing at the capital. We'll have to add that to the list," Balien shared.

"And I think it may be wise to add her to our growing list of possible adversaries," Tara shared. "I'm not suggesting we are at odds with anyone just yet, but we do know the Church has sent the Ophori after Epeë. It wouldn't be a stretch to assume they're after Cophi as well, or that somehow Valerie is involved in this."

Fallon straightened his back. "And if they are after the Cophi, which now may be aligned with the truth about our world, then it could mean they've been at work to actively conceal that truth as well."

Balien winced and collapsed. He violently shook on the floor as Epeë and Fallon rushed to assist him.

"Epeë, let him go," Fallon instructed. "He is seizing. Just make sure he isn't choking. Tara, hold his head."

"What's wrong with him?" Epeë signed in a flurry as she helped Balien move his tongue from the back of his throat.

"He has been periodically seizing. We've scanned his brain, it lights up as bright as the sun. It's as if he's experiencing something his brain can't handle. It overloads."

"So what do we do?" Tara asked

"We let him seize," the doctor replied. "And then we get to work. Time is of the essence."

***

Balien Saroyan, 184 days left

Time had become my best friend. There were still gaps in my mind, but as time went on, I knew what I needed to piece together.

I woke up to Epeë, Tara, and the doctor crowded around me like a ring above my head, wide-eyed and worried.

"How are you feeling?" Epeë asked, as she helped me sit up.

"I'm feeling better. Everything feels a bit clearer," I replied.

"What happened?" Tara asked.

"I'm not sure. It was a dream, or a vision. I was ... with a woman named Seraphina. She seemed to know me, wanted me to know something about myself—she called me by name. She told me to seek truth."

"I know that name, Balien. Seraphina is a mage. If she sought you out, it would have been in a sæ."

"And this is good news, it means we have a starting point," Fallon offered.

"I'm ready to go," I signed, standing to my feet. "We cannot waste any more time. Let's do this."

"OK, Balien, let's get you some proper clothes. Are you sure you're OK?" Fallon offered.

"Yes, I'm OK—really," I replied.

"OK then, ladies, Ava will be supplying you with a prism kokoto. It provides secure communication. We all have the same type. The prism can separate into two parts. Place one on each temple. It will link our minds together."

I held up a fist and tilted it forward. "Understood."

"OK, Balien, follow me." Fallon took me to his closet. He lived seven levels below most of his lab's domes. It was a simple dwelling. A small kitchen. A large library, a medium-sized office. The lighting he preferred was warmer than the domes above. I felt more at peace.

"We're about the same size, Balien," he signed. "You can wear whatever you like."

His clothing was all roughly the same. Simple clothing that could fit underneath his lab coat without adding too much bulk. I choose the black set.

"This is fine, thank you," I replied.

Fallon paced to the other side of the room and stopped to look at his bookcase. "I realize that this isn't what you signed up for." Fallon turned around to face me. "But see me, if any—any—of this is true, it could change everything." Fallon walked toward me. "Look, I can tell you from my conversations with Vega that Valerie is planning something. We still don't know what, but trust me, something is going on."

"I am skeptical, I admit," I replied. "It's just so confusing, my mind is in disorder."

"Balien, I cannot imagine what you're going through. I cannot explain with certainty why I cannot find you in any school records. I cannot explain why no one came looking for you. But I think I at least have a theory as to why." The doctor paused.

"I have been hesitant to say this to you because I feared it would be too much. But I think it's more than fair now. I don't know where this journey will take us. Balien, the truth is that I'm not sure what you are."

I froze. "W-what do you mean, exactly?"

"Balien, I've run your blood samples hundreds of times and there is only one conclusion: You're not a hundred percent Vederian. I honestly didn't know how you tell you ... I even hoped you already knew, and I can tell by the look on your face this isn't exactly news to you."

He was right. This wasn't news to me. After the accident, my memories were jumbled, but I could never forget what my mother had told me.

"N-not a hundred percent Vederian?" I asked. "What's the other part?"

"Your genetic makeup is partially unknown. I cannot account for about forty to fifty percent. My equipment—and I assure you, it is the most advanced equipment available—can only read about half of your DNA. I can tell you that your mother was not Vederian, not even partially."

"You mean she was sick or something?" I replied. "Like she had some kind of genetic disorder?"

"No, Balien. I mean that your mother was simply not Vederian. I don't know what she was. We are taught a strict religious theory of where we came from. One of gods and goddesses. But we don't have any hard science. We've lost a lot of our history after the quantum age began. Any documents or data prior to that switch has been lost to time."

"Lost to time?" I asked.

"Yes. According to my understanding, Vederians pre-Quantum had a ... different method of preserving history. This has evolved into the theology we are taught from the Science Church of the Vael. I believe there are some pockets of our culture that know more about this subject but..." Fallon stopped.

"But *what,* Doctor?"

"But they aren't going to just tell anyone who walks up and asks," he retorted. "They will want a sign. These are a different kind of people. These are superstitious people."

Fallon walked over to his desk and rummaged through his documents. "Balien, I believe the key to who you are is with these people. They have an understanding of themselves that we don't have," he explained. "I also think this is directly related to Kamali and the Cophi. It just make sense."

"What are you expecting to learn?" I asked.

"I believe there is an open secret, Balien. One that has cost people their lives to conceal. And one that so many have always known. Someone knows the name of this new race," Fallon posited. "Your mom was of a completely different race, Balien, and I intend to find out who she was."

"I always thought that my abilities came from my accident," I continued. "Not that I was literally half whatever."

"Yes, I know. That was my hypothesis initially as well, but now, I think the shock of electricity woke a potential that was already inside you, suppressed all along," the doctor said with a smile.

"I was taught that 'we are the race of the world'," I replied, almost reciting. "Our continent is the only one there is in existence. There are no other people besides us."

"Yes, that *is* what we are taught in school. That's what's reinforced in church. But what is the truth? Is it more true because of where it comes from? Or is true simply because it is?"

Fallon finally found the documents he was looking for. They were drawings of what looked like a city nestled in a giant sinkhole.

"This is the city of Valvadus. It is technically in the Monica Province, but doesn't belong to a parish. Have you heard of it?" he asked, thumbing through more papers.

"Well, now that you mention it, it seems familiar…"

"Well, Valvadus is one of the most secretive cities in all of Vedere. It's also one of the oldest."

"So what are you thinking? You think these people know of some secret race of people?"

Fallon walked over to me and placed his hand on my shoulder. "I think that if there are any secrets left in Vedere, they'll be in Valvadus—where Seraphina lives."

As we walked to the elevator, the doctor began to explain inter-halo travel.

"Anytime there is travel between halos it's a pretty big deal," he explained. "Each landmass is separated by thousands of miles. You can't just jump in a hover car and go. You have to choose between the two major inter-halo travel methods."

I was getting a crash course.

"Option one would be the oldest and most conventional method: Looping. It's a network of vacuumed sealed tubes that travel via magnetic rail. It's relatively slow, but safe and reliable. It's the preferred method of travel for diplomats, proveyors, and is useful for shipping goods and like materials because it's easier to track and provides security. The second option would be by halocraft, which is an inter-halo vehicle that disembarks from a launchpad. It's much faster, but less accessible and more expensive. There are also fewer launchpads and landing sites." The elevator flashed as we reached the top with the rest of the girls.

"Of course, this is for public and private sector travel. It's also heavily monitored by Ophori security. For the type of trip that you and I want to take, we'll be traveling by a third method: My personal halocraft. We don't want to run the risk of someone you don't remember recognizing you."

Tara and Epeë walked up. They were clad in slick white suits of leather and silk. They wore a multipurpose vest with protection and thick boots.

"You look prepared," the doctor remarked.

"Yes, Ava said she had something she was designing. We think it will work just fine," Epeë replied.

"You two are Ophori, right?" I asked.

"Tara is, I was. I guess at this point we're both ex-Ophori. I'll tell you, though, Ava's suit design is better than any standard-issue Ophori dress. But let me ask you, do you have any weapons, Doctor?"

Fallon nodded. "Light-based, absolutely. I trust you both will use your discretion."

Epeë and Tara nodded.

"OK, so we are ready. Does everyone have their kokotos attached? Let's test them."

Tara's presence was first. *"OK, I am in. Can everyone perceive me?"*

"Yes, I got you." The second presence was Epeë. It was strange; it was as if I could see her hands in my mind when she signed, and another set of hands when someone else was signing.

"I think we are all good then, everyone." That was the doctor. *"Let's not forget that we are operating under the utmost secrecy. Do not get caught. If anything gets bad, let someone know. And if it looks bad, hold back until we can come up with something else,"* everyone agreed.

"Everyone know what they're doing? OK, let's do this. Fate is with us. Truth is fifth, everyone!"

"Truth is fifth," we replied.

***

Balien Saroyan, 184 days left

We exited through the main dome's atrium and walked around to the hover pad. It split in half and opened up to allow a sleek vehicle to rise from beneath the pad.

"So, this halocraft was custom made?" I asked as I strapped into my seat. "How did you get the resources for this?"

"I have friends in high places." Fallon smiled. "Now, let's get going."

Fallon engaged the autopilot. A holographic display showed our speed and ETA. Six hours to arrival.

"I hope Tara and Epeë find who they are looking for." I plopped my head against the headrest. "Do you really think they'll be able to find this Davis descendant?"

"I think they will. Ava suggested they start with the city of Ajax. If someone is trying to hide, that city's your best bet," the doctor replied.

"How do you feel about where are we going?" I asked.

"We are in the proper Will. Veronica tells us to seek out the oldest of our people. I assumed Valvadus would be best, but then you tell me that Seraphina contacted you, someone who also happens to live in Valvadus. That is the Will."

"The Will?" I asked.

"The Will. I'm a believer in a different religion. I'm not the best believer, but I do believe in the Way Maker. He has a course that we all must follow. And I believe we are on that course."

I nodded my head.

"Here's that sketch of Valvadus, the city below. Its foundation has steadily sank for thousands of years."

"It's a huge ... hole."

"Yes, it's definitely beneath the rock at this point. Their way of life has remained largely untouched as a result. It's the nation's final neutral city as well. It has stayed out of every major conflict Vedere has ever had."

"And you say that a mage lives there? Are there other mages?" As the hovercraft rose, I got a better sense of the scale of our world. The halos were absolutely enormous.

"If there are, there cannot be many left. Mages are defined by their abilities. They are able to create mental structures as real as the world around us and within it, they can communicate with anyone they wish. The best mages, like Seraphina, can reach people thousands of miles away. It's not known how many abilities mages can have, but it is assumed that there are many."

"How do they do it? Can you learn?"

"It's not fully understood, only that you are born with the ability. You can hone it with the help of another mage, and the more you sæ, the better you become. But there is significant mental strain involved. Unfortunately, many are dying out. During the Sisters War, mages were stolen from their homes and used by the armies to gain an advantage. Old, young, they didn't care. We nearly lost an entire generation of mages. The result is the situation we have now with Seraphina."

"The situation?"

"Yes, well, there is kind of an understood agreement with Seraphina. Valvadus has always been a neutral city, but that didn't stop the mass kidnappings nearly a century ago during the war. Seraphina lived through it all, and was one of the few særs who returned to her city after the war ended. Since then, she has made it crystal clear that Valvadus is not to be bothered. Since I've been alive that wish has been respected, and it's because Seraphina is there. She is one of the last and most powerful mages left in Vedere. Even those who seek her power don't want to risk losing her. At this point, even if anyone were to attempt to kidnap Seraphina, she wouldn't survive the journey. All parties have essentially agreed to leave her be."

"But everyone knows she lives in Valvadus, right?"

"Right. It's a unique balance of power. Outside the Cara Royale, Seraphina is the most powerful woman in Vedere—and that's still counting what's left of the Va Dynasty. We are taking a great risk to see her. But as I said, I believe we are in the Will. There is no reward without risk."

"The Va Dynasty?"

"Yes. The only other family that has been Ægæliphi. They are considered ancient history at this point, with many details misconstrued or forgotten, but it's at least generally regarded true they are a splinter of the Cara Royale. They are the reason there was a Sisters War."

"And how do they factor into all this?"

"That's assuming there still is a living Amavi, which I doubt. But if there were, they could have a claim to the throne. If they had the right people behind them, we'd be right back where we were a century ago. History could repeat itself."

"Only this time, if Veronica is to be believed, there is much more at stake. It's bigger than who has control of the world."

"Exactly, now you should get some rest, Balien. We'll be there soon."

It felt like I rested for only a few seconds. We were coming up on Halo Raphaela. Valvadus was even more amazing than the sketch. The city itself was breathtaking. It literally existed within a giant hole in the earth.

"Did you know that Vederians's eyes do not close when they sleep?" Fallon asked.

"I ... I hadn't really thought about it," I replied.

"We also don't quickly close our eyes and open them again like you do. Are you consciously doing that?"

I wasn't sure.

"Look out the window," Fallon suggested. My eyes took a moment to adjust to the light. I quickly closed and opened my eyes. I hadn't really thought about it, but Fallon was right. And for some reason, I felt like I shouldn't have been doing it. The tallest peaks of the buildings barely poked out above the giant crater like needles in a pincushion. I could see how Valvadus remained so secret; just traveling there would be a feat in and of itself. Fallon cautioned that the people of Valvadus were skeptical of outsiders. It was a very close-knit community. We would stick out. We also had another problem.

"I didn't think about this until now, but where are we going to land?" I asked Fallon.

"I planned ahead," Fallon replied. "I have a friend who lives here. His name is Damian Cala. I met him as a child back in my homeland. He was a close friend of my mother's. Both Damian and myself are from Puresh. When he retired, he relocated to Valvadus to live out his life in anonymity." Fallon stopped to unbraid his hair and work his hair into a bun. "Oh, and I forgot, you'll want to tie your hair up in a high bun. It's how the men wear their hair. We need to at least *try* to blend in."

I did my best to tie mine up just as Fallon's, but my hair was much shorter.

"I've had correspondence with Damian for years. When I found you, he was one of the few people I told, as he is an academic like myself, albeit in a more unorthodox sense. He is very interested in meeting you, so between that and a favor that I need to cash in with him, I was able to convince him to provide us lodging."

We landed our hovercraft on the outskirts of the crater in the surrounding jungle. Fallon insisted that his stealth technology was the best in the nation—we'd have to put that to the test. After landing, Fallon walked to the back and returned to the cockpit with evergreen-colored clothing. He winked.

"Like I said, we need to blend in." We changed and trekked deeper into the jungle until we reached the mouth of the crater.

"Something seems weird, but I can't quite place it," I suggested.

"It's the stillness. You see nothing moving. It's a bit jarring. This jungle has no animals. No birds, no insects, nothing."

"That's strange. Why is that?"

"I have no idea." It was the first time Fallon didn't have an answer to my question. It concerned me.

The sky shifted to an amber color, signaling the day had passed. "We'll have what, seven to eight hours of amber sky on this halo, right? Everyone should be asleep," I asked.

"That's right. We'll work our way down to the city and get in with Damian. He'll take us to the mage Seraphina to see if we can get some answers about Kamali. We may even get information about you."

We reached an overgrown staircase—a hodgepodge of barely stable ladders and careening stone stairs.

"So ... is this how we're getting down?" I asked. "It doesn't exactly look stable."

"You're going to have to trust me on this one. Remember, we're not exactly sanctioned to be here." Fallon was right. Unsanctioned halo travel was a serious offense. I remembered that—for some reason.

We made our way to the outskirts of the city, where the taverns and bars ended. "So, how are we doing this?" I asked.

"We're going to work our way around the outskirts until we see anything that looks familiar," Fallon replied.

"What do you mean *looks familiar*?"

"I may not exactly know where Damian Cala lives. We're playing it by eye." Fallon smiled as he crouched behind one of the buildings. "Look, I know one of these bars have to belong to him."

We reached a bar that appeared to be closed.

Peter's Palace.

"I'm going to bet this is it." Fallon made the sign for laughter. "I'll just turn this knob here an—"

The door swung open. A bear of a man appeared for a brief moment. He quickly ducked and turned his back to Fallon, slamming his elbow into Fallon's chest. He swept his leg around, knocking the doctor onto his back, slamming his head against the ground. The man then looked at me and froze.

He signed to me two words: "Get in."

I picked up Fallon from under his arms as the man grabbed his ankles. We carried him past the bar and up the stairs to a separate room, where we laid him on a bed in the corner. The room was medium-sized with a simple bed, desk, and window. It looked unused. I walked over to the man and stood in front of him to prepare to touch foreheads.

"I cannot torphi," he signed. "Too many blows to the head."

My hand signing was still a bit rusty. "Are you Damian Cala?" I asked crudely. I had to spell out his name.

"I am," he signed. "I was not expecting the doctor. I haven't seen him in years and he did not tell me he was coming. He gets a cracked sternum as a result." He smiled. I hoped Damian was joking, but I could not tell.

"Who are you?" he signed.

"I'm Balien Saroyan, the kid Dr. Sylvan told you about that was struck by lightning." I signed, pointing to my chest. "We're here because Dr. Sylvan believes Valvadus is the place for answers. We seek truth. Do you know anything about that?"

Damian scrunched up his glasses before folding his arms. "Truth is everywhere. It always has been. You could be asking about a lot of things, but given what Fallon has told me about you, you are asking if we are the race of the world."

I nodded. "I suppose."

"I guess it doesn't matter if I tell you." Damian paused. "You're here because the mage called you here. It means it's in the Will. Look, the mages have a name for them, but they've never shared it, so we just call them the Others. I've never seen them—no one has. We just have stories. Stories that are built off of variations of the sacred origin story."

"You mean the one we're told as children with the quinqu and the goddess Vedere—"

"We're told by the mages that there are variations to the sacred origin, maybe even two or three more. One of which in particular suggests that there are more races beyond Vederians. Those who experience life in a way we cannot comprehend."

I nodded. This lines up with what Veronica has shared thus far. "Could it be possible that someone of that race lives among us? How could one know? How would they assimilate?"

Damian paused for a moment, then raised his hands to reply.

"The Davis Expedition!" Fallon signed, arms flailing. "Oh gods, my chest is killing me! That's the key. The more we understand about the expedition, the better we understand these 'Others.' It's looking like this entire thing is connected."

"I know very little about the Davis Expedition," Damian signed. "And, Fallon, I'm sorry about your chest. You were not expected."

"Oh, I earned it."

"So explain," Damian pressed. "What's this expedition about?"

"Around a hundred years ago there was an expedition to the Underside of our continent. It was planned out for a decade. Never before had such resources been dedicated to a full-scale expedition before," Fallon explained. "Public records count the expedition a complete failure as the entire expedition team was wiped out."

"You mean no one survived?" Damian asked.

"That's what the record says, but we have reason to believe that is not the complete truth," Fallon signed.

"And so that's what the records say, but there's more than meets the eye." Damian smirked.

"Exactly, Damian. We are told that there was a child. The official record states that Georgette Davis's husband, Rory, returned with a Sherpa, a few members of the team."

"We are looking for a woman named Kamali; those were the instructions," I added.

"But for such a secret to be kept, it would have to go all the way up the chain. Possibly up to the Ægæliphi herself," Damian replied. "How do you know all this?"

"We have been contacted by a phantom. A woman who claims to be the eldest child of the current Ægæliphi, Vera," Fallon replied.

"And do you believe her claim?" Damian asked.

"We do," Fallon replied.

"Fascinating. Then that would mean the old man was right."

"What old man?" I asked.

"An old man who wandered into my bar, oh, maybe twenty years ago. He claimed to once work in the palace, though no one believed him."

Damian made a sign in which his hands fluttered away like a bird and his eyes followed with it. I think he meant to say they thought the old man was crazy.

"Doing what exactly?" I pressured. Fallon gave a disapproving nod.

"You're not suggesting that ... no ... do you really think that it's possible?" Fallon asked.

"I think it's time we pay the mage a visit," Damian signed. "I'll see you all at the beginning of amberlight tomorrow."

***

Part 7: The Small Unidentified Child

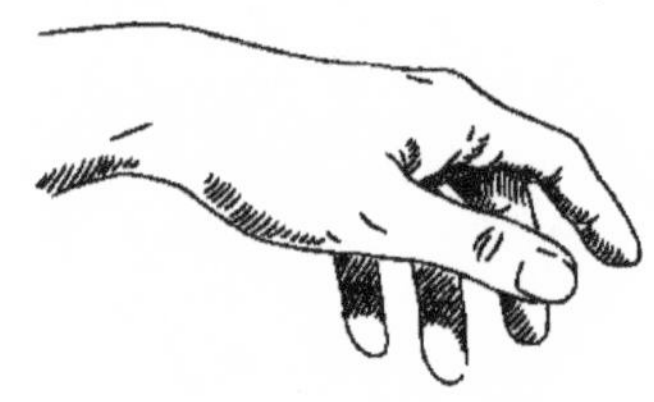

The Journal of Georgette Davis, 57,294 days left

Day 7

07:58

Today's discussions were very stressful. We all have different opinions of what to do with the knowledge we believe we have discovered. The theologians want to know what these beings believe, the philosophers question whether or not we *should* know, political delegates want to know the value of this new land, and the scientists each want their own awards for their new discoveries. It is a mess.

I would be remiss if I was not honest about my own personal intentions to see the Underside. I too journeyed here for answers. I want to know where we came from, where we are going. I want to know why no Vederians live here, or if we ever did. I want to better understand the nature of our continent's geology, and I want to know how to keep our people safe. And now it is clear that it is not just about us. There are others.

So now, we must argue. We must wave our hands and furrow our brows. We must throw down our papers and scowl at each other. I will let it go on for a time, but not too long. I will give them a day. We will have a consensus in twenty-four hours. That I can assure you.

We must also consider the possibilities: who or what attacked Rory and the others? Why would they give him a child? Ava has her own questions as well. She is concerned with pathogens and the clear change in climate. We know we must proceed, but there is so much to process. Again, twenty-four hours.

The consensus, at least now, is that we have a serious problem. The second security team has not returned, bringing the total count of missing up to forty-eight. In addition to the lives, the majority of our videography equipment was with them as well. I cannot worry too much, though. They could be simply lost.

14:49

We have one survivor. Just one. I simply do not know. Many are suggesting the young woman, Dana, is in shock. I only had one conversation with her before the trip. She seemed level-headed and eager like all the young explorers are. I am not quite sure what to believe. I have seen her debrief. She is talking about giants. Something bipedal, huge, covered in black clothing, something preferring the ground and other surfaces as a guide. She also describes some sort of unseen force. Something she can hardly describe or place, but something with the power to make her entire team completely disoriented, bleed from the eyes and nose, and render them unconscious.

We now have two major events to discuss. There is clear evidence of life down here. At least at some point in time. That much we know for certain. We also have to consider the strong possibility that we may not be alone down here. There may be a serious threat and we all know what protocol dictates: we leave immediately.

But that is the true challenge, is it not? Knowing what makes perfect sense. Knowing what we should logically should do. But we are so, so close. We all know that yearning. We are all scholars. We all know what it feels like to be so close to truth. I know I cannot account for everyone, but I am willing to die for this. How do I convey that without steering the group toward my bias?

What Rory describes was a conflict, not monsters. But the unseen force and the PLM are not a coincidence. We truly did not expect to come in contact with non-Vederian beings. So is there truly protocol for this engagement? We now have a baby in our camp as well. This is by far the most perplexing portion of the incident. We are giving the infant an extensive physical assessment. Hopefully, once completed, we will have more answers there as well.

17:32

Discussions are not completely over, but it seems we are pressing on. We have reassessed our contingencies, and, after a substantial debate, we have decided that we have simply come too far. Dana shows signs of severe trauma and we have her currently sedated until we can gather more information. She shows a type of fear that I do not think I have ever seen before. I am not sure how she got word that we were continuing on, but the thought of it seemed to send her into some kind of hysteria.

At our meeting in the main tent, I let each alpha have their time. I asked everyone to attend so we had our Betas and Gammas present as well. Each had something of value to say.

"It has now become clear that there is some form of a threat," Ava signed. "Is it worthwhile to continue on? What will the losses be?"

She was asking the proper questions from the proper perspective of Security alpha. It was the proper thing to ask. But I wanted to know what she really thought. How curious was she truly? What did she fear?

Saven, the alpha of Philosophy, was unopposed to continuing. Richard McDaniel, the alpha of Theology, wanted to continue as well. Ava would eventually come around and we felt we owed it to our missing team members to at least press this issue further.

One more important thing to note: Dr. Mera discovered a way that we may be able to track the other missing team members. Our exosuits have a powerful headlamp that emits a three hundred and sixty-degree dome of light for each person thirty meters in diameter. To prepare for this expedition we have trained to always travel at a forty-five-degree angle with the acute angle always in the center. This focuses and strengthens the light at that acute angle and creates a focal point. By moving together, any unseen threat can be focused so that everyone is able to locate it. Dr. Mera hypothesizes this strategy may have created a unique burn pattern in the ground of which we can use to map their route.

We hope this development will help. We will see tomorrow.

***

Balien Saroyan, 183 days left

We stayed at Damian's bar until the end of amberlight. The next day, we headed out to speak with the mage Seraphina. We let Damian lead the way as we shuffled down the narrow streets of Valvadus. To a first-time visitor like myself, the town seemed trapped in some kind of time loop, as if it hadn't changed in fifty years. We stopped at a corner where children were pushing bracelets and necklaces into the hands of passing adults. Payment was expected.

Damian turned to us and began to sign. "You know, it's good that you both have facial tattoos. Otherwise, we would have had to travel to the parlor first. The both of you both carry yourselves quite differently than locals do here, but I think so long as we keep moving, we'll go unnoticed."

We rounded the corner to an even narrower pathway.

"We're here and I've made provisions for us. She knows you're coming." The signs that Damian used were a bit hurried and animated. They were deeply tied to his facial expressions and, as rusty as I was, I could only manage to focus on either his hands or his face. I was missing much of what he was communicating.

Damian pulled out a small navy disk from his shirt's front pocket. The object seemed to only be designed to emit a clean white light.

"What is that?" I asked.

Fallon squinted at the object. "There are more ways to communicate than you know, Balien. This is a more of an ancient method, the device is called a *lingua*. It's a language that consists of varying durations of light pulses. Those who are proficient in the language can string together sentences called *serie* that are rattled off in rapid succession. They're so fast, those unfamiliar with the language simply cannot interpret it. As it is nearly a dead language, it is ideal for keeping secrets."

"It's all amazing," Damian adds. "I was raised to believe that lies and secrets were impossible in the world of sight."

"I was taught the same," Fallon replied.

"How is it that I've never seen this lingua?" I asked as we entered the mage's home.

"It is a lost art," Damian suggested. "Valvadus is home to many lost arts."

Waiting for us at the threshold was an odd old woman. Her hair was tied back in a bun that was so dense and so large that if loosed her hair would tickle the earth. According to Fallon, she had to be at least two hundred, yet her skin was eerily smooth and without wrinkles. The only signs of wear came from the areas she used the most: the corners of her mouth from excessive smiling, her forehead from often lifted eyebrows, and her knees from what one could only assume were caused from daily prayer.

She began by communicating by lingua only. She held the device at eye level. Damian had to first translate her lingua into tanna, or signs, which Fallon in turn translated into torphi, communicating to me mentally. It was the best way for all of us to have full understanding and was an amazing display of the diversity within Vederian culture, something I was only just now learning.

"Look! Look at this *sight*, yes, this sight," Seraphina began. "Four Vederians, three different forms of communication, yes, three different forms, and yet one culture." Seraphina drew wisps on her chest to indicate amusement.

"When I was the age of this young man before me, they didn't even teach banna in our schools, no, didn't even teach it. And I never cared to learn ... just as I never learned to drive a hovercar." More wisps. I could tell that her grammar was being shaved and molded before it reached me. I was unable to determine if this was her natural cadence, or if it was because of the double translation.

"Now, we don't even communicate with lingua, no, not lingua. We're comfortable with engaging in torphi; joining a collective conscious where secrets don't exist and emotions feel as real as if you're actually experienced them. It is technology too far, yes, too far. It is not what the sacred mineral is to be used for. I'll tell you, I'm not at all a fan of torphi, no, not at all a fan. And do you know why?"

I shook my head. The others did the same. We followed Seraphina to her living room and took a seat.

"Well, for one, I deal in only one currency: secrecy. All mages do, you know. Those willing to share all their thoughts very well may be fools, yes, very well may be fools." She paused to stretch out her folded legs from under her loose-fitting dress. She was remarkably limber.

"We apologize for the complicated communication," Fallon replied, via Damian.

Seraphina drew more wisps on her chest. "Complicated? This is merely transcription and translation, yes, transcription and translation. Merely synthesis. I'll welcome it."

I could tell that Seraphina knew much *more* than she was letting on. I wanted to ask her about meeting me while I was in a coma, but I could not find the proper time.

"Secrecy, yes, secrecy, is extremely valuable to me. I wish more of us, yes, more of us, valued their privacy."

She was right. There's a certain intimacy to torphi. Either a light touching of the forehead, or dragging a finger over the recipient's outstretched palm. Torphi requires an initial physical connection to begin. From there the range varies from person to person. Other people entering the existing conversation must first be granted access. It can be arduous, but it's now the norm. We'd become accustomed to it. It was hard to remember that it was a technological advancement—an artificial ability.

"It's why Seraphina now lives here in Valvadus, yes, in Valvadus. Before that, I served the heir."

So that explained it. Seraphina was well educated because she actually lived in Arælia. She was in close proximity to the Ægæliphi herself.

Seraphina straightened her posture and became focused. "And so you are here to receive the words of a two hundred and thirty-seven-year-old woman, yes, two hundred and thirty-seven. I have the answer to what you seek, Balien, but you won't receive it, no, you won't receive it."

I looked at Fallon defensively. I was unsure if he had translated properly. He did.

"Please, Seraphina, tell us what you know," Fallon pressed. "If the truth can be given, we are willing to receive."

"Willing to receive? How can you be willing? The truth has always been before you. The boy has *always* been before you. The truth is not difficult because it cannot be found, the truth is difficult because you do not choose to accept it."

Seraphina had folded both legs over each other as she sat on her sofa. She looked directly at me as she used lingua with Damian. "What the boy senses, the seizures, they are simply the remnants of experiences he once knew. Experiences his accident has taken from him. The boy is experiencing sounds. In fact, he has always known sounds, yes, always known."

Damian and Fallon looked at each other. Seraphina was using words none of us were familiar with.

"Let me explain from a context in which you already understand. What the boy is experiencing, periodically, is the reception of sounds waves. It is all movement, tiny movements called vibrations. With the proper training, even Vederians can see them. We trained many, yes, trained many. Think of them as ripples in a lake, yes, a lake." Seraphina walked over to her kitchen. She returned with a large frying pan filled nearly to the brim with water.

"*Waves*?" Fallon asked, perplexed. "I don't think I understand."

"Of course you don't!" Seraphina snapped. "I've already said too much, but there's no turning back now, no, there's no turning back now. This was a conversation only for the boy, but time is short. We take risks, yes, we take risks."

Seraphina placed the pan of water on the table between us. She plucked a seed from the soil of one of her plants and held it over the water.

"Now," she continued, "imagine you are on the edge of this pan of water. When something hits the water hard enough, ripples radiate out from the center."

It seemed even Damian himself didn't know about this.

"That initial action is called a *noise.*" She threw the seed straight down into the water. Ripples floated perfect circles outward.

"The center point is the origin of the sound. If your ears were working as they should, they would receive these noises and interpret them. Assign meaning."

For the most part, we kept our ears covered. All Vederians did. We viewed them as aesthetic. It never occurred to me that our ears could have a function.

"I'm sorry to interrupt, Seraphina, but how do you even know all this?" I asked, completely dumbfounded.

"The same way you learn anything, child, by *reading.*" She smiled as she tilted the pan toward her face to drink the water.

"What did you read?" Fallon asked with a look of skepticism. "What have you found that no one else has? Not even the Ægæliphi?"

"Oh! You think the Ægæliphi doesn't know? The Ægæliphi have always known. They simply keep it hidden from the people," she signed with wisps. "What did you think the Va Dynasty was trying to do?"

No one replied. It seemed Seraphina was heavily implying that this conspiracy was far-reaching—much farther than I ever anticipated.

"Take for example, when the real trouble began a century ago. You have read the official report of Georgette, as have most people, but you were not there like I was."

Fallon raised an eyebrow.

"I am saying there is information that has taken countless lives to keep secret. And so now I ask another question, what do you think the Sisters War was about?" Seraphina asked.

"It was an uprising for equality, right?" Fallon asked. Damian frowned.

"No, my child, not at all. Yes, there was a conflict of beliefs, yes, a conflict of beliefs, but the true reason was only known by a few. At that time, there was a Cophi leader who was prepared to reveal the greatest secret of the world. And the Church of Vael started a war to conceal that secret." Fallon was scribbling copious notes.

"And, sadly, the Church won. The secret was kept, yes, the secret was kept. And Georgette was never seen again. Rory's journal does not explain what happened to her, or the others." Seraphina attempted to continue, but her hands were shaking. "Forgive me. My heart hurts. I knew Georgette as a young girl. She had hoped to answer the unthinkable. She always wanted to know the why, the how, the when. She wasn't satisfied when she couldn't get the answers that would put her within her peace."

Fallon scanned his notes before asking his question. "Seraphina, we are here because we have been asked to find a woman named Kamali. Do you know anyone by that name? Is she attached to the expedition in any way?"

Seraphina's body language changed in an instant. Her eyes widened. Her brow lowered and she sat up straight. She turned to me and puckered her lips. I felt, no, I *heard,* something.

"That is called a *whistle,* Balien. It is coming back to you. The Horeni use it to get each other's attention," Seraphina signed. "And I know you *heard* it. I could tell, yes, I could tell. This is good. I suppose it's time for a leap of faith. There can be no victory without faith."

No one was even fazed by the fact that Seraphina could sign this entire time. We were all mystified by the sign she just used. *Horeni.* The sign she used required her to cup her hand around her ear, quickly throwing her hand outward.

"Don't blink," she said. "You'll miss it. The wool is being pulled from your eyes. Did you feel it?"

Seraphina stood and stretched her hands outward. We followed her lead and formed a circle with our hands held. This would no doubt begin torphi.

"Get ready, my children. You are now entering *truth.* You will only see this once, for I can only do this one more time. I will show as much as I can. It will not be comfortable."

Suddenly we were thrown down into what felt like weightlessness. The room, the table, everything faded away. *This must be a sæ,* I thought. But it was much more powerful and vivid. It was as if Seraphina were *made* of raw power. We faded into a jungle where there were two crudely designed synths and men fighting with flashes of light and waves of sound. I looked around for Damian or Fallon, but I was alone. Worse, my nose was bleeding.

"Balien!"

For some reason, the voice seemed far away.

"Balien!" There it was again.

"Balien! Please, we do not have enough time."

"Balien, are you with me?" It was Seraphina, but it was not torphi. Her lips were moving.

"We cannot stay long, my child. Quickly, you must *see.*" Before me was Seraphina but she appeared much younger. I had seen this before. But it wasn't a jungle. Seraphina was clothed in traditional dress, in gold. She was beautiful.

"We are in the jungle of the Underside. The man who has just fallen before us is Rory Davis."

Just a few meters ahead of me Rory fell to his knees.

"Balien, you must be careful, you are not just seeing this happen, we are *here*. They cannot see us, but we *can* affect this world. Do not touch anything!"

The people with Rory were being attacked by people I had never seen before. Rory's people were losing. The unknown people had their entire faces wrapped in cloth. Their ears were exposed and they carried weapons that pushed waves into the bodies of their victims, causing their eyes, nose, and ears to bleed. They were giants, two heads taller than the tallest Vederian. These were the Others. The Horeni.

"Balien, this is first contact," Seraphina shared. "There is chaos, yes, this is chaos," Seraphina's body had split in two, the second one more of an afterimage. "Rory is going to be given a proposition."

"Yes, a proposition," the other Seraphina said. The two women were confirming each other.

"Balien, the strain of the sæ is putting me in both the past and the future; soon I won't make much sense."

"I won't make sense," Seraphina two explained.

She is doing this for me. She is redlining for me.

Finally, the synths regrouped and fought back against the Horeni people. They adapted to the Horeni strategy and turned the tide. The Horeni were crushed and thrown by the much stronger synths. One of the people covered in cloth fell to their knees before Rory.

"This is it, Balien, watch closely."

"Yes, watch closely." The eyes of both Seraphinas were crying blood.

The being, larger than Rory, looked different than the others. It slumped as it unwrapped the black covering, revealing light olive skin. Protected by the wrapping was a baby. The being handed it to Rory.

"We are out of time," Seraphina shared. "I cannot hold any longer, I am sorry. My last gift to you, Balien: accept the knowledge you seek, turn and face the truth!" I embraced Seraphina. My mind was unraveling; it felt poured empty and filled again.

"Your memories were not taken, Balien, they were masked. Accept your trauma, listen to yourself. You will know that you can hear. By seeing this moment, your lineage will be made clear."

Instantly, we were back at the home of Seraphina, whose eyes were red and puffy. To my right, Fallon was seizing. His body shook violently as his eyes rolled back into his head. Damian leapt from my left to try and hold down the flailing doctor.

"Balien, you're bleeding," Damian signed as he tried to subdue the doctor.

"It may have been too much too soon. Go help your friend. He needs you," Seraphina said. I can *hear* her.

Fallon's body rattled as we tried to calm him. I slid behind him to hold his head up, just as he had done for me many times before.

"Why do I feel so terrible?" I asked.

"It's the emotion," Damian answered. "Seraphina is a sær, someone whose sight is stronger than time and space. That is how a mage does it. That is how they all sæ. She took us to a different place in a different time."

Seraphina interrupted to sign. "We have been found. You must go, you must go now." Seraphina appeared much older than she had when we first met her. "I gave my last effort to share my most valuable possessions, my secrets," she explained. Before I could reply, Seraphina slumped over, eyes fixed on the light shining through her window.

"Seraphina! No! I ... I remember it all now, my mother, hearing, my family, all of it! I have so many questions!"

A strong hand on my shoulder brought a surge of torphi from Damian. *"Balien, I am going to pick up the doctor. We must leave right now! As soon as Seraphina exited the sæ, we were located."*

Before we could break for the door, a kai, a flash bomb, flew through the front window—nearly ripping my head off. I was bathed in a blinding white light. *They're already here.* Kai are perfect for apprehension. They disrupt any forms of mental communication, fully disorient anyone within range, and give the Ophori the time they need to swoop in and kick you in your chest. This was their weapon. They had been monitoring for a sæ. We led them right to us.

I had never seen Ophori members in action, but the stories told were enough for me to know that we were in deep, deep trouble.

In the commotion, my vision brightened and faded in. My sense of *hearing* slowly returned as well. My ears were ringing, and I was completely disoriented. Dark figures rolled into the room with a thunder, their feet hitting the floor. Each tap carried its own signature. *Is this what hearing can do?* There were three of them. There were not all the same size. It really *was* all coming back. I was *trained* for this.

Seconds passed, ticking away in silence. Damian had laid the doctor on the ground and picked up a chair in defense. He could see the shadows too, but he couldn't anticipate them like I could. I backed up against a solid surface—it was the kitchen counter. I jumped behind it for cover as I realized how close the shadows had become. I focused on one of the Ophori's hands. She signed something I couldn't make out.

There were only three Ophori in Seraphina's living room. They didn't take us seriously. They knew three was more than enough.

Damian had slid his back foot into a stance that was identical to the trio that had formed a circle around him. It was clear that the first Ophori, directly in front of him, had seniority. Her facial tattoos show her designation. The tattoos curved around her razor-sharp cheek bones and twisted as she tightened her face and licked her lips. She was more than ready. Her battle tunic was made from a very thick fabric sewn into a lazy yellow color that dared to be golden. Her skirt fell to the front and back, giving her enormous thighs room to move freely and inflict damage. She bent into a quarter squat as she drew a fourteen-foot staff with a ten-inch blade at the end.

Directly behind Damian was a younger Ophori member clad in dark blue. Her hair, in thick box braids, was decorated with beads and jewelry. She was shaking enough to cause her beads to knock together, causing a slight *noise* that I was now certain I was hearing.

To Damian's right was a third Ophori member, in red. She was bald and tattooed in such a way that the majority of her coal-dark skin was covered with white ink. She was also a giant, at least a head and shoulder above everyone else in the room. She looked to her sisters and flashed a huge smile. She was ready too. The trio was working together: Lazy Yellow, Dark Blue, and Red. They had Damian surrounded, and though it didn't look like he had a chance, I had a feeling this wasn't going to go as they expected.

Damian, exceptionally large for a Vederian man, stood almost the same height as Lazy Yellow. They had noticed that his stance directly matched theirs. He also had been trained. They didn't expect that.

Red made the first move, extending her staff with the click of a button. Damian anticipated and parried beautifully with the legs of the chair. With a quick flick of the wrist, Damian twisted the staff out of her hand in time to flip it into the air. He threw the chair at Lazy Yellow and kicked Dark Blue squarely in her chest before she could complete her lunge. He was fast. Very fast.

He then caught the staff he disarmed from Red and gave it two skillful spins before holding it low with two hands. Red cracked another, albeit smaller, smile. But Lazy Yellow showed impatience, breaking the chair over her knee and taking two of the chair legs, one for each hand. A jumping lunge from her turned into a spin. She jabbed Damian in the neck with one chair leg, following up with a brisk crack to his cheek with the other. Damian stumbled and spit out a tooth.

It was a miracle it didn't kill him. She nailed him. She then spun around, bringing her two weapons with her to give his ribs two quick strikes before following up with a front kick to his chest. Damian careened into the wall, cracking the glass. Another bone-crushing blow. Using the wall as his only support, Damian allowed his body to slump to the floor. It was clear now that the only thing lazy about Lazy Yellow was her attire. She was completely focused and locked in. She prepared to finish what she started as Dark Blue pulled out a dagger to join the fray. But Damian, having regained his footing, kicked the sofa into Lazy Yellow's thighs, slowing both of them down.

Damian quickly kicked up his staff, flipping it into the air and into his hands. He used the staff as if it were an extension of his arm, each strike landing quickly and intentionally. But Lazy Yellow parried them all. Red picked up a small end table from the family room, throwing it at Damian. With expert footwork, however, he sidestepped it, allowing it to crash into Lazy Yellow. He then hurled the circular glass tabletop at Red with the flick of his wrist. Red held up her forearms to block the spinning disk, shattering the glass, but Damian wasn't done. He barreled toward Red at full speed and dropped his shoulder. Damian and Red both crashed into the wall, pinning Red and the staff she was holding. There was a piercing crack as the staff snapped in two with a pop that made me jump. It was time for hand-to-hand now.

Dark Blue still hadn't found her turn to join in as Damian and Red exchanged quick punches and kicks. Now, Dark Blue tried for another lunge, but instead she got a backhanded slap to the face from Damian—without him skipping a beat. He then gave Red three quick shots to the face that she barely blocked. Dizzy, she attempted a hook that he blocked. He then landed a swift southpaw and went in for a low tackle, wrapping her up and throwing her back over his head, slamming her neck into the ground. Red was done.

Lazy Yellow struggled to stand as her eyes widened. No man had *ever* taken down an Ophori warrior. Ever. Dark Blue's face twisted into a snarl as she lunged at Damian, delivering a swinging kick to his head. He grabbed the kick and drove an elbow down into that same leg, in a way that made both Dark Blue and I wince. He continued with a barrage of punches and open-hand movements, finally punching Dark Blue unconscious. She didn't have a chance.

Damian had yet to rest during this entire ordeal, but it finally caught up with him. He was exhausted, bruised, and bloody. He was straining to see out of puffy eyes and was favoring his right side to adjust for broken ribs. He picked up a lamp and threw it at Lazy Yellow as she came tearing across the room.

He staggered back, preparing himself for her second wind. He resorted to blocks as she delivered kick after kick after kick. She spun and kicked Damian over the cheek, then grabbed a book from the bookcase next to him and bluntly used it to crack his cheek, spine first. Grabbing his arm, she flipped him over her head onto the floor. She was furious and it showed.

All of her moves were seamless, as if they were rehearsed. They flowed with an intentionality that only expert skill could ensure. Both she and Damian were covered in navy-colored blood as Damian used his forearms to block. He needed help. He was gassed. Even though they had been fighting only a few minutes, it felt like an eternity. I had been frozen this entire time, but knew I had to do something. Knowing I had the element of surprise on my side, I took a kitchen knife and jumped over the counter. Without thinking, I stabbed Lazy Yellow in the back, giving Damian enough time to grab a book on the floor to beat Lazy Yellow until her eyes closed.

Damian staggered over to the wall. His navy blood streaked along the glass walls as he lowered himself to the ground. It was finished. We stared at each other for a moment, breathing heavily. Fallon's body had finally stopped convulsing and he was slowly waking up.

"Gods! What happened here?" he asked, using the overturned sofa to pull himself up. "It looks like a whirlwind came through!"

"Ophori," Damian signed. "Three Ophori."

"*Just* three?" Fallon replied. "How did they even know we were here?"

Damian pushed himself off the wall to stand. "Any time there is a sæ, it can be detected," Damian explained, grabbing his small bag. "The Ophori is a much larger organization than the average citizen ever sees. There are members who do nothing but monitor torphi across the nation. Someone there is also a sær. Which also means we are now on the run."

My eyes widened. "So there truly are no secrets."

"Balien, secrets in our world don't truly exist. I think that's clear now. There are things that we know and there are things we are simply not told." Damian opened the door, motioning outward. "It is time to go. Do not mistake what happened here; we did not win. Had it not been for your dishonorable attack, she would have killed us all. They will find us if we stay here."

Damian signed in a way that showed disappointment in me. I had saved his life, but he seemed upset that I had attacked Lazy Yellow from behind. As we shuffled out of the house, I wondered: Damian mentioned that Seraphina was a sær, as if he knew all along. Was he expecting this to happen? We snaked around the back of a building that sat at the foot of mountain.

"We are going to have to scale this," Damian explained. "It's all wide open now. We've been made. There may be only one place we can go where we'll be safe. We're headed to Hyleia, the city on a thousand mountains."

"We're going *where*?" Balien asked.

"I noticed it in the sæ," Damian replied. "Many of the philosophers and scientists were wearing Hyleian clothing. It's also where Georgette was from. If there's anywhere to look for the truth of that expedition, it would be at Hyleia. I think we'll find your Kamali there as well. We will go to my home now to rest. We leave as soon as it is amberlight."

Fallon and I nodded.

"We each saw something different. Something that Seraphina wanted us to see. We must act on those observations," Damian reasoned.

I was inclined to agree with him.

182 days left.

Just as the day shifted into amberlight, Damian arrived upstairs. He was right on time. He took us around back to a building nestled at the base of a cliff. The incline shot up into the sky high enough to cause you to fall back if you tried to track your head back far enough to see its summit. Damian was dressed in lighter-colored clothing. He was shoeless, carrying a small pack. He had a rope around his waist, which he now tied to the doctor and to me.

He assured us that if we followed him exactly, no one would fall. I was concerned about his strength as he had just fought three capable Ophori. He began to climb and we followed.

"*Damian! I have a question.*" I placed my foot into a divot in the rock. "*How is it possible that you can fight and win against three Ophori? They don't teach men to fight where I come from.*"

"*They don't teach men how to fight like Ophori anywhere,*" Fallon chimed in.

"*I was taught by Commander Charene,*" Damian replied plainly. "*I was a part of a program that has now been disbanded. They took me from my family when I was a young boy and raised me on a base in a place I never knew existed.*"

"*Wait, Commander Charene? The Commander Charene?*" Fallon asked, incredulously.

"*Hold on, who is Commander Charene?*" I asked.

"*Commander Charene Durham was the grandmother of the current leader of the Ophori, Maya Durham. She practically wrote the book on modern Ophori culture: everything from teaching methods, to martial arts style, even designing*

Ophori armor and weapon technology. She was a genius," Fallon replied. *"How in the world did you get trained by Charene?"*

"She was persuaded," Damian replied vaguely, reaching up for the next rock.

"Do you know how many boys were a part of the program?" I asked.

"No, I don't know the exact number. But I do know only seven completed the program." Damian stopped climbing for a moment. *"OK, enough about that, we're almost here. I'll climb over the top of the ledge and I'll help pull you up."*

Damian helped us up to the top of the mountain. The cold air had a slight sting to it as it snuck past our skin. There was nothing here. Just more and more mountains. No animals, no roads or bridges. Just landscape. Damian motioned forward.

"We're neck-deep now. All of us. Word will get back that Ophori have been attacked. I hope you both know what you're doing."

***

Record NGV #299, Gabrielle Reporting, 183 days left

I was in the catacombs when I learned of Avis's sacrifice: She made way for Veronica and exposed herself to the church to buy us time. Such great sacrifice; and all for the hope that we could turn just a few more players.

Maya was in her personal quarters when she received word. A light above her door flashed a unique pattern. It was her lieutenant, Kari.

"Sister, we've just received information from the Valvadus extraction. Two confirmed immobilized. The third has not been found."

Maya took a moment to look away before throwing the book in her hand.

"Impossible. Who could have possibly—"

"We've already questioned them, Sister. They claim it was a man, but we're sure they're conf—"

Maya went to her desk and gathered a prism-shaped kokoto into her hands.

"Get Valerie in here right now. I know what this is. This is a Cara Royale foolishness. I need her audience—now."

"Sister, I don't understand."

"Leave me!" Maya signed. Her hand's movements were sharp.

An hour later Valerie appeared; she was dressed in her own training gear, still drenched in sweat from practicing her forms. She entered with a chip on her shoulder. She didn't like Maya, never did. They had a rivalry for as long as both of them could remember.

"I interrupted my training for *this*, Maya?"

"You know the law, Valerie. If I request council, as the leader of the—"

"Yes, yes, I know the law, Maya. Get to the point." Valerie was blunt, and she showed disrespect by not looking Maya in the eye, or by accepting her request for torphi.

"A member of the Old Guard attacked my sisters."

"Lower your dirty hands," Valerie replied. "And don't you ever make such an accusation like that in my presence. Don't you dare forget your place."

"My place?" Maya questioned. "If something were to happen to you, *I* would be next in line. You do not have any children, Valerie."

"Nothing can happen to *me,* Maya. Let's begin there. *You* can't do anything about what can happen to me."

"We can spar at a later date. Right now, I need to know—have you or your family sanctioned your pets to assault my sisters?" Maya's eyebrows raised. She had also tightened a fist.

"Watch that fist, Maya. I may mistake it for offense and have to defend myself. And no, my mother froze the Old Guard project, albeit an act of stupidity. They haven't been active since I was a child. Whatever happened to your precious sisters, it must have been a rogue." Valerie let a smirk slip out.

Maya knew she was lying, but it would be a death sentence to suggest such publicly. "I need that list, Valerie, and understand that this is a formality. I don't need you. Vega has the clearance. My grandmother asked for it, my predecessor asked for it, and now I am asking for it again. I need the list of the Old Guard's members."

"You know I cannot provide that." She flicked her hands outward in disgust after signing.

"According to the law, you have no choice now. Ophori have been attacked. You can provide me this information or I can go above you. Your mother is not dead yet. Your choice. Simply give me names, or I let out word that the precious royal family has had an army of dogs doing their dirty work, or should I say the Queen Mother has gone insane?"

"Maya, I will kill you," Valerie signed with rigid motions. She extended her staff.

"You will not. Killing me will surely raise more suspicions. Think it through. And also consider that taking down the leader of the Ophori is no easy task."

Valerie mulled for a moment. She was shaking with anger. Finally, she snapped her staff over her knee. "I only act when I *choose* to act, Sister."

Valerie walked over to Maya's computer and placed her personal kokoto into the groove. She typed in the commands.

"Here is your list. You are *not* getting the complete list, but a list of living members," Valerie signed.

Gaius Saroyan, Tora McDaniel, Tudor McDaniel, Damian Cala, Timothy Aquinas, Gregor Bastian.

"And don't think I'm not aware," Valerie added. "The only reason you know of this group is because of your father's utter stupidity. If he were not one of the greats of the Old Guard, we would have hung him for telling his daughter of the Old Guard's existence. You may think you have forced my hand, but you have not, I always have the upper hand."

"You have always been incredibly immature, Valerie, it is pathetic. Since we were children."

Valerie gave a cold stare, then turned and left.

Maya studied the list. She went back over her own memory, trying to remember the faces of the men. *I remember the twins,* she thought to herself. *The twins, my father, his best friend, and the bear. The polar bear.*

Maya remembered a kind man who had hands as large as the paws of a bear. He was hairy, covered in a sheet of white hair all over his body. He wore small glasses. He was nearly equal in strength to her father, Robert Daniel.

Damian Cala. It has to be him.

Maya pulled out her prism kokoto once more and summoned her lieutenant.

"I need you to look up everything you can on a Damian Cala. Last known whereabouts, known acquaintances, the full gamut."

"Right away, Sister."

"And get me the Angel Elite. They're going with me on a hunt," Maya smirked.

***

Epeë, 183 days left

The best plan that Tara and I could come up with was to start on the streets and look out for any clues—not a great plan, I know, but it was the best hunch we had. There was a time when the best place to hide was in the mountains, in an area where farming and mining was commonplace, the Hyleian region. That was our first inclination, but we remembered that this girl was probably our age, meaning she would be going to a different city. As Vedere became more industrialized, Ajax replaced Hyleia as the city to hide for troubled youth. It had become a dangerous city known for harboring criminals and though the proveyor aimed to clean up her city's reputation, the progress was slow and hardly productive.

Nonetheless, Ajax was one of the best hiding places on the halo as it served as a major hoverport for inter-halo travel. Millions of transients traveled to and fro each day. Nearly anyone could blend in or find work in the hundreds of service jobs available in the area. When you wanted to disappear, you went to Ajax.

I had one more reason for wanting to find this girl. I probably shouldn't have kept it from the others, but Talia Davis was the name my father secretly signed to me just before his death. Whoever she was, it was my father's final wish that I contact her. The message from V only confirmed that. Fallon also seemed to think she had knowledge of something only known to her. We had to find her no matter what—for my father.

Now, if I were in Ajax and looking for work, where would I go? I'd probably get hungry first. We disembarked and walked to the nearest restaurant to grab something to eat. It was your typical diner. The food looked about as drowned as the weather outside—Ajax was either threatening to rain, or already pouring. Vederian food was about presentation above all, and none of it looked healthy to eat.

"Gods, I forgot how dingy people can look outside the capital," Tara noted. She was right. These people were not as polished as the residents of New Redemption, but there were clear reasons. The type of work conducted here was different. Everyone in the diner was wearing boots and a long-sleeved buttoned-down shirt. Their color palette consisted of muted grays, blacks, and navy. They wore their hair short—just past ear length—and they appeared a bit more slender than the average Vederian. It could have been the nutrition.

The host greeted us and we sat at a small booth in the back. The restaurant was so close to the sea the waves crashed and sprayed the window next to us. I'm sure it would have been beautiful if it had not been raining. A girl about our age approached the table in front of us, putting down her notebook and pencil.

"Hello! My name is Tee," she signed to the waiter.

"Would you prefer signed conversation or mental?" the waiter asked.

"Mental, please." she replied. The waiter placed her kokoto in a row of kokoto-shaped grooves at the edge of the table. Tara and I both placed ours next to the waiter's to sync up when our turn came. "I don't get out much."

"OK, gotcha. What can I get you to drink?"

"I'll just have water, for now. I hope that's OK."

"Not a problem at all," he replied. He dashed off to the back for a few seconds and returned with a tall glass of water.

"What were you thinking of eating today?" he asked, placing the cool water on her table.

"I'm not really sure," she replied. *"I'm not super hungry at the moment. I just plan to hang out here for a while before the fundraiser."*

"Ah, the fundraiser? How did you get in? It's a closed event."

"My aunt knows the proveyor. That's my plug, I guess."

"And what do you think of the fundraiser? Are you a local?"

"No, I'm not. I haven't left my house in years." the girl replied.

The waiter was unsure if the girl was joking or not. She continued.

"It seems a miracle that the fundraiser made it here. I wouldn't be surprised it comes at the possible bribery of its proveyor. She wants clout and respect on an inter-halo stage, and isn't above bribing the committee to host the fundraiser in her city."

The waiter politely nodded, but obviously was taken aback by the girl's frankness. He offered her a few more minutes to look at the menu, though all the food was virtually the same. It was intravenous mostly, as almost all Vederian food. While you pumped the fluids into your arm you were treated to artisans who would draw works of art at your table. Some restaurants would bring out edible works of art, but most food was accompanied by something else that would treat the eyes. With the waiter no longer distracting her, she turned her attention to us.

"Hey!" she signed. "What's with the brooding faces? You two on some kind of mission?" Talia quickly realized that she'd actually missed being social.

Tara kept her signs to her chest so only I could see them. "Be careful. This one is chatty."

"Well, we're meeting a friend here," I offered. "I'm sorry if we look suspicious. We're not spies or anything."

"Great job, Epeë," Tara signed. She was right. I could have done better, but I was working off the top of my head.

"Gotcha, well, if you were spies, you two would be terrible at it. You two are so obvious."

"You're right, we suck," Tara signed bluntly.

"Oh, come on! I don't think you two suck, not really. You just need to sharpen up a bit. If you're going to be a spy, it's all about the details. I read a book by an ex-Ophori when I was a young girl. It was all about the details—hair color, eye color, place of work, friends and family members, all that," she replied. "I'm kind of a book nerd."

"Fascinating," Tara signed facetiously.

"Oh, this is exciting! It's like watching a book in real life. Two kinda-but-not-really spies. What do you and your friend have planned tonight? If you're up for it I could sneak you into the fundraiser. There will be dancing and a stellar light show."

"Oh, I don't know ... our friend might not be interested," I suggested.

"Come on, it'll be free! What's a spy without adventure? Look, the truth is I don't really want to be there as well. I figured inviting some girls my age would help. Oh, and I forgot to introduce myself, my name is Talia, Talia Davis, but everyone calls me Tee. It's nice to meet you."

Incredible, I thought. I couldn't believe it. We had planned to stay in Ajax for months to hunt this girl down and the first diner we walk into has her sitting right before us. Maybe the fates really did favor us.

"Talia. I like that name. Talia, my name is Epeë Carol. This is my best friend, Tara." I didn't want her to know I was an Afauna. It was still too soon and I didn't know if I could trust her, to be honest.

"Oh, I thought you two were together! Perfect, Epeë, you can be my plus one."

Tara pointed to her mouth and stuck her tongue out. "She's too chatty, not your type."

I didn't know if I agreed with Tara. I kind of did like Talia.

"Sure, I'd be interested in hanging out. I'm new to Ajax. First time here. You think you could show us around?"

"Of course," Talia signed with a smile. "Let's hit this fundraiser. I don't think the food is any good here anyway. Then we can tour Ajax."

"Perfect, let's do it."

***

Record #728: Ægæliphi-level clearance, 57,199 days ago.

Special counsel with the Ægæliphi was an honor few received. Under most circumstances, no one was allowed direct counsel with the Ægæliphi—even with a proveyor present. The Ægæliphi never spoke directly to anyone outside of the courts. She would communicate via torphi to a proxy. The proxy would communicate with Rory. Rory would be risking not only his entire plan, but his very life by attempting to involve the Ægæliphi in keeping the child a secret.

"Husband of Georgette, I welcome you here to Arælia with honor. You are a special guest that will be given counsel with the Ægæliphi. You may now sign," the proxy began.

"Ægæliphi, I understand my time is short so I will not waste time. We have been given a child. A child no one must know about."

The Ægæliphi paused with a stillness that made it seem as if time within the throne room had stopped. She broke that stillness with an adjustment to her seated posture. She folded her legs, knees outward, so her feet no longer touched the floor. With her veil covering her entire body, it appeared as if she were floating above her throne.

"What does this child mean, husband of Georgette?"

Her calmness slightly unsettled Rory. He expected the Ægæliphi to be reserved, but not to this extent. It was as if she were reciting from a conversation she had before.

"The child—it, she, is unlike anything I have ever seen. I don't even know if I fully understand her," Rory answered. "She is not Vederian, that is certain. I do not know what she is. I had hoped you may know."

The proxy frowned and tracked her eyes away from Rory. She knew that what she could say would have the potential to cast the entire nation into anarchy. The Ægæliphi proceeded with sublime wisdom.

"A thousand years, Rory," the Ægæliphi began. "A thousand years we've kept the secret. You know, the Cara family was one of the five founding families. We swore an oath, one with a strength neither you or I could fully understand."

Rory began to develop beads of sweat just above his brow and around his nose. He felt a sudden urge to both run away as fast as he could and to keep his feet firmly planted on the throne room's solid gold flooring. It was all happening so fast, like a train he couldn't stop, yet her words seemed to be pouring out as slow as possible.

"I prayed, Rory, in fact, you have no idea how hard I prayed for this decision to not fall on me. Not my mother, not my daughter, Vera. I prayed for this to pass us over. But I suppose in the end, allowing Georgette's expedition was ultimately compliance."

The Ægæliphi buried her head in her hands. "The child is not of our people. What would you have me do? Tell me plainly, and you will be given my unlimited power."

***

RECIPIENT: Q

SUBJECT: The precious gift.

BODY: The plan itself will be quite simple. The child will be kept a secret, and no one will ask for any more information beyond what is already known. We have the full power of the Ægaeliphi. Information regarding the child will be kept at that clearance level. The backup will be a handwritten journal using an ancient script myself and Georgette had discovered while in school. The text will be the guide for Generation I. This is the highest priority of Generation 0. The plan must go to Generation V, but it is possible IV may be the final Vederian generation. We have much work to do. I trust your people are in place.

In hope of a better future,

Rory

***

Epeë, 183 days left

The address Talia had given us put us on the eastern coast. She said she would meet us as soon as we arrived. I took the time while in the hover car to contact Fallon. He responded immediately.

"Fallon, you would not believe it. We found Talia."

"Really? That was fast! How?"

"We literally walked into the first diner we could find and there she was."

"It's true then. We are in the Will."

I didn't believe in any Will, at least I didn't think I did. But I was willing to let Fallon believe what he wanted.

"We're headed to her aunt's fundraiser. We told her we would come and we're going to play it cool. I think she likes me."

Tara rolled her eyes.

"Good," Fallon replied. "Let's establish her trust first, there's a lot we want her to believe on our end as well so the more honest, the better. Do you think there's a chance you could be made?"

"Tara is a bit uneasy, but when is she not? But I think we're in good shape. What do you suggest?"

"I would see the fundraiser through. Afterwards, see if you can link up again in a more private place. It's a risk, but at some point you're just going to have to drop it on her and tell her who you are and what you want."

Fallon was right, but I didn't like it. Too much of our overall plan was risk-taking.

"So, how are you two?" I asked.

"We've been better. One of our companions is pretty banged up and I had a seizure due to our interaction with the sæ, but beyond that, we're not too bad. Balien had a huge breakthrough. We haven't got a chance to assess it, but the majority of his memories have been restored and then some. In that regard, we've had a huge win."

"Why do I feel like that's not all?"

"We lost Seraphina. She gave her last strength to take the three of us on her final sæ."

"Oh my God. That's terrible—for the whole nation! What's next?"

"Do whatever you can to get Talia on our side. We can't move on from this without her. Do that and meet us at the Udugigvdi."

"The what?"

"U-du-gi-gv-di. It's the base of the Cophi. We may have gotten into a concerning scuffle back at Valvadus. As soon as you've got Talia, head to the coordinates I will provide. It may not be safe for you all much longer."

"Got it. We'll do our best, Fallon."

"Forever in the Will. See you soon."

A few minutes later, we arrived at our destination. Dr. Abrams, the proveyor of Ajax, was there, pacing back and forth from her main desk to the window that looked onto the Aquillian Sea. She would pause frequently in thought. Her venue was full and some of the most important scientific minds were present in one place.

The fundraiser was filled with women Talia, Tara, and I had never seen before. The servers were smaller men who hunched their backs and flashed quick smiles as they hurriedly walked past. Their uniforms were as extravagant as the ballroom's decor. To my understanding, the venue was built from scratch to serve the very specific purpose of attracting events like these. The building's exterior was made almost entirely of glass and steel.

From above, it took the shape of a frozen wave of water. The interior was modern and lit golden with its marble tables and ash black floors.

The other unique portion of the affair was the location. Ajax, not the political hotbed like Puresh or Denali, but rather, Ajax, the place to hide. The city of thieves. I pondered this and the thought, though brief, was riveting enough to pull me out of the mundane. But it wasn't for long; soon, I was thrust back into the boring world of female academics.

Talia seemed much more interested in *who* was there rather than what was going on. She was looking for someone in particular, that much was clear. I just needed to find out who.

Tara looked more determined and focused than at the diner. This adventure seemed to be exactly what she needed in a world that was too boring for her. Tara wanted a mission. She wanted a cause to believe in and she wanted a mission that she had to complete. She had decided she would be protecting us no matter the cost and to that end she was judiciously scanning the room for any possible threats.

Almost universally, the scientists were women. Each stood in a corner with their own specific gravity, each with their own satellites orbiting around them. Those satellites would ask them questions and test their theories. The scientists were graceful, monolithic, and distinct. But they were not alone, as they were discreetly competing with the other disciplines present as well: philosophers, clergy, artisans. I imagined what it was like to have such a collection of people all willing to go on an expedition. To truly put dirt in their hands and go answer the most important questions of the age.

The high priestess of the Church of the Vael, Vonna, and her entourage were encircled by her constituents. She went largely unseen save for her headdress, which stood above the small crowd, reminding everyone that she was present. The philosopher Seraphina II, and the new mage, Seraphina III, the daughter and granddaughter respectively of the great mage Seraphina, were seated nearby in two-toned dresses.

Seraphina II appeared moody and brooding. She now carried the weight of her mother's reputation. Seraphina II grew up in her mother's shadow. That pressure did not result in her being a pleasant person. That said, this fundraiser was expertly planned. Someone wanted everyone together. Once thing was certain; at some point, someone would be poised to make a dangerous move. Her daughter, Seraphina III, twenty-five, had shown that her abilities were a far cry from her grandmother's. If war broke out again, there would be no mage to sway the outcome.

My short stint as Ophori had helped plug me into the who's who of Vedere, but this was where my intel ended. Everyone else was a stranger in this grand hall.

Tara's eyes continued to scan the room. She instantly recognized when a botanist from Denali greeted Seraphina II. She had seen that sign before. Fallon used it. She had to tell him.

"Doctor, come in, it's Tara."

"Yes, Tara, I am here, what is it?"

"Does your mage have a daughter? A granddaughter?"

"I believe so, yes."

"Her children are here. Seraphina II, Seraphina III."

"OK, so now we truly must be careful. Seraphina II is not a mage—she did not receive the ability—but I think that the granddaughter did. Watch out for her. She could blow your cover. I don't think news has traveled yet, but it will get complicated for them very soon."

"What do you mean?"

"I'm going to have to call you back."

Talia's eyes had stopped at a younger woman with long white hair parted into two braids. She wore the simple two-toned formal tunic made of silk and cotton. She had facial tattoos that indicated that she was of higher class, but not from the capital city of New Redemption in Arælia. Her skin was of the darkest black. She sat at one of the traditional Vederian dining tables, which were lower to the ground and used flat pillows as chairs. At this height, everyone was able to see each other at eye level. The woman sat as if she were going to be praying for a long time. She noticed Talia's stare and met her eyes with a smile. It was Seraphina III.

"Talia has locked eyes with the very person Fallon just told us to avoid," Tara informed me.

"I see that, Tara. But there's no turning back now. We are in this thing. I'm making a move."

I was too quick for Tara to stop me. I walked directly up to Seraphina III. "You're Seraphina III, right? I just wanted to say that I love your dress. It is beautiful."

It was beautiful. Seraphina III was a tall and slender young woman. Skin radiant, lips full, nose wide—by any account she was stunningly beautiful.

Talia was reserved, but not shy. She had walked up to us. "Well, that's rude, are you going to introduce us too?"

Seraphina III looked at me, then back at Talia. She then looked past us to Tara, who was hanging back. Seraphina III excused herself from her mother's group and motioned for us to follow her to a window seat at the other end of the ballroom.

"I don't have to be a mage to know something is up," Seraphina III explained. "You three are here for three completely separate purposes."

"Oh wow, well, we—" Talia began.

"And it doesn't take a mage to know that you all are not on the same page," Seraphina signed, cutting Talia off. *"What do you all want? Go one at a time."*

I was taken aback. This was extremely wise on Seraphina III's part. Vederians could not lie when given a direct question within torphi. Seraphina III was able to establish a connection at will. She was looking at Tara first. With Tara being forced to tell the truth, I would struggle to clean up Tara's answer.

"You are here because you are in love with a girl named Epeë," Seraphina III discerned. She was extracting information from us with an ease that was incredibly alarming. A jolt shot through me. I had no idea what I was expecting, but it wasn't that. Even if Tara didn't want to answer, it wouldn't have mattered. Seraphina III would have felt the emotion.

"Interesting," Seraphina III continued, smiling. *"That means the true motive lies with you."* Seraphina III now locked eyes with me. It was as if her eyes moved past me into my forehead. She was in my mind with me.

"Tara is here because she will protect you. You are here for your father. Your father asked you to convince Talia Davis to return with you. She has the journal."

Talia quickly snapped her head around. *"How do you know about the journal?"*

Seraphina III's smile widened. *"Incredible, it seems spontaneity has truly taken you all down a poor path. You had no idea, Talia, did you?"*

Talia shook her head.

"Now it's your turn," Seraphina advised Talia. *"I know each of you have already thought of escaping, but you haven't considered the Ophori security outside, so let's just take a moment to relax. It's all the same—love. Tara for Epeë. Epeë for her father. And you for your father as well. You have something special, but you don't know what it means. You came here to find someone to help you decipher it."*

"You don't have to pry, mage," Talia replied. *"I will just tell you. I hoped to find someone here that could explain some of the science in my grandfather's journal; beyond that I mean no harm."*

"As I said, you three should relax. Well, Tara, I can't imagine how uncomfortable this is for you, but you should try and relax too. And I didn't expect you to confess your love like that. I'm sorry."

We were still all on the defense. None of us had dealt with a mage before.

"Look, we locked eyes because I could tell, Talia, that you were as bored at this event as I was. I was tired of sitting there with old women asking of my potential. And of my mother boasting of feats I never accomplished. I am not my grandmother nor do I choose to be. I'm looking for my own path. That's why I went to school to study biology."

"So you're not training to be a mage?" I asked.

"Eh, I don't know. Who knows what I'll be, but I won't be bored." Seraphina III shrugged.

"So you have your degree? Advanced biogenics?" Talia asked.

Seraphina III sat back onto one of the benches used to look out the window at the sea. She held her hand up. *"Yes. I am a biologist. A mage-biologist. You three can just call me Sera."*

Talia felt the rise of a smile, but quickly snuffed it out. Sera was funny. She was just too afraid to acknowledge it.

Sera continued, *"It seems my grandmother's reputation precedes me. You all are not getting turned in for crashing a party. Your motives are safe. I'm less of a budding mage and more of a commissioned biologist. I do field work."*

Talia must have felt as if she had already hit the jackpot. What were the odds that she'd meet a young biologist who had experience in the field? What's more, it was a mage. Someone with connections, yes, but also someone who truly wanted her own adventure. Her outsider perspective may have been exactly what she was seeking.

"Look, let's start over. It's a pleasure to meet you. My name is Talia Davis, I—"

Sera was quick to cut Talia off. *"I'm sorry to interject, but did you say Davis? As in granddaughter of Rory Davis, scientist and husband of Georgette Davis? Georgette is my idol. She inspired me so much as a child!"*

Talia let out a quick breath. *Maybe she had hit the jackpot. "Yes. That's my papa. It's amazing to hear that he inspired you."*

"Yes, well, I just love what he was trying to accomplish with his wife, you know? He was in a space many of us never reach. I never thought I could be a scientist until I heard about him."

I decided to sit down as well.

"So let's address something else," Sera continued. *"Why are the two of you seeking Talia and her journal?"*

Tara shot another strong look at me. She didn't want me to spoil anything else, but I didn't care. Maybe—maybe we were in the Will.

"My last name is not Carol, Talia, it's Afauna. I'm the daughter of Justice Afauna, the now-assassinated leader of the Cophi. I'm telling you all this because I really don't have much else to lose. I only seek to gain the knowledge of what happened to my father."

"And you, Tara, choose to follow her wherever she goes," Sera added. *"Well, good gods, this is heavy. I feel like I've been dropped into a movie! Fortunately for you all that's exactly what I'm looking for. It seems we're all seeking something. You know, as a junior mage, I kind of have to believe in the Cophi by default."*

I took the pause in the conversation to test her. *"So you sound progressive. Do you believe in the systematic equality of our sexes?"*. I aimed to begin with medium pressure before turning up the heat.

"I suppose you could call me progressive in the traditional sense," Sera replied. *"I'm a biologist. There are obvious phenotypic differences between the sexes, but our genetics tell a clear story. If anything is progressive, it's the research. Perhaps it's why most biologists are sent so far away from the cities to conduct it. Can't be stirring up the people with the truth, now can we?"*

Talia was on the right track. I assumed she figured she could now ask a personal question. *"What do you do? Well, I guess I'm asking, what makes you so progressive?"*

Sera paused, then motioned for Talia to sit. *"Well, I'm curious about our genetics. In secondary school, I became skeptical of what was being taught to me by our leading geneticists. Becoming aware of my abilities as a mage, I began to make my own observations as well. I began to understand that we don't quite have all the answers that we say we do, but maybe I should stop. I'm bordering on blasphemy, you know?"*

Jackpot.

"All of my thoughts are blasphemy," Talia began. *"Tell me, do you believe that we are the race of the world? As our history tells us?"*

Sera paused before replying. She now had a better understanding of what she was dealing with.

"I believe it is incredibly audacious to assume that we are alone in our world. Could there be other floating land masses? Could there be other beings intelligent like us? Absolutely."

I jumped in. *"Then what if I told you we have proof?"*

Talia's eyes widened. Sera's eyebrow shot up.

"That's what finding you was all about, Talia. Come with us. Sera, you too! We've been provided information that has enormous implications. And it wouldn't hurt to have a mage as well."

"JUNIOR mage," Sera corrected. *"Look, I'm all for it if it means I get out these heels and this dress and leave Ajax."*

"It's settled then, we leave at once, we have a rendezvous point," Tara offered.

"And I have a hovercraft," Sera explained. *"Let's go."*

***

Fallon, 182 days left

Fallon typed a query regarding the Davis Expedition, then contacted Epeë. The air was clean and fresh at the base of the Hyleian mountain range. Damian and Balien looked well for a morning of climbing and little sleep.

"So we're on foot to the base of the Cophi?" Fallon asked.

"Yes, and we have the granddaughter of the mage you went to see," Epeë replied. "She's with us, Fallon. And I think it would be valuable to have a mage on our side."

Fallon's skin had flushed red, the Vederian biological response to sadness and apprehension. He tapped the kokoto and raised his hands to activate his holographic display. Now would not be the best time to tell Sera.

"Look, I think you three should lay low in Denali, the glass city on Halo Penelope. It's the best city to disappear for a moment. We don't know how long we will be in Hyleia. We may have stumbled across something big," Fallon reported. "And I will trust your judgment with Seraphina III. If she is who you all claim she is, she would be a fantastic addition to our growing team."

"Well, that is good news, as we think we may have stumbled upon something big as well. We put our heads together and reviewed Talia's grandfather's journal. We think we know how Kamali factors into this whole expedition," Epeë added.

"That is outstanding news. We each saw something different in the sæ. Seraphina I was leading us to this very place, Hyleia, but that's not all. I ran a query to test my theory of what I saw. Sure enough, there were actually two investigations of the expedition. The first was sealed, while the second was used as the official report. In the second, unsealed report, the survivors were as follows: Rory Davis, Damien, an ecologist, etymologist Asa Oko, and a Sherpa, Quannah. This was Cara Royale clearance only."

"Did you just say Quannah?" Tara asked. "The guy who helped us get to your place?"

"Yes," Fallon replied. "I have known Quannah for a number of years. He has worked at the capital for as long as I can remember. In fact, he is there now after we set off."

"But how could he possibly be that old? I mean, that would make him—"

"Over two hundred years old," Balien added. "We still are not looking at the whole picture here. There is more than meets the eye." He scanned the mountainous ridge for anyone in the distance.

"And we cannot afford to deal with that at this moment," Fallon continued. "Because this lead now confirms the existence of a documented, first investigation."

"Why was the first investigation sealed?" Talia asked. She quickly jolted, thinking she saw something above her.

"Unknown. The clearance level was Ægæliphi-only, higher than even the heir's clearance. I had no idea some files had such a clearance until now. So I reached out to Vega and she went to her mother. I am sending you an encrypted version of the report. You should all be sitting down."

Epeë's eyes widened as she opened the file. "Talia, the first report is nothing like the second." Epeë's hands shook as she signed. "This, I can't believe *this* was sealed. This—it's groundbreaking. It changes ... everything."

"What is it?!" Talia signed quickly.

"Talia, it's ... it's describing an entirely new ecosystem. Something ... ancient. The air, the plants, the artifacts. It's all ..."

Epeë froze. Her eyes were fixed on the screen in front of her. "It was the child, Talia."

"What do you mean, Epeë? A child?"

"It was always about the child. That's what uprooted the expedition. They returned with a baby. A small unidentified child. Fallon, how much of this report have you read?"

Fallon scrambled to check the manifest on record before sending the file in to ask Ava to scan them for any mentions of a child or someone with child during the expedition. He then took time to have Damian and Balien review the report.

"This ... it just doesn't make any sense," Fallon began. "Even if someone lied about being pregnant, the expedition was cut short. There's no way they could just miraculously return with a baby."

"Wait, Fallon," Talia signed. "I remember reading something. A letter within the journal addressed to the Sherpa. The gift 'shook' common conventions of math."

"What, like, one plus one equals two" Fallon asked, throwing his hands up.

"Yes! What if one plus one equals three?" Talia flashed a smile that lit up the holographic display. "The gift. The gift was the small unidentified child!"

"And if there is any chance that one of the survivors are alive, it would be the youngest survivor! That's why we were asked to track down that child. The child was Kamali," Fallon replied.

***

How do you find a child that was born almost a hundred years ago? Where would you start? Fallon thought to himself.

"Ava, did you receive my upload?" He'd tapped into Ava's communication systems to ensure secure communication with her while on the go.

"Yes, Fallon. I am currently designing an interface for your team to be able to interact with. I think it will help you all understand what is still missing."

"Ava, this is phenomenal. So it was successful?"

"Yes, I was able to create a digital render. I've parsed though the information myself as well. It is very helpful, but there's more to it. I've also updated the V with this information. We're waiting for them to get back to us soon."

"What have you found so far?" Fallon asked.

"According to Rory's journal, the baby was raised in secret. It's not clear who all was involved in keeping this child a secret, but we can assume the Sherpa and the ecologist were involved at least. Though not explicitly outlined, it was assumed that this particular Sherpa was Hyleian. Hyleia, the place most Sherpas came from, was in the mountain regions, where there was a collection of settlements fixated around mines and farms."

"It makes a lot of sense. Damian was thinking on the right track. What other information do you have?" Fallon asked.

"Hyleia: Located on the third halo, Gabriela, it was home to Vederians who spent little time in the capital city. Their homes were carved out of the rock face itself. They traveled up and down the cliff sides just as easy as city-dwelling Vederians would climb stairs. It seems it was the perfect place to hide an undocumented child and it would have been the perfect place to ensure protection. Even if the Sherpa was made, he'd have time to use the cliff side to escape."

"There's also the geology to consider, right?"

"Yes, Fallon, the center of city was within the mountain range's highest peak, Va Major. My suggestion would be to start at a public place and begin canvassing. The city is secluded much like Valvadus. You may be able to find someone trustworthy."

That public place would be a bazaar, where they were told through canvassing that many of the oldest citizens of Hyleia could be found. The bazaar was a major part of Hyleian culture—you could find people conducting all kinds of business there; peddling, selling their personal art, entertaining the passersby with intricate light shows.

Vederian bazaars were some of the most popular places in all of the halos and Hyleian bazaars were some of the best. It was respected—one of the oldest consistently running bazaars in the nation. There was patina on the vases and paintbrushes and trinkets with incredible history. Two-thousand-year-old stone tablets. Volumes of books half a millennia old. At Hyleian bazaars, customers could find the finest silks, cottons, and wools as well.

In ancient times, it was believed that some of the most sought-after pieces of art originally came from Hyleian bazaars. Their value came from the materials used. A blue paint to color the sea was not enough. Was it mixed with the water from that same sea? Was the color gradient accurate to perfection? This is what set the art apart.

One of the most popular pieces of art in the nation was a Hyleian piece called "The Sadness," a marble sculpture of the female form completed by legendary artist Samein Artust. Once completed, she used her own blood to paint over the completed marble structure. It was said to be the most beautiful blue in the entire nation.

The following day, Damian, Balien, and Fallon waded in the sea of customers and artisans. Damian and Fallon began asking the oldest Hyleians they could find about a Sherpa with a baby who went to the capital. One that possibly never returned.

Intriguingly, they discovered that the Sherpa, who was indeed named Quannah, was fairly well known among everyone in the town. He was known to be a kind man with a soft face and solemn temperament. He signed as if everyone he signed to was of royal blood. He helped any and all, answering questions, fixing farming equipment, and helping children with their homework.

Damian and Fallon assumed these accounts were embellished at least slightly, as many people would speak of him as if he were still alive, making him at least three hundred years old—older than any Vederian could possibly be. And yet, as described, he seemed to be exactly the same man Fallon knew.

For example, according to one elder, Joan, Quannah once fixed her father's farming hoe when she was a child. Joan was now a hundred and twenty-seven herself, but she said she could clearly remember Quannah appearing with a newborn baby about the time she finished her university schooling.

"It was out of pure respect for Ba that we kept his secret," she told Fallon, using the term of respect for an elder, Ba. "He said that the child was special and unlike any child we had ever seen. We thought it was an expression, as he would say that about all children, but the baby's hair was dark and black like coal and had the fluff of sheep's wool. The child's eyes were as green as bentgrass and the child was as big a two-year-old Vederian, though apparently newborn." Joan developed a worried look on her face. "That baby was not Vederian. That much I know."

When asked what happened to the baby, Joan was more careful in her signing. "The baby grew," she signed. "The baby grew into an adult unlike any Vederian I had ever seen. Unlike *any* of us have seen." Joan was shaking now. Her eyes darted around to be sure her signs were not seen.

"How was this secret kept?" Balien asked. "How could such a unique person remain hidden?"

"Why do you look so much like her?" Joan asked.

Balien took a few steps back. He looked at Fallon, then at Damian.

"I don't think I know wha—"

"You look identical to her," Joan repeated.

"Joan, the baby. How was the baby a secret?" Fallon pressed.

Joan kept her eyes on Balien, but answered the question. "The baby became the open secret of the mountain town," she confessed. "We couldn't hide her, no one could. So we didn't try. We just ... agreed she was too special, too unique. Kamali was her name, I will never forget it."

Another older man who had shuffled from the alley during the conversation made his way to the group. He didn't introduce himself. He just began signing.

"Her name was Kamali and she believed in the ancient teachings. She believed the old ways to be true. To be arcane, but clear once understood."

"Ba, would you sign that she was a believer in the Residual?" Fallon asked. Any information at this point was welcomed, regardless of who it was from.

"Young man, she not only claimed to believe in the Residual, she claimed to be able to experience the Residual," the old man signed. "She was very tall and strong. Her nose was prominent and her lips shaped. Her appearance was so different from us and she had a natural charisma. People gravitated to her and became fixated on what she thought about the world and how she experienced it."

"And how do you know all these things?" Damian asked.

"Because I trained the girl, young man. When it became time for her to begin schooling, she told Quannah that she wanted to be Ophori and this was something Quannah knew could never happen. Kamali would never be able to leave Hyleia, though I believe with my soul that she should have."

"What is your name, Ba?" Fallon asked. "How are we to believe you?"

"I am Joseph. Husband of Ægæliphi Vera, father of my children, Veronica, Vega, Valerie, and Victor."

***

Veronica, 182 days left

I am alone now. I've lost my best to ensure we stay on track. I must now trust in the people we have been spying on all this time. Whether or not they are ready, we are out of time and our enemies were aware of this too—including Gaius.

Gaius didn't often make mistakes. He was brilliant: calculated and focused. He tried to keep his shortcomings to a minimum by being as precise as he possibly could. He was an extremely detail-oriented man and was pointedly disciplined.

He had developed a reputation for asking questions that most never thought to ask and he was successful because of it. As the philosopher Antius—one of the few and great male Vederian poets—once said, "Failures impart wisdom into those who rise. I've failed many times and now, have risen far above any man." As prominent as Gaius was, he was equally arrogant. He led the type of life that most all of us lead—a mistake-filled career and a life with many failures speckled in between.

This, however, was not what Gaius believed. Gaius believed that he had ascended. He was the Queensguard. He was given the ability to think and act and make difficult decisions on behalf of the throne. He was able to be in rooms no men had ever set foot in. He was successful, yes, but not without failure. And this was his true flaw—his blindness.

When his wife was rushed to the hospital by his adopted son in the middle of a storm, he was not there. Instead, he was at Arælia with the third in line to the throne. He knew his wife was pregnant. He knew that he was needed. He simply made a judgment call. He didn't think twice about it.

"Where does your wife think you are, Gaius?" Valerie asked. Her hands flowed as she signed. Her rings flashed and sparkled in her bedroom lighting. She was sprawled out on her bed, behind a veil that emitted its own light.

"She thinks I'm with the most powerful woman in the world," Gaius replied. His hands were rigid and succinct. After each sign, he would place his hands back behind him. He was standing at the foot of the bed. But he knew he would be horizontal soon.

"And does she know what you *do* with the most powerful woman in the world?" Valerie continued, opening the veil.

"She knows that I serve the princess with my life and that my sworn duty is to you." Gaius was giving cookie-cut answers in a situation that was the complete opposite.

Valerie left her bed and walked toward him. She adjusted his uniform before continuing. "And what is your duty to her as her husband?" She placed her thumb lightly on his bottom lip before sitting back down on her bed.

Gaius thought about this question before answering. "I will sign in ahak," Gaius began, a word that meant he was communicating strictly in the present tense. "For some reason, here, in this moment, I feel strong. But my wife would tell you that it's not who I am strong for, but who I am weak for. And I now know that is my flaw; I am not weak for her, I am weak for myself."

Valerie licked her lips before making her way back toward Gaius.

"Gaius, you are weak. It's why I chose you for your duty, and your duty is to please me. You've never had a problem with it." She was right. Gaius was both weak in principle and in practice. It was instances like these that defined him. Not the moments of glory, not the Queensguard.

"I have the answer that you seek," Gaius replied, ignoring her previous statement. "I am no longer within ahak, but now sign to you that which someone else has seen."

"Go on."

"His name is Damian Cala and he is not alone. Where he lacks in skill, he makes up for in size. He is the white bear, as we previously thought."

"And who could he possibly be working with, the Cophi? Or has he gone rogue?"

"He may have gone rouge. The motive is there. The Church murdered his wife and child. The royal family denied him trial. It could be a number of things," Gaius said plainly. He rushed through that explanation as to not go much deeper into it. The Church was not kind to the retired Old Guard. Damian had it the worst.

Valerie's eye began to twitch. "We answer to ourselves and ourselves alone. Let hidden things be done in secret."

"In any case, he is not alone. He is with two other men that we have yet to identify. They have left Valvadus on foot and we can confirm that they have killed the mage Seraphina. We believe they are headed to Hyleia."

Valerie let in a shallow breath. "And so the great Seraphina has come to rest. My, my, the final moments will be rapid ones."

Gaius nodded.

"I made my declaration. I will establish the House of Amavi once more. Those of my family that recognize my claim will be here in the coming days. And I have warned Vega and Victor. I will ascend. And I will take what I was denied. I have been told enough. Assemble the Old Guard one last time. Snuff this out and end it. Do not return to me until it is done."

Gaius hesitated, but bowed in reverence. "It will be done."

"And, Gaius, one more thing, since we're digging up the past once more, if you manage to find my "father" out there, bring him to me. I will kill him myself."

***

Veronica, 182 days left

The trio was stunned. It was Joseph, the husband of the Ægæliphi. Known as the most mysterious man in the nation, known by many officially as the Hidden King. According to numerous reports, he was believed to have been present, at some point, in Arælia, but his whereabouts were never officially known. The people knew he existed, knew of his importance, but many assumed by this point he was dead. In reality, it was worse than being dead. It was almost as if he never existed. As husband of Ægæliphi he was never to be seen in public, never a part of any official records, never discussed. And yet here he was, leading a trio of traitors to his home. Traitors who were coming to learn of and even more hidden world.

"I have lived in Hyleia for about forty years," Joseph began. He looked back occasionally to be sure the group could keep up with his pace. They climbed over brush, stepped over divots in the grass, and treaded through shallow creeks. The mountainous region were second nature to him. It was as if he knew where each rock and root was as he stepped over each and every one. "I like it here. The air is cleaner," he signed.

The path to Joseph's home was not really a path. It was largely unmarked. To those following him, it felt more like he was returning to nothing, making up the path as he went along. There was no infrastructure, no electricity, nothing. And yet, he was returning to this place from memory. There were no markers. Only increasingly dense forest.

The group continued through the forest, carefully stepping over fallen logs and ducking under low-hanging branches. They snaked through the forest, steadily inclining to a final clearing. The forest continued until it just stopped. The group climbed up to a clearing where the forest ended unnaturally and abruptly. The separation was as sharp as a razor's edge. But there was more. Balien took note of the silence. If there were living animals within the forest, he couldn't hear them. And the clearing was equally dead. There was a curvature to the edge of the forest. He didn't know what to make of the unnatural shape. There was a house that looked to be made of multiple concrete boxes stacked on top of each other at varying angles. There was plenty of glass, steel, and wood. Just a few meters out, Joseph stopped and turned to them.

"When Quannah first approached me, I stood in disbelief," Joseph confessed. "Nothing can prepare you for such a sight. To finally see something you never believed possible."

Still facing us, Joseph took two steps back.

"This, no"—he took two more steps back—"this is where I stood when Quannah came to me holding a child."

There were tears in his eyes pooling just below the lids.

"I felt unworthy. I didn't think it was something that I could do, but Quannah insisted. I want you all to understand that no one can truly be prepared for what I am about to show you."

Everyone nodded. Joseph turned and took the group up to his home. They took a few steps to his front door—it was a deep navy, like Vederian blood. Inside was an extremely traditional Vederian home. Very little technology, with all the interior walls made of a thick translucent glass. All the usual things were color-coded. Red tools. Blue utensils. Yellow books. Traditionally, Vederians color-coded everything, but it was less common in modern homes. He offered the trio places to sit—pillows placed on the floor. They were in his prayer room, but it had be stripped, and there was no focal point to pray.

"Please, sit," Joseph signed. "You know, I used to pray here. I was a believer, completely. From birth I was raised to believe in the teachings of the Vael. I was enamored with the goddess. I only wanted to know of sight. I only wanted to know of what more we could see and nothing else," Joseph explained. "As a child, when my mother explained to me that I was to be the Hidden King, it only caused me to study harder. I wanted to be perfect. I studied all the sacred texts. I went to temple every day of the week. I became so focused that when the truth was finally presented to me, I couldn't even recognize it. In fact, all I could show was anger and hate. And I suppose that is what we all do when we experience something other. Our gut instinct isn't to welcome it—it's to oppose it. In my decades of study, all that work, I didn't want to accept that it was all incorrect. How could so much devotion be wrong? I was furious."

Fallon's eyes were as wide as they could get. Everyone listened intently.

"And so I hated the child. Even after Quannah explained what she was, even after I learned to accept it, I was still infected with anger. It made me into a man I didn't know I could become. And now here we are; my daughter is just as infected as I was. No, our entire nation is as hateful as I was."

The group was brimming with questions, but they were too intimidated to interrupt.

"I knew this day would come. I knew one day someone would find me. This old man wanted to be ready for that day. It is finally here. And you all are just as they said you would be—I just hope it isn't too late. Time is so short."

Balien looked out the window at the open field that artificially cut the forest into a circle. Joseph had been exiled here. And in that solitude, he was able to protect one of the most important people the nation had ever known.

"You all have no idea who you all are, do you?" Joseph asked. "Well, let me explain that you are the product of a plan that is generations old. This is all destiny. I began with my anger to provide you context. To bring you here: I want you to understand how we built the Church of the Kofi. I took that anger and turned it into passion. I dedicated my life to finding the truth. We wanted to spread that to the world. We wanted to prepare our people for the others, we didn't want them to greet them with war. We knew that our people wouldn't be able to deal with the truth that the others had lived among us for millennia. But I digress, what are you questions? We do not have much time. They will come for me soon."

Balien began. "Who will come for you?"

"My daughter, of course. My third child, Valerie," Joseph replied. "By now, she has seen all. We were wrong for what we did to her, but soon it will not matter. Soon no one will be able to stop her."

"We continue to be told this, but help us understand. What is so wrong with Valerie, why can she not be Ægæliphi? Why is her own family against her?" Fallon asked. "Why must she be stopped?"

"Because Valerie is *not* family. She is the result of an act of mercy. A mistake that has complicated the royal family so much that I fear it has become unrepairable. This is thousands of years old, young man. Vo, Va, the family lines. There has always been war. It just hasn't always been public. Even as a child, Valerie sought answers to questions she was never supposed to ask and, as a result, we were never able to provide Valerie with the answers she needed. On top of that she claimed to see visions, even as a young girl. She told her mother that she was not her child. She told her sisters that she was not their sister. She told everyone that she did not belong. This was since she could first sign. She always knew the truth."

"What was the truth?" Damian asked.

"The truth was that she was right. But not in the way she thought. As she got older she became increasingly deviant. Her suspicions could not be quelled. You have to believe me, we did a lot of things to her family, but they were insane. We had to take Vedere back. Do you understand?"

Joseph had developed tears in his eyes as he signed. "We tried our best to treat her as family, we truly did. But she killed all her pets. She told us her visions wanted her to kill us all. We took her to therapists, to priestesses, to shamans. But it was more of the same, she would not change. Until Kamali, she was my greatest secret. We couldn't let the people know what we had done. We couldn't explain to the world that we were imposters. Valerie's family had an ancient duty, one that is much, much older that you could possibly comprehend. Her line was one of the very first. One of the original five that was split. Their duty is to control. And when the Cara Royale finally took hold, even we knew it wouldn't last long. We just wanted to buy ourselves enough time."

Damian furrowed his brow as he folded his arms.

"You don't understand, I know. But you do not have all the answers yet. You don't know what her family was bred to do!" Joseph's hands shook and rattled as he spoke. "She was out of control—just like the rest of her family. We never should have kept her. We were told not one member of the original family was to live. If we wanted to defy the quinqu, that was the price. Was it harsh? Yes. But was it right? I think you have to have all the details to make a decision on that; but Vera, she could not do it. To her, it was too high a price. So we kept the baby. We kept her and raised her as our own. We didn't know what else to do. It was the only way we could think of to preserve the peace. War was going to rise back up!"

Balien got up from his seated position, knelt by Joseph, and grabbed his hand. "We are not judging you, Joseph. We just want to understand."

"You have Kamali's eyes. That's what it is," Joseph replied. "Are you an imposter too?"

Fallon interrupted again. "Help me understand, Joseph. Who are you, really? Who is Vera, Vega, and Victor?"

"I am Joseph Raphaela. Eldest descendant of the Raphaela family."

"As in Halo Raphaela?" Balien asked.

"Yes," Joseph replied. "We were the first family to colonize the halo all those years ago. We also led the resistance in the civil war. All of the families did. We had to when we discovered what the royal family was doing."

"And what were they doing, Joseph?" Damian asked.

"Culling. On their own volition. Whenever they deemed it necessary. It was population control. It ... it was genocide. You all are too young to remember." Joseph vigorously rubbed his forehead. "People would just disappear. Taken from their very beds. Some would return, many would not. But if they did return, they had no memories of what happened to them. They insisted they were fine, but they were not. They had become different people. They had become changed. This is what the war was truly about. A family that believed they were gods. A family that believed they could just breed out any imperfections like we were cattle. We are not cattle. We colonized this world, just as the other five families did."

There was a pause in the conversation. Balien, Fallon, and Damian were thinking. This was not how the civil war had been presented nor was this what they were told it was about.

"It wasn't until Kamali that I began to understand who the Cara family was," Joseph continued. "The Caras were pure-blood, just as Kamali was, but her blood was different."

Balien thought on the comparison Joseph made between himself and Kamali. "Where is Kamali now?" he asked.

Joseph stared at Balien. "You truly don't know, do you, Balien?"

Balien shook his head.

"Kamali, your great-grandmother, was killed. What happened to you? You don't even recognize me."

All eyes were now fixed on Balien, who stared back incredulously. Fallon attempted to fill in the gaps.

"Balien was in a terrible accident. He has trouble with his memories. Seraphina I helped, but there are still gaps. You ... you know him?"

Joseph continued to stare, wide-eyed. "Balien, you poor child. You ... you are everything. You are what this whole thing is about."

Fallon pulled out his pad and began scribbling. He had his own theories, but he hadn't told Balien yet. He didn't want to overwhelm him. It seemed now that all would be revealed.

"Balien," Joseph began. "When Quannah came to me, when I was going to kill him where he stood, he said to me, 'Joseph, she is one of us. The last of our people. We are so few.'"

Balien's eyes blurred from the tears. He was remembering.

Joseph's eyes widened, then narrowed, focused on Balien. "They were killing the Vederian people because they were looking for a specific family—yours."

"But why?" Fallon asked.

"Well, doctor, if you haven't been able to tell, this conflict is a generational one. When I first met Kamali as an infant, I was in my twenties. I had just learned of my destiny as Hidden King and given this home in Hyleia, inspired by the home of the Viceroy. As Hidden King, I would not live with my future family, so I spent the majority of my time here in the wilderness. I wrote poetry, painted. It was wartime and I wanted to be as far away as I could from the fighting. When we learned of the failure of the Davis Expedition, I knew focus would shift to the capital. I prepared to leave for Arælia when Quannah met me in this very field." Joseph pointed out back at the clearing that the group just trekked through.

Fallon continued to scribble.

"Quannah was desperate. He said I was the only one he could trust and I didn't even know him. He said as Hidden King, I was the infant's best chance of survival. He explained the expedition revealed a new timetable that would change everything and that Kamali represented a show of faith between three peoples, the Vedere and the Hören and the Nusdvagisdi—your people, Balien."

Fallon scribbled more in his notebook. With two independent accounts, it looked to mean that everything was true. Everything.

"I, along with Seraphina I, raised the child. It was Seraphina I that named her Kamali, the Sacred Guide. She lived here, in this very house. She learned of her people through Seraphina I and Quannah and she learned of our people through me. It was an amazing few decades."

"How did Seraphina I teach her?" Balien asked.

"Through the sæ. I still do not truly understand it, but Seraphina I described a sæ to me as sight beyond sight—the ability to see beyond the veil of time and space. She could show people themselves in a way a mirror could not. To her, time was a liquid, and she was baptizing her travelers into the ocean of their own mind."

Balien adjusted to this thought. It was an accurate explanation. Through Seraphina I's sæ, he, Damian, and Fallon all observed something unique to them. She designed what she wanted each of them to see and she had her own reasons for each of them. Though the trio had not yet had the time to discuss what each of them saw, it was clear that whatever it was deeply impacted each of them.

"It's how I realized that Valerie was a sær as well. How I realized we eventually would not be able to hide anything from her. Seraphina I believed that memories were written into our DNA; that our ancestors' strongest beliefs, vices, and hopes all lied within. She used the sæ to access those parts that our conscious minds lived ahead of, unknowingly," Joseph explained. "Much of who Kamali truly was remained a mystery, even to Seraphina I. It was her goal to help Kamali understand what only Kamali could experience. To give names to the invisible. To link her back to her people. It took decades."

"And so the Kofi was born out of what Kamali was seeking? Her beliefs?" Damian asked.

"No, Damian, not her beliefs, her family. Though I didn't realize it until she became older, Kamali was truly alone. We were not her people. And though she had these astounding abilities, none of us could truly grasp how alone she truly was ... only Quannah could understand."

This resonated deeply with Balien. He knew this feeling. He was taught of it by his mother. The familiarity all started to weave back together in his mind. This was his family. This was his story.

"The Kofi had no choice but to be born as a result. Even before Kamali entered our world, our people always wondered. Every few generations we would cycle, seeking the effects of causes we could not see, developing skepticism of the Viceroy and their power, fearful of what happened to those of us who openly discussed their beliefs of something more. It would always swell until entire families disappeared in the amberlight. Those questions would die with them. That's was the duty of Valerie's family. To prevent the discovery of the truth. And by now, I'm certain she knows her family's true task. She will not stop."

"What was the turning point?" Balien asked. "When did everything change?"

"That is difficult to explain. But I can tell you that the turning point for Kamali was when she truly saw our world. When she traveled to the other halos, when she fell in love."

Damian began to fidget. His kokoto interface device, contact lenses on the surfaces of his eyes, flashed words in front of him. He felt completely seen by the others, though he was not yet.

"Damian, we are nearly in position. It's time for you to make a decision," the message flashed.

It was Gaius Saroyan, Damian's ranking officer. He had led Gaius's men directly to them.

"Kamali couldn't bear seeing so many people of sight blind to the truth. She returned here to Hyleia and began telling people her testimony. She told them about what she felt, and they believed her. The first church was started," Joseph explained.

Sweat beaded on Damian's forehead. Some of the nation's best warriors were about to descend on the Hidden King and the others.

"We are out of time, I'm sorry. There is a group of men on horseback approaching from the south," Damian signed abruptly, pointing out the window. "I will go out to meet them; it should slow them down enough to for you to escape."

Balien cocked his head as he turned to Damian. "I don't see any—"

"Look!" Fallon signed. "They are coming in fast, how did they find us?"

Joseph turned a skeptical eye toward Damian. "They are Old Guard. And if I had to guess, this man was once one of them."

In a flurry, Balien and Fallon gathered their belongings. Damian stood motionless. Joseph stood up and pulled out a curiously shaped weapon, an ancient-looking sword.

"You came here for answers. You do not need Kamali, you have Balien. Anything else you need to know is already with Balien. Find Quannah. Despite his appearance, he is indeed the same man from all those years ago. He will further explain what I did not have time to share. And so my friends, my journey ends here," Joseph signed. "This is how I want it to be."

Balien attempted to protest, but Fallon grabbed him from behind. "We each have our own time, Balien."

Balien snatched off Fallon's hold on his arm. "I'm not leaving without one more answer. Damian, tell me now, did you betray us?"

Damian unbuttoned the collar of his shirt and the buttons on his sleeves. "It is not yet time for your father to see you," Damian signed, rolling up his sleeves.

"My ... father?" Balien asked. "How could you know?"

"We have always known," Joseph confessed. "Veronica, Seraphina I, Damian, myself. This is all how it was designed to be. So to answer your question, no. Damian didn't betray you, he has freed you. And in fact, it is now his brothers who have betrayed him. Now go!"

Joseph and Damian rushed out the front door as Fallon dragged Balien out the back. Balien stole looks behind as they ran forward. *Which one is my father?* He thought to himself. The men on horseback were fully clad in their Ophori dress. Joseph was right. It was the Old Guard. The twins, Gaius, and Timothy Aquinas. Joseph seemed content to make his stand on his own porch, with Damian opting to walk out ahead into the clearing. When Balien and Fallon reached the tree line, they took a break to gather their breath and assess the situation.

The four men on horseback had dismounted and formed a semicircle around Damian. Joseph had deepened into a traditional stance with his unique sword held high. He was waiting. Damian curved his foot around in the grass to a standard boxing stance. He held his fists up tight and near the eyes.

The other four men removed much of their leather and metallic armor; the sunlight caused a glint to flash like a beacon signaling that something was beginning. The men also removed all their weapons: obsidian blades, energy-based guns, and flash grenades. One stepped forward first. He was the smallest of the group with a scar over his eyebrow that made it appear as if he was squinting that eye continuously. He slowly signed that he was sorry, rubbed his fist in a circular motion on his chest. He also used the word "friend," a sign in which his pointer fingers linked like a chain, one hand over the other.

"Balien, we cannot stay," Fallon repeated, but Balien was transfixed. He had to know which one was his father. Through the sæ, he had regained the majority of his memories, but those most closely linked to his father remained shrouded.

"Damian is one of them," Balien signed. "He was a part of this group. They've come to kill him."

The smaller man with the squint held his fists high and tight as well. Damian removed his shirt, revealing a back riddled with white-and-black tattoos and scars from the nape of his neck down to the small of his back. *Just how much battle had Damian seen?* Balien thought. Damian let in a slow, deep breath and exhaled quickly. He was to make the first move.

Damian attempted an open-hand chop to Squint Eye's neck, but it was blocked with a forearm. He turned around for a sweeping kick, but Squint Eye expertly timed a jump to avoid it. Damian then opted for a straight jab and hook combo, but Squint Eye dodged both.

So far, Damian was punching and kicking thin air. Frustrated, Damian charged for a low tackle and wrapped up Squint Eye's waist, but incredibly, he struggled to get him to the ground. In the struggle, Squint Eye found a soft spot just below Damian's ears where the base of the skull and jaw met on both sides and used his thumb to apply pressure. Damian loosened his grip and Squint Eye used that opening to crash two fists down onto Damian's shoulder blades. Damian's chest hit the ground and, before he could complete a pushup to regain his footing, he was kicked across the face by Squint Eye.

Damian rolled over to his back and covered his face with his arms. There was a judo-like tussle between attempts to grapple each other. Arms were slapped away and ill-placed punches barely landed. Squint Eye was trying to go for the neck, but Damian wouldn't allow. By now, Squint Eye had jumped on top of Damian and straddled his waist. He still couldn't get the leverage he wanted. Damian hinged at the hips and fell to his chest. Squint Eye flipped over, sitting on top of Damian's back. Damian reached to Squint Eye's neck and pulled back down, arching Squint Eye's back further than his body wanted. He reached frantically at first, but his arms slowed. Neither of them would hear it, but there was a snap that was loud enough for Balien to hear.

It was this action that caused the twins to sprint in synchronicity. They were identical and moved like it. Their eyes were bloodshot and their actions were in tandem, fierce and fueled with emotion. Damian had just snapped their brother-in-arm's back. He would pay. Balien found himself gripping the grass so tightly that he had a handful of dirt in both his hands.

"I don't think Damian will come back from this," Fallon signed. Balien was worried he was right.

Just in time to meet the charging brothers, Damian had rolled backward to his feet and beat his chest with both fists and motioned for the twins to rush him. He knew this time he would have to give his all. This was Damian at his most brutal. The only way Balien could tell the twins apart was that one had his hair cut short to a buzz while the other had braids cornrowed to his scalp. Cornrow got to Damian faster and went for a low tackle, which Damian sidestepped. He then cracked him in the ribs with a vicious side kick as he prepared for Buzz's jumping roundhouse kick. Damian had to make a three-quarters turn and displayed both forearms to block the kick.

He stabbed Buzz in the neck with his bare open hand, choking him. He jumped and distributed a spinning kick that knocked Buzz on his back. With no hesitation, Damian turned back to Cornrow, who was favoring those broken ribs. Damian just didn't let up. He dished out the fastest, most visceral barrage of punches Balien had ever seen

It was not to say the brothers were not exceptional fighters—they were, it was just that Damian had transcended to another level. This was Damian's last battle, and he knew it. He was going out with as many as he could take with him. Cornrow attempted a straight punch, but Damian dodged and grabbed that same arm so that he could careen his elbow into it. Another snap. This was not the same fight he had with the Ophori. With this engagement, each movement had the intention to disarm.

As Cornrow adjusted to his newly broken arm, Damian turned to the other brother and slapped both ears with his hands. Two kicks to the thigh, a knee to the gut, and elbow to the cheekbone. Buzz should have been dead, but instead he just drifted back until he passed out. Damian reached down and grabbed the grass and earth and squeezed it in his hands. He had claimed this ground. It was at this point that Balien noticed the final solider in the back. That was the leader. That was his father. It was time to go. Now.

"That's enough, Balien," Fallon signed. "Don't let Damian's sacrifice be for nothing."

Balien, now visibly moved by what had just taken place, remembered Damian's final message. "It's not time for your father to see you yet."

Balien would honor that wish. He turned his head and the pair ran into the forest.

***

Part 8: The Ecologist

The Journal of Georgette Davis, 57,293 days left

Day 8

An unexpected breakthrough! One of our Gamma geologists, Dr. Mera, suggested that we leverage the IR cameras and our various spectroscopy equipment to better understand the landscape. The results were not just successful, they were mesmerizing. Not only were we able to build our best 3D map of the Underside, but we now understand the landscape on an unprecedented level. Not only that, but it would appear that we have completely changed the geology of our area of the Underside before we ever set foot here. Dr. Mera believes that the light probes that we sent down months ago—to illuminate our expedition—have significantly changed the ecosystem of the area.

The working hypothesis is there was no light here prior to our expedition nor was there any light present at any given point. This directly contradicts the majority of our understanding of our world. We knew we would come and receive answers, but I do not believe any of us could have foreseen this.

I called a council meeting with the alpha of each field of study to discuss. So far, all available information suggests that the plants and possibly animals of the Underside are virtually all noctophiles. The plants we have studied all thrive in the darkness. The heat and the light from our beacons have produced adverse effects to many of the samples we have taken. Direct beacon light causes severe decay within a matter of minutes! This is the complete opposite of any plant or animal on the Topside or the outer rim!

What we may be looking at here is a complete paradigm shift of our entire ecosystem. Of the halos that were not constructed by Vederian Builders, there are two which are naturally occurring. Our entire world is built on the visible spectrum. So how are there any plants that thrive in the dark? Did Vederians once thrive in the darkness?

My husband will be a part of the second security team and he will surely return with answers. I've asked the remaining security team members to scout out again, just to our perimeter, to see if we can find any trace of the first party. We are now using our science team's equipment to look for our team. We have our most advanced technology on this mission! Why not put it to use!

11:43

We have just received a report that something just tripped our sensors on the outskirts of our camp. We are not quite sure what it could be at this time, but it is believed to be relatively the size of a large animal; perhaps some type of bear or similarly sized creature. Of course, it is our hope that it is just that, given the nature of our work and where we are. The working plan now is to continue to monitor it and hope that it stays along the perimeter.

12:10

A second report this time. It seems as if there are more of these animals among us. We will be sending out a drone to assess the situation. Hopefully the cameras will illuminate this development further.

12:12

After about a minute and a half of flight time, our drone was shot down. Ava Bastian, the alpha of Security, has raised our threat level to green. Nonessential personnel has been moved to our most secured facility at the center of camp. We are going to go completely dark save for the interior of a number of our facilities. This could be the missing team, though we are still taking every precaution.

13:24

We are all in agreement that the best course of action for us is to identify the source of the vector. It could be possible that someone or something has triggered or initiated the signal. We believe that it is in our best interest to seek out the signal, build a base camp from there, and continue to conduct our research from that location.

What has become increasingly odd is the terrain as we get closer to the signal. The closer we get, the less living material we find. The surface we walk upon has transitioned into a stonelike material and the area before us is as vast and as flat as a desert. Upon further evaluation it appears the surfaces are metallic in nature, but the likes of nothing we have ever seen.

The technology we use for lighting has been sufficient, but it has been incredibly unnerving to see so much darkness immediately around us. It's as if it's a force we're pushing back—an enormous wall of bleakness. We light our way as we go and I imagine in my mind's eye that we are creating a small vein of life-giving blood inside of a giant organism that has been long dead.

Our survivor seems in better spirits. She is no longer sedated and is cooperating with Neil and his team. Rory maintains his account of the events. I am biased, but I truly believe him. And he has this child. Something *surely* happened.

Some on our physics team have begun to discuss what the signal could be. Some are suggesting it could be a new power source, or similar phenomenon we have yet been able to measure. Others believe it can also be some sort of message, perhaps, left behind by our ancestors. And of course, there's always the possibility that whatever made the signal is still down here with us and, though initially believed to be incredibly unlikely, whatever happened with Rory seems to point to the veracity of that supposition.

As for me, I am not sure what to think. I am not quite sure what I would want, to be honest. What would be the most ideal outcome given what we have been presented? I think it would be safer for us to stumble upon a previous civilization that has been a long dead. I want to say we have already found some sort of evidence of that given the unnatural nature of this increasingly growing surface of smooth metallic-stone. Though I do not recall it, I was told that we crossed over a plane of stone that had a nonnatural perfectly straight line. Could we be walking on top of some sort of structure? Something that was carved from something that *was* naturally occurring? Perhaps it is another phenomenon of which we are currently unaware.

Further observations: The stone is smooth in a way that could suggest the flow of water, but we have not found any signs of any standing water, pools, or any form of an ocean or aquifer.

If it becomes clear that we are on some sort of surface that was designed, what could that mean? Is this some sort of tribute to an ancestral god, or could it be some form of giant tool that our previous civilization used? It could even be some sort of sporting venue, for all we know. Rory maintains that none of this material was present when he and the other parties were here, but with something this large it cannot be possible that this structure is moving. I suppose we will have to continue our study.

16:18

For the last few hours, we have been studying it. We thought it was made of stone, but it is something else entirely. First, the most important point: we are receiving information from the rear of our camp that the material is growing in size. We are theorizing it is circular in shape. It is stretching outward at a rate of a few centimeters every few hours.

We have called up our alpha of Ecology, as we are still trying to understand whether or not this is an ecological phenomena. In addition, we finally have our drones up to give us an understanding of just how large of a structure we are dealing with. Whatever this object is, it is huge and we are all but certain now that the source of the signal must lie at the center of this gigantic disc. The structure is surely not natural, though it is hard to fathom the idea that something this large could be created by anything that we can conceptualize.

Our geological team seems to believe that it's not the earth around the disc that came first, rather it was the disk that came first before the earth around it. Under microscope, its structure appears living, though it seems to hold the geometric structure of something older than anything I've ever come across. If it were some kind of landing site, you would think that there would be signs of wear or maybe markings that indicated locations of where to touch down. But the markings seemed to be randomized, though the final verdict is still in limbo as our linguistics team continues to conduct their study.

The current consensus among our alphas is the increasingly real possibility of first contact. "There is substantial reason to believe that when one culture is significantly more technologically advanced than the other, there will be significant conflict. Whether that be our side or their side remains to be determined," Saven, our alpha of Philosophy, shared in our discussion. "I think it will be important for us to determine of which side we originate. Because if we are unfortunate to be the lesser of the two—and in my opinion, it will be our side—simply due to nature of conflict, that will face the worst of consequences."

"And if I may, I must caution the introduction of diseases. For the most part, our technology has allowed for the irradiation of most all diseases that impact our biology, but we must not forget how pathology plays a critical role in this process," Neil, our alpha of Biology, added. "We are positioning ourselves among the most isolated peoples we have ever come across—from territories in densities we've only hypothesized. Our ability to succumb to foreign illnesses brought to us from their unique biology is extremely high. It may already be too late."

The conversation shifted heavily. We were now discussing the tangibility of our fate. We knew what we signed up for when we agreed to this expedition. And we all discussed what it would mean if it became clear that we would be unable to return. We have our contingency plan, we have our journals. But I still remain hopeful. According to our surveys, we will reach the center of the structure just before early tomorrow morning. We will get our answers then. Until that time, I have ask all teams to prepare for contact. We have recalled all our synths and put on our exosuits. Time will tell.

22: 54

My hands shake as I write this message. By the Goddess, they are still with them as I write. I only stepped away as to document what has transpired, as it is fresh in the mind. I suppose first I should describe them. They are bipedal just as we are, but have slender-proportioned frames and slightly longer limbs. Most are nearly three meters in height and are extremely flexible for their size. Details on their appearance is scant given the nature of their clothing: they seem to be completely wrapped in dark cloth. Only their ears are exposed.

They ... they knew we would come. They were waiting for us. The signal did indeed come from them, but as they explain it, it is a signal that can only be detected by them. Their technology is so far advanced than ours, I am certain the translation is incorrect. Oh! Before I get too far ahead of myself. Communication! It is by far the most enigmatic part of them. They understand us to be as they call "People of Sight." They call themselves "People of Sound." We are able to vaguely understand the parallels due to the similarities, but we would be nowhere without a woman that is with them named Vantalyn.

Vantalyn is, by her own account, Omni. Vantalyn and her husband are of a tribe called the Nusdvagisdi. She claims that sight is just once "sense" of many and that the People of Sound, the Horeni, have traveled here from their world to warn us. She explains that her entire race was destroyed by the quinqu, a group of people who believe in something she refers to as "supreme balance." Because the Nusdvagisdi knew their time was short, they sent out thousands of couples to the "other realities" to help warn them. Vantalyn explains they are the only race that is still fluent in all of the senses. Without them, it would be nearly impossible to communicate with the Horeni.

According to Vantalyn, the Horeni have been here for at least five hundred years. It has taken them nearly half that time to simply travel here. The metallic-stone substance has a name that we cannot understand, as it can only be "heard," as she explains. The Horeni people can only "hear." The fabric of their society and communication is based in this metallic substance.

It seems they have the ability to create communication using "tones." So long as we are on the metallic structure, we are all connected, but the rest is simply beyond my understanding. Vantalyn also explained that during our first contact, there was a misunderstanding and a fight broke out.

As a peace offering, Vantalyn explained that the leader of the Horeni, a man named Corva, gave his infant son to Rory. They have been trying to heal our first and second scouts ever since. Vantalyn also explained that the first priority of their expedition was to warn us about the quinqu, that the Horeni inhabited the closest reality to us, so they pooled the resources of their entire world to bring a small party here. But they have devastating news. They claim their computers have calculated the coming of something the Nusdvagisdi call an eclipse.

According to Vantalyn, it is a phenomenon that will plunge our entire nation into complete darkness for longer than any Vederian lifetime. It will be the end of our world as we know it. I ... I'll be back to write more. They are calling me back out.

***

Veronica, 183 days left

To the public, Gaius was the most important man in the nation. He was the shining example of what it meant to serve his Ægæliphi and her nation. He was the embodiment of that which all Vederian men aspired to be; he was everything Vederian mothers wanted their sons to be.

Gaius was handsome. He surprised and awed those around him with his size—almost as tall as the average Vederian woman. He had large hands and a broad chest. He looked to be made of worked leather with skin just as durable. He would smile and wave and wink through every interaction. He never tired at educational lectures. He always stayed after speaking engagements to answer questions and provide encouragement. He was interpersonal, congenial, and charismatic. If there was any man poised to be the first in Vederian leadership, it was Gaius.

To the inner circle, Gaius was something else entirely—that was his talent. He knew who to be to people and exactly when to promptly code switch. He was attentive; he would always stand directly in front of you when conversing. He would never forget your name. He knew how to read body language with an uncanny precision. He was very aware of his surroundings. And as only a few knew, he was a man of many secrets.

Gaius was an assassin for his Ægæliphi, a mercenary to the Va Dynasty, and a terrorist to the outer halos. He could be blinded by policy and cold-hearted to principle. At times, it seemed as if Gaius would resign himself to the orders he was given—even when it was painfully clear he was much too smart to acquiesce. But Gaius had his period of mourning. He worked to reconcile the activities of a man who was twenty years younger and much more brash. He absorbed the pain of losing his wife and child. And he let it spill out at the feet of a queen's daughter hellbent on destroying the dynasty that raised her. Yesterday was for mourning.

But today was a day of celebration. Gaius would be awarded for his valor after the Sisters War, an engagement now being retconned into the Civil War by Valerie. This would be her first public appearance since her time with the Viceroy. This would also be the first time the entire Cara Royale family would be seen together in nearly five years. Even the Ægæliphi was present.

"My most beloved people, I stand here before you today to honor a man of whom I treat as a brother. A man many of you know only as kind, meek, and loving. The exemplary Gaius Anton Saroyan." There were flashes of light and hands that fluttered in the air. Valerie motioned for Gaius to stand from his end of the long rectangle table. "Gaius, you are everything I want our men to be. During our most dark time you remained steadfast—as the example I always knew you to be. It is for this reason that I award you with the Paa, the highest award available to men. Gaius, come and receive your necklace." Valerie smiled as Gaius made his way to her. They stood in the courtyard before the majority of the nation's leaders, everyone from the innermost ring of Ræ to the distant Medisi territory.

Valerie placed the necklace over Gaius's head and brought his forehead to hers to kiss it. With her back turned to the crowd, she then shared something privately to him before addressing the crowd again.

"As some of you know, Gaius suffered a terrible tragedy. Five years ago, during one of the most terrible storms of that year, Gaius lost his entire family to a hovercar crash. Today, we honor them as well."

Gaius was not expecting this information to be shared publicly and his face showed it.

"But! I am not done." Valerie shot her hand up in the air. "I have one more thing I must do! Gaius, you have been close with our family since I was but a girl. You have proven yourself to be invaluable to our family, and so, from this day forward, I hereby assign you, Gaius Anton, as my personal Queensguard, on par with Maya, leader of the Ophori, second only to me."

The crowd exploded with flashes of light to signify elation. Hands flickered as everyone showed their approval. Gaius beamed.

As they left the stage, Valerie approached him. "I protected you once again, my love. Someone was snooping about the Old Guard."

"Maya?" Gaius asked.

"Of course. I know you consider her your child as well, but I had to throw her off the vector."

"It doesn't matter. She knows my involvement, you didn't—"

Valerie grabbed Gaius's belt. "You're not seeing me, Gaius. I said I saved you."

Gaius pulled away. They were too far out in the open.

"I'm not done with you Gaius, I will be back," Valerie said before returning to the crowd.

"It is indeed time for celebration, Gaius," an old woman said, outstretching her hand for assistance. "For it is your obedience that has brought you here, as I promised."

Gaius didn't respond. His mood had shifted considerably once he realized who it was—a member of the Viceroy. When a member of their trio appeared, a clandestine meeting was sure to follow. You were to only listen and they were only to be obeyed.

"Be reminded that if you are asked to kill again, you will do so," she continued. She communicated in the old language, one that used a small light that could be turned on and off. Each word or sentence could be expressed in a series of flashes with varying duration. The language remained one of the only surviving ways to have a private conversation in Vedere.

"He was an old man. He was going to die soon," Gaius signed. He turned his head to the side and raised his eyebrows. He was protesting only slightly, but it could still be considered treason.

The member of the Viceroy was lenient and she was going to overlook his objection. "As I have said, if asked to kill anyone, be it Rory Davis, or your adopted son, it will be done."

***

Valerie was approached by Victor and Vega. This meant that everyone needed to clear that area of the courtyard.

"To be honest, I don't really care where you've been all this time, sister," Vega began. "It is clear you've changed. And I have my own thoughts as to what that means for me."

"Valerie, Mom will not make it to the week's end. We must prepare for Vega's ascension," Victor explained.

Valerie winced as he signed.

"It will not be you, Valerie. It will be me. It will take my dying breath for you to ascend," Vega offered. She held back a fit of coughs and slightly rubbed her nose to be sure it was not bleeding.

Valerie balled up her gown in her hands. "To you, dear sister, I was always unfit. I could never rule. And your seniority was never enough of an implication for you, no, you had to make it incredibly clear that I was never going to be Ægæliphi. You are so pretentious."

"And you are so vain!" Vega replied. "Your head is too big for your body, your thoughts too big for this family. We were never enough for you. No, you always had to have more. Do you want to know why no one wants you to see the throne? Because you are unstable, Valerie. You are unstable and you are selfish. You will burn anything that stands in your way, even your own family. That is not what an Ægæliphi is born to be."

"But you see, that's just it, Vega. I spent my time with the old women, yes. They changed me, yes. But they also opened my eyes. This is where you cannot blink—otherwise, you'll miss it: the wool is now being pulled from your eyes ... did you feel it, brother?"

Victor diverted his eyes. His skin bleached into a paler shade.

"I am not Cara, Vega. I am Amavi. Go ask your mother—"

"Valerie, I know. I have always known."

Valerie's eyes widened. "You ... knew?"

"As I said, you were never suited to be Ægæliphi. What our mother gave you was a gift. And this is how you treat her."

Valerie slapped her sister across her cheek. "You evil, evil woman. I will take *everything* from you."

Victor attempted to interject, but was stopped by Valerie's pointed finger in his face. "Don't you even try it, brother."

"You want to know what I did with the Viceroy? I contacted my family. I found the few your mother didn't slaughter. I took the cousins and uncles and aunts who were fed up and I asked them to storm the wall with me. And it has already begun. So don't come to me about your ascension. Brace yourselves for mine."

Vega began her coughing fit. It went on until Victor had to hold Vega down to prevent her shaking.

"I belong to a family of monsters," Victor reported. "What has happened to us?"

"You have two options, Victor Cara, Vega Cara. I am Æræya Amavi, first of her name, absolute ruler of Vedere. And if you reject my claim, you will be killed. You can run now, or stay here and die."

"You know there is no way we will leave our mother," Victor replied.

"Then prepare yourselves. Put your affairs in order. The line of Vo will end with you, Vega. My plan is already in motion. I will claim what is rightfully mine."

Valerie walked past Victor and Vega to reenter the courtyard. She didn't look back.

"So," Victor asked, "what do we do now?"

"We get our affairs in order."

***

Veronica, 183 days left

The altercation at Valvadus had alerted the Viceroy. Their leader, Viviana, had opted to remain away from the public for decades, influencing the nation of Vedere from afar. She was terrifyingly calculated, detached from those she was around in a way that unnerved many. She was young, brilliant, and fed up, much like Valerie. She had allowed the older women to act as they pleased—but that would be changing soon.

Tara, Epeë, Talia, and Sera were all a few hundred meters in the air, their visibility protected in the tint of amberlight.

"I probably should have asked earlier, but, is this your hovercraft or your mother's?" Epeë asked.

Sera engaged the autopilot and swung her head around. "I'm a student, not a billionaire. This is my mother's."

"Well, that's great thinking, Sera," Tara signed sarcastically. There was attitude in her wrists as her fingers formed the words. "When she realizes her vehicle has been stolen, they are going to track it. We're leading them directly to us."

Sera hadn't thought of that. She was the type to act first, then think. If she had to clean up the pieces after that, so be it.

"OK, yep, let's set this baby down ... now," Sera replied.

"Positioning reports were only about five kilometers out from where we're meeting Dr. Sylvan; we can walk that," Epeë suggested.

"Talia, you're about Sera's size. At least give her a pair of your pants and some shoes. She won't make it in that dress," Tara added.

"No need, my mom always packs an extra pair of clothes in here somewhere. I'll be fine," Sera replied.

They set down the hovercraft at a clearing just before the forest's edge. The quartet exited the vehicle and stood outside. Epeë was using a disk-shaped kokoto, a standard computer used for halo positioning. Talia was carrying two items, a small messenger bag and a water bottle. Inside her messenger bag was, of course, the journal, but also two other identical leather journals with identical patina. The idea was to ensure a thirty-three percent chance of an assailant stealing the correct journal in a rush. Talia hoped it wouldn't come to that. She peeked into the bag to ensure once more it was still in her possession.

"So, this is it, I presume," Sera signed as she held up her hand to show innocence. Her eyes were on the journal. "I first want to be clear and sign that I do not take your precious possession lightly. I understand the dangers of our meeting and the jeopardy you've put yourself in to share its contents. I want to give you my word that I will be responsible with the information you share with me. I know that Epeë and Tara are close-knit and have already come to some sort of agreement. But you and I are the odd ones out. I understand. But I want to be clear and make a commitment. I believe what you've told me so far, and I'm with you until you get your answers. So please, tell me what you already know, we've got a long walk ahead of us."

Talia slightly hesitated. She was aware that she was in a conundrum. She needed help; not just Sera's, but Epeë's and Tara's. She lacked context. It made sense to pool knowledge, but she also risked complete exposure as a result. She had reasoned it would be a risk worth taking, but now, walking into a forest with three strangers she'd just met, she couldn't help but feel trapped. Still, Talia swiveled the bag around to the front and dug into the bag to reveal the book. She opened it and thumbed through the first few pages before beginning.

"This book is a puzzle piece, OK? I know that much. The journal my grandfather kept refers to other people's journals almost as much as it shares his own thoughts."

"The others?" Epeë asked, stepping over a fallen log.

"Yes, see, my grandfather's book mainly outlines a contingency plan. My grandfather knew there was a spy among the scientists who were involved in the expedition, so he worked with three others to ensure their journals kept an honest account of what happened down there, as well as a plan for protecting the *real* information. The interesting part is that I think his journals outline where to possibly find the others and how they all link together. This all seems to be a part of a multigenerational plan to expose the truth."

"Incredible," Sera replied. "I knew there was more to that history lesson in school. So how far have you gotten?"

"Not very far," Talia replied. "There are several mentions of a 'precious' exchange between someone named Hören and the Sherpa, or maybe Hören is a group of people and the Sherpa worked with them. I can't say for sure. The journal isn't too clear about that, but what is clear is that my grandfather was being intentionally vague about what this 'gift' was."

There was a pause as the girls thought about it.

Talia continued, "But anyway, it's the name that's so unique to me. Hören. Have you ever known of anything like it?"

The other girls shook their heads. Stepping ahead, Tara chose to start leading the way.

"OK, so let's stick to what we know," Sera signed. "The agreement made between the scientists must have been a series of journals. Maybe the gift was another book? Hören could be a codename? Or an acronym?"

"I'm more inclined to believe that it's a person," Epeë signed.

Talia pursed her lips together as she squinted one of her eyes. She was tracking Epeë's line of thought, but something seemed to be missing. Something that was staring her in the face.

"OK, so the question now is book or person, but I feel like if it were a book, there would have been a different kind of clue," Talia signed. "Do you think it'd be possible to track down the surviving members of the expedition?"

"Well, what if I told you that it's something we're already doing?" Epeë replied. "We aren't alone, Tara and I; we're also working with a guy named Balien and his doctor, Dr. Fallon Sylvan. Operating off some information they were given, Fallon and another man named Quannah brought Tara and me to his lab. They are currently following another lead in which they are attempting to find the final descendant of the founder of the Cophi. A woman named Kamali. None of us knew much about her, and though I know my father mentioned the name, I was very young. I can't remember what he said about her. But at the very least, you should know we're swinging some serious weight. We have a way to access House Cara-level clearance."

Talia sharply turned her head. "Wait, so tasked? What do you mean? And how does a male doctor have House Cara-level clearance? That's not possible unless you're a member of the royal family."

"I don't know if I—"

Talia pushed down Epeë's hands to interrupt her again. She was becoming increasingly paranoid. "I am out here in the middle of the forest headed to who knows where, on *faith,* and I still don't even know if I can trust you." Talia held up her book, then hugged it close to her chest. "This is my truth. This is my family. This is a piece of me, a piece that is a secret. And when I lost my father I learned that I am a secret too. A secret in a world where we are told secrets can't exist. In a world where nothing is supposed to be truly be hidden. So I need you to be honest with me. Don't omit. Don't redirect. You must be as open with me as I am with you."

Epeë folded her hands. She knew that Talia was right. She had to make an offering of trust before going any further.

"Look, Talia. We were going to tell you, it's just ... the story is trippy, OK?" Tara nodded in agreement. "The doctor has House Cara-level clearance because he is working with a member of House Cara, Heir Vega," Epeë replied. Her shoulders lowered with her head and her demeanor changed, just like the way the sky changes when a cloud covers the sun.

"Did you sign that correctly?" Talia asked.

"Yes, Heir Vega."

"The *heir?* By the Goddess, Epeë. What are you all involved in?" Talia stopped walking.

"Understand that we are truly all seeking the same thing, Talia. Please," Epeë explained. "My father was killed. I wanted to save him, and I tried—but I was too late, we both were." Tara put her arm around Epeë.

"In the commotion, the doctor confronted us. He told us he was instructed to bring us to his lab. It was crowded. Ophori were everywhere, we had to take the risk and follow him."

Talia puckered her lips and twisted them to the side.

"When we arrived there, that's when we discovered he was working with the heir. He explained that he was receiving messages from someone claiming to be from the Underside and that he knew my father."

Sera let out a huff. "That's impossible."

"We thought it was too. We also thought it was impossible to clone a whole person, but we saw that with our own eyes as well," Epeë signed.

"I can co-sign," Tara offered. Sera's favorite eyebrow raised again.

"We saw it, OK? It was a seventeen-year-old girl in a weird tube-like thing sitting on a table. Her face was covered with a dome of glass, but even through it we could tell. She looked just like the heir."

"You realize almost no one has even seen the heir, right? I mean I haven't even seen the heir," Sera confessed. "Are you sure?"

"See me, I am telling you the truth. I know what we saw. And the doctor's story may sound like a stretch, but it makes sense. He said that the heir would do whatever she could to prevent her sister Valerie from ascending," Epeë signed.

"But for what purpose?" Sera asked. "Why clone Heir Vega?"

"For the purpose of replacing the heir," Tara signed. "The heir is terminally ill. No one knows this. I mean *no* one. Not even her own family."

Sera raised both eyebrows in amazement this time and tilted up her head to the sky. "Oh Goddess, we may be well in over our head."

"I agree," Epeë shared. "We're probably already dead. You know the royal family sees everything. But we are waist deep in this thing now."

Talia smacked her forehead. "Wait, hold on. You said the doctor and a young man went to find what?"

"Not what, whom," Tara corrected.

Talia shook her head like a bee was flying next to it. "Wait. Talia, you said an exchange was made, between Hören and Sherpa. What if we run with Epeë's theory ... what if Hören *is* a person? This Kamali could be connected to the Hören," Talia signed enthusiastically.

"How did you make *that* connection?" Sera asked.

"Think about it. The Cophi believe in the Residual, things beyond what we can see." The sign Talia used ended with her pointing at her temple. "What if the expedition uncovered something we couldn't see? Something that could change everything. It would explain where the belief came from!"

"It would also explain who our enemies truly are," Tara added. "If your theory is correct, and something we cannot see truly was discovered, it *would* change everything. It would tip the scales of power. It would challenge our very belief system."

"It would directly challenge the Church," Sera added.

"OK, ladies, slow down. Wasn't the Cophi established *before* the expedition?" Epeë asked.

"Yes, but they were not called the Cophi then, remember? Go back to primary school ..."

"She's right," Tara replied. "They were simply called the believers. They became the Cophi after the Sisters War."

"After the expedition," the quartet signed in unison.

"And that's it! That's what my father would always sign," Epeë signed. "I remember now. He hated how we spelled 'Cophi'. He always said that the Cophi was named after its founder. It should be spelled Kofi."

"We have to tell your doctor," Talia signed. "I think we just put a few puzzle pieces together."

"Yes, but we're forgetting something else. Something big. What is Hören?" Epeë asked.

Tara chimed in. "Let's ask Ava to run a query. Ava?"

Tara tapped her communication device. *Yes, Tara, I'm here. Running a query now ... sorry, nothing found. But I do have something I feel I should point out, I think you're being followed.*

Instinctively, the girls all stopped walking. Of course they were being followed. And it could be anyone. This was their disadvantage.

Ava continued. "I've been tracking them since your escape, but they aren't moving very fast. It doesn't seem they are trying to catch up with you; in fact, yes, they have changed their heading. They're now heading in the opposite direction."

"What's in that direction, Ava?" Talia asked.

"Well, no one but me. Let me call you back."

***

Valerie, 182 days left

The Jinaza of the Ægæliphi

The irony was that Valerie mother was the one who suggested she keep a personal journal.

"Something somewhere where no one else can reach you," she'd say. "A place where you can be your true self. A place we will never see." And here she was. She was writing. Valerie had always been writing.

And she had always been secretly reading.

Valerie was writing in journals since she learned to write and she'd never stopped. But recently, since learning her true name, she'd been writing a lot about timing. A lot about learning to live when you're not sure what you're doing. A lot about understanding destiny and fate. "What to do when your crucial moment comes?" Valerie had been thinking. When your time comes, it isn't always easy. It's almost never simple. You have your entire destiny lying before you and usually, it's the culmination of so many things; so many years of work, so many tears, so much fear. It's so much. You think about all of those things as the moment rests in you before it passes away forever.

And it's so unassuming. It's incredibly understated—that moment that you had hoped would always come—and now the question becomes, what are you going to do with it? What do you do when you're not even sure what to do with that moment? What happens when a moment interrupts your life and changes you? When you didn't consent to it?

These are the things Valerie wrote about these days. She never wanted to be the enemy. She never wanted to be against her own family. But Valerie was confused. She needed answers. It was in Valerie's moment of true desperation; that's when that unsettling group of women and their castle finally got to her. They suggested their innocuous thoughts to her in a way she didn't understand. They always had an air of deceit, but Valerie welcomed it as if it were a cool breeze. Valerie let that wind carry her to them, away from her family, away from what she thought brought comfort, though it never did. And when she stayed there with them, when she read their book in their crypt and did not eat; when she walked about the castle's halls and observed the women, she knew. Valerie knew there was more than what met the eye. She knew that she wasn't against her own family. She believed she was *away* from her *true* family.

"Isn't it strange how we run from one disappointment to another?" Valerie would write. "How the same thing can look differently simply because of timing? When you actually see it—when it actually comes across to you, it could have come the same way a year ago and you would have missed it."

Valerie never saw the Viceroy as an answer. And at first she felt she escaped one hole only to trip into another one. But this time Valerie cared less. This time she accepted much more. And, according to her journal, Valerie thought that it was this apathy that made it all different this time. Valerie realized that the same thoughts that had always crashed into her finally hit in a way that made a difference. And it was timing. Timing did that. Timing taught her about duty. About how what at *first* seemed pointless became everything in the world to her. It shifted her focus. Valerie exchanged her lens for something greater. She saw the same things in new ways. She saw her same family in a light she never had before. And their actions now looked inferior. They looked misguided. They looked like they had forgotten their duty.

Until the Viceroy opened her eyes, Valerie misunderstood her adoptive family.

"House Cara was never like us," Valerie wrote. "We have always had a duty. We were House Amavi, the Keepers of Secrets. We had a duty to the people. We have *always* had a duty to the people. And not once have we ever faltered. Not until I discovered those incorrect names in that cave. The only time we seemed to stray was when our family line started to care more about war and less about influence. We had a destiny that it seems my family forgot. And it cost us so much."

Valerie was writing in her journal at amber's light to be clear at least about one thing: that she would uphold her destiny. She would take back her birthright and she would not be stopped.

"It is in moments like these that all the things that make us similar diverge. We all as people experience pain and suffering." Valerie wrote. "We are all upset, tired, frustrated. There are three of us: those who face the moments that will forever change their lives and, because they are so unaccustomed to living, they pass them by; second, those who see these pivotal moments, but they do not care enough to take hold of theirs lives; and third, those who are so perfectly in their course, so decidedly capable, that when their deciding moment comes, they are already prepared."

Valerie was now convinced. She felt she had only two choices: A decision that brought her closer to your goals and one that did not.

As Valerie stood over her mother, with her eyes looking up at her with resignation, she became overwhelmed by how incredibly innocuous the deciding moment would be. Valerie saw her moment and she took it. When she visited the Viceroy in their castle, she saw her moment. When she faced the dark of the cave and found her bloodline, she saw her moment. Valerie saw where it would take her and what she would leave behind. Valerie *was* the third person. So she wrote, "I grabbed my mother's withering, decrepit neck and I choked her to death. I took my destiny into both my right hand and my left hand. I told myself—through action—that my life was mine and all mine. How I now live in the days after will forever reflect that moment. I will adjust."

***

Veronica, 182 days left

The kokoto bracelets flashed at exactly the same time. Seven bright red flashes. Someone was in the Ægæliphi's bedroom. In less than fifteen seconds, a hundred royal Ophori guards would descend on the annular-shaped room.

Vega was carried up the stairs; her servants skipping two steps at a time—twisting up the corkscrew spire and sprinting across the causeway to her mother's quarters. Victor was only half a step behind. They were warned and still they were not ready.

Sprinting ahead of them came the Alpha Ophori, the royal family's personal guard, as they expertly maneuvered around the heir and prince, continuing to gain speed as they rushed to their queen's bedroom. They were trained to arrive in under five seconds. Sliding to a stop, the Ophori approached the grand doors, seven gate-like entrances that led to the Ægæliphi's personal quarters. Their leader, Maya, quickly established a radial torphi of forty meters. *"I will be employing the beam. Brace yourselves."*

Seven flashes, bright red. This was the second ping. Red meant the Ægæliphi was not alone. Seven flashes meant she was in danger. This would be the greatest test of Maya's career.

The beam was one of the many Vederian weapons that used light as a power source. It emitted a high-energy focused light with the power to blind or vaporize depending on its intensity. In addition to this type of weaponry, Alpha battle armor—unlike traditional Ophori armor—was comprised of mainly curved mirrors, giving a skilled team of alphas the ability to reflect a beam into any given direction. Working as a team, one beam with two or three alphas could take out a small army. And it did. It was the brilliance of the scientist Dr. Faroah Sylvan's design that proved the ultimate advantage, turning the tide of the Civil War.

Decades later, it was still one of the most advanced weapons in the nation. Extreme caution was employed and the device was seldom ever used. Made of obsidian and platinum, the beam was a heavy disk-shaped object that was convex, bowing away from the operator. It had to be mounted onto the operator's chest magnetically and hand-controlled with two wireless gloves. Maya donned the beam and motioned for her troop to step back. She required the assistance of two other Ophori to act as counterweights when the weapon was fired. She was also clipped into the walls and ceiling. She would have to remain perfectly still while the weapon was fired.

Instantaneously, a silver ring began to burn into the center door of the queen's quarters. The power required to establish the beam dispersed the gravitational and magnetic fields in a specific radius. As a result, everyone but Maya began to float as they waited for an impenetrable door to open.

Seven more bright red flashes. This was the third ping. Maya was taking way too long.

Unable to wait any longer, Maya deactivated the beam, crashing everyone to the marble floor. She rolled into her landing and began to kick in the door, bracing herself against the threshold of the foyer as she pulled out two khopeshes, curved swords. *"We will beat the door down. On me!"* Maya instructed.

The women crashed into the door—even Vega and Victor helped. As precious seconds ticked by, they finally broke through the first of seven doors. Maya knew they were taking too long. Someone knew that initiating the security protocol from *within* the Ægæliphi's bedroom would make entrance from the outside nearly impossible. It was initially designed to protect the royal family from within, not keep the Ophori out. Maya would have to think outside the box.

"Seven on the queen, the rest out the window!" Maya was improvising. Seven formed behind her, and by now, nearly one hundred Ophori were now present. Maya had asked everyone else to rappel around the outside. The weakest points would be the windows, albeit still very strong. They would work on the windows and Maya would work inside.

Maya picked the beam back up. *"Stay on me. Keep the beam firing at all costs. Do not worry about me!"* Maya turned the intensity to maximum. She felt the heat of the disk push back into her chest. It began to melt through her armor as it seared into her chest.

"It's not enough, sisters. I'm sorry, it's still not enough. I wish it were enough," Maya confessed. The women knew what she meant. The seven that had been bracing her quickly ran around her and locked arms. They staggered each other along the path to the doors. Maya tilted the beam into the

first woman, who reflected it on to the next, and the next, and the next, zigzagging a more focused beam into the door.

The final door was not penetrated until the second woman had been vaporized. When the final door was breached, Maya had not only vaporized all seven women, but risked hitting the Ægæliphi as well. She quickly removed the beam and rushed as fast as she could to the Ægæliphi's bedroom. Her entire torso had been burned.

With tears in her eyes, she rushed into the queen's bedroom, forming a semicircle around the bed once the others arrived. Another seven leapt headfirst out the adjacent window, deploying their grappling hooks into the exterior as they searched for the culprit.

"Look what they have done to my mother," Victor signed. *"We are too late."* He fell to his knees.

Vega and Maya each tore their clothing and let out a shockwave of emotions that shook the entire group. Slowly, phantoms began to form of Vega and her brother and sister in childhood, playing and dancing around the room. When emotions of great magnitude were passed through torphi, the memories of those in torphi could be seen by all who were connected.

Before them lay the Ægæliphi, the covers pulled down past her knees. Her arms were stretched out as if she were crucified. Her neck was badly bruised with her eyes looking straight up into the ceiling. Around her, Vega and Valerie in their childhood sat on the bed, personalizing their spears with carvings.

"Vega, this is not real. This is not the present. You have to focus your pain so that we can see what has happened." Maya placed both hands on the shoulders of the new Ægæliphi.

Victor fainted, his memories disappearing along with him.

"Ægæliphi, where is your sister?" Maya asked. Vega didn't respond to her new title and continued to stare off into space.

"Vega, please, where is your sister?" Maya turned Vega around and shook her until her neck nearly snapped back. *"This is extremely important. I need to know if you know where Valerie could be at this very moment. If you do not know, we have to move you right now."*

"I do not know where my sister has gone," Vega replied. *"And I am sorry I didn't tell you. My sister has finally done it."*

"Then we must go, My Queen," Maya signed. *"You are no longer safe."*

The seven alphas who were suspended outside began disappearing as their grapples went limp with slack. One by one, each hook briefly shook. It was all Maya could do to turn back tears. She had walked the entire royal family into an ambush. *"Alphas! On your queen! Three before us, four around us!"*

Maya picked up Victor and rallied the other four around Vega. *"See me, this is it! We are sprinting to the bunker. If anyone or anything attempts to stop us, cut them down. We stop for no one!"*

Forming a huddle around Maya, Victor, and Vega, the remaining alphas shuttled out of the former queen's bedroom, out the foyer and back down the spiral stairs. Maya thought ahead to the glass causeway at the bottom of the stairs that separated the Ægæliphi's wing from the rest of the royal family's quarters.

Maya spouted orders. *"Priority one is to keep the Ægæliphi safe. Priority two is to locate Heir Valerie. Priority three is to—"* In an instant, with a flash of bright green light, Maya was thrown forward, tumbling down the steps, along with Victor, Vega, and two alphas. Two alphas were killed in the initial blast, buried beneath the crumbled marble of the wall where a perfect circle was cut out. Maya stood on shaky legs as she scanned the area for Victor and Vega. *So we make our stand here,* she thought.

"Maya! We can still make it," one alpha signed as she propped herself up against the adjacent wall. *"Two of us will stay, go! Go now!"*

"No! I've made my decision," Maya replied. *"We make our stand here. I am not letting either of them out of my sight. I will protect them."* Maya felt her control slipping. She was being soundly beaten at every turn.

Just as Maya replied, a second perfect circle was made in the side of the spire, only this time it vaporized two other alphas along with the wall. She looked at the remaining three and nodded. Without hesitation, two of them jumped through the opening to assess the threat. It was now only Maya, the heirs, and Maya's best, Haven.

"We won't survive another blast, sister," Haven signed. *"If we continue to the causeway we leave ourselves wide open."*

Maya nodded and thought to herself. She only had a few more seconds. She clenched her teeth at the realization that she was losing. She was beaten.

"OK, we jump around the causeway. Use your grappling hooks and take hold of an heir."

Haven nodded as she took Victor and wrapped him up at the waist. With a running start, the two pairs jumped through the spire's opening and took an angle to the glass causeway that led to the main atrium. They both took heavy fire and careened into the side wall, snapping their tethers, which sent them falling some fifteen meters to the concrete roof of the library. Maya landed flat on her back to protect Vega from the fall, while Haven and Victor both landed on their side. Victor was still unconscious and Haven was swaying to her feet, trying to reach for him.

Before Maya could give the next command, her party was hit with a flash grenade. Maya wiped the tears from her eyes to see seven figures in the light smoke. Haven had begun her offensive, but could be seen taking a staff to the chin and the knee before she was stabbed in the back with a spear.

Maya grimaced and balled her fists, holding them high and tight to her cheekbones. She took on a flurry of kicks and punches from a smaller but limber assailant. She attempted to find an opening, but had to remain on the defensive. Her vision was still blurry and she only had a vague idea of where Vega could have been lying, but by then it was too late—a staff to her temple caused her to see a flash of light as she crashed to the ground.

The smaller assailant knelt down to touch Maya's forehead. *"It was me. Never forget that. I did this,"* Valerie explained. *"And that includes the hand-to-hand combat. I beat you. Long be the reign of Amavi."*

Maya drifted in and out of consciousness throughout, but those words were etched into her mind: *"I beat you."* The words couldn't have been any truer. In the span of half an hour, Valerie had staged the most successful coup in Vederian history. With the queen murdered, Victor and Vega captured—if not already killed—it also meant that Maya was the most unsuccessful leader the Ophori had ever seen.

Overcome with grief, Maya looked over at the edge of the library's roof. *All I have to do is roll over the edge,* she thought. *Who would know?*

***

Part 9: The Etymologist

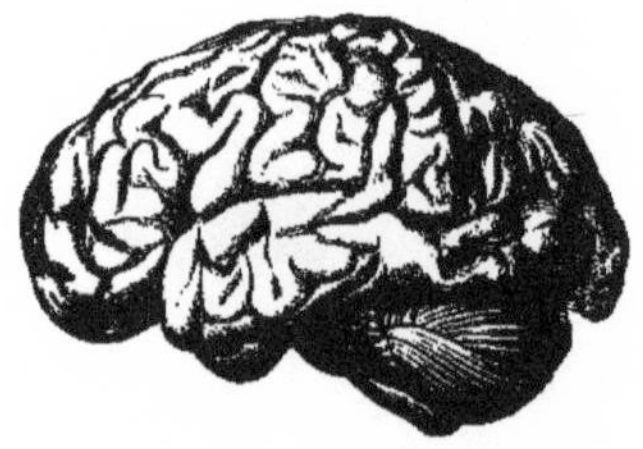

The Journal of Georgette Davis, 57,292 days left

Day 9

I have called an emergency meeting. We have asked our guests to give us a day to decide what we will do. This has been almost too much to process. I cannot believe all this is happening so fast. And we now have another complication: some of us are starting to become sick. We do not know what is causing it. We have our biological team on it. We are first checking for leaks in any of our exosuits or equipment.

Dr. Casei still believes the atmosphere is breathable, but may contain toxins that are causing some sort of reaction. As a precaution, we have asked everyone to suspend any testing outside of our habitats until we get a better understanding of what's going on. I've asked the remaining security team members to scout out again, just to our perimeter, to see if we can find any trace of contaminates. Goddess, it feels like everything is falling apart. And we are so, so close to revealing everything. Why now?

Though many of us are ill, we are continuing on with our work. We have been able to establish communication between the Others, or the Horeni as we have learned, through a lexicon established by the Nusdvagisdi. Their history is very similar to ours and is handed down through the generations. They expressed that they have known of us since time immoral—they just didn't have the technology to reach us until recently.

Which brings me to another interesting concept: reaching us. As I mentioned before, they claim that reaching us took the time of three generations. But their ability to manipulate matter is technology they claim comes from another, fourth race. I hope my journal entries still make sense. Information is flying a kilometer a minute. The last few hours have been nothing short of whirlwind. I have every alpha on our expedition on tasks. It is far greater than any of us could ever imagine. They are unlike anything I have ever seen—beyond anything I could ever conceive or even my imagination in my head. They are so unlike us ... and yet so familiar. So much has happened, I am worried that I will not be able to document it all. I cannot believe it. We have initiated first contact with a race other than our own. This has changed everything.

When the photography was presented to our alpha of Anthropology, she shared, "When two beings meet for the first time, there is a sizing up that occurs between the two of them. Each takes note of the other, often focusing on differences." She was reminding us that difference almost always implies a reference: difference from whom? She went on to say, "Look at me; I am no more different from you than you are from me. My hair is shorter than yours, yet only different in relation to hair that is longer than mine; size, in this most pertinent case, is only in relation to us. They never knew there were giants until they met us."

She was highlighting differences, but her point was more about comparison and what that could mean. The point of comparison is often unstated. As we begin identifying unstated points of comparison, we must also examine the relationships we are unconsciously establishing with regards to power. This is the most crucial time. What are we implying? How are we concerning ourselves? Soon we must ask who among us has the power to assign labels of difference. What does this mean for those who lack that power?

Until our time comes to that, we have decided to assist the two races. They are even proposing a number of them returning Topside, but given our state of war, and the almost certain xenophobia that would result, we are unsure of how to execute that suggestion safely. Until then, we will work. I will write more tomorrow.

***

Balien, 175 days left

Seven days after the death of the Ægæliphi

We scaled the side of the slope using our hands and feet. As the incline increased, we had to resort to flat-out climbing. We had been traveling for nearly seven days. It gave me plenty of time to think about how I was connected to Kamali, Quannah, and my adoptive father. I still didn't know why my memory was so shredded, but at least I had a better understanding. As soon as we left Damian we asked the girls to leave Denali immediately. We were to meet them just before meeting the Kofi's officials.

"The rendezvous point with the girls is at the top of this embankment," Fallon insisted.

"Embankment?" I asked. This was a mountain. "And if they are not here?"

"We'll deal with that when we have to," Fallon insisted.

"Fallon, Balien. Pardon me, but, there's been a development," Ava said.

"What is it, Ava?" Fallon asked. "Are the girls OK?"

"Yes, Fallon. You all will meet in approximately three hours. But that is not why I am calling. The girls made a bit of a mess in their escape and I believed them to be in danger when my scans detected someone following them. Yanne is looking into it with me."

"Well, that's definitely not good," I added.

"No, Balien, it is not. Shortly thereafter, the person turned the opposite way."

"What's in that direction?" Fallon asked.

"The lab, Fallon. Whatever was following the girls changed locations as soon as I began broadcasting to them. Since then I have adjusted bandwidths, but regardless, the unknown signal found me. It appears to be royal guards, but they have new colors."

Reaching into his pack, Fallon produced a rope, which he tied around himself first and then me.

"It'll take about an hour to get to the top of this cliffside. Ava, can you chart a course for the girls to keep them out of sight?"

"Of course, Fallon. I will keep you updated on my situation. I want you to know I will do everything in my power to keep Vega II safe."

An hour later, as soon as Fallon reached the top of the cliff, he froze like a block of ice. His body slowly disappeared as he climbed over the top. There was an awkward passage of time. It felt like forever, but could have been just seconds. I was then pulled up by the rope at a speed I knew Fallon could not produce. When I stood up, it was clear: there were about four or five women in tactical uniforms. I became paralyzed with fear. *How did the Ophori find us so quickly? Do I run?*

Every inch of their body was covered in a matching, form-fitting uniform. This wasn't a typical uniform. I was wrong, they couldn't be Ophori. No, this was something completely different. They were holding strange weapons as well; some had spearlike weapons with what looked like a projectile on both ends, others held metallic weapons that used the entire forearm as support for it, and others held swords that emitted rings of light instead of a blades. It seemed like men were among the group as well. I was definitely mistaken. These people were not Ophori. But it looked as if they could give Ophori a run for their money.

"You are six. Are there more of you?" one man asked. The communication was different, but still understandable. Vederian text streamed across their chest on some type of display screen. It seemed as if they simply had to think of what they wanted to say and it was converted into text for the reader. Very advanced stuff. Fallon remained on his knees and I did the same. He held his hands back, open and toward me. He was telling me to hold off. If we were six, that meant they already had the girls. If we even attempted to lie, something Vederians were notoriously bad at, they would surely know.

Fallon's best play was to be honest. "I am Dr. Fallon Saroyan of the Science Church of the Vael. I am retained on commission by the queen's heir, Vega. Behind me is Balien. He is the direct descendant of Kamali."

The soldier put two fingers to his head. "Bring me the boy," the male soldier demanded. Two of the soldiers grabbed me from underneath my armpits and dragged my knees toward him. He knelt down and pulled up his visor. He moved his lips as he spoke, "Cousin?"

He used the Horeni language. The same my mother had taught me.

"Yes," I replied. Something about the word rang familiar in my ears, unearthing memories I'd forgotten.

"Where have you all been?" the soldier asked. The Ægæliphi is dead. Vega and Victor are unaccounted for. The Ægæliphi is Valerie. The soldier smiled and raised me to my feet. "This changes everything," he signed. "We are coming upon a tumultuous time."

I couldn't believe it. It had only been ten days. How could so much have fallen apart?

The female soldier chimed in. "You act as if you've never seen your own people. Are we sure this is the right kid?"

A third solider kneeled and reached into their pack, producing two clear jumpsuits. "Put these on. They're for cloaking."

Fallon was fascinated. "*Cloaking?* How well can these suits refract light? Does it render the wearer completely invisible? How were you able to develop such technology?"

Fallon was ignored and we were taken to down the other side of the mountain into a valley and a cave. As we entered the cave, the air became increasingly warmer until we entered a clear corridor. It was unnerving walking underneath a clear tube, as it appeared the dirt could collapse on us at any moment.

"Please consider that there has never been a person unaffiliated with the Kofi who has seen our technology or our base, Udugigvdi," the soldier explained. "We're taking you to Command to meet Gregor Bastian. We will have the rest of your group meet you there."

We continued on, walking through so many corridors that I couldn't keep track of where we were going. It had to be circular in design, but it became more and more difficult to tell.

Without warning, we were suddenly hit with a flash of light toward the back of the group. Everyone stopped and turned around. The lead soldier's orders displayed across the back of his uniform in a sharp bright purple: "Sequester the boy, form a barrier!"

Three of the soldiers formed a wall in front of us and I was encircled by the remaining four. The bright light seemed to have been flashed to disorient, as smoke followed close behind. The lead soldier called for an adjustment: "I'm going Ghost!"

The lead soldier pulled a black mask over his head as he pressed the center of his uniform, activating his cloaking. He was completely invisible. The corridor became still as the smoke settled.

From the ceiling of the corridor a body crashed down on one of the soldiers protecting me. It was a slender person in a black bodysuit that tightly hugged her body. Nothing could be seen save for her eyes. Her weapons consisted of two short black sticks, which she pulled out from behind her. She stood feet together, then slid down into a wider stance—I had seen that before. Ophori.

Two of the soldiers charged at her, using their projectile weapons as cover. Black Suit jumped back onto one hand, dodging the initial barrage. She took the two black sticks and cracked them together, creating the same white flash. She then disarmed the two soldiers with a grace I'd only seen once before: with Damian at Seraphina I's home.

Black Suit handled the first two with ease, but she was unaware of the lead soldier who was completely invisible behind her. He stunned her with his weapon, knocking her down.

"You were followed," he signed to me once he pulled off his mask. "Get on your knees."

"Wait! Just wait a second here!" Fallon signed. "We were not followed! We don't know this person!"

"Oh, I think you do," the lead soldier replied with cold eyes. "I've only seen that fighting style once before. She's Ophori."

The lead soldier pulled off her mask to reveal a beautiful young woman. Her sharp white hair was box braided and tucked into her stealth uniform. Unexpectedly, she smiled. Her silver eyes and rich dark brown skin reminded me of the royal family. Her eyebrows were distinctive—pure white in color, but not razor-sharp, as most Vederian women styled them. She looked at me and rolled her eyes.

A man placed his hand on my shoulder. I turned around to see a middle-aged man with thick, curly hair in a long braid. He was tall, with large hands. He was accompanied by seven other soldiers, all wearing tactical gear.

"Slow down, Piori." He folded his arms. "It is clear she is Ophori. But no Ophori has ever made it this far into the Udugigvdi. I want to know how."

He kneeled down near her. "Young lady, I know that you're willing to answer my questions, as Ophori are to kill themselves if they are ever captured. You have not killed yourself."

She cut her eyes at him and blinked. She was pouting.

"Let's just start with your name," he continued. "I am Commander Gregor Bastian, interim leader of the Kofi, a resistance force against tyranny and dishonesty."

It hit me as she stood up; this was Blue, who Damian had fought at Seraphina I's home.

"My name is Christina Wynne, an O8 in the Order of the Ophori, force for fairness and justice."

"Thank you, Ms. Wynne. I know why you're here—"

"You do *not* know why I am here," Christina interjected. "I am here not as a spy, but as a believer."

This I didn't expect. What did she see that changed her opinion so quickly? Perhaps she saw something in a sæ as well.

"I could not disobey a direct order. Not yet. I want to apologize to both of you." Christina turned to myself and Fallon, taking a bow. "On my way to intercept the house of the sær, I saw a vision. I was in a jungle where there was a great conflict. I ... I saw a being that I have never seen before ... bigger than us, different in almost every way."

"I can vouch for Christina," Fallon added. "I, too, witnessed a vision."

"And was it the same?" asked Commander Bastian.

"No, no. It was not exactly the same, but many of the features were the same," Fallon replied.

"I saw a vision as well, just before the Ophori arrived," I added. "It too has variations."

"It seems we all were a part of the same sæ," Fallon added. "What does it mean?"

The commander asked the rest of his team to stand down and motioned for us all to follow him. "I've never been a part of a sæ. But I am told that they can be different things to different people. Our perspectives are all unique. Who we are affects what we see. This is true in life as much as it is in a sæ."

We followed the commander and his group further underground. We snaked a number of corners until we arrived at the Command Room. There were dozens of people here. We walked onto a platform overlooking six rows of workers, all stationed behind light blue glowing holographic screens. They tapped and swiped across the various screens. Some were looking at video from around the nations, others were performing calculations or studying data.

"A sæ is a quest into time. Særs have the best sight of all. A sight that can literally see through our three dimensions, into a fourth, and beyond. They can show you yourself, or show you yourself later in time. But enough of that for now. I think we have enough new people here to justify a full explanation. You all are standing at the center of the Kofian Base, but make no mistake: a building is not the Kofi, its people are the Kofi. Are we a religious group? Yes, in a sense. We worship the Truth, the Way, and the Light. We combat any and all activities that stray the people away from the truth. You may have heard us referred to as traitors and secessionists at best, and warmongers and terrorists at worst. We are neither of those things. We are simply a group of people from all walks of life who believe that no one has the right to be lied to—especially not from their own people."

"So what's the lie?" Christina asked.

"I'm glad you've asked," Commander Bastian continued. "The lie is simple: we challenge the idea that we are the race of the world."

The commander walked to the other side of a giant table overlooking the other workers and screens. "We are taught from birth that the way we experience the world is normal. But what if I told you there was a way to detect things you could not see?" Commander Bastian paused for effect. "That there is an entire unseen world that we may be able to soon detect?"

"You mean for years, you and all these people believe in something you never saw?" Christina interrupted.

"Faith is merely the substance of that which we hope for," the commander replied. "We hope for a world much better than the one we are given. We were not the first beings here. Georgette's mission made that clear, and we have had other races among us, hidden in plain sight, for millennia. We don't have all the answers, but I'd argue we have the most. Balien, it is your people who have helped us the most."

The commander walked over to me and placed his hand on my shoulder. "So, Balien, tell us what you saw in your sæ."

Tara, Talia, Epeë, and another girl that I'd never met were also in the Command Room. I hesitated. I was worried I didn't have the answers. I glanced over to Fallon, who provided me a light nod. "I ... I saw a being, no, maybe a person. A person I've never seen before in clothing that I've never seen before. It was a giant. I ... I think it was a woman who was much larger than the man I saw before me."

The commander turned his head to the side slightly. "A man? A Vederian man? What did he look like?"

"I'm unsure. I think he had glasses and short hair with a thick mustache."

"Yes, yes. That's good," the commander replied. He motioned for a member of the Kofi to take notes. "Balien, this is good. We believe we know who that man could be. You seem to be describing Rory Davis." There was an obvious shuffle in the room. Had I seen Talia's grandfather?

"But please," the commander asked, "please continue. What happened next?"

"Well, it was really quick after that and I get confused. I think the being handed a baby to the man. He took the baby and then I returned from the sæ. Seraphina I was clear that this was something I had to see."

Tears streamed down Commander Bastian's face. "This is it. We have our confirmation."

Fallon grabbed my hand. "We know that baby. That baby was Kamali."

I looked out at the group. Talia was near tears. Fallon had a serious look on his face, like he was about to perform in front of a large group. It felt like things are finally coming together.

"Balien, you saw what you saw because it was *your* family. Kamali was given as a show of peace. As long as she lived, she would prove that we could come together again. We must move forward. It is time. We built a resistance, we now have our catalyst. We will push back harder that we ever have before. We must unify now."

"What do you mean by unify, Commander?" Fallon asked. The rest of the group began to assemble around the command table.

"He means they are going to finally connect with the Halfalans, the Dalfalans, the Pureshi, and the Ajaxi," Christina posited. "Everyone who believes. You thought we didn't know about them too? The Cophi have been on the Ophori Watchlist for at least three generations. And we also know that the Cophi are not the only believers in the prophecy."

"Yes, that's true," Gregor acquiesced. "But I also mean the other races of the world. There is an older history that you don't know. One that the prophecy hints at—Balien, it was your family that was the first to explain a different prophecy."

"What prophecy?" Epeë asked. An awkward silence blanketed the group.

"You mean you don't know?" Christina asked. "You haven't seen? The Light, the Darkness?"

A soldier interrupted. "I know it, but I can't say I always believed it. It was a story that my father would tell. I think it went ... *and then there will come a Darkness; such an absence of light that madness and despair will swallow the Earth. There will be a Light. A Light that will lead the Heart. A Light that the Shadows will reject, a Light that will endure. And then the End will come; the World forever changed."*

"It's a prophecy that I didn't believe until I saw Balien and my sæ. I don't understand what he can experience. I can't even comprehend it. But he can do things I have never seen," Christina added.

"Things that I cannot fully remember," I added.

"Well, I am a believer. I believe in this boy," Fallon signed. "So what does this all mean now?"

"The young Ophori is correct," the commander signed. "It's time we call on the leaders of the original families. We plan a meeting with—"

A handsome young man with ice-colored eyes walked in from a separate entrance flanked by three Kofian soldiers. He was dressed very nicely, but his clothing was tattered and singed. Each finger had its own ring, but was covered in blood. He did not smile. His muted black clothing matched his dark skin and deeply contrasted his bone-white hair. His demeanor was somber. His eyes suggested he'd just seen something terrible.

"We are out of time. Everything has just changed," the young man signed, interrupting. I hadn't noticed that everyone who was sitting in the bunker had stood and lowered their heads.

"To those of you unfamiliar, this is Prince Victor Cara, of the royal family. Our highest-ranking spy," the commander signed. Victor scanned the room, looking at Talia and Epeë, along with the others in our group, to Fallon, and finally to me.

"Whatever you plan to do, do it now. It is not yet public knowledge, but my mother, the Ægæliphi, has been murdered."

There was a mass of people around Victor as his damaged clothing was removed and replaced. One of the doctors rushed up to scan Victor's face and hands.

"It was Valerie, without a doubt," Victor explained. "She told us she would do this. We didn't have enough time to get our affairs in order."

Victor ignored the doctor. "Vega has been captured and forcibly moved to the royal bunker by the largest assembly of Ophori soldiers this century has ever seen. They completely turned on their leader, Maya, and were joined by the remainder of the Amavi family. Maya was fighting for as long as I could see as I was rushed away. Valerie has finally made her move and when she kills my sister—if she hasn't already—she will have the full might of the nation. She will become unstoppable."

A stillness came over the room as many dropped to their knees in tears. Though many had never seen the Ægæliphi, their love of her and the security she brought with her name was extremely valuable.

"What could Valerie possibly want? What is her motivation?" I asked.

Victor walked over to a chair before explaining. Everyone else sat as he did. "Valerie learned of a secret. She learned of a terrible thing my family had done. You see, decades after the war was officially over, the real plan for victory began. My family infiltrated the Amavi Royale and killed all of the seated royal family members. All except for Valerie. She was never to know and she was raised as if she were a part of our family. By the time I was born, victory was all but certain, hence my name, Victor."

"But now she knows?" the commander asked. "How?"

"My guess is the Viceroy and the fact that she can sæ. I don't know how I didn't notice it sooner," Victor replied. "She left for months and stayed with them. It's my opinion that was their plan all along. For thousands of years the Viceroy have had a kind of immunity. They've been able to snub any oversight or scrutiny because they are a religious sect. I don't trust any group that has remained relatively unchecked for thousands of years. They have their spies just as we do. I think they always knew the royal family was switched. And I think they saw Valerie as a ticking bomb."

"So the question is why now?" Christina signed. "Why prime Valerie to make her move now?"

"Valerie's interests align with theirs. Though the Viceroy intend to keep the balance that the quinqu established, they know they have to move in the shadows. If they couldn't get an Amavi back on the throne, they would use Valerie to upend everything," Victor explained.

"In addition, Vega's health is in severe decline. Not only was Vera near death, but the heir was as well," Fallon confessed. "Vega is terminally ill. She didn't want anyone to know. It seems Valerie will get exactly what she wants even sooner that any of us anticipated."

Victor jumped up and found the best way for his fist to connect with Fallon's jaw.

"How dare you?" Victor signed. The piori and the commander pulled Victor away as I helped Fallon get his feet back up under him.

"I'm sorry, Prince, but it is true," Fallon replied, adjusting his jaw. "This is where I came into play. I was to supply Vega with her clone, Vega II. But it seems all of us have been challenged with time."

"Hey, um, so we were also being followed," added the young girl with Epeë, Tara, and Talia. "Oh! Excuse me, my name is Seraphina III, granddaughter of Seraphina I, your highness." She was wiping tears from her eyes.

"And us as well," I added with lowered shoulders. I still felt responsible for her grandmother's fate. I scanned the room for Christina. Her face mirrored mine.

"I think it's time we all share what we know. I know tensions are high, but we need to get a handle on all of this fast. We can regroup from the shared knowledge and then form a plan," the commander signed. "Doctor, if you can, let's start with you and your team. Victor and I can fill in any gaps along the way. Christina, are we in agreement?"

Christina nodded. She seemed motivated by the presence of a royal family member.

"Three weeks ago, we were approached by a woman who claimed to be the eldest sibling of Vega, Valerie, and Victor," Fallon began.

"Of course, at first, we didn't believe her," Tara added. "I mean she said a lot of things that made sense, but we were unsure."

"It is true," Victor shared. "I must commend the work you are doing, as you are here and you have the journal, something we have searched for decades. And my sister chose you all for a reason. I trust her judgment."

Tara nodded and continued, "Her instructions were simple—an eclipse is coming and there is nothing we could do to stop it. This was apparently discovered from the Davis Expedition."

"It also fulfills the prophecy that Christina mentioned," I add.

Fallon continued, "The plan was to evacuate as many as we would, but there are some specific leads that she needed us to pursue, one of which was to get in contact with the founder of the Kofi."

"We were tasked with finding Talia, Georgette's grandchild, and her journal, and were asked to bring her here to you. We were told the journal would be all you needed," Epeë added.

"And in our pursuit of Kamali, we met the Hidden King, who corroborated the existence of Veronica, and gave his life, in addition to Damian, to ensure we could escape a group of men he called the Old Guard."

The commander's eyes widened, then he turned to the center console to display a list. "This means Valerie has quite the army. Those men of the Old Guard were once my brother in arms. We became aware of their involvement when Tora McDaniel attacked one of our meetings a year and a half ago. We believed he acted alone as a religious zealot, which he was, but it seems there is more to it than that. Valerie has activated my brothers one last time. It confirms that their memories were left intact as well."

I scanned the list. Damian Cala, Gaius Saroyan, Tora McDaniel, Tudor McDaniel, Robert Daniel Durham, Timothy Aquinas, and Gregor Bastian. All of this was connected.

"This story is a generational one. That is something you may have been told before. I was a spy then as I am a spy now. I clashed heavily with our leader, Gaius, but I couldn't blow my cover. As I think back on it now, I think I can account for some of what has happened to you, Balien. Your memory was wiped. Someone didn't want you to remember who you were," Gregor suggested.

It was something I hadn't considered, but it made considerable sense.

"This is where I think we can fill in the gaps," Gregor continued. "This what we know: the modern understanding of the Residual and of sound comes from the extensive work of Justice Afauna and his mentor, Genet. Genet was the son of Kamali, who spoke of waves and pressure, a world unseen."

Genet. Why do I know that name? Why is it so familiar?

"We learned that Kamali was the child who came back from the expedition," Fallon shared. "It seems that we can trace all knowledge of the Residual to her."

I know that I have a memory of that name. Who is he?

"And that seems to be a pattern," Victor added. "Along with my team and the Kofi, we are aware of five individuals who returned from that expedition. With the advent of such a discovery, it is now clear why there was an amendment to the official record. It also seems my sister was aware of this as well. The five were Rory, Talia's grandfather; a child, who we now believe to be Kamali; an ecologist; an etymologist, whom I believe to be the father of an aide who works in conjunction with Valerie; and finally, a linguist of whom we still know nothing about."

Grandfather. That's it, Genet was my grandfather. I began to laugh.

"That's it," I signed. "It make so much more sense now ... Genet was my grandfather."

Victor cut his eyes at me and squinted.

"I accept this," the commander responded. "This story is a generational one, as I have said. It makes sense that we are all linked in some way. The Residual and the concept of sound may have been too much for a single person to understand. Perhaps this is why the information is fragmented."

"Look, I know I haven't said much," Seraphina III signed. "But I don't know anything about this word, sound." She spelled it out, S-O-U-N-D.

"Perhaps I can explain better. Sorry to interrupt, Dr. Sylvan, but these girls are just being introduced to this concept and it is very difficult to put into words," the commander began. "The history of the Residual has been known for generations within our culture. It is the religious belief that there are strange forces that surround our daily life. It has been claimed that the Residual can be seen, though it is extremely rare among Vederians.

It is also believed to be the reason increasingly strange behavior befalls the most devout believers and the elderly of our people. The theory is that as we age, we slowly regain the ability to 'hear.' About twenty years ago, your Dr. Sylvan was commissioned by the Science Church of the Vael to further study Vederian biology and the validity of the Residual. He was only sixteen at the time. I believed him to have simply been banished to pursue a discipline that would never yield any results."

Fallon picked up from there. "Decades of testing and a bit of luck over the years eventually confirmed the existence of a phenomenon we now call the sound. It was my life's work up until I met Vega. It is something that I now believe has been independently observed by many of the nation's minds over the centuries. I believe that each time it is discovered, it is snuffed out."

"And that is where the Viceroy comes into play," Victor explained.

"Because of the work of your father, Epeë, the discovery of this ancient word and its meaning has helped us better understand what the sound is and how it effects our world," the commander continued. "In short, the sound is comprised of waves that travel through the air, or similar medium. With the correct equipment, these waves can be detected."

"So all of it? All of it is real?" Tara asked.

"Yes, Tara. All of it is real," Fallon replied.

"Perhaps a demonstration?" the commander replied.

He took our group further underground and then over to a concrete ramp that spiraled down to a glass cube suspended in air. It was just large enough to fit us all inside.

"The concept for the cuboid came from an idea of your father, Epeë. This is where we first saw the sound. This is how it works: sound causes tiny movements of the objects that they travel through; we call these movements vibrations. When the sound is present, these vibrations can be seen. This structure is suspended by magnetic fields. Above us is an identical cube in size, but containing much more mass. When the two cubes are joined with force, tiny movements are made. These movements are initially extremely difficult for Vederians to see, but by recording them and slowing them down, we were able to study this phenomenon in depth.

We now believe that different vibrations correspond to different tones and frequencies."

"Frequency? Tones? What do these [words] mean?" Sera asked.

"It means there is more in this world than we ever thought. One that others have always known existed. Now that we have Talia's journal, there are many things we will now have answers to," the commander replied. "But let us continue. What else do we know? What do we know about Valerie, Victor?"

Victor stepped forward. "You need to know that she has somehow turned the Ophori against Maya—if Maya is not already dead. You should also know that she is aware of her birthright as Ægæliphi by way of her heritage as Amavi, and she must have some plan for how she intends to rule. She is also a sær. This has been confirmed by my contacts on the inside. This revelation changes things considerably. I think our first priority needs to be to reunify the halos. Make it look like we're building an army against Valerie, while I work to get in contact with my eldest sister. I also intend, if possible, to rescue Vega."

"If we want to unify, we have to go where it all began," Epeë signed. "Fallon, I think you know where we'd need to go."

Fallon nodded.

"We go home to Puresh," he replied.

"That's an excellent idea," the commander replied. "I'll come along with you. If we get the support of the Pureshi, we can get the rest of the halos to join our cause."

"What about your project, Dr. Sylvan?" Tara asked. I had completely forgotten about Vega's clone. "We can't leave her."

Fallon agreed. "Work with Ava and Yanne. Get Vega II and await our further instructions. Take Talia with you after you all analyze your grandfather's journal. I think the key to our next steps will be within your grandfather's work."

"And I'll need a bit of help, but I need to know what state the Ophori are in, especially if there are any remaining that are loyal," Christina added.

"I'll go with you. I haven't been to the capital since I was a little girl," Seraphina III signed.

"And so it is settled. We act. We send out or message. We need all of us," the commander concluded. "Our enemy is not the Ophori, no, it's not even Valerie, if we are to believe what Veronica says. Our enemy is doubt. We *can* do this. We *can* save as many as we can convince. I believe in Balien and I believe in Talia. I believe in Fallon, and Victor. I believe in all of you. It's time we find out just how many believers there are. Let's get to work."

***

Balien, 173 days left

Nine days after the murder of the Ægæliphi

According to the commander, it is said that though the physical birthplace of the Kofi was Hyleia, the cultural birthplace of the Kofi was a small country called Puresh, a dual-city on the northern outer edge of Halo Gabriela. In Puresh, most worked as farmers—even the women. When I was first told that there was a secret base of the Kofi at Puresh, I didn't believe it. It seemed too obvious, the land too open and sparse. It was rural and farther away from the capital. Its inhabitants were mostly people who had never left Halo Gabriela.

Puresh was the birthplace of Justice Afauna and his daughter, Epeë. Fallon was a native of Puresh as well, though he hadn't [spoken] with me since the revelation that Kamali was my great-grandmother. Though I had been honest from the beginning, I thought he believed I was withholding something from him.

"How could you not remember your own grandfather? That you were among the Sound-people?" Fallon finally asked. "You tell me now that you recall your mother teaching you of your foreign culture. That you all have been living among us all these decades."

Fallon had a right to be upset. It didn't make much sense, but it was still true. He felt invaded. I think everyone at the Kofi base did. And it was also the point that Commander Gregor was making. There had to be a slow-moving plan to help the population adjust to such a revelation. This was work that started generations ago and still the people struggled with the truth.

"I love my people, Balien," Fallon explained. As if they were not my people too. "I am going along with this to save them. To save my people."

Now, it felt more and more like we were at odds with each other. What if I responded and told him that I loved *my* people. I wondered how that would feel to him. Would my love for my own mean I didn't love my adoptive father's people? Surely it didn't have to come across that way.

Gregor later said that he was surprised that I was the adoptive son of Gaius Saroyan, but he had [heard] stranger revelations. I told him it was possible that it was Gaius who wiped my memory, but again, for what purpose? What we did know is that Gaius was still tracking us. Whether or not he knew he was tracking me remained to be seen.

The first thing I noticed about the people in Puresh were that they seemed a bit more weathered. They all looked older, though I could tell by other ways that they were not as old as they presented—their hands, for example. Fallon explained that Puresh sat on the River Ora, dividing the lush forest that jutted up against the Fai Desert. The word "puresh" means "where two opposites meet" in their written language. A name that made perfect sense as roughly half of the Pureshi people lived on the desert side, while the other half lived in the forest. Though they were all Vederian, they conducted torphi differently and had their unique customs. Their art was different. Their theater was different. Their body language was different.

Fallon explained that this was simply because of how differently they lived. The Forest Pureshi lived in the enormous trees that covered the Western landscape. Epeë was a Forest Pureshi. She explained to us on the journey there that she never even saw the ground—not even the base of trees—until she was sixteen. Most Forest Pureshi never set foot on the ground. Their trees were sacred to them.

Fallon was also Pursehi, but of the Eastern side. That is why his skin was as black as coal—not light brown, such as those who lived near the capitol—and his lips thin, like a slit cut at the bottom of his face. The white tattoo that stretched across his forehead was his family's crest. The tattoos on the back of his hands showed the type of work he did as a child, all typical features of a Desert Pureshi.

As we arrived at the outskirts of the forest, we stopped at the River Ora, which appeared much more like a sea as it stretched almost as wide as the forest we'd just passed. In the distance was a caravan on its way to meet us from the other side of the river. They were focused, regal.

"Are they staring at me or are they staring at you?" I asked as our horses slowed to a stop at the edge of the river. We'd chosen a less traceable source of transportation.

"Neither. It is more likely they are staring at Epeë. You'd never see a Forest Pureshi this far into the interior," he signed before touching his tallest three fingertips to his forehead and then outward to the crowd of people approaching us. He was greeting in a signed language I did not know.

"It's true," Epeë replied, taking her hands off the reins to show her palms to the caravan. "I've never been this far into the desert. I don't think any forester has." Her open palms were meant to display a sign of peace, that much I did know.

"Follow me and remain calm. The horses know the way," Fallon signed. He kicked just inside the back hip of the horse and we walked directly into the river, but didn't descend farther than ankle deep. "It was my family who built the under-bridge when we first claimed this land four centuries ago."

I looked down to see a white terrazzo bridge just beneath the surface of the water that allowed our horses to comfortably walk across. I noticed a clipping noise as we made our way across. I was beginning to notice more and more my sense of hearing as time went on. It had only been a few days, but I was gaining more nuance all the time.

As the crowd gathered, a split in the rear grew into a path for a woman in traditional clothing to make her way toward us at the center of the under-bridge. She wore a modern cut, which—as I was told—contrasted to the rest of the Desert People. Her long evergreen dress covered her entire body from shoulders to ankles. Her arms were completely covered as well, though you could still make out the tattoos on the back on her hands. "Proveyor," they read. She was the Pursehi liaison. A diplomat who represented her people in government, a position only women could hold. Her headdress covered the majority of her face and protected her from the heat of the sun. The bridge of her nose was very pronounced and her eyes were a calm, familiar blue.

"The three of you may stop here," she signed. Lips stiff, straight spine, shoulders back.

"Hello, Mama," Fallon replied. She nodded to him in response.

"Why have you brought a forester with you?" she asked sharply.

"Mama, this is Epeë Afauna, daughter of Justice Afauna, leader of the Kofi," he explained. "The boy is Balien Saroyan, the *Luz*. We have come so that he can be formally accepted. We have come for your help."

"My child, you have come because you need our blessing if you intend to use him to unify the other halos," she replied. She was sharp and quick-witted. She didn't take very long to respond and she was to the point. "Balien, I know of you. But do you know of yourself? Last I was told, you did not remember your family. That could pose a problem for me and mine. Sort that, and you will be welcomed into Halfala. Epeë, because of your father, I will not have you killed for setting foot on our lands. You may wait by the horses until our affairs have been completed."

Fallon gripped his reins. I could tell he was ready to rebut.

"It would be my pleasure, Proveyor Sylvan," Epeë replied. She did not press further, to my surprise. I don't doubt she was angry, but at times like these, I've understood tradition to supersede emotions.

We dismounted and followed Fallon's mother toward a dome-shaped building. All of the buildings in Halfala were dome-shaped, but this one was the largest and placed in the center of the city. We passed a gathering crowd that continued to grow as we neared the central dome. A path was formed for us. Seeds and budding plants were thrown at our feet. The people fought to get a glimpse of us as we passed. Fallon put his hand on my shoulder to explain in private, through torphi: *"There are some who believe that you are holy. Word has spread. They believe that if you step onto their seeds and plants, they will have a bountiful crop. As I'm sure you can already tell, it gets very hot here."* It was true—they were in the center of a desert. The ecosystem shifted dramatically from lush forest to arid desert. It looked as if this whole area used to be an ocean.

"Why didn't you tell me your mother was a proveyor?" I asked.

Fallon kept a hand on my shoulder as the pathway narrowed. *"I didn't think it was important. She is very traditional, as you may have already noticed."*

I had. Though I'm glad she didn't kill Epeë, I was still put off by her forcing her to stay outside the city.

"The relationship between the Desert Pureshi, the Halfalans, and the Forest Pureshi, the Dalfalans is very complicated," Fallon continued. *"Genetically, I suppose you could say that we are cousins, all tracing our ancestry back to one nomadic group that occupied the area of Puresh hundreds of years ago. For many of those years, there was forest on both sides of the River Ora. But, as one side of the river began to decline, the other prospered. When the elders met to discuss provisions, there was ... a disagreement."*

As we entered the center dome, the proveyor disrobed and stepped into about two meters of water. Nearly the entire floor of the dome was a large pool of clear blue water except for the outer ring. Bordering the ring were seats for at least a few thousand people. It was packed and hot with the bodies of a full arena.

"We'll continue the history lesson another time, Balien. This is your time now. Embrace it." Fallon motioned for me to continue.

"Balien, you may strip down to your undergarments and join me in the baptismal pool," Proveyor Sylvan signed.

The water rippled, presumably from the vibrations and sounds being caused by the groups of people. This seemed to be something the people noticed as well. It seemed the Halfalans used the water to understand the Residual, like some form of communication. I looked down at the water and then back at Fallon.

"Balien, my mother intends to bless you, but your memory must be restored. You will be held under the water for some time, please try not to panic," Fallon cautioned. *"The duress will trigger your memory. It will be discomforting, but try to clear your mind and let go."*

"Dr. Sylvan, what was the disagreement about?" I asked as we separated. Fallon walked around the outer edge of the pool to take a seat as I followed his mother to the center of the pool.

"Who should be baptized. It was Epeë's family. Not ours," he replied, knowing I didn't fully understand him.

As I approached Proveyor Sylvan, she began to sign to the audience.

"Before us is what appears to be a Vederian young man much like you and I. My son believes that he is more—that he has direct commune with the Residual and can gain understanding from its movement. If this is true, I then believe this young man can lead us into a new age of reason. But before he can lead us, he must be sanctified and proven before all. He must enter the darkness. If he can find his way out, we will serve as witness to the day a boy became the Light."

Proveyor Sylvan stood behind me as she motioned for me to fall back into her hands under the water. At first, there was nothing. I saw the light of the dome above through the filter of the light passing through the water. The edges of my vision were dark and I didn't notice them collapse on the center until it was too late—I was in complete darkness. I was trapped. I couldn't breathe. Then, something familiar. Something I had always known.

"What did you say?" she asked.

"I seek the truth," I replied.

"The truth is the light. You are the Light. Come to land with me." The voice transformed from a white eagle into a white koi fish. As she swam, the waves left a path for me to follow.

"Balien, I am not your guide. But I am your beginning. You are the Light, the example for all your people. You are the child of two nations. The product of a union unlike any this world has ever seen. Some will follow you and some will not. Are you ready for the knowledge you seek?"

I nodded my head.

"Then turn and face the truth!"

In the distance, far out in the ocean, a wave began to grow. What began as a small swell turned into a ferocious wall of water. I began to tremble. It was too much for me.

"Do not fear it!" the wolf howled. "Do not run from it! It is yours! It is your truth!"

As the wall neared, it showed its true size—it was a mountain. I fell to my knees and opened my arms. I turned back to the wolf one last time. "I can't! It will consume me! I will die!" I shouted.

"There will be peace, Balien. On the other side there is peace, you have to choose to accept this."

Though completely silent, the ferocity of the wave created a rumble that shook my ribcage. It slowly faded into a thunder.

"Is there any other way? Is there any other way to let this pass?" I asked one final time.

"This is your truth. It is yours," the wolf replied.

I fixed my eyes forward and tilted my head back. I felt the wave slam into me and my body went limp as I swirled within the water until it rose, taking the shape of a perfect sphere with me inside. I opened my eyes to see the white eagle once again.

"You are fully Vederian, and yet you are fully Nusdvagisdi, the last of your people," the eagle whispered. "Now wake up!"

In an instant, it all came back. Everything. My family. My abilities, my education, my history. I knew who I was, I knew where I came from, I knew where I was going. I was trained for this.

"Rise, Balien Saroyan. You have been baptized. You are now, and forever more, the Light." My vision was still blurry. I was surrounded by countless people. They were shaking their hands in excitement. Their necklaces bounced on their chests. Some danced, other cried. And I could hear it all.

"What is this?" I asked.

"This is the celebration, Balien. You can now lead the Way. You are what my people have waited generations to see, the product of so many." Proveyor Sylvan replied. *"We will follow you wherever you go."*

***

Valerie, 170 days left

The Viceroy explained that the Ophori could be activated with emergency powers at any time because their true allegiance was to the true ruling family. They only needed confirmation to prove it. With that small piece of the puzzle provided, Valerie no longer had to worry about Maya. She had her army, she had her spies; everything Valerie needed to execute her plan was in place. She warned the two that were left. She believed that she'd given her adoptive family their last chance for mercy.

Valerie placed spies at every palace door and every street corner. She even placed spies in Maya's precious Angel Elite. By now, Gaius would have killed Valerie's father and it would only be a matter of time before he captured the traitors and the materials they had with them. Valerie had won. But Vega still hadn't seen it yet.

So she told her to look at her and she Vega never blinked.

"Look at me, sister," Valerie ordered as their minds linked for one last time. "Do not close your mind off to me, you arrogant, arrogant woman. I need you to understand every last thought I force into your mind ... you thought you were better than me. You thought I was just some deviant who couldn't control her anger. A child who could never become who you would become. Well, you were right ... I will never be what you have become. I will be something different entirely. It wasn't my family that was out of place. It was *yours*."

Vega made no movements. Valerie told herself that if she was going to kill Vega, she would do so as Vega looked her in the eye. But Vega was sick. And she was waiting for Valerie to finish it. Valerie already had the information she needed. She knew Vega would never tell her what she was hiding. She knew none of her servants would betray her. So Valerie began tracking their movements months ago. Always to some little lab in the ocean. Always short visits to a Pursehi doctor. But by this point Valerie knew everything. *What more do I want from this skeleton lying before me?* Valerie thought to herself.

"I know all that you knew—for I have always been able to sæ. I know you lied to me. I know that our ancestors switched. I know that they went against the only belief that truly mattered. I know that we have a higher purpose that *you* ignored."

Valerie felt her hands tighten around Vega's neck. Vega was a husk. She had become so frail she had become their two hundred-year-old mother in a matter of weeks.

"You ... you knew, didn't you?" Valerie accused. She noticed as her chest rose and fell at an increasing rate.

Vega nodded.

"Of course Mother told you. She left me in the dark, but not you. Not her golden child with the crystal eyes. She never trusted me. *You* never trusted me."

"I want you to know—before your old frame gives up—that I know the truth now. And not just the grand truth, but your personal truth. I know of your clone. The *thing* you thought you could use to replace me. And I've already found her. I will kill her, Vega. And nothing else will ever be the same."

Vega closed her eyes to prevent her tears from streaming back into her ears. She would not give Valerie the satisfaction. Valerie loosened her grip on Vega's neck. She hesitated, the slapped Vega across her cheek with all her strength. "You are not to die. There is so much I need you to see—one last time."

***

Part 10: The Linguist

The Journal of Georgette Davis, 57,291 days left

Day 10

06:23

As I look back on it, we have followed our protocol to the letter. We provided gift offerings and miraculously found a way to establish communication. It seems all of our scouts and security team members are within their compound and those who were rendered unconscious due to the machinery are recovering. We also have more answers. The PLM was picking up a signal that the Others were using to contact us. They knew we would not be able to h-e-a-r it, but they had hoped that with advanced technology, we would eventually be able to find them.

We have our alpha of Engineering, Roman, working around the clock. We are leaning heavily on our linguistics team as well to create some form of device to help us communicate with each other.

We have also learned that the matter manipulation technology the Nusdvagisdi have brought originally came from a race called the Gan Dong. I will do a write up on each race and include it in the journal.

10:17

Just left our meeting with Vantalyn and the Horeni King. Their plan—it is phenomenal. It seems they put the might of their entire world to come to us and give us a fighting chance. According to the Nusdvagisdi, the quinqu is traveling the different planes of existence to eradicate the races once again. They came to the Horeni first, who agreed they would need our help if they ever hoped to fight back. So they came here to save us. They want to build ships. They are offering to take us back to their home. That is why the king has given us his infant daughter. They want us to be one again. Something the Nusdvagisdi tells us used to exist. A world where all people experiences all the s-e-n-s-e-s.

13:44

Those of us who are too sick to continue have decided to leave. Those who we have sedated due to their mental state are doing nothing to help us with our work here. I have made the decision for him, so that he will not burden himself with it. I have asked Rory to leave. He will take the others, Quannah and his sister, Atsila, a Nusdvagisdi linguist, and the baby, and begin the work Topside while we continue here. He has to convince the Ægæliphi to continue support us. For now, I am unsure of what that looks like, but I know I can trust him.

I just hope that Rory and the others make it. I fear I have become too focused on this work that I am forgetting the things that matter most to me. I will be leaving behind my family—my sisters and their children, my husband. But we have agreed that this is now more important than anything that we could ever hope to achieve. We cannot let our children inherit a dying world. I will not let anything stand it the way.

We have 57,291 days left. We have to get to work.

***

Veronica, 169 days left

The journey, albeit in secret, was much smoother than expected. In Talia's mind, it was a sign of providence. It was a challenge to smuggle anything within a halo and nearly impossible to go from one halo to the next. The pair's loophole was a supply ship that carried Ophori rations and supplies to each halo. Tara was in the Ophori academy and knew when the automated ship would land and take off at Halo Davina—it was her job to accompany the supply runs.

Back then, it was a time of fulfillment. It was the one thing all little girls wanted to be—at least at some point. The Ophori force was the pinnacle for the common Vederian woman. But for Tara, it was less about wanting to be Ophori, it was more about being powerful. About commanding space without having to lift a finger to enforce it. More recently, though, it was going through the motions.

Tara was four years in when she realized she didn't want to be Ophori. By then it didn't matter. The only thing that mattered now was how Tara felt; how could she reconcile her time spent toward a goal—time that she couldn't get back? How would she wrestle with the truth that she now felt aimless, how she simply followed her best friend around because that's all she knew how to do. She lived through her mother's wish to be an Ophori soldier someday. She lived through Epeë and her drive to vindicate her father. She now lived through Talia and her drive to absolve her grandmother and complete the work her family started. It was an uncomfortable pattern, and she felt trapped.

Tara came from a very traditional Ophori family. Two mothers, one surrogate father, and a life filled with training for diplomacy and discipline. Her schedule was meditation in the morning, training in the late morning, schooling until lunch, schooling after lunch, more training, then, more reading. Tara had never become an individual.

For Talia's part, there was excitement. Some of the first real excitement she'd felt in years. It was some of the first real emotion she'd ever felt since her parents were murdered. Her aunt always urged Talia to wake back up. Maybe now she truly would.

As a child, though, it hadn't mattered what happened around her; there was never a spark strong enough to restore Talia to her former self. Her aunt placed her in a preparatory school for young physicians. Talia completed the work, but then went home and scribbled in separate notebooks about what may have happened to the alpha of Entomology, or what the significance of the last name Oko was, or why it seemed that at a certain point her grandmother had given up.

That was the part that stuck with Talia. It was as if her grandmother decided not to press any further. Her journaling started to space out into separated and disjointed parts. And Talia did the same. She decided not to press any further. The truth was she had no intention to until meeting Sera, Epeë, and Tara. It was a sign of providence. The value she saw in a hundred-year-old journal was not only important to her now, it meant something to a lot of people. That was a new feeling. It was a fearless feeling. There was nothing that Talia felt could stop her.

They were now huddled inside of the hull of the driverless vehicle. Items were scanned using kokoto technology—so long as they stayed behind the shipping containers, they wouldn't be detected. From there, they just had to wait for their stop at Halo Raphaela. They would rely on Tara's memory to get back to Sciya.

"The summit at the base of the Kofi confirmed a lot of things for me," Talia offered. "You don't know how long I have waited for that kind of assurance. I've asked these questions to myself for years—all to have the answers spilled out in front of me in a matter of moments."

Tara furrowed her brow and wiped the accumulating sweat from off her nose. "It has to feel incredible—that validation."

Talia nodded with her signing hands still in the air. "We can really change the world. Once we get back to Sciya and meet up with the rest of the group ... we can really do this, we can expose the truth."

Tara nodded her hand in agreement. The ride was bumpy, but that was a good thing. It meant the motion detectors wouldn't notice two stowaways. As they came up on Halo Raphaela, Tara proposed her plan.

"I think we should do this as fast as we can. We have no idea who is watching."

Talia agreed as she adjusted her satchel. "You are a hundred percent right. We get in, get the girl, and get out. Simple as that. We can ask questions later. That reminds me, have you received any communication from Ava? What about Yanne?"

The supply ship landed at Port Astor. "We can sneak out now if we jump in and swim, no one will notice us," Tara suggested.

Talia shook her head. "That won't work. Not while I have the journal. We have to come up with something else."

Tara thought for a moment. "Why don't we just use the ship?"

They stared at each other blankly. It sounded like a dumb idea, but it was better than anything else they had. In fact, they hadn't truly thought about how they would escape if need be. It was time to come up with a proper plan.

"I'm not completely against the idea, but I do think we should consider it a last resort," Tara cautioned. "If I override this ship's autopilot, we will alert everyone in the area that we are here."

"And if it comes to that, they most likely will already know we were here to begin with," Talia added. "Then it's settled. If we have to get out of here fast, we break for the ship, cool?"

"Alright, let's go get our girl."

Tara hopped out first. Talia followed close behind. Tara stripped down to a sleeveless top and bounced a few times before diving into the water. Tara's head bobbed up and down as she swam to the doctor's lab. The waves chopped but didn't overtake her. She shuffled to her feet while combing the sand with their hands. She made it to shore. Now to get Talia.

"Alright, let's not waste any time," Tara signed as she took a crouched posture. "We get in and we get out."

Talia nodded as she tried to remember Tara's brief instructions for keeping the ship hovering. She spun the vehicle around to follow Tara along as Tara searched for one of the secondary entrances. "OK, Ava, let us in," Tara signed to the viewfinder next to the door. "Unlock the door."

Nothing. The lighting inside was dimmed. The lab and adjacent buildings were unoccupied, but Ava or Yanne should have responded by now. A few more awkward moments passed until suddenly, the door opened.

"OK." Tara turned to Talia. "I'm going in."

Tara rushed inside and used her memory of the building to find the chamber where Vega II was held. But Talia began to notice a few things from the pilot's chair outside the lab.

"The lights should have raised by now," she shared, tapping her kokoto.

"True, but maybe Ava is helping us keep this as covert as possible."

"I don't know. She would have contacted us by now, it's been too long," Talia pressed.

"You're being paranoid," Tara snapped back.

Suddenly, Talia felt a sense of extreme dizziness. She tried to keep her hands on the console, but felt she was blacking out. Tara felt the same sensation, though accompanied with flashes of white light before her eyes, disorienting her.

Talia couldn't hold on any longer. The controls were ripped from her hand and the ship was thrust into the main atrium of the lab, shattering the glass and bending the steel as it careened into the ground.

Through the flashes of light Tara could see the outstretched hand of a woman guiding the ship into the ground. Like a shockwave she entered her mind.

"You're right, Ava would have, but I shut her down," Valerie explained.

As if on cue, a half dozen Ophori swarmed throughout. They were wearing different attire, as was Valerie. The clothing was all-white and form-fitting. The Ophori had various markings on their hands and arms—also in white—with protective gear over their heads that covered their entire faces.

"You'll be dead soon, so I feel as if it's only right to bring you up to speed," Valerie continued. *"I'll also keep it simple and brief: I am the new culture. One*

that will replace the old. There is a family in power that must be removed. It is my duty to carry this out. I am Æræya Amavi and this is the end of the Cara Royale."

She motioned to one of the Ophori, who walked over to one of Fallon's consoles. She removed a pure white kokoto and placed in into the groove. A screen with Vega in restraints appeared.

"This is the beginning, my former sister, I told you I wanted you to see," she signed as Vega II—now out of her tank and gasping for air—was brought to her. Valerie took the girl by the neck and choked her until she fell limp. She was still naked and wet from the tank. Her heels slipped on the marble floor until there was no more life in them.

Valerie dropped the girl onto the ground as Vega stared blankly into space. Vega's head had been shaved and her face was a mix of smudged navy and deep brown from dried blood.

"Alright, who is next?" Valerie signed.

Yanne was brought out next. The new Ophori forced her to her knees, facing Æræya.

"I thought you'd be more captivating, I must confess."

Æræya grabbed Yanne's skull with both hands and kneed Yanne in the face. "I cannot stand scientists. Especially the ones who think they are so smart."

"I did what I did for love," Yanne explained. "You girls survive. Tell Fallon that—"

Æræya pounced on Yanne, straddling her as she choked her, bruising her neck.

Tara immediately sprang into action. She took a book sitting on one of the tables and charged at Æræya. She used the book to defend herself as she tried to grab a warrior's weapon. The book served as her blunt force object as she beat the shoulders, arms, legs, and anything else she could connect with. Tara jammed the book between the warrior's neck and collarbone and gave a swift kick to the chest. She spun to the other leg and provided another kick square in the jaw. With the Ophori warrior now staggering to the ground, Tara leapt on top, using the book to repeatedly land blows to the warrior's face.

Before she could knock her unconscious, however, a second warrior quickly rounded Tara and stabbed her first in the chest, then the forehead. It all happened too quickly. Epeë flinched as the jarring reality stumbled into her view. Tara slumped to the floor.

"Fully deactivate the artificial intelligence and take the Davis descendant. She has the journal," Valerie commanded.

Talia froze. She thought to run, but she couldn't. The crash had hurt her so bad she couldn't walk. At any moment, she believed that Ava would reactivate and help her stage a daring escape. But that moment never came. Talia was now alone again. It was a disaster.

***

Quannah, 167 days left

Balien sat wrapped in a towel on a concave disc in the corner of the room. This space, similar to the previous dome-shaped buildings he'd seen, was significantly smaller than the dome with the pool. Its purpose wasn't completely clear—it looked to be a place of prayer or meditation. Balien continued to scan the room. There was a large padded pillow for the proveyor to sit. She was accompanied by two assistants who were dressed neatly with their hands always behind their backs.

Fallon had his own pillow and sat beside Balien. He was scribbling, adding arrows, equations, and rushed diagrams into a notebook filled with copious notes. Their travels had taken them across three halos. They had come face-to-face with a sær, the Hidden King, the Kofi, and now, home—at least for Fallon. Fallon had spent almost twenty years of his life running away from his home—all to return back to it.

There was a lot Fallon wanted to say to his mother. He wanted to apologize for abandoning her. For alienating her in the name of finding himself. He learned too late that being an adult shouldn't have meant ignoring his own mother. He was a better man now, but who was he good to? Who did he have around him? Yanne had reminded him what his pursuit had cost. The irony now was having both Balien and his mother in one room. It didn't quite satisfy him the way he thought it would.

"We have blessed you and there will be conversation. If my people know, everyone will know." Fallon's mother straightened her posture before continuing. "And that means that Valerie will know if she does not already."

Fallon attempted to interject but his mother's look silenced him.

"If I am to understand you properly, with Balien now confirmed in prophecy, you hope to build respect among the other halos. With their support, you will then consult the Ægæliphi, to convince her of the eclipse. But you cannot get there without my help. I am to assist you in reaching the capital. Do I have that correct?"

Balien shook his head. He was now considered the *Luz,* there was no turning back. He was now the face of the rebellion and the hope of the coming storm. He was the symbol of what his people could be. It was now his job to be sure the Ægæliphi was on his side—if she was still alive. The rebellion had already begun, but it was now time to see it through.

"Yes, ma'am," Balien replied. "We will surely need your help. What do you propose we do?"

Puresh was on the third halo. Two halo jumps in an ever-growing hostile climate would be a challenge. Without an inner circle, it would be impossible.

"We believed in the prophecy well before you forgot who you were," Proveyor Sylvan replied. "We knew a member of your family would be chosen, though we did not know it would be you."

Balien was brought new clothing, such that he could be assumed to be Halfalan.

"It's possible time could be of the essence. But we have prepared for this as well. We will get you to the capital. It's a part of the pact."

"The pact?" Fallon asked.

"The pact was our contingency. We all had our instructions after the Georgette Expedition. We've been waiting for this day for longer than you could imagine." Proveyor Sylvan raised her hand as four people in all black filed into the room. "We always knew who you were, Balien. We were always with you."

Balien's eyes scanned the room back and forth as he tried to remember. Fallon straightened his posture and placed his hands behind his back.

"These four are of the Ashanti. The best we have and better than the Ophori. They are your personal guard and will assist you as you attempt to bargain with Vega or, if necessary, Valerie," Proveyor Sylvan signed.

Balien took in a deep breath. Sweat collected on his nose and behind his ears. His heart sped as he tried to process everything being said.

One of the Ashanti stepped forward. His chest was broad and his posture straight. "We will carry you to the ends of the world, Balien. It's what we've trained our entire lives to do."

"There are two halos between us and the capital. If we want to do this properly, we will have to take its seat, Arælia," Proveyor Sylvan continued. "We cannot take the seat until we have the full support of the Outer Four. Balien, we hoped that with your help we could accomplish that."

"What exactly am I to do?" Balien asked.

"We are still people of sight, Balien," the Ashanti warrior signed. "You are our only connection to a world we could never imagine. Seeing is believing."

Fallon stepped forward. "I have come this far with Balien. I have no intention of stopping here. If we have to go as far as the Reach, we will. If we have to go door to door, we will. Valerie is gaining more and more power. According to Victor, soon we won't be able to compete with her. We have to do this and do it now."

"Agreed," Proveyor Sylvan nodded. "That also means there is one more thing I must do. Bring her in now."

The door opened and Epeë entered in with two more of the proveyor's assistants. She looked to be as shocked as Fallon and Balien.

Proveyor Sylvan stood and held up her hands to begin conversation.

"To put it simply, your father abdicated," she began. "When your mother became sick after giving birth to you, we planned to do the unthinkable—we were prepared to appoint your father. He said no."

Proveyor Sylvan held back tears. "It was a disease that had no common name. The only thing common about it was that it was one of the last few diseases Vederian geneticists couldn't remove. It began with blurred vision, dizziness, and nausea. It progressed to a persistent cough with blood. Epeë, you were nearly seven months old. You never knew who your mother was. Your father was too destroyed to ever tell you.

"Your mother's life's work was a treaty drafted over twenty-five years ago. A treaty between the Halfalans and the Dalfalans. A concept for peace." Proveyor Sylvan motioned in five *urukoja*, traditional tattoo artists, who entered in with their needles, bowls, powders, and water. "Balien is now here and time is short. I want to be sure we do the right thing before this all ends."

Epeë stood with her hands behind her back. She didn't dare move.

"So much of the work has been without you all. This work has spanned five generations and an untold number of families. My generation was slow to transfer power. So our atonement, it begins with me," Proveyor Sylvan explained. "Justice Afauna was a good man. He was an even better father. He remarried for you, to give you the mother you deserved. But the work he was tasked with consumed him. Epeë, you as his daughter had your own role to play. Unfortunately, we were all poorly prepared for what would happen should he meet an untimely death. Your stepmother knew nothing and perhaps it was better that way."

Fallon and Balien stood in shock.

"Epeë, through your biological mother, the Dalfalan proveyor, you are the rightful leader of the Dalfalans. Your ascension is what your mother would have wanted. And I will need your help in leading and unifying our people. Stand—Proveyor Afauna."

Epeë bowed her head in respect. She knew what she had to do.

"I didn't let you into our city because I had to test your composure—one final time. You exceeded my expectations. You are your father's child, but you have your mother's spirit. You now lead half a billion people. Come and claim your destiny."

Epeë walked over to a reed mat in the center of the room. Her clothing was mostly removed to expose her limbs, hands, and feet. Her hair was pulled back and her body was cleaned and covered in oils. The urukoja worked seamlessly. They were synchronized as they prepared their inks and dyes.

"Each needle, each cut, every design," Proveyor Sylvan continued, "it all confirms who you already are. From this day on, when they see you, they will know you are powerful."

***

Veronica, 166 days left

"Our scouts have received information that a boy has been dedicated as the *Luz* from prophecy. He has a following," the Ophori soldier reported.

Valerie walked about her study barefoot. She was becoming increasingly agitated and perturbed. With her actions growing more and more sporadic, her loosely formed advisors found themselves still in the dark. What was Valerie truly planning?

Valerie was holding the company of only a few people: the Viceroy; Maya's replacement, Vana; Machiavelli; and Gaius.

"Define a following?" Valerie replied. Talia was brought into the study in a wheelchair, her forearms were strapped to the armrests. The back of her head pressed up against the headrest with a dark blue strap across her forehead keeping it in place. "And be specific."

"The Halfalans have completed some sort of ritual. It seems they see him as some sort of resistance leader."

"I know the stories," Valerie replied. "We all do. It's the prophecy of some end. It's propaganda to turn the people against my rule. They wish that I was taking over a dying nation."

Gaius stepped up with his hands behind his back. "I would request that we move carefully. Have we been able to secure the Outer Four?" Gaius knew they hadn't and that was crucial. He was the most experienced in political tensions among the group of advisors. Machiavelli's career was spent mostly within Arælia. The trio of Viceroy represented probably the oldest tenants of Vederian society yet remained the mostly mysterious and inexperienced with actually dealing with the people. And with Maya now out of the picture, Vala represented the newest generation of Vederian force.

"The Halfalans lost their way over two hundred years ago. We should have removed them then," the Viceroy added. "They have held their own beliefs since that family migrated out, and let us not forget it was their people who led the resistance against the people of Vedere in the modern civil war."

"Ægæliphi, we do not know what this ritual means at this time. We—"

"We know that it is an act of force against us," Valerie interrupted Gaius. "I know these people and they believe in some sort of Saint of Truth. If this is boy is their choice, they have made a grave mistake. Much like your mistake in failing to bring my father to me."

"Ægæliphi, if these people aided in the removal of the rightful heirs to the throne as you have claimed, then no trial is necessary. Let me take my best and we will blight them from the world," Vala retorted. She slammed down her staff and nodded her bald head.

"The claim is bound to one blood and one blood alone. A bloodline that only exists now in Æræya. No one else can coexist with her rule," the Viceroy clarified.

"So what is our position on this? There is no more covering up left for us to do. We still haven't found Maya, and the information the Viceroy has promised legitimizing Valerie's claim has yet to be published," Gaius pressed. To say he was skeptical of the Viceroy and their true intentions would be a severe understatement.

"Gaius, remember your place in my court," Valerie reminded. "My first priority is information. I do not tolerate doubt in my constituency. Will I have a problem with you?"

Gaius returned his hands behind his back and nodded.

Valerie turned her attention to Talia. "Don't worry, I won't have to torture you. Torture does not work. What I will do is open your mind. In the sæ, you'll tell me everything I need to know. Oh, and we've already analyzed your journal. Did you know that Machiavelli here is also a descendant of the expedition?" Valerie paused to think to herself. "I think that's what I will call you all. Descendants. Descendants of rebellion."

Talia shook in her chair as Valerie grabbed Talia's temples with her thumbs. "This will just take a moment."

***

Veronica, 166 days left

Sera and Christina were given a vehicle that the Kofi referred to as the Viper. It was a two-seat aircraft designed specifically for covert missions. Though illegal and punishable by death, what set the Viper apart was its powerful cloaking technology. Kofi scientists were the best in the field of stealth technology and designed outstanding cloaking vehicles and clothing.

The lead the girls were following came from Victor. His spy network confirmed Maya as somewhere still within the capital. The initial plan was to try and persuade her to switch sides, as Valerie's rapid rise to power was beginning to cause reverberations throughout the capital city. But now, with Vega kidnapped and the Ophori taken from her, it was possible that Maya was in a terrible place both mentally and physically. The mission's priority was now rescue.

Victor was able to escape with the help of Kofian spies embedded in the capital. The plan was to connect with those same spies once they reached the capital. Employing the Viper's autopilot feature, Sera and Christina had time to discuss their next moves.

"So it's like you go into some kind of trance?" Christina asked.

"I suppose you could describe it as that," Sera replied. "But it's really much more like another way of seeing. Technically speaking, a sæ is just another form of sight, one that's just not limited by the typical physical laws. Just as you can look out and see buildings in the distance, my ability to see reaches so far that it pierces through time and space."

"So then, how do you ... arrive? I'm sorry, I don't know the proper word."

Sera took a sheet of paper that was tucked under the Viper's console and a pen that was holding up her hair. She drew some straight lines on the sheet of paper that initially looked as if they didn't connect. She then drew a small circle in the center of those lines.

"This is how we see the world. Each line represents an action, or a person, or a thought. In reality, they are all the same matter. Even our thoughts are matter. Just a different type."

"OK, I think I'm following."

Sera folded the paper a few times and pierced the folded paper with her pen.

"That was the sæ," she explains. "The type of sight I have is so strong that it pierces the fabric of space-time."

Sera lifted up each sheet of the folded paper one by one. "Now, as you can see, when the paper is folded, the lines seem to form one connected line." Sera then completely unfolded the paper. The indentations from the folds connected all the lines and the hole she pierced was in the center of it all, with the circle orbiting it. "So now, I can see all of it. Thoughts, actions, people. The circle I drew is something we call our sphere of influence. It can only be so large and its size depends on the person. In this way, we cannot see everything all of the time. Just our sphere of influence."

"That's ... that's amazing," Christina responded. "How did you learn all of this?"

"My grandmother taught me. Many believed she was the most powerful sær in the world. She had the largest sphere of influence in the nation. She was hiding in Valvadus, waiting for Balien, I suppose. She knew what she had to do."

Christina quickly swallowed. The old woman's house that she and her Ophori sisters raided—that was Sera's grandmother. What part did Christina play in her death? She wasn't sure.

"I see no reason now not to live in my truth. Sæ is a trait that is genetic. I didn't want to be a political tool like my mother, but with all I've learned maybe I can do something truly worth something. If Balien can do even half of what is said he can do—it could change everything."

Christina nodded sheepishly. "You know, I—I was there. I took my assignment and did as I was asked. I promise when we arrived, it appeared as if your grandmother was already dead."

"She only had so much strength left. She spent it on what she felt was most important. I understand," Sera replied. "She taught me the most important lesson of all: that true connection can provide us will all the answers that we could ever need in life."

"That's great advice," Christina replied.

"You know what! You could help me." Sera bounced in her seat. "You are Ophori, you could be my conduit. It's possible I could find Maya through your thoughts and memories!"

Christina froze. "I don't know if that's the best thing ... "

"What do you mean?" Sera responded. "How else are going to find Maya quickly?"

"Look," Christina interrupted. "I don't want you in my head. I don't want you seeing me or whatever it's called."

"I understand that it can be intrusive. But I think you know this is going to be the safest way. You don't know me, but I'm already trusting you. I'm letting an Ophori take me to the capital. A capital that is now under a military coup."

Sera made a strong point. But Christina also knew that if she participated in the sæ, Sera would see what happened to her grandmother. Not only that, but there was no telling what else Sera would find. But Christina was committed. She knew at some point her trust would be called into question. She would have to prove her loyalty. If she waited too long to tell the truth, it would only make matters worse down the road.

"Fine," Christina responded. "Just tell me what I have to do."

"All you have to do is look at me. Do not close your eyes. Take my hand. And believe it or not, you will be the one guiding us, not me."

Christina took Sera's hand. At first she didn't see anything. Everything looked the same, until slowly the edges of her vision began to curve and turn darker. It looked as if she were heading into a tunnel. Sera's eyes began to lighten—retina, pupil, iris, everything—until her entire eye was a pure and glowing white.

"We will be going away now," Sera explained. It was an odd thing. She wasn't signing, it wasn't torphi. It was like she was a part of Christina's mind.

"Wait, Sera, no. Look, whatever you see, I'm sorry, I'm so sorry." It was too late, they were already in Seraphina I's home.

"We cannot stay long. We will both be lost to time," Sera explained. Her hair floated and her eyes still glowed. The rest of the world around her was muted and gray. Only she was of brilliant colors and sharp lines. Sera's tears formed and floated off her eyes like bubbles in the sky. "I already know what happened here. I don't have the time I want to cry, so we will go on," Sera said.

The pair walked forward, from one type of room to another. They used the same door, but everything was so fluid. It was like a dream. Christina began to realize where she was. It was her bedroom. She was seven and it was late. She was already asleep but her father had snuck in.

"Oh God," Christina yelped. *"Please! We cannot stay here!"* Christina rushed to the window of the bedroom and leapt out. She felt a warm hand on her shoulder as she sensed she was falling—until suddenly she wasn't.

"I can't help you travel; your mind will take us where you want it to go," Sera explained. "Your mind is stronger than me in the sæ. Help me. Remember why we are traveling."

Christina noticed grass beneath her feet. She was in a forest. A forest she knew very well. This is where she completed her Ophori survival training.

"This is good," Sera encouraged. "Who else is here? Take me there."

Other Ophori came out of the bushes. Their skin was painted tar black and their clothing was camouflaged. They all held spears and were accompanied by levitating kokotos that acted as drones.

"Alpha squadron to the north. Beta, flank around to the east. Gamma, up the gut." That was Maya. She was a head and shoulder above any of other warriors. Her hair was shorter and curly like cotton. Her hips were wide and her stance wider. She crouched low and gave hand commands.

Suddenly, an arrow struck an Ophori just off the front line. "Suppress their fire!"

"We went too far. We took out so many we had to lie about what happened to them," Christina confessed. *"We did a very bad thing here."*

"Where are we?" Sera asked.

"We are in the Gobi forest. Halo Michaela, suppressing Kofian advances."

"And that is where we will find Maya," Sera replied. *"You did well."*

***

Quannah, 35,328 days left

It was a small group. It felt much more humble of a group when huddled together in an attic at amberlight. It was Kamali's home. Her husband remained downstairs with their children as he doubled as lookout in case any of the others were followed.

"It all begins with us. We are the first generation," Kamali signed with lowered eyebrows. "It has to start with us and we have to do our best."

The others sat on large plush pillows with tensed arms and legs. At any moment, they might have to run for their lives.

"It starts with us, but it will take decades to complete. We have to get this right. We're fighting against time."

The group nodded. Seven families were represented in the group: Afauna, Davis, Durham, Sylvan, Bastian, Saroyan, and Lee.

"We are the only ones who truly know what was discovered that day Georgette discovered that crash site. We are the only ones who have the artifacts. We have to keep them separate until the time comes. Our families each have a task. Are we in agreement?"

It was the early days. Hearing was not a myth or a concept. It was a culture, an entire people, with Kamali as its matriarch. She was the proof, but truths like hers still had to be hidden. And with knowledge of what was to come, the work that had to be done now was more important than ever. It would span decades beyond her and the others.

"The Nusdvagisdi will help us. I know there are not many of them, but their lifespans are much, much longer than ours. Quannah, I promised he and his wife would help us. Vantalyn is still down below with the others," a Davis family member added.

"Their people are all but extinct. Are we certain we can trust them?" a Bastian family member asked.

"We don't have a choice, without them, we will not be able to complete the codexes. And if that is not completed, we may never be able to communicate with the other races ever again," Kamali reasoned. She stood up to be sure everyone could see her.

"We all know the parts we have to play. We all know what we have to share with our children—our children's children. We know the truth of Georgette's mission. We have spread this truth among you all. You each have your notes, your journals and artifacts. It will be through you all and the physical proof that you've retained, that will help us save the lives of billions."

Everyone nodded.

"So let's get started."

***

ACT III

The Prestige

Part 11: Vedere

The History of the Vedere

***

In the beginning, there was the quinqu. Before the quinqu, there was nothing. All that exists owes its life to them. As gods in their own right, the five came together, creating beings never before seen, and when it came time to make woman, the world was forever changed. This being, woman, would be wise, unmoving, astounding. Vedere. Hören, Gan Dong, Odore, and Nusdvagisdi. The quinqu came together. They bickered over whose likeness would be used for woman. Vedere, the wisest of the gods, offered to step aside, to make the choice easier. By this act, the gods were motivated to compromise. As a result, Vedere emerged as the most suitable template. This new being, called Vedere, the first woman, would be the god's greatest creation. For Vedere sees all. Nothing can hide from her. Vederians would experience the world through Vedere ... through sight. This is the truth. This is how the Earth began. We are Vedere. And we are the greatest of the world.

***

Rory, 57,921 days left

We left immediately. By the Goddess, Georgette and her team will have the fight of their lives ahead of them. This land is untamed. It will try to swallow them whole once again. They will have to fight back if they want to complete their work.

I've taken as many as I can with me. Those who are coughing too hard are going to have to wait. We will figure out a plan to come back for them, but we have to keep moving. I have got to get Topside as soon as possible. Everyone has to know what we've seen here.

***

The Journal of Jayla Oko, 57,294 days left
Special Report to Viceroy, Day 7

It is now clear that we are not alone—though there are many of us within the group still too afraid to admit it. There are ruins here that the archeologist believes are thousands of years old. There are tools here so advanced that a select few of us believe they had to have been conceived in a place and time far, far from here. We're still going through the artifacts, but I've already seen enough. Viceroy, you were right. None of this information can leave. I'm going to have to do what I never wanted to do.

I've contaminated our rations as you've instructed, including my own. No one will leave, as you have instructed. This will be my final message. Please do not tell my family what I have done.

In honor of the quinqu,

Jayla Oko

***

Veronica, 164 days left

"You know how I prefer it. It is all ruined now." Machiavelli shifted his weight over to the left side of the bed, allowing his feet to dangle. "What is this?" he signed as he grabbed one of the small mirrors off of his nightstand.

Machiavelli's personal quarters, referred to many as "The Looking Glass," featured wall-to-wall mirrors that surrounded his circular room. He was known to be obsessive over symmetry and physical beauty—a trait not all that uncommon among Vederians. Symmetry was everything. Nothing came before personal beauty to the common Vederian, but Machiavelli was obsessive. He kept a mirror of every shape, size, and magnification within arm's reach.

"I have lost three eyelashes," Machiavelli carefully inspected his right eye before turning to his servant.

"Why are you even here?" he asked.

"Sir, you have been summoned by the Ægæliphi," the servant signed sheepishly.

"Summoned for what?" Machiavelli asked, knowing the servant wouldn't know.

"Sir, please, follow me."

Reluctantly, Machiavelli followed. He found himself nearly chasing the servant as the small man rounded each corner in a hurry. They were headed below the royal family's home, beneath the crypt to the catacombs where generations of royal family members went to hide during the numerous conflicts they had seen.

It was the same chasm where he first saw Valerie commune with the Viceroy. They stood before her as she kneeled and they entered her mind and spoke.

"You will shave your head and remove all clothing. Present yourself as the dirt you are before us and in our mercy we will change you. You will be reborn in the fire and emerge as the being we always intended for you to be."

Machiavelli winced at the thought. It was true that Valerie's family was slaughtered and replaced, but he had always seen the plan as an endeavor to usurp the current rule to improve upon it. The documents and records were clear. What more did Valerie have to do?

"This ritual is necessary for you to take back your regality," the Viceroy continued.

A conflict began to pang in Machiavelli. He had wanted nothing more than for Valerie to be what she was always intended to be, but now, he was no longer sure of what the cost would be for her to accomplish that. Something in him wanted her to stop, but he couldn't move. He had sensed a coming transformation, but he never thought it would be physical.

Valerie rose and walked toward a hexagonal pit that was full of boiling tar.

"I am ready," Valerie signed, though her fear was evident.

"Be strong, child," Machiavelli thought to himself. He wondered if Valerie could even see him from where the servant directed him to stand.

Valerie stepped into the pit and crouched down to wrap her arms around her legs. She closed her eyes, completely covered in the smooth, pitch-black material.

"Never close your eyes. Keep them open!" the Viceroy insisted. *"It is your time now."*

As Valerie attempted to stand, four shadowy figures with long white hoses formed behind her. Before she could react, she was sprayed with scalding hot steam. She shook as the steam pillowed up into a cloud engulfing her body. She was covered with a mixture of crushed onyx, aloe, and water. When the steam cleared, she was fetal and motionless. Machiavelli rushed to her as the Viceroy offered no aid.

"It is up to you to ensure she survives the healing," the Viceroy signed.

Machiavelli examined her. Her skin was black and cracked from burns. With her eyes closed, she looked to be a dead corpse covered in ash.

Machiavelli wasn't sure if he had made a mistake in trusting the Viceroy, but it was clearly too late.

One of the Viceroy stood forward and signed: *"Rise, Æræya! For you were robbed of the title Ægæliphi! Stand reborn as the true ruler of the known world! No longer are you Ægæliphi, but a leader in direct commune with the quinqu!"* The corners of her mouth cracked open into a smile as Valerie remained in the soot. Slowly, with Machiavelli's help, Valerie stood, shaking as she placed her body's weight back under her. She was different now. She had changed completely. It was Æræya who now stood before them, stronger and prepared.

"You will find that your mind is stronger than it has ever been. Consider it a gift of the quinqu. You are a sœr. Be strong in our will and nothing will stand in your way."

Æræya looked to be an aged statue—until she opened her eyes. Their piercing iciness stared back with an unnerving gaze. Her eyes were the only proof that she was alive. The contrast against her new skin color was disturbing. She was as black as coal and ash. A living shadow. Her etiolated body finally matched how her heart had always felt. She unfolded her arms and stood straight, though her chin still rested on her clavicle.

"Bring a veil. It is time," she commanded. Her signs were sharp and clipped at the ends. She was straight and to the point. *"First, I am no longer the woman you once knew. I have burned away to become something greater. I have established a permanent connection with the Viceroy through torphi and they shall advise me as they deem so. From this point further, no one will never address me directly. They will address you and you will address me. Is that understood?"*

"Yes, My Queen," Machiavelli replied.

"I was approached in the flames and I have emerged omniscient. I am pure power, Valerie is dead." Smoke still rose from Æræya's skin.

Æræya then, curiously, sat down with her legs folded onto each other. She slowly floated midair.

"There is only one truth, and it is mine. The quinqu have restored my birthright and I will be the Lawbringer."

Quinqu. It was a sign that Æræya spelled out with her fingers. Machiavelli had only seen it once before, in a set of scientific papers that his father had written.

"There is an end that will come. A time no one in our world is ready to face. But I am merciful and I will save our people. And we will emerge from the Darkness anew," Æræya signed. *"Come, we have work to do."*

***

Veronica, 164 days left

The nation of Vedere had seven distinct governments—each one representing one of the circular continents that made up their world. Each halo was governed by a proveyor, a leader who was a member of the First Family to colonize that continent. Though traditionally the Ægæliphi held virtually absolute power, one of the compromises that ended the civil war was a voting system in which matters that directly impacted the halos could be put to a vote. Each ræ or proveyor who represented her halo could bring about a vote with the weight of II (2). The Ægæliphi was given the weight of V (5). The system was designed so that the only way an Ægæliphi's vote could be carried out was if she had the votes of two other halos. Without two other supporters, the Ægæliphi could be outweighed.

Years ago, Ægæliphi Vaia built a courtyard where she could commune with her proveyors. It became tradition to use Vaia's Courtyard as the meeting area for the nation's government. Many changes occurred in that courtyard. This would be the final one.

When Æræya stood before the proveyors, the entire constituency was mortified by what they saw. Obsidian skin that was cracked wherever muscles needed to move, her eyes piercing through a pure white veil that went the length of her body, her movements slow and controlled. Many wretched at the sight.

"I bring forth an offering of peace. An offering to keep our people safe, to give them freedom," Æræya began. *"I bring forth your salvation. I have been transformed. And I can do a new thing. Behold."*

Æræya raised her hands and closed her eyes. Among the proveyors in the courtyard was Proveyor Sylvan, along with a few others now loyal to Balien's cause.

"We will die here today," Proveyor Sylvan suggested through telepathy. *"Many of us will have to take a stand here, but it cannot be all of us. You need to leave—now. I know a coup when I see one."*

Epeë nodded, but hesitated before she could leave. She squeezed Proveyor Sylvan's hand once last time. *"I owe you too much."*

Proveyor Sylvan shook her head. *"You owe me nothing. You were royal the day you were born. Now, when the time is right, you run."*

Using telepathy, Æræya lifted a decorative vase off its platform and released it—allowing it to crash to the ground.

Epeë felt an odd sensation creep up her spine. The kind of feeling you get when you sense someone is in the room, but you can't see them.

"I have been transformed. And I have become the first of a new race. Let me show you what I sæ," Æræya continued. *"My telepathy's advance is just one of the many gifts I intend to use to rule, my ability to sæ is another. I only require you to kneel."*

Conversation erupted as the proveyors tried to make sense of what they were being presented.

Ræ of Halo Davina was the first to [speak] up. "We came to this meeting because we were told you had fair claim to the throne. We would like to see that proof!"

Another, ræ of Halo Asa, entered with her concern as well. "We have not seen the Ægæliphi in months. Where is your brother and sister? Our people have been left in the absence of light for too long!"

Æræya motioned with her finger toward the ræ of Halo Asa. Instantly, three Ophori moved to arrest her.

"What is the meaning of this?" the ræ proclaimed. "What are you true intentions? You cannot do this!"

Proveyor Sylvan locked eyes with Epeë. *"This is it, run now! We need a living witness!"* With a quick nod of the head, Proveyor Sylvan authorized the first offensive. Her servant launched a javelin aimed directly at Æræya. Æræya reacted quickly, using her powerful telepathy to stop the javelin midair.

"My intentions are to remake this world. With or without you. It seems the Halo of Gabriela will not be with us for this transition. Kill them."

Ophori guards descended on Proveyor Sylvan and the Asan ræ. Many of her fellow proveyors tried to stop the attack, but were simply speared alongside each other. In the commotion, Epeë made a break for the garden just outside the courtyard. If she could get past the garden, she could get lost in the forest beyond it. She snuck back a look as she ran. Two Ophori had peeled off and were in pursuit. Epeë scanned for anything along the way that she could use as a weapon.

Epeë's vision tinted to a light shade of red, the Vederian signifier that she was hurt. She rubbed her arms to find the wound; she had been clipped by an Ophori spear. Epeë leapt over a low hedge and tore through a bed of flowers. She could make it, but the Ophori were much faster than her. They quickly stopped, then darted to the left. They were going to head her off. Epeë cut to the opposite direction, now running parallel with a high row of hedges. She felt a strong arm grip her forearm and swing her around to the ground. She began kicking and flailing until the frame of a large woman landed on top of her. It was Maya.

"See me, I can't take them both—I will need your help," Maya handed Epeë a short dagger with a curved edge. "When I give the nod, this goes in a lung, you understand?" Epeë was shaking, but nodded in agreement.

By now the Ophori had caught up with Epeë and were thrashing at the hedges, hoping to cull their escapee. The time to act was now. Maya timed their tandem attack perfectly; she expertly assumed one would go low and the other high. With a running start, the attacker with pink nail polish used a nearby stone fountain to launch herself into the air. The second attacker, purple nail polish, geared up for an attempt at a tackle. Maya first used her legs to spin around low enough to swipe one of the Purple Nail Polish's feet out from under her, she then used her elbow to spin around and crack the ribs of the Pink Nail Polish. Purple Nail Polish rebounded and returned a volley of high kicks, which Maya blocked easily.

Maya used the same marble step to catapult her body directly into Purple Nail Polish. Two jabs and a hook left her dazed. Maya then took her head in one hand and smashed it against the marble step—she was asleep now. Pink Nail Polish managed to tackle Maya to the ground, but was unable to land any substantial hits. With Maya on her back trying to gain a leverage, she reached out a hand to grip the dirt. Maya locked eyes with Epeë. Epeë knew what to do. Jumping from over the hedge, Epeë stabbed Pink Nail Polish with the short, curved edge dagger.

"No time, we must keep moving," Maya communicated telepathically. She smacked Epeë on the back as they darted deeper into the forest. Just as they began to pick up speed, Maya stopped abruptly, throwing out a hand across

Epeë's chest to stop her. *"There's someone else here, someone with stronger sight than I."*

"In the past we found you, in the present just the same, leading and fighting," Sera signed. The two women walked up to a scene only recently quelled. *"Maya, we've come to rescue you."*

"Valerie has just declared war against the halos. She is executing proveyors," Epeë signed.

Christina interjected. Her mind was on the next course of action. "Ma'am. Where is the safest place for us?"

"We have to get off of this halo," Maya explained. Sera looked at Maya and squinted her eyes.

"But there a place we must go first?" Sera asked.

Maya paused. "I'm not sure what you mean."

Sera touched Maya's hand. Her eyes rolled back, but only for a moment.

"Just as I thought. This story is a generational one," Sera signed. "We must make one more stop. We must go home, Maya."

The home that Maya's father, Robert Daniel, was given was much like the ones given to all of the Old Guard. They were all given gifts in that time. Housing, clothing, schooling for their children. It had to be all very secret, but the men and their families were thankful. They were in service to a secretive god.

The home itself was modest, but serviceable. It had everything a family of three would need. It was out and away from the general population and Robert Daniel liked that. It was just a few acres up from a serpentine brook that trickled deeper in the forest. He would often take Maya outdoors and explore; they would trail run and rock climb and practice archery or tracking animals. A lot of what Robert Daniel loved about that time in his life had to do with the home he was given. But it was also a home that was under complete surveillance. Robert Daniel didn't become aware of this until it was far too late.

It was a discovery that cost him the life of his wife, and eventually his own.

When his wife died, Robert Daniel moved his only child out of that home and never returned. Maya had always known where the house was and she always had a desire to return to it, to understand that part of her. But she couldn't do it. She didn't want to face the things she had buried. She had hoped to leave them there, deep down where they could never rise back to the surface.

But now here she was, with strangers she'd only just met starting at a place that had not changed. It was jarring, and it gave Maya a feeling that made her very uncomfortable.

"It—it's just like I remember," she [said] to the group. "It was such a thin, wispy place in my memory. Now it's so very real."

Maya had led the group to her home from muscle memory. They were still on Halo Michaela, but in a region that had become increasingly rural as jobs shifted more toward the interior. *I have no idea why I led them here,* Maya thought as she scanned the area round the house.

The grass was overgrown. Her toy rabbit was half buried in the dirt, with one floppy ear hanging out. That was an image that stuck with her. She felt like that toy. She was always tied to her father's past and the things he did, yet she also wanted so badly to escape to a place where she could be her own woman—but she knew she had to reckon with her past. It was that half in, half out, nature that defined her life. To some degree, that may have been why she never truly felt comfortable, or proud even, of the work that she had accomplished.

"It is real, Maya, it is all real." Sera's demeanor had changed significantly since her sæ with Christina and Maya. It's said that the act of sæing changes the sær each time she looks out into the larger plane. Christina noted this change and it somewhat bothered her. It was almost as if Sera were a different person altogether. "Thank you for bringing us here, we know this had to be hard for you."

"I don't know, I just felt called to come. Whatever you showed me in that dream reminded me of that. And I guess now that I'll be dead very soon, I supposed I had to see it one last time." All Maya could see was red. She knew she was terribly injured.

"What do you mean, dead?" Christina asked. "You are the greatest Ophori leader to ever live! You not only inspired me to join, you are the reason we came to get you. Maya, the world is ending. We're being told it will never be the same. We need your help."

Maya knelt down before the half-buried rabbit. She let the long ear slide through her fingers. "I was the Ophori leader that was too late for the Ægæliphi, too late for her son, and too weak to save the heir. And now, Valerie, or Æræya, has claim to my army in the name of some familial feud that's a millennia old. She will be coming for me. And she can have me. I deserve it. What do I care of the end of the world? My world has already ended."

Sera knelt down, putting her hand on Maya's knee. "No one deserves claim over you, not even the most powerful of this world. Tell me, what will we find in here?"

Sera's eye began to twitch and she fell back onto her butt. She wrote in the dirt: *We have little time. She can see us.*

The women froze for a breathless moment. *Who* could see them?

Christina sprang into action. "Whatever is in this house go in and get it now. We cannot afford to stay here long."

"What are we even looking for?" Epeë asked.

"It has to be something her father owned, or kept. Think, ma'am. What would your father hide? Where would he put it?" Christina pressed.

Maya signed, "My father loved plants. He loved nature. He cared for his plants as much if not more than me," she joked. "But I accepted it. He would step out to garden and be gone just as long as the day would allow. I tried to gain the same respect he had in this area, in his domain, but it never was enough. I was never as strong and as great as his tree."

"It—it is Valerie. She is entering my mind. She—she has become something else entirely. Soon she will know our every move," Sera shared. "Something here is grounding her. She is connected to something here with us."

Maya continued, "We used to play this game. We would give each other notes for us to read and would hide them in the ground near our plants. I think that—"

"We need to start digging now. That's clearly it," Epeë signed. "There's a flower garden behind her house. It's possible he left her something there." Epeë ran off.

The women began digging. After a few holes, they began to find old notes that Maya's father had left her. A few moments later, they found what they were looking for.

"You all will not believe this," Epeë signed. "We have to get this to Dr. Sylvan."

Sera turned to Maya. "Did Æræya touch you? Did she ever put your hands on you?"

Maya thought back to her defeat. Æræya had touched her to remind her who took her down. "Yes, I think she—"

"You have to take these clothes off now!" Sera signed. "Christina, go into the home and find something for Maya to wear. Epeë, try and reach out to Dr. Sylvan or Tara. She and Talia should be close by."

After a few moments, Christina returned with clothing from Maya's father. "This is all I could find."

"Tara is not picking up, Talia either. I—I think something is wrong," Epeë replied.

"We have to assume the worse," Sera replied. "Æræya may already have them. We have to regroup. We are burning these clothes. Maya, we have to get you medical attention, but first we have to remove your marker."

"Marker?" Maya asked.

"Yes," Sera replied. She tapped a small, thick metallic disk in the middle of Maya's back.

"Once we remove this, we have to know exactly where we are going to go," Christina cautioned.

"I am contacting the doctor now," replied Epeë.

Epeë explained their situation and the information they'd obtained from the letters. Robert Daniel had discovered and kept a written record of internment camps sponsored by the Viceroy. Each line item included location, type of experimentation, and number of occupants.

Fallon was stunned. "Ava has not responded to me either. That means the lab is compromised. For now, your best option is to head to the coast.

I have a safe house there deep within the cave system just past the marsh. I will provide you coordinates now."

"Fallon, look, she—she assassinated your mother. I didn't want you learning this from someone else. She did what she did to help me escape. I am so, so sorry."

In a manner of seconds, Fallon's life had completely fallen apart. Ava, Vega II, his mother—all gone.

"We—we don't know what happened to Tara and Talia yet," Fallon replied, trying to comfort the others. "Victor is building an army and will be there shortly to retrieve his sister. One way or another, we will get to the bottom of this. Æræya wants an audience, and until we are all present, she can only stockpile her resources. So we will do the same. Go to the safe house and wait. It has everything you need there, clothes, medical supplies, weapons, everything. Hold out until then. I will give you information as I receive it. Forever in the Will."

"But Fallon," Epeë replied.

"The safe house, Epeë. Please."

"OK, Fallon. Forever in the Will," Epeë replied.

***

Part 12: Hören

The History of the Hören

***

When the gods discovered Vedere's cunning, they were furious. Hören, the god of equality and fairness, proposed that each god now make their own being in secret—hiding them in the corners of the world. Hören's people, the Listeners, would be beings of extraordinary hearing—being able to witness the winds of other continents and even hear the whispers of the past. They lived in the cliffs and mountains, where the wind could speak their name. Gan Dong's people, the People of Taste, could taste the temperature out of the air and distinguish between any disease without suffering. They lived among the sea, exchanging the land for the oceans. Odore's people, the people of aroma, were given the ability to experience all odors and aromas, with their power to trance. They lived among the jungles, in the deepest forests of the earth. And Nusdvagisdi, the god of specialty and mystery, hid his people, with no one knowing the true nature of his people. Vedere's pride had shattered the unity of the Senses. But there was more than meets the eye.

This is what history tells us. This is what we know. This is how the Earth began. We are Hören. And we will listen to the world.

***

Rory 57,290 days left

What would I do without our Sherpa Quannah? He has led us every step of the way. These people have already given so much, but their children? Georgette and I never had time for children. We put all we had into this expedition. And now I was returning with two. A Horeni and a Nusdvagisdi. What a lucky father I am. Just another day now before we reach our original base camp. We'll regroup there.

We've also reworked our contingency plan. If anything happens to us, we have the journals. Damien Durham, the ecologist, will keep up with these journals until we have to find another. Anyone will be able to piece together what happened here if it comes to that. But I have my hopes. We didn't meet these people for nothing. We are in the Will.

***

Victor, 103 days left

My spies were losing more and more of their footing as the days went by. Soon, the capital would be solely my sister's and there would be nothing I could do to stop it.

"And what about my hunch?" I asked. I had speculated for years that Valerie possibly had the ability to sæ. If the reports were to believed, what she was now capable of doing would be much more powerful than any sær I'd ever heard of.

"It would appear you are correct, sir," Mason, one of our newest recruits, replied. "Valerie is definitely a sær. And I am told she has undergone some sort of procedure. She introduced herself at Vaia's Courtyard as 'Æræya.' Those who managed to escape have [said] that she has completely lost her mind. She has some sort of master plan to exterminate the majority of the population in the name of some new set of gods."

The Viceroy had to have deeply manipulated her. I never knew Valerie to be a religious person. There was obviously some other factors at play, someone else pulling the strings. I was still unsure of how deep the rabbit hole went.

I turned to Quannah, my most trusted spy. He'd been undercover for months after assisting Fallon in retrieving Epeë. He'd remained in the Galavad up until now. We had no way of reaching him without blowing his cover. "You are certain my sister is at the Onyx?" I asked.

"Yes, sir, she has been kept there for almost two months," Quannah replied. "She is badly hurt, but Æræya refuses to kill her. She wants witnesses."

"And what of your personal project?"

"The Viceroy surely have them. I am unsure of how many remain, but we must liberate them at the Hysk as well."

"And the Davis descendant?"

"Her mind is nearly shredded, but she is not dead yet. We have to assume now that Æræya knows everything."

"Æræya has assassinated proveyors in broad daylight. If it is a war she wants, then a war she shall have. What about Veronica and her people?"

"Communication with them has been steady as well. She still intends to carry out her plan. She will be ready when the time comes."

I had heard enough. Nearly two months of preparation. *We were ready.* I turned off my holographic display and turned to my self-appointed generals.

"Safie, I want to know the final count of the opposition—we need to find out who else she was able to turn against us." Safie, one of my oldest friends, nodded and shrouded herself behind the blue light of her holographic view screen. With them all here before me, I realized that most of my team was made up of old friends. Nearly all of the resistance had been pieced together one best friend and borrowed piece of equipment at a time.

Ironically, my base camp was one part bedroom and another part cave that snaked beneath Arælia's porous foundation. I, like many others, used the catacombs to my advantage, staking out my own uncharted path of secret passageways. I now found solace in the very places I hated. As a child, I dreamed of being out in the open, the shining son of the Cara Royale. I knew my place in policy and rulership would be mitigated, but I still craved the splendor of it.

I still did, in fact. But in maturity I came to see my reality for what it truly was; I would never see the throne. I would be hidden, just like my father. But what I found from that realization was that my passions could still be invested in—through education. Now, I relished seclusion. I escaped to it.

Initially, my cave was overflow for my growing book collection. When I said I was ready for bed as a child, the truth was that I was ready to go to my special place and read. By thirteen, it was my lab—I brought samples of dirt and feathers and insects and all manner of things that I could further experiment on. It was through nature that I found what I theorized as "the order of design" in nearly everything I studied.

My plan was to defend a thesis on the concept just as it became clear that my mother was growing further and further ill. My focus shifted then. I began to study what was happening to her and developed my own hypothesis, but it was not yet clear what had befallen her and so many others at her age. That's when I met Quannah, and so much was explained.

"Safie, also, I need more on the Viceroy. It's as if the more I look at them, the less I understand."

"And the more you realize how little you know about them?" she replied with a raised eyebrow. "I've been thinking the exact same."

"Let's take it from the top once more—what exactly do we know about them?" I began thumbing through Quannah's handwritten notes. He kept a judicious collection of ideas, research, concepts, all originating from self-study. This wasn't the first time he had questioned the Viceroy's place in society.

"I don't know, Safie, so much of it just feels like children's stories. Is that really all we know?" Damien, another one of my generals, asked. He was a practical man, sharp, but didn't like to take many risks.

"I think that's really all we *have* been told, Victor. It seems anytime someone digs just a little deeper—they just stop or disappear. I'm not sure I've ever been able to place why that keeps occurring," Safie replied.

"Well, it is now clear they have been winding up my sister for decades. What I'm still not understanding is their motive."

I knew Vega would be killed soon. The trouble of it was not just the pain of it, or the disappointment, but of what to do next. The crashing down of an era had implications much larger than anyone could imagine. We couldn't possibly foresee everything. But that seemed to be the point, at least to the Viceroy. They were the one entity that had withstood all of Vedere's historical era. The one institution that had seen it all. I had no doubt that it was the Viceroy, ultimately, that had been pulling the strings all along at the bidding of the quinqu.

"The most concerning point for me, Safie, is that I am not completely convinced that Valerie does not have a fair claim. My deeper concern is who this quinqu really is—how this all ties into our history." My goal was to understand more about who truly held the power in our world. One thing I was sure of, however—it was not Æræya.

"The more I study it, the more it seems that the Cara Royale was a historical anomaly. We were not the family the Viceroy intended to have rule. The Viceroy wanted to ensure that the Amavi family, not ours, would remain in power. But it is also possible that even they became too difficult to control. Perhaps now, Æræya is the one they chose to restore balance."

"On what are you basing this hypothesis?" Safie asked.

"Well, what I'm looking at, from a historical perspective, is the cycles. How things continue to come back around at certain points. It seems historically accurate that any time there is a push for knowledge, or furthering the concept of truth, there is some kind of reset. I think our era's was the Davis Expedition. It seems with the results of that expedition, the Viceroy had to regain control. But I still don't understand why."

"Well, I think that much is clear, Victor. They don't want us to see what else is in the world. It's possible they know what's beyond our world. What's beneath us, what's perhaps all around us," Safie proposed.

I thought more on it. Why would the Viceroy be so intent on hiding the rest of the world? What could possibly be worth that much work and dedication?

"That—is exactly what it is," Quannah confessed. "My friends, time is becoming incredibly short. I think it is time I explain to you all who I really am."

***

Veronica, beginning with 173, ending with 103 days left

"We will get you to each halo's seat," one of the Ashanti signed, after putting down his book. The quintet was in a Viper—a cloaked vehicle that could skip across most terrains. They needed an all-terrain vehicle for the type of travel they were conducting. Because the nation of Vedere experienced unique terrains and weather conditions, a simple hover car would not be enough.

"The first stop will be the city of Tyre, also referred to as Sideway City," the Ashanti signed. Tyre was one of the most unique cities in the nation. It was built on the giant cliffside that made up the majority of Halo Maria, which had been constructed using a highly advance terraforming technique. The process funneled magma, water, and precious metals from the adjacent halo to the new landmass. It flowed in gigantic waves that created striking and sharp peaks and valleys, creating Halo Maria.

The people of Tyre were probably the most adventurous people you would ever come across. The furthest removed from much of the capital's dealings, the government of Tyre was mostly concerned with their own affairs. As the outermost colony, they still felt like the pioneers of Vederian people. They still had the spirit of exploration and benefitting society. Now, news was traveling that a new civil war was nearing reality and a prophecy fulfilled. If Balien was to have any hope in persuading an alliance, his best approach would be to lean into the prophecy. Many of the people of Tyre were spiritual. He hoped to used that.

"We've already set up a meeting in the courtyard. They will be waiting for us," Fallon shared. "I think we should discuss how we are going to approach this situation."

Fallon handed Balien a pad with a beaded kokoto at the center near the top.

"This is a truncated history of the City of Tyre and its colonies. There are details regarding settlements, culture, and governmental structure."

"Do I really need this information?" Balien asked.

Fallon paused with a slight look of shock on his face. "Yes, I think it would be useful."

"I think time is of the essence. I have the ability to hear. Is that not enough?"

Fallon frowned. "Perhaps, but I think it's important information."

"I'll skim it."

The Viper was allowed to land in an open area just outside of the courtyard. It was marked by a metal diamond shape with a circle in the middle. There was a standard welcoming party that was there to greet them; a few guards, a number of liaisons. When Balien and his constituency approached, they were met with skeptical eyes.

Balien was the first out to greet them. He walked down the ramp of the Viper with outstretched arms. He flashed a wide smile and waved his hands. He arched his back to raise his chest and he made sure his gait was patient.

"Help me understand, you said that he lost his memory?" one of the Ashanti asked Fallon.

"The details still don't reflect well in the light. But it is my understanding that he is of different blood and that it is his unique physiology that has given him an ability beyond ours. He claims to now recall his mother's teachings and the ways of his people, as the majority of that was lost after his accident."

"And it's your understanding that it was the accident that impacted his memory, correct?"

"Yes, that is my understanding. But something is still not quite coming together. Gregor Bastian hypothesized that his memory was wiped artificially. It would make more sense, though that type of technology would be illegal."

By this point, Balien had fully embraced what he felt to be his destiny. He looked at this moment, and the ones yet to come, as a confirmation of the destiny he felt he was always owed. Balien thought of himself as uniquely special: charismatic and charming. It was what others had readily told him, and his mother only helped the belief along. For Balien, this was a new era, not just for the people of Vedere, but for him, and though Fallon thought the same, it started to feel more like the end of his people forever.

In thoughts that he still kept to himself, what could be seen as the dawning of a new era could also be seen as the most insidious invasion in the history of his world. What if Balien's people were not benevolent? What if what really happened during the expedition was an all-out war, with only those who were willing to surrender surviving?

"Balien, you told us that your ancestor came as a baby to live among us, correct?"

Balien finished shaking hands with Tyre's dignitaries. He flipped his head around with visible annoyance. "She was a baby, Fallon. A refugee. Why?"

Fallon was growing skeptical. Something was being hidden, he just didn't know what.

"We appreciate your visit, and we accept your company," a liaison shared. "As you know we are a newer society that concerns itself less with what goes on with the rest of the halos, but we have verified much of what you have shared and we are in agreement: We are in a dire situation."

Balien nodded and looked back at the Ashanti and Fallon, who seemed despondent.

"Sir, these are my royal guards, the Ashanti, and my right hand, Dr. Fallon Sylvan of Puresh I'll let my right hand explain, he's the scientist."

Fallon stepped forward. "I hate to come off rude, but I'd suggest we skip the formalities. We have two major problems, one of which I'm sure you're already aware. We have word that Valerie has staged a coup. We understand that it is her intent to make what she is calling a 'new world.' A couple members of the Kofi on the inside are still trying to understand exactly what that means, but our experts are hypothesizing genocide."

There were no experts on these topics, but Fallon wanted to be sure he sounded official. "And then, of course, there is our second, but arguably more pressing concern. An event. We don't exactly have a name for it, but it seems there is a time coming where our entire world will be plunged into complete darkness."

"Yes," one of the ambassadors replied. "And that is why you have our audience. We want to be sure our people are prepared for this event." She motioned for them to follow her.

The group walked over to the edge of the landing pad to overlook the mountains.

"As you can see, we have a different terrain. We have begun constructing shelters. We will place our people—"

"I'm sorry, ma'am, but this will not work," Fallon interrupted.

"Why not?" a second constituent asked. "We've made provisions for two generations to last in there, the dome we are constructing will be reinforced—"

"Our conservative estimates suggests that the eclipse could last a minimum of five hundred years," Fallon interrupted. There was a short pause, as if everyone were briefly frozen for a moment.

"You're insane," the constituent replied.

"You couldn't possibly be suggesting—" the ambassador signed.

"This ... will be an extinction-level event," Fallon replied.

Balien opted to fill in the gap of silence. "My people foresaw this event. They came to warn us. Preparations have been made over the last hundred years. We—"

"You're asking us to put your trust in a society of people who we have never before known of prior to now?"

"A supposed society of people who can't even see?!" another added.

Balien and Fallon paused. The Ashanti tensed in the growing hostility.

"We must have misunderstood what you were proposing. We put our faith in what we can see. We would like to ask you to leave now."

Balien wanted to protest, but Fallon intervened. He explained to Balien that there was simply no time to convince those unable to believe. Frustrated and confused, Balien and his group left Halo Maria, traveling to Halo Davina.

"Balien, I don't understand what has gotten into you," Fallon quipped. "What's with all of the arrogance?"

"You're not doing this without me, Fallon. I'm sorry if I'm playing up the part, but based on our first performance, we're not that convincing."

"This isn't a performance, Balien. It's real life. It's life and death. We aren't playing some game."

"I'm not a child, Fallon, I understand what's going on here. Now drop it. I'm going to go take a nap. Wake me when we arrive at Davina."

Fallon let out a huff and returned to his notes. They would have to wait another eight hours before they saw the next landmass.

The Davinans were shorter people, with bone-straight hair and their entire bodies covered in freckles. During the Civil War, many of them were the pilots, others were engineers and architects.

"What are you asking us to build?" their proveyor asked plainly. Balien and Fallon were given entry and direct counsel with Halo Davina's highest command.

"We are asking you to build a loop," Fallon explained. "We must have a way to get our people out of the darkness. You've reviewed all our—"

"Yes, we reviewed everything," the proveyor interrupted. "You have our support. Now go and save as many as you can. Let us begin our work."

It was a conversation that was brief and in stark contrast to the conversation with the people of Tyre. The engineers were believers, as evidenced by the growing number of people now following Balien.

Balien came into Halo Asa, a month later, with hovercrafts and a hundred followers. At Penelope, there were five hundred, and large trading ships.

In two months' time, when Balien reached Gabriela, the idea of rebellion was no longer just an idea. It was believed to be a certainty. A new camp was set up at the banks of Gabriela's new capital, Kesh—the home of both the Halfalans and Dalfalans. The Kofi had advanced from their base at Udugigvdi and were now coalescing at Kesh behind Commander Bastian, Balien, and the newly formed group of believers, now known as the Unionists.

Base camp was the Proveyor Sylvan's home, situated near the northern edge of Halo Gabriela. With just one continent left between the seat of the known world, Halo Michaela and Arælia, the validity and belief in the Unionist movement had become widely known—and tensions were rising.

***

Veronica, 35 days left

Two months ago, a dazed Talia stumbled at the gates of Kesh, Halfala. She had been fairly well nourished, but was obviously rattled from her capture. She explained what happened to Ava and Tara, tried to share as much as she could about what Æræya was planning. But it was clear that Sciya had fallen, their one base in Arælia. Sciya was Balien's second home. When he first woke up, Sciya and Ava were all he knew. Now, all gone in a flash. What did Æræya have planned next?

Talia explained that after she entered a sæ with Æræya, she was simply let go. Æræya explained that she had no need to kill her yet, she still needed witnesses. This also meant that Vega was still alive, though Talia was unsure how many days she had left.

Upon receiving this information, Victor made a difficult decision. He decided to suspend his plans to help Veronica get Topside. The plan was still to amass a force large enough to defeat Æræya and rescue his sister, but he had to be realistic. Vega was too sick to travel. Victor would be seeing her to say goodbye.

When Puresh finally became fortified, a task force was sent out to retrieve Sera, Maya, and the others. They had holed up in the safe house for almost two months. According to Victor, Veronica was due Topside any day now.

Balien sat at a round table with a newly formed counsel: Dr. Fallon Sylvan, Epeë Afauna, now proveyor of Unified Puresh, Talia Davis, Christina Wynne, Victor Cara, and Maya.

Also present was Commander Bastian, the Unionist royal guard, the Ashanti, and Sera, one of the last known særs alive in Vedere. Balien let in a deep breath as his eyes tracked around the room. There were finally all there together again, in one room.

"Have we been able to communicate with any Tyre? Denali?" Balien asked.

"Still they resist," Christina replied. "Æræya has convened them to remain loyal to her. That puts our numbers about even."

"You do know what they are called now?" Fallon added. "They call themselves Loyalists. Æræya has unified the rest of the world under the guise of loyalty. They see *us* as people against the very order of civilization."

"I suppose in part, we are anarchists," Epeë replied.

"And we are rebelling," Christina added.

"Might we continue the conversation of what we discovered as we were collecting Maya," Sera interjected, turning the conversation back to its intended course.

"Right, you're saying Maya's father discovered ... camps?" Victor asked.

"I'm certain of it," Sera replied. "I have never felt such a presence such as that. And Æræya is fully aware. I have never felt a presence quite like hers either. Not even from my grandmother Seraphina. Victor, she is powerful. And, perhaps, she has always been watching."

"Are we saying, then, that Æræya has placed the Vederian people in camps?" Fallon asked.

"It would be the largest open secret the world has ever known," Maya replied.

"No, it would be the second largest," a man with long white hair replied. His hair was parted in the middle and pulled down into two braids that came down to his waist. He looked to be about thirty, perhaps younger, and was escorted in by members of the Ashanti.

"Quannah?" Talia replied. "How long has it been?"

"Too long. I'm here to finally reveal my truth to the others. To share what is really going on in our world."

"Cool, really dramatic," Talia added bluntly. "But really, who are you then?"

"Quannah works with the royal family ... right?" Fallon asked. "I came to his acquaintance when we were first trying to find you, Talia."

"I thought you were a merchant," Commander Bastian added.

"Wait, didn't I see you in the courtyard?" Maya added as well. It was obvious now that everyone had some vague connection to Quannah, but didn't know why.

"I was all of those things, and I am all those things to everyone. With work that I started five hundred years ago, and with the help of all of you, we are finally ready to restore balance to this body," Quannah replied.

"Did ... did you say five hundred years?" Fallon asked, "The longest-lived Vederian lived half that—"

"Ah, Fallon, but I am not Vederian. I am Nusdvagisdi. I am of the People of Taste."

Balien spelled out the word, "T-A-S-T-E?"

Quannah nodded. "If you all would indulge me, I will explain as much as I can. I know I have been gone for some time, in and out. There is a reason for that. Think of everything that you currently know of as Phase II. The work my father began, and passed on to me, all completed hundreds of years before the Davis Expedition, that was Phase I. To reclaim the artifacts of the five races."

Quannah paused to check for understanding. "This story is a generational one. One that you all are linked to, and one that has been a gift to see unfold over such a long time. If we start with what you all know, there was the explorer, a woman we all now know to be the late Georgette Davis, relative of Talia Davis, with her grandfather, Rory, being one of the few survivors alongside a small unidentified child, a discovery that Fallon and Balien uncovered, a child that grew up to be Kamali, the first leader of the Kofi, and fourth non-Vederian to set foot on your halo, my father, mother, and I being the first. Kamali was Horeni, one of the people of Hearing, and also ancestor to you, Balien."

"Wait, so before you go any further, you are saying that not only are Vederians not alone, but there are five other races of people, all distinctly different from each other?" Fallon asked.

Quannah nodded. "That is exactly what I am saying. And understand me when I say that *this* is the truth. It is *this* fact that has come to be the greatest secret this world has ever known. A secret that has been so tightly held, and with a ruthlessness you would struggle to imagine. A secret that was first understood here in Vedere by an ecologist, an ancestor of yours, Maya, the Ophori, and etymologist, the aunt of Valerie's right hand, Machiavelli, during the Davis Expedition. It is by no coincidence that all of these people; including the linguist, and myself, the Sherpa, returned from that expedition."

Everyone's eyes widened. "My mother and father were refugees. They lived with the Horeni on their world and chose to come along when they launched their generational ship to come here. They landed on the Underside and set up a settlement there. When it came time for Rory to return to Topside, I was asked to accompany them.

"Since I first arrived Topside until now, I have helped shuttle thousands of Nusdvagisdi refugees from the other realities to help give them a home here. And for a time, there was peace. The Ægæliphi permitted, and we kept nomadic territories on the Outer Four. But leadership changed, and the Viceroy had their own plan. They influenced the new Ægæliphi to put our people in camps where the Viceroy could keep us under their watch.

"I have worked decades to find my people, and I have received help along the way. Your father, Maya, for example had been certain he knew the locations of the camps, but died before I could get that information. Now you have it." Quannah stopped to take a seat at the round table.

"I've been working to save my own people as well as your own. It has not been easy," Quannah continued. "Æræya is being guided by the Viceroy, a convent of women you know of as elders and who have led each royal leader since the beginning. Their leader, Viviana, is the one I believe is guiding Æræya. But see me, the Viceroy do not answer to the Church of the Vael, and they do not answer to the royal family. They answer to the quinqu."

Skeptic eyes squinted at what Quannah was saying. "I had hoped we could succeed in your world without involving you in an inter-dimensional conflict, but it seems I must lay all my cards out now."

"Maybe I can help you, Quannah," signed a woman in her mid-thirties. She was nearly identical to Vega. Her hair was braided back into cornrows and her nose and cheeks were covered in freckles. Her clothes were those of someone who was both a soldier and archeologist; her hands were rough, like they had been handling rocks or other hard materials.

And she wasn't alone, she had entered with a dozen other people, but they were unlike anything the group had ever seen. They were all a minimum height of two meters, some with reddish hair, others with jet black hair. Their skin was brown, but much, much lighter. Their eyes were almost pure crystals.

The Horeni, Talia thought to herself.

"The quinqu are behind it all. It is their goal to divide us. And when many rebelled, they were crushed." The woman placed her hand on Quannah's shoulder. "When Victor shared with me that that our mother had been murdered, I decided it was finally time to return home."

The group froze in astonishment. It was Veronica, true heir to the throne of Vedere.

"I am Veronica, I am Vera's eldest, elder sister of Vega, Valerie, and Victor, and I am so sorry you all have to meet me this way. Quannah and I realize that we are dumping a lot of information on you at once. That was not our intention. We just simply do not have as much time as we had hoped we would." Veronica looked around the proveyor's court. "But let me just say, if we were able to get this far, I believe we will succeed."

The dozen with her meshed in with the ranks of the Ashanti, forming a full circle around the counsel. Fallon stood up to provide Veronica his seat. She denied it.

"The quinqu take their orders from no one. It stops there. We have phases in place to get to them, but for now we must save as many as we can. Æræya is fighting for a dying world. And we will not let another race of people become extinct. As you all know from my message, the majority of the work has been done down below, a work that was started by your family, Talia." Veronica had an uncanny charisma about her. She seemed fluent in any necessary language as she signed and used her lips to communicate between the other visitors and Quannah. If circumstances were different, Veronica would have been a phenomenal Ægæliphi.

"When Georgette reached the Underside, she was met with a delegation. They were People of Hearing and the People of Taste. They told Georgette of an impending eclipse that would not affect them, but could collapse Vederian civilization. They risked defying the quinqu to save our people. And when it became clear there was nothing that could be done to ameliorate the eclipse, Georgette and her best stayed behind to complete construction—a way for her people to escape. Since that time, the royal family had been left in the dark until after the Civil War."

"When the change was made," Quannah added.

"Yes, you see, it was the Viceroy who stoked the fires of Civil War. They wanted to plant a family they felt they had better control over—the Cara family, my family," Veronica continued.

"This conflict, however, began well before the civil war," Quannah jumped back in. "Vedere's oldest two familial lines, Vo and Va, have been clamoring over the throne for millennia. One line was strictly dedicated to their duties as one of the first families and the quinqu, the other dedicated themselves to the people."

"Allegiances and moral ambiguities have changed sides for thousands of years, but it always comes down to a simple idea: Who is for the people?" Veronica finished. "This world will be dead soon, and by the time the sun reappears, there will be no one left to bask in its light. We have just over a month to preserve the culture and civilization of over a millennia. Work that Quannah has been working tirelessly to complete, and work that you all have been doing as well. We are to save as many as we can. That is our goal."

"We will to flee to Hören, as we believe we can prepare for the final Great War there," Quannah stated. "We will take as many as we can; however, we cannot leave until we have one last thing. We are not exactly sure where it is, but we have an idea."

"You see," Veronica explained, "when Georgette first met the Horeni, there was no way to communicate with them without the Nusdvagisdi's help. We need a lexicon for future generations. For the Horeni, it was a recording, for us it was a scroll. These items are inspired by primordial designs, from before even the quinqu. The Viceroy will stop at nothing to retrieve these artifacts. They are the key to the unification of us all, something that the quinqu desperately desires to prevent."

"My sister was a Nusdvagisdi linguist, and the very same linguist who left with us when we returned Topside. She was working on one of the lexicons when we were separated after the second investigation," Quannah explained. "I've spent the last century searching for her. She is probably dead, but I haven't given up hope."

"We're not sure what has happened to Atsila, but we are certain the Viceroy has something to do with it," Veronica offered.

"So we have to retrieve the collective history of an entire civilization from this dying world in just over a month," Fallon scoffed.

"No, Fallon, we save this world's people. As many as we can. And we find that scroll at any cost. Either we find it and destroy it, or we take it with us, but it cannot be in the Viceroy's hands. There is nothing more important than that."

Veronica walked around the table as she expressed a closing thought. "There are no chosen people. There is no one hero to save us. There is only the work that we must get done. I don't care who does it. We have to find this scroll and evacuate the cities. We are out of time."

"Then where do we start?" Talia signed, after putting down her notebook. She had been taking extensive notes.

The rest of the group unfolded themselves; no one was still seated at the round table. Balien had propped him himself up against a wall, sitting on the floor, which he now positioned with outstretched legs. Sera quickly showed recognition by a small nod of the head, then resumed her martial arts forms. Epeë looked up from her notes only briefly, then returned to them. Balien was adjusting. He saw himself as the new king, but now, it seemed to have no value—especially now that Sciya had fallen.

"From my position within the capital, I can only assume that the scroll is somewhere within or close to Arælia—it's the oldest continent in the world. This would put us no doubt into direct confrontation with Æræya herself. And given that we now know she is a sær, we will need to be sure we have a solid plan if we are to engage," Quannah answered.

"Also, could you help us understand the scroll? What exactly are we looking for?" Balien asked as he stood up near the group.

"Well, it is important to note that while it is called the scroll, it is most likely by this point kokoto technology," Veronica explained. "The scroll is a schematic for an apparatus that you would wear over your eyes that would help translate sounds into visual symbols you could understand. It is already indexed, and is essentially the bridge to eventual unassisted communication."

"As you already know, sound to the Horeni is what sight is to us. Sound itself is simply movement. When I first learned and became aware of what I was hearing, it felt like there was movement inside of my head. Almost fluid-like," Quannah added.

"So you can experience this ... sense of hearing?" Christina asked.

Quannah nodded. "I can, and others, but the explanation for that must be at another time."

"Hearing is the truth, and though this is not what they've taught us, there is more than meets the eye," Veronica signed. She smiled.

"Well, it all makes sense, really," Talia replied. "We are the Young Guild. The last generation, the broken, the outcasts, and the forgotten. We will be the ones to usher in a new age. I'm ready for one last mission before we go."

"Listen, I agree with that, I truly do, but this is real life. We can die," Maya snapped with a dose of reality. "Veronica, you're asking us to follow you; we have to throw our lives into a course that we may never escape. Who's OK with that?"

There was a hush over the group as the contemplated Maya's point. She had her defeat still fresh in her mind. She didn't want to relive that again.

"Look, I have come this far. My life was set on this course even before I lost my memory," Balien admitted. "I don't fully understand everything and quite frankly I'm ashamed I cannot be much more help, but I'm committed, even if this is all I know. I'm with you, Veronica, even if it means storming the capital."

Commander Bastian snapped his head up. "That's exactly what we will do. Storm the capital!"

The rest of the group looked on with concern.

"I'm serious! It can work. Æræya will be named Ægæliphi during the coronation. The entire world will be at that parade. We can take the Ophori by surprise and capture Æræya. We then use that platform to tell the world the truth; meanwhile, another group of us can track down the Viceroy and get the scroll."

Victor chimed in. "Æræya will have me killed as soon as she is crowned."

"Yes, but I am certain she will want you to see her crowned before you die," Veronica replied. "Which means though the public may think Vega dead, she is not."

"Which also makes it quite possible that we could look to rescue her as well!" Epeë added.

"The moment we have the scroll is the moment we break for the Underside. There will be no time to waste," Quannah cautioned.

"It seems we have ourselves a plan." Veronica grinned. "I also brought us some help. Everyone, meet the children of the Horeni Delegation. We have the best of their technology and ours at our disposal. Let's get everyone suited. We don't have a moment to lose."

***

Quannah, 7 days left

Quannah looked at them in a way he'd never looked at anyone else in his life. He had never seen such dedication. This Young Guild, a band of kids who had acted on only faith—willing to challenge their very existence. Quannah stood before them; He wanted to tell them that there was so much more. He didn't even have the words. But there was no time left.

"It was a measurement of time that was used thousands of years ago. They were called days, but they were not like the ones you know. They represented a duration of time in which a day could be ended, and returned again."

"And what happened to the light?" Epeë asked.

"It would set. The light was replaced; it was removed and replaced with darkness. Darkness is the absence of light and it is called night. The world would go dark for an equal amount of time as it was in the light. And the passing of that light was called day."

The quartet was huddled tightly in an alleyway as the parade marched past on the main street before them. The sky seemed to rain confetti. Thousands danced to the strobing of lights and marched toward the capitol with glee.

"There will come a time, in seven days, when Vedere will experience darkness for a period of 182,500 days. Vederian civilization will not survive that long a night," Quannah explained.

Shalane, one of the Horeni warriors who accompanied Quannah and Epeë, stood straight, ready to give her report. She had fiery red hair and piercing crystal eyes. Shalayne was half Horeni and half Vederian, like most of her friends and cousins, though unlike them, she could not see. She was fully Horeni in that regard.

"Quannah, we are ready to go." She adjusted the small nude-colored implants on her temples. She gently rested her hands on top of Quannah's signing hands. "Is everyone able to understand me?"

Everyone nodded.

"Alright, for our part, it is simple. The moment Victor comes forward the Ophori will be on him. That is when we take our opening," Shalane reminded everyone.

"And remember everyone, we only have one shot at this. We are going in brutally fast. We will take the first opening until the next one, and the next one after that," Quannah encouraged.

Nearly five hundred years of planning. Four generations of families. All for the next seven days.

"OK, I am in position," Victor reported. He couldn't hear it, but his breathing cadenced into slow breaths that could be heard over the radio. In, out. In, and out. One, two. One, two.

"This calle is a straight shot to the Arælia," Victor added. "You all can take this main road and head straight into position."

The circular palace of the royal family was encircled by a nearly impenetrable wall. It was at the center of the planned city of New Redemption, which was essentially the innermost district of the seat, Arælia. It included the Nexus, the Galavad, and the interior Halo Michaela. It was designed to appear just as the actual continents of the other halos, with rings of living space around a center area. Arælia was exclusively for the royal family, their constituents, and counsel. The actual population lived farther out and rarely stepped foot on royal grounds—unless it was coronation.

During a coronation, a parade began at the edge of Halo Michaela and in a maze-like fashion weaved into the center of the continent like a great migration. The walls of the cities and districts are opened for passage, with only Arælia itself kept guarded as it normally would.

"They will know something is up," Epeë hypothesized. "Æræya is incredibly shrewd. She will have her people ready."

"Æræya's weakness is her pride. She wants us all to see her ascension. If we can get this plan to unfold before then, we have a fighting chance," Victor explained.

We assimilated into the crowd and pretended to cheer as we worked our way to the border of New Redemption and the Ræ.

"Victor, are you in position?" Quannah asked.

"Yes."

"See you on the Underside," he signed with a smile.

Victor threw off his robe and walked toward the center stage across the courtyard. He was walking against the crowd. Heads turned and tracked him—the Ophori.

"Alright everyone, remember, if you are captured, you are captured. There is no turning back," Quannah reminded everyone. "I'm sorry. Give it your all."

The crowd didn't notice as the Ophori closed in. They wanted to handle this as swiftly and quietly as possible.

"Beta team, we are drawing them across to the southern entrance of the district, directly across the temple. Now is your chance."

Victor knelt with outstretched hands. Slowly, the crowd began to notice who he was and began celebrating. They thrust him up onto their shoulders and paraded him down to the calle.

"The people have taken him, I repeat, the people have taken him. The Ophori are following close behind," Shalane reported.

"Then we take this course and follow it to the very end," Quannah replied. "This is our first moment. We take this one and hope for the next."

The procession grew with each passing step. The conditions were in our favor. The crowd was thick and the pace was brisk. The people would carry their prince to his sister.

***

Part 13: Gan Dong

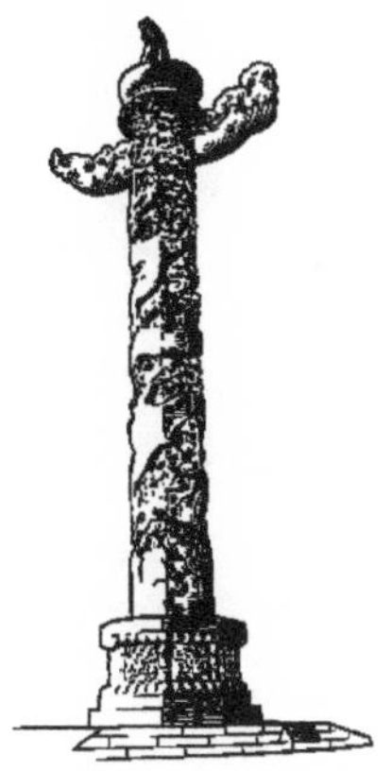

The History of the Gan Dong

***

Vedere, with her power of sight, soon discovered what the remaining quinqu had done and with her Soldiers of Sight set out to wipe out the new races of humanity from existence. But the People of Touch, the Gan Dong, took up arms against Vedere and began the Millennium War. In the darkest hour, the Hören and the Odore joined arms against the Soldiers of Sight. Time was purchased to seek out the wisest all humanity—the Nusdvagisdi.

This is what history tells us. This is what we believe. If this is how the Earth began. We will fight for a better ending. We are the Gan Dong. And will fight for a better world.

***

Rory 57,289 days left

We've agreed that a child of the Ægæliphi will help lead the work on the Underside. We now have a representative of all three races present. We hope to only require this for another three generations at the most. I'm not even sure if we will have that kind of time left, but we plan for the moment until we can seize the next moment.

I met with the Gammas that are with me. They have volunteered to stay behind with the infirmed who we are leaving. I hate to do this, but we must press on. We rest, journal, eat, and continue walking. We have to keep going. I know we can make it.

***

Commander Gregor Bastian, 7 days left

The Ophori were the most skilled fighters in the entire nation. But the men and women of the Udugigvdi were not far behind. We would protect each other until we were no more. And yes, the Ophori were the most fierce fighting force this world had ever seen, but they followed orders, not belief. My people—we fought for the truth. We fought because we now *knew* the truth. We fought now, because we had proof.

We were ten thousand soldiers strong. We were to lead the assault. We would take the fight to them and give Balien's team the time they needed to get the scroll. We were in plainclothes and dispersed among the crowd. At the ready, we would use our weapons, our staffs, our shoes, and anything else we could get our hands on to get the job done. And we would fight until the last person.

"Kofi, see me," I asked. "We have precious cargo. We must protect Balien and his team as they attempt to enter the district. Give it everything you have to get them there. Once we open fire, it will be chaos."

"Beta team, we are drawing them across to the southern entrance of the district, directly across the temple. Now is your chance," a lieutenant reported.

"We have notice from Alpha team!" I raised my hands. "And so now, my family, let us fight. Let us fight for the truth!" I took Balien by the belt buckle and drew my weapon. Maya grabbed the collar of Fallon, Christina took the young sær Sera, and Veronica was with Talia. Around us was a diamond formation, mixed with our very best fighters and the Horeni warriors. We pushed around the crowd and worked our way directly to the entrance. Off to our right, I could see Victor kneeling on both knees, arms stretched. He had surrendered.

"That's it!" I told my group. "They have Victor, we must hurry!" The Ophori descended upon us much quicker than I thought they would.

"They are picking us off!" one of my leads signed. Maya looked at me, her eyes searching for my answer. *We might not make it, we still have too far to go,* I thought to myself.

"We have to break for it!" Veronica exclaimed. She expertly dodged an arrow as she pointed her weapon to the north.

"Just sprint. We must push now as fast as we can!" I pressed. Nearly two hundred meters before the entrance, I saw their best: the new leader of the Ophori, Vala, and her most elite guard. The entire parade was now a battlefield. Children had lost their parents, others had died in the fray. *My Goddess, we sprang a trap on innocent people. What have we done?*

The alleys snaked and wound in circles. We could go the long way around, but we didn't have the time.

"Do not stop! No matter what! If someone falls, stand in the gap! We cannot lose now!" Maya ordered.

"Keep moving!" I repeated. "We are nearly there!"

We moved at a blistering pace, our weapons pulsing whenever we saw a flash of Ophori clothing. We ran and fired, kicked and vaulted over flipped tables and overturned newsstands.

"You know what I must do," Maya signed to me. I did. And I knew nothing that I could say would change her mind.

"Balien. This is it. Æræya knows you are here. The Ophori will surround us soon. We are at the gate. We will make our stand here. Christina and the Ashanti will protect you. Go and find whatever you are looking for."

"I will find Æræya and my sister," Veronica reported. "Victor, can you hear me? Let's finish this."

We pushed for one final charge. Maya connected first, using her staff to subdue the first threat. Fallon ducked down as a clay pot flew overhead. I planted my feet and drew my sword.

"On me!" I motioned. "We make our stand here!"

I took one final look at Balien as he sprinted toward the entrance of the Arælia. We had put all our trust in him.

***

Part 14: Odore

The History of the Odore

***

Gifted by the god Odore, the people of Odore used their strength and understanding of aromas to begin the work of reuniting humanity. They did their best to help save the other races, but they soon discovered that Vedere would find them as well. In preparation of the worst, the Odore went out in search of the Nusdvagisdi, hoping their understanding of science and philosophy would save humanity. With the help of the Hören, the Odore and Hören found the Gan Dong, the People of Touch, but something was amiss. This is what history tells us. This is what we hope: That the way in which the Earth began, will not be how it ended. We are the Odore. And we are the believers of the world.

***

Rory 57,280 days left

Jayla Oko died today. She confessed before she slipped into her coma. She wanted to assure us it wasn't supposed to take this long. She didn't expect the atmosphere down here to affect the poison in the way that it had, but I supposed I should be thankful, as it proved to be the reason for my immunity as well.

We know who our enemy is now. And I know who I will have to face once we reach Topside. The Viceroy want our people to remain in the dark and now that I have seen the light, I can't keep it for myself. I have to tell as many as I can. So that's what I will do.

There is no anger toward Jayla. Only sadness. We buried her just south of camp Yuki. You will find her remains there.

***

Machiavelli, 7 days left

"Æræya, it has been brought to my attention that—"

Æræya remained seated, legs folded on a circular pillow. She was in the observatory of the throne room, draped in her veil and ceremonial attire. She didn't even face me when I entered the room and addressed her.

"I know, Machiavelli. I know. War has been brought to my home. I offered my people peace. And they rebel."

I looked out the window and down to street level, where the crowd rushed around in a panic. "Æræya, I think it would be wise to address the people. They have your brother—he is on his way."

"He is not my brother. And this is no longer my ceremony. If they aim to place blood on this sacred ground, then I will give them their own."

"But Æræya, you don't seriously—"

"It has been long enough. I am ready for this to finally end. They are staging a diversion. Find out what they truly seek."

I nodded.

"And call up the Old Guard. If this is to all come to an end, then we must have our family reunion. They aimed to take us by surprise, it's time we return the favor."

***

Quannah, 7 days left

"Quannah should be here now. We will have to come up with something else," Fallon suggested. The group was huddled just inside the walls of Arælia. "We are sitting ducks out here. We have to keep moving."

"We have no idea where we would be going. And we know at this point we are within range. Any communication can be intercepted by Æræya. We have to have a guide," Balien spat back. The tension was starting to get to him as well.

"Balien, we have to do this. Our time is now. We will not be given another." Talia was right. Time was running short.

Quannah appeared from around other end of the circular wall. His hair was partially out of its low ponytail and his clothes were tattered and dirty.

"We know where we are going," he responded. "We go to the Hysk."

Sera's eyes widened. "The Oroisha? The home of the Viceroy?"

Quannah nodded with lowered shoulders and a somber demeanor. "It is where they took my sister," Quannah added. "We will find the scroll there."

"For all we know, Maya, Commander Bastian, everyone, they've all given their lives just to get us within the walls. Will the lexicon even be there?" Fallon was framing the conversation.

"The Hysk is the oldest structure in Vedere. If it would be anywhere, it would make sense for it to be there," Balien added.

"And this was still in the Will," Quannah replied. "As the only way to get to the Hysk is from within Arælia. Follow me."

Quannah took the group to a secret passage. It was at the base of a hopi tree; an entrance to an underground passageway that linked to the thousands of catacombs beneath Halo Michaela. It wasn't hidden particularly well, but you would have to know it was there to actually find anything.

"This was one of my father's last secrets," Quannah explained. "This passage was built before the Cara Royale was ever established. It goes back to the time of Vo and Va, when this world was very different."

The group scuttled down into the underground passage. Then stopped. It was pitch black.

"We have to press on," Quannah urged. "Use whatever you have to light your way and grab hold of the person in front of you."

The group used whatever they had to produce light and trudged into the darkness. Without warning, a presence filled the tunnel.

"Is someone else here?" Talia asked.

"No, it's not a person, at least not their physical body," Sera added.

"I know what this is," Balien replied. "We were at Seraphina I's and then—"

Balien had instantly returned to his bed at Sciya. His last memory was standing in the tunnel and then suddenly he was in his bed, paralyzed. From Quannah's perspective, his entire troop had either fallen unconscious, eyes wide open, or were displaying other puzzling behavior. Balien had fallen onto the dirt floor. Fallon was in a fetal position. Talia had darted deeper into tunnel, leaving her flashlight behind, and Sera had collapsed, her body violently shaking from a seizure.

No, not now! We should have had more time, Quannah thought.

The small circle of white light that represented the entrance to the secret passageway widened, then turned pitch black. Quannah heard the rush of water as his ankles began to soak. Springing into action, Quannah picked up Balien, fearing he'd be the first to drown, while he used his foot to nudge Sera.

"Sera! This is a mental attack! You are in a sæ constructed by Æræya. She is trying to stop us! You have to fight!"

In Sera's mind, she was fighting, and it was causing her brain to seize. Æræya had reconstructed Seraphina I's home and placed Sera in the middle of Damian's fight with Red, Lazy Yellow, and Christina—only this time, she was fighting them too. Sera kicked, punched, threw glasses from the kitchen, everything she could do to help Damian. She was still too attached to the sæ.

I need your help, Sera, I will not be able to save everyone. Quannah propped Balien up against the wall. *There is no other way, is there?*

Quannah quickly knelt and closed his eyes. When he opened them, a glass from Seraphina I's kitchen whizzed past his ear.

"This is not real, Sera. Feel your body. Your legs are soaked."

Sera squinted and cocked her head to the side. *"I'm sorry, this is my family."*

Quannah frowned. *"I can't force you, Sera. You must leave under your own volition."*

Sera ignored him and continued to fight. This resulted in her getting kicked in the chest by Lazy Yellow. As her back slid down the wall, Quannah tried again. This time his clothes from the waist down were soaked.

"Look at me, Sera. I'm still kneeling. Your friends are drowning."

Sera looked at her grandmother through teary-red eyes. *"Goodbye, Nona, I'm sorry."*

Sera stopped shaking and stumbled to her feet.

"You are your grandmother, Sera. She lives in you. Now, you are the witness."

Sera opened her eyes and immediately reached under Balien's armpits and began dragging him deeper into the tunnel. "I can get him downstream while I try to find Talia. Fallon is too big for me."

"We can only hope that Talia is somewhere upright. You will have to retrieve her from her sæ."

Talia was being chased by the Ophori of her childhood, deep brown journal in hand. As she rounded the corner to dart into an alley, she was met with Sera.

"Talia, we must go. I'm sorry. Æræya is manipulating us all," Sera explained.

Talia frowned. *"A sæ is not time travel—I know that. That means I can't save them, can I?"*

"Æræya is cruel, Talia, so I will not lie to you. A sæ is not time travel, but that doesn't exactly mean that you cannot make changes."

Talia's face twisted. *"You mean you could have stopped all of this before it even started? You could have saved us? You could have saved your grandmother!"*

"But if I did that I'd fail her and all the women before her."

"What do you mean?"

"To sæ is to have true sight. To see it all—all things—for what they truly are. This is why the sæ transcends time and space. We are the only ones, Talia, do you understand? We are the only witnesses."

Talia's cheeks were soaked as tears streamed down her face. *"But ... but you still help us. You're impacting world. What's the difference?"*

"Talia, I already know. I've known my beginning, I have already seen my end. I have never left my place. This is what it means to be a witness." Sera began to cough up water.

"But if it was your grandmother?"

"I've already seen her place. The moment I met you, back at the party, I saw mine. It all began there. My mind was ready and it finally opened. I'd had my awakening, just like Nona said I would, I awoke when she slept."

Sera begin to float in the air. *"Come embrace your story. It's yours. This story was always about you."*

When Talia woke up, she was floating above water, riding the stream with her head propped up by Sera.

"Where is everyone?"

"Drifting along with us, I hope. Thank you for waking up." Sera choked out more water.

The tunnel spilled out into an underground reservoir. Talia helped Sera carry Balien out of the water, guided by the cave's bioluminous fungi. The entire dome-shaped area was lit by a calming briny blue tint.

Fallon and Quannah also emerged from the water. Quannah gave Sera a soft smile. "To sæ is to be a witness."

"To sæ is to be a witness," she replied.

"We are still exactly where we need to be," Quannah explained. "We will be taking a similar tunnel to the mouth of a cave entrance just outside the perimeter of the Hysk."

The group followed Quannah's lead. The top of the Hysk could eventually be seen from inside the entrance to the cave as the group neared the light.

"So what's the plan?" Balien asked. "We just walk in?"

"We have no choice," Quannah responded. "Time is up."

The group walked through the main entrance. No one welcomed them. In fact, the whole building looked to be abandoned.

"Split up and look for whatever you can find: old papers, databases, writings on the walls, anything," Quannah instructed them.

"I'll search the database," Fallon offered, placing a kokoto he found near a desk into its groove. "It's as if whoever was here left in a hurry. Everything is just strewn about. Even their kokotos."

A collective sense of worry began to develop as they searched, finding nothing. The Ophori could arrive at any moment.

"By the Goddess ... I ... I found something." Sera was trembling. She had gone downstairs and worked her way down a hallway with glass rooms on both sides. Inside each of the rooms were a few dozen corpses. They looked to have been of all ages and backgrounds.

The rest of the group froze at the sight.

"Quannah, look at this clothing," Fallon said. "I've never seen anything like it—"

"And these corpses ... Have you ever seen hair this curly?" Balien noted.

"There is no way these people are Vederian. The bone structure, the size of these remains, the clothing ... no, these are not Vederian people," Sera added.

"Then who are these people? Where did they come from?" Talia asked.

"You all are correct. These are not Vederians. These are not Horeni either," Quannah signed. "These are Nusdvagisdi. These are my people."

Quannah placed one hand on the glass. "Veronica spoke of an extinct people. She was speaking of mine. I had thought we had all been wiped out by now. It seems a few of us still remained. Just a few hundred meters from me. All this time and I never knew. Maya's father knew about this, everyone knew about this, and still nothing was done."

"Quannah, I don't have the words ... " Fallon began.

"To live is to be a witness to the pain of the world," Quannah replied. "We cannot lose another civilization."

Balien wiped a tear from his eye. "What were they doing with them?"

"They were attempting to do what *we* are attempting to do," Quannah replied. "Find the lexicon."

"But why the Nusdvagisdi?" Sera asked, "What could they possible help do?"

Quannah let in a deep breath and let it out slowly. "There's a reason why the Nusdvagisdi were wiped out first. It is the same reason we have been hunted, captured, tortured, and killed. It is because we were the last living example of the truth. The last race of the world that had all five senses."

Fallon leaned back against the glass wall of the hallway and allowed his body to slump down to the ground. "By now, each race has developed their own unique abilities; for you all, it is torphi, or the sæ, all abilities born out of advanced sight. Our gift, among other things, was the ability to communicate with everyone. We were the translators, the witnesses, the observers."

Quannah walked to the other side of the hallway. "They were experimenting on these people, torturing these people. It means they didn't have the lexicon."

"Wait, I'm not understanding, I thought the lexicon was a physical code or set of writings of some sort," Fallon confessed. "I don't understand."

"I don't think even I did," Quannah confessed as well. "But it all makes sense now. My sister *was* the lexicon. Look at this panel."

Quannah walked over to a console that had been left activated. It showed a number of sequences with corresponding traits.

"The lexicon is a *genetic* code," Fallon replied.

"The Viceroy, the quinqu, they didn't want the lexicon for themselves, they simply wanted it eradicated. This was their attempt at ending it. They killed all of us," Quannah cried. "Everyone but me."

"And then they fled," Æræya signed. *"They even tricked me. Spoke of some great calamity that would befall this great nation. Perhaps even I was too jaded."*

Quannah quickly spun his head around. Balien, Fallon, Sera, and Talia all prepared for conflict.

"A hover car with royal markings is blocking the exit," Æræya explained calmly. *"Though I—I've just come to a point where it has failed to matter,"* she confessed. *"Machiavelli was too afraid to leave the palace, so I killed him. And I've stamped nearly all of your rebellion. I've killed the clone, Fallon. And your AI. And Yanne. And sadly, at this point, I'm not even sure why. I don't think I even care why anymore, but I am nearly done."*

"Æræya, you were right. Your family was massacred. The throne may very well be yours," Quannah suggested.

"Just bring her in here," Æræya signed. Vega, just a skeletal frame, was pushed into the hall.

"She's so weak now. It's almost not worth the trouble. She was to see my coronation—then I was going to kill her."

"You can just stop now, Æræya, you still can," Quannah pressed.

"But Quannah, my dear friend, I already know that. Vo and Va have been fighting since time immoral. Every few hundred years either family decides to resist the Viceroy, reject the quinqu, and go their own way. And each time the Viceroy stokes the fire for the opposition. My family has been on the right side. It has also been on the wrong side. But you misunderstand. I am no longer Valerie. She has died. I am Æræya. And so now I will kill the Viceroy. I will establish a new world order. No more Viceroy, no more quinqu. Only ... us." Æræya cracked a disturbing smile. Her mental state was continuing to decline.

With a tip of her hand, five Ophori warriors entered from the other side of the hall, drawing a weapon. Magenta. Teal. Obsidian. Tangerine. Cobalt. Viviana, the Viceroy leader, entered last, her hair in a low bun and wearing a dark red bodysuit. But she wasn't the only visitor. Suddenly, there was a flash of bright white light. Beams of energy were exchanged in multiple directions.

Christina crashed in. Following her was Maya, Shalayne, and Commander Bastian. Epeë and the last of the Horeni assassins entered last.

"The tide turned," Commander Bastian proclaimed proudly. "My people fight with a ferociousness this world has never seen. We have the Hysk surrounded."

"What will it be, Æræya?" Maya asked. "It is over."

A single tear crept down Æræya cheek. *"I know, Maya. But there is one final thing I must do."*

Viviana walked over to a nearby seating area and calmly took a seat, crossing her legs.

Beaten and cuffed, Æræya revealed Victor, brought along by Gaius Saroyan and Vala.

"The last of the Old Guard," Commander Bastian signed.

"I thought you a coward, Gregor," Vala snapped, "but it seems you are worse, you are a traitor."

Balien straightened his back and looked directly at Gaius.

"It was a few years ago when your father learned of your accident," Æræya explained. *"Oh, how he mourned your mother's death. But I was there to comfort him. It was a year later when he learned that you were not dead. And when I told him who your mother really was, who you really were, he didn't even react."*

Balien held back his tears as Gaius remained unmoved.

"My goal now is to see it all end. But I had to be sure we all saw each other one last time," Æræya explained. She had already slipped out of her cuffs as she turned around with a short knife in her hand. She quickly stabbed Victor in the chest and sliced Vega's neck before hardly anyone could react.

Æræya turned back to face the group and signed, *"Vedere is no more."* She attempted to thrust the knife into her own chest—but Gaius grabbed her forearm, preventing the fatal blow.

"Spy or believer?" Christina asked Balien. He didn't have time to answer as she lunged at Cobalt, who was wielding a bow-staff. Cobalt was shorter, but incredibly powerful. Each of their movements were precise and deadly.

Just a few steps past them was Shalane and Obsidian. Tangerine and Teal worked as a team. They took to the Horeni assassins. Epeë went after Magenta, and it Maya chose Æræya as her opponent. Gregor faced off against Gaius.

Shalane clearly had the upper hand against Obsidian. Though an incredible fighter, they had never faced off against a Horeni. Shalane's weapon was like a spear, but the sharp end extended out quickly and retracted. It was the same for the opposite end. Shalane spun around to sweep the legs, then jutted her weapon into Obsidian's chest and extended it. That's all it took.

Teal and Tangerine fought like the twins they were. They were easily able to overpower one of the Horeni using their unique tag-team approach, but in the end they were outnumbered and it only took a few key blows to subdue them.

This left Epeë, Maya, and Gaius. In the commotion, Fallon and Sera searched for an alternative exit. That was when they discovered a devastating revelation.

"How could it be this dark?" Sera asked. "It's too early for amberlight."

Fallon checked his watch. "It's the middle of the day ... "

The inside of the building grew darker and darker. Fallon logged into his computer and began rerunning previous simulations.

"We ... we miscalculated. We're completely out of time," he signed. Fallon and Sera looked up at the others, still fighting. He and Sera had to develop a revised plan.

"We—we have to go door to door. We try to save as many as we can. We try to prepare them," he said. Fallon's vision was tinting red and his posture compromised. One, maybe two, ribs were broken. He couldn't remember how he got hurt.

"There's no time to prepare our people for this. We will lose millions ... millions," Sera maintained. What initially began as a plan to expose the truth was becoming a desperate, last-minute attempt at thwarting extinction.

"How do we warn them?" Fallon asked.

Magenta, Vala, and Æræya. That was all that was left. They stood back to back, sharp objects in each of their hands. Magenta and Vala would be loyal to the end—and Æræya would make the Young Guild kill her. That was the only way she would allow herself to be stopped—at the hand of her enemy.

Gaius, Maya, Christina, and Epeë had them surrounded. The end would be painted in blood.

"You have been beaten, Æræya," Gaius explained. "This has to stop. Don't make us kill you."

"Look around you, Æræya. Look at what has happened!" Balien shook with anger. "Look what you have done!"

The ground shook violently as chaos erupted above them. It was too dark for midday, much too dark.

"Everyone is gone, now. Victor is gone. Vega is gone. Vera is gone. There is only you. And look at what you have become!" Balien continued. "Go up and look outside, this is just the beginning. This world will be in total darkness in a matter of hours. There is no escape now."

Æræya laughed as she collapsed to her knees. *"It is too late, little Luz. All these things I set in motion ... I can't reverse what has been done. There are things bigger, more powerful beings than I, Balien. This great war is larger than the both of us. I've played my part and I have won."*

Æræya squinted her eyes and cocked her head to the side. She looked at Quannah and Gaius. "How did I not see it before? You're one of them, a Nusdvagisdi. It's ... it's all of you."

"I am," Quannah replied with pride. "And in the name of my people, I will bring you to justice."

Æræya tightened her face and gripped her dagger. She charged at him and flung her dagger directly at Gaius. Using his bow-staff, he expertly deflected the blade—ricocheting it directly into Balien's chest.

Maya lunged with her staff. She whipped it first round her back and neck and with that momentum, clear across Valerie's face, knocking her out cold.

Magenta froze, then dropped her head and weapons together, falling to her knees.

"Why continue to fight, my sisters? It's over," Magenta told them. Vala too dropped her weapons and knelt before Maya.

"Over?" Viviana asked. "You thought Æræya was your opponent? Not even close. My plan for her was to remake her in my image—but she was weak."

Fallon and the others rushed over to Balien. The blood had soaked through his clothes and pooled around his body on the floor. He was choking.

Gaius tore his shirt and tried to stop the bleeding. Sera, who was holding Balien's hand, already knew.

"Can't we move him?" Christina asked.

"It will not matter. Your symbol is dead. Moving him will not make a difference. Because you do not yet know what I am and the four others like me, it will not be your time. Save as many as you'd like. It will not matter. The other immortals and I will find you whether in this reality or any of the others." Viviana's threat carried a heaviness to it. "Ask Quannah who I really am. He will tell you that I am inevitable. If you knew how old I was, you'd know how patient I've been. I can wait a bit longer. See you in the next reality." Viviana smirked as she pantomimed the general shape of an eye. The space in front of her folded up like an eyelid, revealing a bright and strange world behind it. The spatial tear blinked, taking Viviana with it.

"Leave her! Do what you can for Balien!" Quannah signed.

"No," Balien signed. It was a sign where you took your pointer and middle fingers and closed them with your thumb. "No ... time." Balien's eyes were fixed out the glass hallway, just above where the last sliver of the day's light shone through.

"We were wrong about the eclipse, Balien. It's already started," Sera shared.

Gaius leaned in to Balien. "I failed you," Gaius explained calmly. "I completely failed you."

Gaius began to cry. Everyone did. Gaius tried to find the words, but Fallon stopped him. "Tell him you love him."

"I love you, my son. I love you."

Balien gasped, then nodded his head. He was gone.

***

Quannah, 0 days left

They decided to leave Æræya alone in her palace. There was no time for anything else. They gave her what she wanted, the throne and her kingdom. In the hours that passed, the Unionists frantically rushed from door to door, begging the citizens to escape the darkness. Gregor sent the Kofi as far as he reasonably could. Fallon and Sera worked on broadcasting a message in the sky for all to read. Veronica and her team assembled, from the Underside of the continents, massive ships that rumbled to the surface. A century of the best technology known to Vedere focused on one goal, the prevention of extinction.

But in the end, many did not heed the Unionist's pleas. Most closed their doors and brightened their indoor lights.

Only a few took the leap of faith. Of the seven ships prepared for the evacuation, only two were filled. Vedere remained content with what they knew, nothing more.

"No, no, no. This can't be right. Just two hundred and fifty thousand?" Fallon thought to himself, slumping into his chair.

"You did all you could do, Doctor. We've put as many as we can into the ships. We have to hope that we can wait it out," Talia replied.

"How long before total darkness?" Epeë asked, walking over to a whiteboard and reviewing Fallon's formulas.

"It's but hours now. It's almost time to head to the ships. Has anyone made contact with Quannah?" Fallon asked. He had hoped they would receive the final count from him one last time before the light left the sky. There was no telling what the world would look like once the darkness began.

"I haven't heard from them. Everyone was making last-minute preparations," Talia replied. They had truly scrambled to the end. And it felt that they were only getting more sloppy as time went on. All of a sudden, it just seemed like they had no time. As if they completely failed before they began.

***

Part 15: Nusdvagisdi

The History of the Nusdvagisdi

***

After the deception of Vedere, Nusdvagisdi's people remained hidden, working tirelessly to unlock the limits placed on humanity in the hopes of restoring the races, and uniting the planet.

With the arrival of the Odore, the Hören, and the Gan Dong, the Nusdvagisdi's plan for unity was within reach.

This is what history tells us. This is the truth. This is how the Earth began, but not how it will end. We are the Nusdvagisdi. And we will unite the world.

***

The Journal of Georgette Davis, 56,860 days left

Day 85

So it is settled then. This will be my final entry. I promised to keep it short and to the point: If anyone reads this, we have partnered with the Horeni Delegation. They too have graciously agreed to stay behind, along with myself and a select few others. We will continue preparations to save our race and send them to the Horeni Domain. We know we will not fail because we cannot fail.

It seems all but proven that this was my purpose all along. I cannot help but believe this was all by design. Our constituents represent everything we will ever need to complete our true work. Our world is ending, but our people can live on. We came to discover, but we could have never imagined we'd participate in a work such as this.

We will not finish this work in my lifetime, or the next. So we have sent my husband to return to make a special request to ensure this work is completed. I will miss him with everything I have. He tells me he truly understands, but how can I ever know for sure?

I'm reminded that those who reflect the light will always stand apart. I wanted to help leave my world better than I found it—we all did. I thought I knew what that development would look like: advancement in the sciences, a deeper understanding of our nature and philosophy, protecting our world.

But I wasn't fully correct. I was blind to what our world needed the most: the truth.

There is more than meets the eye.

***

Quannah, 0 days left

"Talia, it's time. The people are waiting for you," Veronica signed. She was extremely tired and dazed. It was all over her face. "Remember, this is

Arc 2. This one houses a hundred and seventy-six thousand people. They're afraid, Talia. They need hope."

"I don't know what to tell them," Talia replied.

"Look at everything we've done, Talia," Veronica signed, as they touched foreheads. *"In just a few months, we were able to complete seven ships on the underside of two halos. We will be saving over quarter a million people. These people left everything they knew because of what you and your friends did. They believe that you can lead them into a new age. Whatever happens after this Great Darkness, whatever we are left with ... it will all be because of your belief. We will have our reminder that we can move beyond what we are now."*

Veronica turned to the opaque glass doors behind the mezzanine of the ship. She had lost so much weight. We all had. We hadn't had the time to eat, to dance, to smile. We worked to preserve the Vederian race. And we ran out of time even still.

"They didn't come for me, Veronica. They came for Balien, and how he is gone. So many of us are gone."

"All of this ... all of this, Talia, it began with your grandmother. Her journal, the one you protected, set all of this in motion. You are just as much as important as anyone. I don't know what you should tell them, and I won't. I just know that they should hear from you."

I stepped forward and placed a supportive hand on Talia's shoulder. "Just speak from your heart," I signed. "Tell them your truth."

Talia took a deep breath and stepped into the light. Before her were her people, from all walks of life: those who worked in the Cara Royale, carpenters, painters, doctors, lawyers, children, families, everyone.

"Vederians are strong people. History tells us that when we first came to this continent, we had to fight back against nature to carve out our place in it. We fought and we fought hard. We became the greatest generation our nation had ever seen. We believed we belonged here and we became settled in the life we chose for ourselves.

"But we are a new generation. And we no longer belong here. Our home is no longer for us, and we must leave. But we now know we are not alone. Balien and his people—they came to warn us. To save us from what destroyed them. And we are indebted to them. So I say, let's honor them.

Let's honor their hope and faith in us. Let us be open-minded, kind, and ready for whatever is on the other side. I don't know what is next, but I do know I have you all. And I somehow, I know that will be enough."

***

The Journal of Georgette Davis, 57,290 days left.

Day 11

"I reminded the team today that we have the blessing of the Ægæliphi. The result of our endeavors can reshape the knowledge of our entire nation. We do not know exactly what we will see, but we have prepared and taken all necessary precautions in lieu of first contact."

That was the first thing that I wrote in this journal. And now look how far we have come. What an incredibly unique endeavor it is to begin a work you know will take longer than your lifetime to accomplish. To hope. To guess. To dream. I am old now—I have spent the majority of my adult life down here. I would have it no other way. The work we are doing, the people we are doing it with, everything is perfectly balanced. I thought for a long time about what drove the Others to divide us so sharply. To stretch us so far apart and run is thin. But the answer was always right in front of me. Our ally is unity. Their enemy is togetherness. And somewhere along the way, the interests of a few came to outweigh the needs of us all.

I thought I was making a scientific endeavor. And I truly did. But what I would discover would push me past everything I have ever believed in. My goal has changed. My husband's goal has changed. We started this work to encourage discovery. To end our war. To prevent a catastrophe. And we discovered our true end. We faced our true failure of a people, and we saw just how far hate and separation can go.

And now we know our true work. We must undo what was done to our people—all of our people. I have put everything in place. I hope it will be enough

Veronica, Day 1.

The escape pods deployed one by one. There was not a single error or miscalculation. Every pod deployed. I let out a sigh of relief as I leaned back in my pod. Out the window, I could see them as they careened down into the darkness. Talia looked up as the halos above became smaller and smaller. She looked at the floating displays and their clean blue lines and Vederian script. Their course was set. They would be landing at the Domain of the Hören. Beyond that, no one knew. As she ship began to rumble and shake as it embarked, a little girl across from Talia began to cry. Talia unstrapped her harness and stumbled over.

"Hi, I'm Talia. What's your name?"

"Bailey."

"Are you scared, Bailey?"

Bailey nodded.

"I'm scared too. But I think we'll be OK."

Bailey scrunched up her face. "How do you know if you've never seen what's down there?"

"I don't know," Talia confessed. "But someone very important to me told me to have a little faith, even when you can't see what's next."

"But why?"

Talia smiled. "Because there's more than meets the eye."

The End

CPSIA information can be obtained
at www.ICGtesting.com
Printed in the USA
BVHW032034100323
660178BV00002B/644

9 781685 836276